P9-AOF-182

AGUAHEGA

Kathleen Snow

9/23/90

For Betty,
"A book is like a garden carried in your pocket."
thanks for being a wonderful friend.
love
Kathleen

AGUAHEGA

a new novel by

Kathleen Snow

Acadia Press
Bar Harbor, ME

This book is a work of fiction. Names, characters, places and incidents are either the product of the author's imagination or are used fictitiously. Any resemblance to actual events or locales or persons, living or dead, is entirely coincidental.

 Address inquiries to Acadia Publishing Company, P.O. Box 170, Bar Harbor, ME 04609.

First Edition Published September 1990.

Library of Congress Cataloging-in-Publication Data

Snow, Kathleen.
Aguahega : a new novel / by Kathleen Snow. -- 1st ed.
p. cm.
ISBN 0-934745-13-7 : $19.95
I. Title
PS3569.N623A74 1990
813' .54--dc20 90-578
CIP

Printed in the United States of America
10 9 8 7 6 5 4 3 2 1 90 91 92

For the Family Snow:

Charles
Katherine
Carolyn
Marina
Georgiana

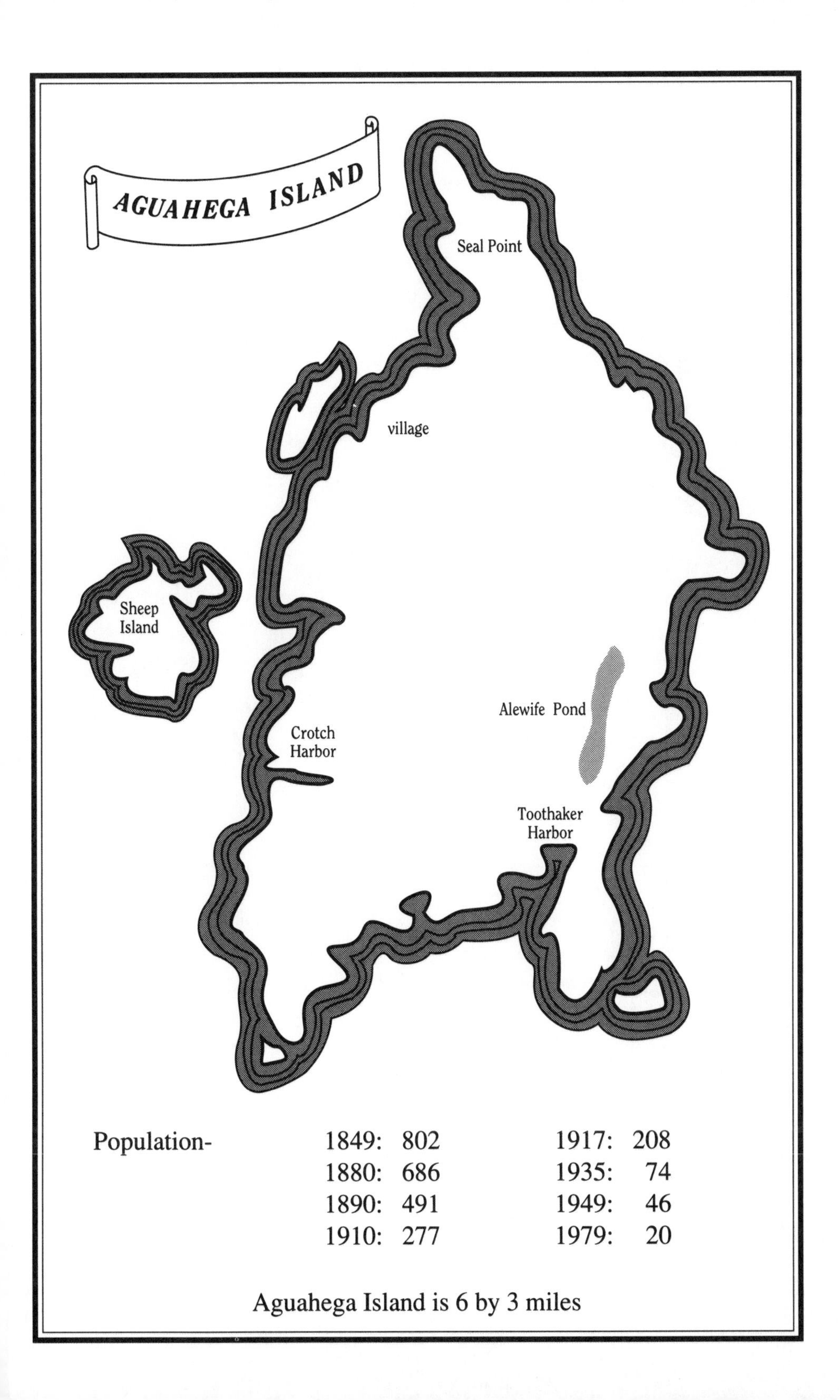
AGUAHEGA ISLAND
Seal Point
village
Sheep
Island
Crotch
Harbor
Alewife Pond
Toothaker
Harbor
Population-
1849: 802
1880: 686
1890: 491
1910: 277
1917: 208
1935: 74
1949: 46
1979: 20
Aguahega Island is 6 by 3 miles

PROLOGUE

1524

Aguahega Island, "the landing place," didn't belong to them.

They called themselves Abnaki, "the people of the dawnland," for Aguahega was as far east as people could go. It was a mountain that had drowned, the island highest in a frigid blue bay, outermost. Its pink granite spine arched bare above forests of green. Lichens spun bullseyes of yellow across its 1000-foot cliffs. In its mossy depths seventeen species of orchid hid, the shyest with a tiger striped lip, lavender pink petals, and three rows of golden hairs. At its root, lobsters five feet long swarmed leopard-spotted blue, green, and orange. Its mud flats spouted clams, its coves shrilled with seabirds: food to dry for the long mainland winters.

For 5300 years, they had belonged to Aguahega.

1788

"How much *occopy* for the high island?" Amariah Beal called. Amariah, his wife Mattie and fourteen children were tired, grimy after sailing down east for eleven days from overcrowded Gloucester, looking for a cove, somewhere to settle, a home. And now, Amariah thought, they had found one. The high island was like a stronghold in which no harm could ever intrude.

"Worth very much." The Indian Sagamore, in his birch bark canoe, squinted up at them from under a stovepipe hat. "Three gallons *occopy*."

Amariah looked his question at Mattie, heard her familiar mocking voice: " 'Take what you want,' said God, 'and pay for it.' "

"To Amariah Beal:
...a parcel of land commonly
called by ye name of Aguahega,
lying and being a Island in ye
sea, bounded with Duck Isld on
ye West, Burnt Isld and Barred
Isld to ye East, Cape Andrews
on ye north.
By the Hand of Joseph
Quaduaquid, Sagamore."

CHAPTER 1

1904 - Aguahega Island, Maine

Gooden was the first of the Aguahega Beals to sell his birthright to someone from away. But tonight nothing could have been farther from his mind. His long square-tipped fingers reached for Mary Stella's waist, eyes shutting for an instant as the message of soft pink calico hot with the body beneath flashed through his palm, up his arm, racing into all the convolutions of his brain.

He had never held a girl's waist—other than a sister's—before. He always stood in the background braced by some wall, watching.

He opened his eyes, blinking through a sting of sweat. Mary Stella's pink and gold face danced before him, her blue eyes laughing up at him, her blond hair flouncing on the round white bertha collar that caped her shoulders, her black stockinged feet in the soft kip leather shoes flying to the music. He stumbled frantically to keep up.

On a box in the center of the room, the bowlegged fiddler, suspenders dangling in scallops from his waist, leaned precariously forward as he sawed away at *Lady of the Lake*. Beneath Gooden's heavy kag boots, the rough planks bounced and thumped as they swept around with the others, finishing *Lady* and starting *March and*

Circle, down the long second-story packing room of the defunct lobster cannery. Through a haze of cigar smoke, he glimpsed his father, Perley, and his mother in the crowds that lined the wall, and four of his seven sisters clapping their hands from their plank seats suspended between two kegs. Evelina, the youngest, crammed sticky brown dates in her mouth, spitting the stones back out on the floor.

Despite the thrown-open windows, the heat was fierce, the reek of sweat heavy on the fog-dense night air. Mary Stella's face was red, glossed with moisture, but on her, even sweat looked good.

She was an angel, Mary Stella. She was his angel, should he go thinking of a bride some time soon, his mother kept hinting. For Gooden's eighteenth birthday, Perley Beal had given him 100 acres of his own to build a home on. He could clear the field for six cows, a yoke of oxen, fifty sheep, a couple of hogs. Mary Stella could tend the poultry while he lobstered, and every night they would go to sleep in each other's arms.

Because everyone knew Mary Stella was his.

Gooden saw Reverend Witney, the young new preacher who'd been trying to make time with her, watching them with his pickle face.

Jealous! This time as he spun her around he gave her an experimental squeeze, his blood pounding when, coy as a herring at the mouth of a weir, smooth as a smelt, she sideslipped in his grasp, smiling wider up at him. Did she like him? Or was she laughing at him—skinny stick Gooden with his too big head stuck like a pumpkin on a six-foot scaregull, his big ears jutting out in front of lank brown hair.

"Oo, Gooden, stop, stop!"

His heart stopped in panic, his hand dropping from her waist.

"We've just got to rest, can't catch my breath." She splayed her small pink fingers out against her collarbone. "I'd just love some of that nice cool lemonade before it's all gone."

"You wait just a second, Mary Stella. Fetch you a mug right back." He ran to the blue-painted wooden pail, dipping up two mugs and spilling it as he whirled, eyes searching in confusion the spot where she had just stood.

It was the *Virginia Reel*, the fiddler was tapping his toe, and Mary Stella was whirling down the floor in the arms of the preacher.

Angel? Angel? Mary Stella simpered, eyes narrowed up at the preacher, looking at him from under her brows. The Devil take her, she was the Devil's own!

The tune was no more than finished when the preacher waved a halt. "Friends, I have a happy announcement. Mary Stella here's kindly agreed to become my wife."

Through the cheers, Gooden heard only:

"Got a powerful big thirst of a sudden, have you?" Harry Smallidge mockingly eyed the two mugs.

Gooden jerked away, the lemonade penetrating the front of his woolen pants, clawing down his legs in fiery cold lines. His family was looking, children laughing. He stood in a gray mist ringed with sound.

He fought his way down the narrow stairs, past the men stumbling up from the store below where they had fortified themselves with Ernie Taggett's keg of rum sweetened with molasses. He fled down the cart path.

The night air was blessedly cool on Gooden's cheeks, hiding him in tattered islands of fog. It had been the longest fog mull on record, driving the mackerel schooners, with the fiddling sailor aboard, and a ship from foreign parts into the Aguahega village harbor. The Thoroughfare was a forest of masts: schooners, lobster smacks, the mysterious ship from far parts tallest of all, and even the floating junkshop of a trader in whose shingled clapboarded miniature of a house on decktop Gooden had swapped clams, ten cents a quart, for the new doll buggy for Evelina, his favorite sister.

Faintly now, for the second time this evening, he heard a violin, but this one's voice was slow and tremulous. Gooden felt its sadness merge with his own. It was coming from the other world of Aguahega, the summer world of Seal Point, where the rich had built the first great shingled estate called Tenhaven. In his torment, he followed the music, avoiding the ornamental iron gates, the boardwalks strung like beads with pagoda-roofed gazebos that rollercoastered over the hill. He pressed through the silent wet skirts of evergreens to Tenhaven's garden wall, peered through its round Moon Gate.

Colored lanterns smudged and winked blue, green, yellow from every tree. They ringed the fountain in the middle of a greensward whose flower colors faded into mist. People sat in wicker chairs and crowded in groups and the violin's playing, the most beautiful sound Gooden had ever heard, swelled from somewhere in their midst.

He stepped closer, hiding behind a stone pedestal ringed with frogs, on which stood a statue of a naked boy, stone blind. It was the girl he stared at, and he felt suddenly angry despite his fascination because she made him realize Mary Stella wasn't beautiful after all. The girl's back was arched against some sort of tension, the blue glimmer of a paper lantern flickering over her hair. She wore a long gown of pleated white lawn and a man's hand like a decoration around her waist, hidden out here at the edge of the crowd. The man's fingers were beginning a slow, arduous ascent up the sheer face of her ribs. Higher they climbed, pioneering their way pitch by pitch, one, two, three fingers gaining altitude, regrouping, now setting forth boldly again, higher, higher, closing inexorably toward the overhang of her breast.

Gooden thought his blood would burst from his ears.

Underbrush crackled behind him.

His body poured sweat as the man's fingers ascended the first foothill of the final peak.

The underbrush in the woods behind snapped alive. A boyish voice hissed out at him, and then another, and another.

"Edward, do you *notice* something?"

"Why, no. Oh, could you possibly mean that sudden stink?"

"Old lobstermen don't die. They just smell that way."

"Why'nt they take a bath?"

"They haven't got a bath!"

"Turpentine wouldn't get that off. That's fish stink. They all stink, all the natives do. Tell them coming a mile away."

"Reek, rank, runk, all the lobstermen stunk. Runk, rank, reek, their mothers also stink!"

There were seven of them in their teens, like him, and though Gooden was half a head taller than all but one of them, they were strangely awesome, these children of the rich. He was trespassing, and he backed away through the Moon Gate into a maze of boxwood and Blackthorn hedges.

"You were *spying*, weren't you?" He was the most muscular of them, redhaired with white eyelashes, in knickerbocker pants and knee socks. His stiff finger jabbed Gooden's chest.

"No."

"Come here to steal, you stinking sneak thief?"

Gooden turned around but there was one of them behind him, short with slitted eyes. Gooden pushed through a narrow arched opening in the hedge. Ahead was another wall of yellow stucco, again with a round doorway, and Gooden ran through. But inside was enclosed, without exit, a graveyard with miniature headstones and urns sculptured of privet with roses.

"Meant you no harm."

"Planning to steal, huh, sneak thief? Just pop right in and pinch a few things?"

"He stinks worse'n a garbage pit."

Shame pushed Gooden harder than their jabs and shoves, rode him as closely, as indelibly as his smell. He had discovered it the first time he ventured inside Tenhaven, delivering a package from the village post office to earn some change. The endless front hall was fragrant with waxed wood, sunlight gleaming on the polished floor and carved walls, shining through the window in a room at the end of the hall, the biggest window he had ever seen.

The woman's straight small nose had wrinkled as he stood there, she in her black uniform with an apron lacy as a doily, and it was then he was first aware he had a smell.

The smell. But then they all had it, all of the fishermen. The fish smell that clung to clothes, penetrated the skin, breathed out of your pores no matter how hard you scrubbed. "It smells like money," his mother said. "Now you hesh up and don't go giving yourself airs."

Now, at Tenhaven, Gooden watched the short boy wrap a handkerchief around and around his knuckles. The boy flexed his fingers, making a fist. "If I saw a snake coming at me and a native, I'd let the snake go free."

"Let him go!" The boy was taller than the rest, in tweed kneepants and matching tweed cap. "Charles, it's my property. I say let him go."

"Shut up, Fairfield!" The redhead spared him no glance. "You're just chicken. How about you, Edward? What do you say?"

A fist spun out of the air, colliding with Gooden's chin. The darkness in his head exploded into light. He felt his thighs bunching, he was sailing through the air, and his own fist connected with someone's hard bone. But abruptly he felt his arms pinned back, four of them twisted his arms higher, higher, until he fought to keep from shrieking with pain. The redhead and the short one approached him from the front. He stared like a deer shined by gunners: it knew it was going to get it, transfixed.

When the beating was done Gooden found himself flat on his back. Moisture soaked up into his shirt. Or was it blood soaking down into the ground? He struggled to breathe. There was a shivering deep inside him, as if his intestines had come loose.

"Oh, Charles," one of them said, falsetto. "Whatever are you doing now?"

Gooden felt the urine land spattering on his pants leg, hot as it soaked through the sieve of cloth. The sound of the last few drops ratcheted through his brain. He tried to get up but his legs didn't work, his brain swam through a new endless sound. It was a sound like rain falling. It fell on his knees, his stomach, his chest, it sluiced his face. His body steamed with it, vapor rising like midwinter's arctic smoke.

When they had been gone awhile, Gooden dragged himself to his knees. The spruces spun and blurred, and then he saw the one in tweed again.

Fairfield Chancellor of New York and Tenhaven, Aguahega Island, Maine was staring at him as if he were a strange marine creature washed ashore. But his voice was kind. "I tried to stop them. I'm sorry." A new dollar bill fluttered in his outstretched hand. "Can you get up?"

The pity Gooden saw in his face was the final shame. It brought him roaring to his feet. The tweed kneepants vanished through the round doorway in the wall.

Gooden rolled in the clipped clean grass, dragged his wet arms and legs over it and through it, pulled it up, crushing it, rolling it over his face. His cheeks streamed with the green juice and his tears. He ran stumbling away from the formal gardens, park, woodlands surrounding Tenhaven, followed the ridge trail down the mountainous backbone to Aguahega's south end, *his* end, to the fishing community of Toothaker Harbor, to Alewife Pond. Without removing his clothes, he jumped in, swimming through the icy purity of white lily pads, splashing deeper in his clumsy dogpaddle until the numbing cold sank too deeply into his blood. He came out pouring wet and stood trembling on the hill above Perley's House, the home where he had been born.

Like Tenhaven, the old two-chimneyed cape was covered in shingles. But it looked huddled and bulky, like a man wearing two overcoats. The curve of the gambrel roof covered its walls down to its only decoration, an oak-ribbed fan above the front door. A lantern welcomed on the stoop: Mother had left it for him there.

But he couldn't go in. Shame burned him dry. He smelled the smell of urine even in his hair.

He knew it would never wash clean.

Gooden closed his eyes and let the train take him westward, deep into the main. The black rampart of Aguahega was far away, fog covering it like a shroud. But the voices of the rich boys pursued him, faster than the train, louder than its wheels.

"Reek, rank, runk, all the lobstermen stunk. Runk, rank, reek, their mothers also stink."

Again he drew out the folded document, squinting in the sun where he lay on top of the boxcar, reading the incomprehensible words.

> This indenture made the thirteenth
> day of the eighth month in the year
> of Our Lord nineteen hundred four.
> Between Gooden Henry Beal, herein
> designated as the party of the first
> part and Altoona Land Company, herein
> designated as party of the second part.
> Witnesseth, that the party of the
> first part granted, bargained, sold,
> aliened, enfeoffed, released, conveyed,
> and confirmed unto the said party of
> the second part, heirs and assigns,
> ALL that tract and parcel of land...

It sounded like the Bible, but it didn't mean a thing. He could feel the land in him indelible as a birthmark, as deep as sin. You could never wash it away.

His fingers felt the $200 the Altoona Land man had given him; it was unbelievable but there it was. He remembered the chalked message on the schoolhouse blackboard: "Seest thou a man diligent in his business? He shall stand before kings; He shall not stand before mean men." He would be diligent in his business, Gooden thought, see the world, make a fortune as large as any at Seal Point. Then he'd return. And the money in his pocket was the spark that would start the flame. . . .

By nightfall, there were four travelers preparing for uneasy sleep in the depths of the "side-door pullman," the rattling boxcar. A red-haired woman lay down beside Gooden, her dark eyes with the deep circles searching his, and spread her one thin blanket over them both. Under the blanket he felt her fingers fumbling, tugging at the buttons on the front of his wool pants.

In the blackness she pulled him suddenly on top of her, her bare thighs breaking around him like water, like waves. He looked down into the denser blackness where her face should have been. It seemed he was looking at Mary Stella's face, pink and gold and then snuffed out, like a candle flame between finger and thumb.

When he woke in the morning the woman and the $200 were gone.

In Erie, Pennsylvania, he joined a one-lion traveling circus as a general handy boy. There was lots of peculiarly scented manure to shovel, and the spangles of the aerialist's costume, so beautiful at a distance, came off on his hands. During a rainy spell he developed a cough and congestion, and thought of his mother filling the jar with violet blossoms, covering them with water, letting them set for a day and adding two cups of sugar, dosing him every hour from a big tarnished spoon—afraid it was consumption, the "island disease."

It seemed to Gooden that he could taste violets, feel the prick of salt fog on his tongue. That same night, still coughing, he packed his few belongings and caught another train.

For the next five years, he wandered across the northern midwest, working for a teamster and then for a traveling cobbler, finally striking out on his own as a handyman, farmhand, day laborer. Thoughts of home came farther and farther apart until the fog of memory descended on Aguahega, its outlines blurring, steepled church vanishing, and then the whole of it lost altogether in a swirling white cloud.

Then one May a passing freight to which he clung thundered into the cool green dairyland of Wisconsin. Friedrich Schleicher, who owned one of the largest dairy farms near Madison and could pay the highest wage—$13 and board a month—took a liking to the tall, lank-haired young man with the big ears, guessing rightly that his broad shoulders could work tirelessly for hours.

And he did, for two more years. Old man Schleicher reminded him, in a way, of his father Perley Beal, and that made for easier dreams at night. He had given up the hope of making a fortune, he was 25 and happy just as he was, when he thought about it, until Schleicher decided to get himself a wife.

CHAPTER 2

1911 - Germany

She was watching the ice again.

When the summons came Clara Bittens was looking for the first signs of breakup in the pond, the ice-out that meant spring. *The* spring: she had just turned fifteen, and she was the prettiest girl in Schleswig-Holstein, Joerg had said. Her glossy light brown hair was braided in a crown around her face whose skin was thick and opaque, all the same creamy hue.

The shouting brought her head up. Her black brows pinched together in amazement as she watched her father hurtling right through the middle of the potato field, leaping like a young goat.

Otto Bittens brandished the white envelope over his head, and she could hear the excitement in his voice—a letter! From America a letter!

America. In America there were streets paved with gold. You could pick up glittering chunks big as your fist right at your feet. In America there was even a street named Gold in New York where young John Jacob Astor, born right near here in Heidelberg, found a job pounding skins, and then went on to make twenty-five millions of dollars in the fur business. Of course, this sum was as incomprehensible to Clara as if she had been told the distance to the moon. But she had heard it spoken over and over, reverent as a catechism, by the men beside the fire over their juniper-scented *Bommerlunder* brandy, counting what was left in their homespun pockets after market day.

The entire family gathered to hear the letter read in the low brick cottage, whose sharply sloping thatched roof nearly reached the ground. With her ten brothers and sisters, Clara sat cross-legged on the side that was family living quarters, the fireplace and oven in a commanding position in the center beneath the high peak of the roof. Facing her were the now empty stalls for the grazing dairy cattle, a loft piled high with fragrant hay above.

He would marry now, Friedrich Frans Schleicher had written. He wanted a bride from the Old World, of course, from home—someone young and strong, not afraid of hard work, who could bear him many sons. And of those of marriageable age, Clara was the youngest, *nicht wahr*?

Clara's parents, Otto and Ermgarde, were flattered. It was an opportunity, they said, for an ignorant young farm girl like herself. Everyone knew about Herr Schleicher, how he had crossed the great ocean to America some thirty years before, and now he was wealthy and wished to share his good fortune and grand dairy farm in the place called Wisconsin with a wife. Oh, how lucky for you, *Mädel*. You silly goose, why do you cry?

When the loaves were finished baking, they ate them with a special dish to celebrate: *Labskaus*, a stew of cured pork, mashed potatoes, and herring served with poached eggs and pickled cucumbers. But Clara's throat refused to swallow.

Herr Schleicher—someone had hastily figured it out—was now sixty years and three.

And because gloomy news gathers ballast, someone next remembered that there were wild Indians in America who snatch young girls into captivity and never let them go. And there were snakes in every stream, called Cotton Jaw, who crawl up out of the night and into your bed!

America.

After the meal had been cleared away, Clara crossed the marshy stream on the plank nailed to pilings, climbed over the hill of dikes and down to the tumbled sand dunes with their patches of wind-blown grass. A soft rain was falling through the worn places in her brown woolen cloak. She shivered as she stood looking out to the North Sea. Behind her stretched the flat farmland of Germany's northernmost province, the cottages clustered at the center of rich fields: vegetable, potato, and wheat, and soft green heaths starred with black and white cows.

She stood on her toes: if she could just see far enough, she could look right across and see it—America.

But Herr Schleicher was 63.

It never occurred to her to resist her father's decision. Marriages were arranged; that was the usual thing. But she knew the way she felt looking at Joerg, how her heart beat faster and palms grew sweaty—and also how most of the village boys stirred as much interest in her as her brothers. It was just that she hoped Herr Schleicher would make her feel as Joerg did.

But what would *he* think of *her*? Would he grow to like her, would he approve? She had strong arms and wide shoulders, could certainly cook well and clean, and her laundry was famous for five miles. And from the cattle she knew all about mating and birthing, what to do, how it went.

Because she was frightened, romantic thoughts filled her head, gradually soothing the fear to an aching sweet excitement. Herr Schleicher—Friedrich—would be tall and silver haired, and infinitely gentle and kind. He would wear velvet and fine linen and smoke a long pipe while she mended beside him in the evening candle's glow. And then he would put down his pipe and together they would go up to the bed....

In a clear low voice she began to sing.

Unter der Linden, Auf der Heide,
Wo mein Liebster bei mir sass,
Da Könnt ihr finden
Gebrochen beide
Bunte Blumen und das Gras,
Im nahen Wald mit hellem Schall,
Tandaradei!
Sang so süss die Nachtigall.

Under the linden, On the heath,
Where my sweetheart sat with me,
Where you can find
Broken, both
Colorful flowers and grass,
In the nearby woods, with ringing sound
Tandaradei!
So sweetly sang the nightingale.

Someone had come up behind her. "You won't be singing soon," her married sister Uschi said. "Just wait till a man gets the rights of you."

Clara Bittens lay as she had for the past four days on the canvas hung by hooks from iron tubing, unable to lift her head, not sure if she was awake or asleep. In the ghost light of the candle bracketed with its tin reflector to a timber, she stared down the lumped length of her body under the thin blanket to the hill of her feet. It swung up in an arc higher than her head and then plummeted in a dizzying descent that threatened to spill her from the bed.

The small steamer had no more than departed Hamburg when it encountered the storm and thirty foot waves. The door twelve steps up from the aft steerage compartment had been tied with rope from the outside, sealing them in so no one would get swept overboard.

Clara closed her eyes, trying to wall off the seasick agony, to move away from it. But it moved with her, pushed upward in a rush with the arc of her feet and again she doubled up, reaching for the tin plate they had given her, which wasn't large enough.

She was going to die, that was all. She had seen pigs die, and new young calves still wet from birth, and her grandmother and two little sisters. It would be a relief to die, she prayed for it.

The six-foot high compartment was filled with the weak groans of the ill, children crying. Without portholes or ventilation, the air was thick with the smells from the ship's galley, human excrement, the sharp sourness of vomit. The men were separated from the women only by a few blankets tossed over a sagging line. Beneath her own blanket, Clara had not dared remove her best gray woolen dress, which covered the new store-bought underwear drenched with sweat. She stared at the ship's timbers close above her face and her eyes—hot, red, swollen—like a sore, oozed clear liquid too devoid of feeling to be tears.

"Paved with gold!" a man shrieked beyond the blankets. "You poor fool. My brother went over last year and he got a job *doing* the paving. It was certainly stone."

On the seventh day, the storm let up and Clara, weak but recovering, found herself summoned to the office of the ship's doctor. He was fat and shiny-bald and red and smelled of peppermint *schnapps.*

"Liebes Fräulein," he said. He frowned sternly, wagging a finger at her.

"Yes?"

"You are a woman alone."

Under her chemise, the steel and whalebone corset pinched sharp as a bee sting into her side.

"Many young women of purest virtue *think* they are coming to be married in America. But alas, *Liebes Fräulein*, a fate worse than death awaits them."

"The wild Indians capture them, *Herr Doktor*?"

His lips, the color of overripe raspberries, pursed. His thick finger banged once, twice against them. They opened obediently. "Ah, a humorist I have here. There is the Mann Act in America, prohibiting the transportation of young women across state lines for—Do you know that which I am saying, *Fräulein*?"

"Yes. A man gets the rights of you."

He smiled. He planted the stethoscope tubes among the tufts of gray hair in his ears, and with the other end approached her chest. "Please to unbutton."

"What for?"

"There is the matter of the examination. A requirement for everyone, my dear."

The cold metal disc pressed among the frills of her corset cover with rhythmic lunges, and then he suddenly reached in with one huge hand. Through the armor of her underwear he squeezed her large breast twice before, in her stunned disbelief, she realized anything was happening. If she screamed, would he cuff her, throttle her, rape her, kill her, send her back to Germany in disgrace? She felt a wave of passivity like water close over her head. His fingers wedged under the top of her corset, straining to pry it away from her chest. She felt the starched frills pull, finally give way and tear. The sound was loud in the hot close air. His fingers found her nipple and his breath pumped hot against her neck. Somewhere down by his lap, his other hand kept time with a furious motion.

She wasn't here; this wasn't happening at all.

Sounds like a rutting bull tore from his mouth.

In her mind she saw herself running, felt her legs carry her away safe at home. The sand sank cupping after her bare feet, but she ran faster than it could seize her. And then her hands fell spread on the tall round warmth of *Trotz*, the huge balance rock poised by the sea. Her toes found the small bulge there, the tiny cleft here as she scampered up and around and over to his sun-warmed lap, a ledge six inches wide facing the sea, where no one could find her.

Trotz, her father had named the rock. Defiance: "You see how he defies the sea."

Clara felt a tightening in her stomach. In the doctor's cabin she seized on it with her mind, concentrating down through the floor to the pitching, rolling of the steamer in the sea. Her mouth began to water, sweat sprang out on her face.

The doctor's hot fingers slid wet over her cold puckered skin. Just as he made a sound like a stuck pig, she accomplished her mission: very suddenly and very completely vomiting all over his clean braid-hung brass-buttoned jacket.

Clara Bittens walked out the back door of the Great Hall of Ellis Island, down the stairs, down the wire-enclosed path to the ferry landing. The dark little interpreter gripped her arm.

She was "a woman alone."

Inspectors had boarded the ship in New York harbor looking for white slavery, finding only women seasick, yellow as lemons. But Clara could not be released from Immigration Service control until she was safely married.

Now, in the crush of languages—Arabic, Armenian, French, Italian, Polish, Spanish, Yiddish—her eyes searched shyly at first, then frantically for the silver-haired gentleman. Around her couples embraced, children fled into welcoming arms, and everyone seemed to belong to someone who waited for them, wanted them, and loved them. She felt her heart contract. The milling landing was emptying, the first rush of people spreading out onto the ferry and away.

Toward her came an old beggar—lank pieces of white hair descended unevenly from a shiny bald pate, baggy wrinkled clothes were knotted together at the waist with a rope. He carried a stained carpetbag, his back stooped, and his eyes seized on her as he drew nearer. Scornfully she turned away, smoothing her skirt from the touch of his garments as he passed.

But he didn't pass. The guttural sounds of the fatherland came from his mouth, in which loomed a few yellowed teeth. Her own mouth opened in horror.

"Wie heissen Sie?" he said. What is your name?

All she could do was breathe.

"Wie heissen Sie?"

"Clara Bittens."

He bowed. *"Sehr angenehm."* Delighted to meet you. *"Darf ich mich vorstellen: Mein Name ist... "* May I introduce myself, I am..."

But she knew that already.

They were married at City Hall before an alderman who inserted lewd asides into the reading of the vows, much to the amusement of two politicians who hung around to watch "the mail-order bride." From Pennsylvania Station, Clara and Friedrich Schleicher boarded a train.

The dining car swayed and clicked, the rumble oddly soothing as Clara drank cup after cup of coffee to keep them at the table. Outside the window, the towns appeared, blazed by, and were gone. Friedrich rose out of their silence, staring down at the crown of her braided hair. His fingers closed upon her upper arm.

He was not gentle, and it seemed that each part of his body had its own peculiar smell. When it was over, he immediately fell asleep. Clara lay bruised and quivering, eyes staring at the berth above. When she awakened he was on top of her, and she flinched as he entered her again.

She thought: I am no longer a woman alone.

The farm was the only part that resembled her imaginings. On its lush green acres, three hundred head of dairy cattle grazed. The bank account was fat as cream, and there were many outbuildings and a tall Victorian farmhouse. Friedrich showed Clara the upstairs, and then their bedroom with its high four-poster, one bedpost carved with a sun; the other, a moon. He would sleep on the side with the sun, he said. He stared at her with the signs she had already come to know: eyes bulging moist and glassy, a redness suffusing neck and cheeks. He pushed her back on the bed. The curtains were open. He surged over her body, the rough material of his trousers abrading her thighs. She turned her face away, staring out into the brightly lit freedom of the yard.

A man stood there staring up at them. His name was Gooden Beal.

CHAPTER 3

1912-1914, Wisconsin

When Clara was 16, Wilhelmina Elisabeth Schleicher was born. She was undersized and red and cried incessantly. Clara tried to love her. She carefully fed her and bathed her and rocked her to sleep, but no emotion for the tiny body stirred in her.

In Willi's face it seemed she could see Friedrich's eyes.

Friedrich wasn't cruel to her, treating her as well as any of his possessions. There were a few nights when, eyes squeezed closed, she felt a warmth flush through her body that was almost like pleasure, imagining he was Gooden Beal.

Gooden was one of three men, unkempt and unshaved, who slept in the bunkhouse. He was taller even than Joerg, with hugely muscled shoulders and thighs, a shock of straight brown hair that fell thick as fur around his ears. When he smiled, which she had witnessed just once, his eyes flashed at her like fish through blue waters.

She sat at her sewing room window more and more now, mending, darning, and knitting, glancing out from time to time across the yard. Soon she could sense his entrance from the corner of her eye—as if the farmyard were in two dimensions while he leaped out in three.

Once he had looked up and seen her; she waited for his smile. Instead he scowled fiercely, brows drawing together. But after that he looked up all the time.

Clara began to take an interest in the farm, asking Friedrich about it, wandering around its outbuildings and pens.

Gooden was raking out the floor of a stall in the birthing shed when she paused in the doorway.

He looked up, eyebrows drawing together. "Oh! Hullo."

She watched him rake a few more mounds of soiled hay.

"Uh, how does he call you, Mädel? But that means just girl, Sam said. What's your name?"

She stared at his face and then shook her head, gesturing toward her mouth. Her eyes filled with a sad aloneness.

"I know, I know. Don't speak English, hey? That's what I heard. Old devil keeps you cooped up like a setting hen, afraid you'll steal a nest. But here, now, if he won't learn you, want me to try?"

Her face brightened at his smile. She had a very nice face, he thought.

"Okay. Now—uh—let's see here. My name is Gooden." He thumped his chest with two fingers. "Goo-dun."

She pointed at him. "Goo-dun."

"Ah-hah! Learn fast, do you? Okay now. My name is Gooden. But you, you are—" He pointed at her. "My name is—. Go on. Your turn now."

Her pale gray eyes, so light beneath the thick black brows it was almost as if they weren't there, stared up at him.

"Oh, girl, I don't know no more about how to...Okay, now you look here. Pay attention to me." He tapped his chest with two fingers again. "My name is Gooden." He pointed the fingers at her. "My name is—" He nodded, pointing again at her.

She tapped her fingertips against the white collar of her ankle-length brown dress. He nodded violently. "My name ist—" More nods. "My name ist—Clara!"

"Clara! Clara. Well, now, that's a good, solid, sensible name as I ever heard there, yessir."

"My name ist Clara!"

"That's right! A good name you got yourself now, Clara. Now, let's see..." He looked around for inspiration. A large Guernsey cow which had been circling restlessly in the next stall was now staring curiously at them. He pointed to the cow. "Cow! Cow! Say it, Clara, go on and try it. Cow."

"Cow?"

"Cow! That's right, by gum. Cow!"

The cow chewed its cud, jaws moving left-right, left-right, eyes unwaveringly fixed on their faces. Clara pointed suddenly at its head. "My name ist cow!"

The cow paused, chewed, paused as if reflecting, and then belched.

They laughed. The sound was sudden and its joy seemed to hang in the air.

Clara turned and fled back toward the house.

Once more in her sewing room, she looked again from her window into the yard. "Cow," she said softly, experimentally. She held up the piece of mending spread on her wooden darning egg, straightening its edge. Then her fingers moved nimbly with needle and thread. Her voice was quiet as a whisper. "My name ist Gooden."

Over the next few months she learned "good morning" in the big round dairy barn and "How are you? I am fine" in the chicken house. She learned "What time is it? Quarter past ten. Eleven o'clock. Twenty past six. It's late, Clara, oh my God," in the kitchen, when Friedrich had driven the two bay geldings on his weekly trip into Madison.

Then came the thunderstorm and Friedrich not yet back from town. In a moment the sky blanched from gray to a fierce yellow, the wind tearing her dry laundry from the line. Last night, Clara had set the stiffened, work stained clothes, the grimiest sheets soaking. At dawn she hauled in wood for the fire, bucket after bucket of water for the washing machine and the boiler and every pot that could be crowded on top of the cookstove. It had taken all morning. And now, in just a few more moments, her laundry—ready to fold in the linen closet stacked to the rafters with sun-scented white—would be soaked again, draggled in mud.

Clara ran out into the yard, the first huge separate drops pricking her face like darts of ice. Tears of frustration ran down her cheeks as her fingers struggled with the thick wooden clothespins, the long white sheets punishing her black stockinged legs.

Suddenly she halted. Between the endless double lines of white and blue, another person was pulling sheets off and rolling them out of reach of mud beneath one arm—a man.

They met in the middle, drops spattering closer and closer now, spreading circles of wetness intersecting circles on the sheets piled in her straw basket. Gooden's hand, hot against her cold red skin, closed suddenly on her fingers. His pale blue eyes stared down at her, his eyebrows drawn together. He pulled her suddenly against him, his body heat searing through her damp clothes which felt suddenly fragile and thin, the clinging membranes of the few remaining sheets whipping her body as if it had no covering at all.

His hand seized her arm and they ran awkwardly, carrying the basket to the dark square of the harness room. Inside, gasping, she let her basket drop to the rough plank floor. He closed the heavy door, sealing the room into darkness. The small window was gray, lashed now with the staccato of driving rain. As she rubbed her arms, eyes adjusting to the dim light, the shadowed shapes of hanging harnesses and saddles, bridles, and halters swam into focus. The sharp scent of new leather, the waxy scent of saddle soap filled the air.

Gooden bent over her, and she felt the clean dry towel from the line rubbing and warming her arms, her face, her throat. He knelt down and unlaced her black ankle boots and drew off the soaked black stockings. The towel rubbed away at her ankles, her calves, her knees—the most wonderful sensation she had ever felt. He spread out some horse blankets from the pile in the corner and she lay back on their scratchy wool, the soft deep animal scent of horses breathing out around her head. He took off her dress and she lay shivering in her white, now patched chemise and the full-skirted underdrawers.

And then they were gone.

She heard his indrawn breath. She half sat up, propped on her elbows. She looked proudly at the jut of her full breasts and then up at his face. She thought, I do not want to be a woman alone.

Her exposed breasts felt damp and cold and then his chest seared heat down upon them. She had time to question what she was doing, and why.

She heard a voice saying, "*ja, ja, ja*."

From outside in the yard, she could hear the few sheets they had abandoned on the clothesline angrily popping, lecturing her in the wind. And then, after a time, the temperature fell and they hung frozen and still.

A fly buzzed in the summer heat.

Gooden's eyes were shut and his mouth had sagged open. He had a bulky way of lying just as he did moving, standing.

She knew she had to tell Gooden today. But how?

Clara peered out the dim cobwebbed glass of the window high in the enormous round barn. One hundred and two feet below she could see men and horses like insects, crawling in isolation out to the horizon. In Germany, farm families lived together in villages, coming and going from the fields. But in America, it was so lonely: each family as far apart as possible, walled in by lonely fields.

The familiar smells drifted up from the square opening in the loft: grain and manure, sweat, animals, rotted straw, sneezy hay dust, and the fatness of milk. Hay was forked down from the loft into a central bin from which stalls radiated like spokes of a wheel. A round barn, Friedrich said, kept the devil from hiding in the corners. But the barn was deserted now, all the cattle out grazing. The only devil was within herself.

Gooden's eyes opened. He brushed a fly from her loosened tawny hair, fingers lingering against the opaque whiteness of her face.

The squared ends of his fingers felt rough and warm.

She had to tell him; it would wait no longer.

"That tulip tree Friedrich has bringing back from town? He told me water it. I have good. But it has dying. He has angry."

Clara's eyes looked at him, and he saw the violence and bite in them. He had learned not to look too deeply in her eyes.

Her voice came soft and gentle. "But I have watering it, Gooden. Every day. With the boiling teakettle and the laundry soap!"

"Clara, what is it? What's troubling you?"

"It has nothing doing good."

"It's bad? What's so bad I couldn't hear it?"

"You have hating me. You have leaving me now."

"Clara—"

"The old maid has not."

"What the devil are you taking on about?"

"The old maid! It has not, at the time!"

"What old maid?"

"I have—there has coming a child."

In his silence she heard her happiness shatter, its pieces scattering, winking back at her from memory like a dropped glass.

If this was what sex was, she didn't want it. She renounced it. What was it worth: the greedy itch, sweating palms, just like with Joerg. It was this that made Friedrich write her father, want to marry. It was this drew her to Gooden Beal. It was this joined a man and a woman together, so that the man could destroy her. It was for nothing more than this that all her happiness was crushed and gone.

"Clara, Clara. How could it have happened? Minded my pull-backs all these months."

She remembered the sudden sting as scabs on the small of her back scraped off again. She knew what to expect: his sudden cry and then the violent abrupt withdrawal, spilling the wetness onto the dry porous boards.

In the barn she looked at him. Did he not know? Friedrich had demanded his rights of her, did Gooden think she could have stopped it? Did he think Friedrich too old now, had given up the marriage bed? Humiliation filled her. Uncertainty growing day by day, week by week, despair crossed out by hope replaced by despair. And finally the certainty and that was worse.

She was seventeen. At this rate, there would be twelve children by the time she was 27. She had tried to speak to Friedrich of her wish to wait before the next child, begged him to use masculine restraint.

"Dr. Mott warned me well, Mädel," he had said. "It is dangerous to interrupt Nature. Debility is caused and jaundice, sleeplessness, weak back. And childbearing is God's purpose for woman."

Oh how she hated Dr. Mott. Stone blind, he had delivered Willi, and Friedrich had called him for just that reason. It made him a better doctor, people said, more sensitive to his touching. All the doctors conducted their female examinations and deliveries under cover anyway, by touch alone. The jokes of old midwife Jutta in

Germany had been replaced by this—an ugly man's cold formal probing blind fingers. Yet even in Germany village women talked, most with broods of children numbering into the teens. Yes, they said, if no one would ever know. If you could be certain no one would ever know, they might do what Lotte had done: strangle her sixteenth, a newborn babe.

Clara thought of the thing growing relentlessly within her, lodged firmly as a peach pit.

"But Friedrich, the cows in the barn, the calving, God limits it to certain periods—but not for women. God must have intended women to limit it themselves."

"*Halt die Schnauze!*"

It would be better to be a woman alone.

In the barn Clara dared a glance at Gooden lying beside her. His eyes had softened.

"Never had me a child, you know, Clara. I want him, our child." His hand reached out, tentatively stroked her belly which he saw now was slightly round. "Can't rattle around in a buggy now, of course. Just up and wait a bit, wait it out until he gets born."

"And then?"

"We'll leave then. Can't weld cake dough to cast iron. A young girl to an old man."

"Gooden, you have meaning it? But where going?"

He turned over on his belly, chin on his hands. "Place I know of. Rich enough to put butter on your bacon. You'll have you a rhubarb patch there, beans and potatoes. And walk out to the pasture with sixty sheep, and strawberries growing sweet as all sweet. Past the pasture you come to blueberries, then cranberries in the bog, and then farther you're standing on clam beds squirting at your bare toes, and farther it's cunners and flounders you can handline right off our dock.

"And you get you in a boat, Clara, and go out to the ledges off Hobbomocca Head where lobsters crawl, so thick in my daddy's day spread 'em for manure on the fields—lobsters grew biggest squash of all. And then sail farther, two miles out for mackerel, cod, haddock. Everything you need."

"What has the name?"

"Aguahega Island."

"And the baby has no trouble, Gooden, I making sure. And Willi, she has quiet, and—"

"No."

"No?"

"Willi must stay here, of course. I'm sorry, but Willi is *his*."

"Gooden—"

"Willi's old enough to be without you now. The babe must suckle, but Willi eats at the table. The babe is mine. We'll take the babe, but Willi stays behind."

"It has wrong. I have afraid, Gooden. Leaving him, wrong. Leaving her, wrong. You, me: wrong."

"Your duty is to me now, Clara, and to our child."

She watched one of her hands, holding the other.

"You'll be happy, Clara, I promise you that, my girl. In time you will even forget."

She said it just to hurt him. "What if it has changing, Aguahega?"

"Does the sun go from west to east?"

1914

Johann was born in January. Deep in February, Clara Bittens Schleicher knotted her grandmother's feather pillow in her extra dress. Then, from the darkened kitchen she took a slab of cake and climbed the stairs to Willi's room. Slowly, fearfully, she pushed the door open, expecting to find her asleep.

But Willi was gripping the wood bars of her crib, standing stockily in a welter of bedding and a rumpled white nightdress. The two year old stared soundlessly at her mother.

Clara's hand reached out, offering the cake. The child stared up at her, refused to take it. It was as if she knew she was being left behind.

"*Willst Du noch was?*" Clara whispered. Do you need anything?

Still the child stared, brown eyes pulsing like candle flames guttering in a breeze.

Clara pushed the cake through the crib bars where it lay brown and falling into crumbs on the white sheet. She hurried to the door, paused, looked back.

Willi seized the cake, which oozed lumpily through her gripping fingers. She flung it away to the floor.

Clara felt something break inside her—what was it, grief? Conformity? *Broken, both colorful flowers and grass.*

She couldn't leave. She couldn't leave her firstborn.

And then she felt Gooden's hand on her arm.

CHAPTER 4

1914-1918, Aguahega Island, Maine

Aguahega was a blue cloud on a blue horizon, then a green cloud, finally granite-edged reality. The bare mountaintops rose flushed as dawn above the firs. For the first time in ten years, Gooden looked at his home again.

"Clara, quick! Bring Johnny up deck. I want my son to see his birthright."

"Your son and daughter," Clara said. Willi fussed as usual, one hand dragging at Clara's long skirt, not even happy to have been brought along. It was the last day of February, but she climbed with the children to the mailboat's deck. It was one of the newfangled little gas boats whose warm cabin reeked with fumes.

"Just look," Gooden said. Something ached in his chest, and against it he felt his heart drum, shattering the ache and sending it shooting through him. Wheels of gulls revolved above him, bawking their fragile welcome into the wind. The smells of home reached out to him: ammoniated smell that was cat spruce, freshrot of clam flats, the clean scour of salt washing it all from the sea.

"Don't she look just like I told you now?"

Clara clutched the infant Johann to her chest, his heart tattooing rapidly down on hers. She tried to be brave as she examined this, her next new home: an island swept by wind. In the cold bite and freezing spray, she watched the village houses swelling white and gray through the wisps of scudding vapor. The village lay piebald with white, the blue of winter shadows stretching on the snow. A freezing rain was just beginning and she watched a slab of ice loosen from a roof, sweep soundlessly to the ground which met it with a devouring roar. To the south, the bare walls of an abandoned quarry frowned between the trees. She looked at the muck and rubble left by the low drain tide.

"Is there always with the wind, like this?" She tucked Johann's shawl tighter around his reddening cheeks.

"Wished we'd come when it was warmer, Clara. You'd fancy it then. Come summer, pick you lady slippers just the color of your fingers, blooming in the bog. But a snowy February, that's promise of a fine summer."

He pointed at the tall white Congregational steeple. "Ship's bell in the belfry. Hear it ring and you know it's death, disaster, or Sunday: same thing! See top of the steeple? Codfish made of gold, some say. Real cod's good as gold: smashed bone from its head stops female hemorrhage; bone in its stomach cures kidney stones. Or failing that, go in the church and pray!"

Gooden was looking at the lobster sloops drawn up on the Thoroughfare's shore, bare masts reaching high as the firs. In his mind he saw their sails bellying taut as he beat back racing the others all the way in from the lobster ledges off Killdevil Island. He always won, of course.

The gas motor pounded the mailboat's frame all around him and suddenly in his mind he saw its snubby prow pushing ahead, faster than the sloops. Fear stilled his blood: damn infernal combustion, what did his hands know of that? And the sloops—there'd been many more than this when he left.

"Unless it's a February like that year," he said, "had no summer at all. They called it eighteen-hundred and froze to death." It seemed he could hear voices crowding out from shore:

"Reek, rank, runk, all the lobstermen stunk."

"It smells like money, Gooden, now don't take on airs."

He wanted to cry out to her: *Mother*. Would she hear?

He couldn't remember where the lady slippers grew.

The mailboat captain was a stranger.

Weren't nearly enough lobster sloops on the shore.

"Why your face has all red?" Clara was peering up at him.

"Wind, freshening into a williewaw for sure. But I'll have all three of you wrapped snug to home by then, and Mother will fix you a hot mug-up. And wait till summer. You'll be happy as all happy then."

The captain rowed them in the little skiff toward the heron legs of the village wharf. But Clara stared up above the cliffs at a stone and shingle expanse, its many panes of glass staring back at her over a columned piazza out to sea. Its center clawed skyward with gables and chimneys, turrets and towers, high as the Great Hall on Ellis Island, maybe higher still. "Gooden, up on the hill. Is it the village, yes?"

The captain craned his rough-red face around to peer at her. "What parts do you hail from, m'am?"

"She's from Germany," Gooden said.

"Germany?"

"What is it—that place, Gooden?"

"Nothing. Just what they call Tenhaven—Seal Point. Set foot up there and I'll break every bone in your hand."

Willi's fussing escalated into cries. Her face was round red noise.

Clara patted Willi's head while looking again at the house. It was more beautiful than the Pennsylvania Train Station, more awesome than Schleicher's great round barn. Just let Gooden try and stop her. He could not rule her anymore than Schleicher did. She would do just as she pleased in this, her new home. The first chance she found she would satisfy her curiosity. She would go to this...Seal Point.

They trudged with their bags through the wind. "Island wind," Gooden explained, a steady force solid as a wall.

The wind was the same, he thought, but the road was new-graveled, the schoolhouse rebuilt, hung with a sign scrolled in loops and swirls: *The Lorelei School.* Lorelei? It had needed no name before. The road bent south and finally he saw it: Toothaker Harbor. His lungs forgot to breathe. Its houses sat doll-like against the soaring ridge of spruce, pine, cedar, and balsam that led up to high meadows swept free of snow. Smoke flattened westward from one of two chimneys on Perley's House.

It had waited for him: just the same.

But then he saw the schoolhouse, the second one for the community of Toothaker. The glass in the windows was gone and the roof hung cracked down its midline, a timber dangling loose.

Gooden walked faster. He saw the waterfront now, the salt water ice pushed up on the rocks by successive tides. The rain changed to snow, dusting the now black firs as the afternoon waned, powdering the granite ground with white into which Perley's House seemed lost.

"That's home." He pointed. The shingle flounces of the roof that had sparkled with ice just a few minutes ago were now dull. "Smashed rum on the roof when the neighbors raised her, Clara, for luck."

Clara stared up at the fan structure above the door, the baby in her arms. The fan's oak ribs radiated out from an embedded horseshoe. She felt her exhaustion, the strange place dry her tongue. And behind it was fear, a growing fear. "The horseshoe, it is down pointing. Down is meaning your luck falls out."

He turned abruptly away. He was looking at the waterfront and she saw a red-faced man in high red kag boots digging with a clam hoe. Not knowing who they were, still he raised his hand in welcome.

"Uncle!" Gooden ran toward him as if he were 8, not 28. He heard his boots ring like iron on the frozen ground. "Uncle Tobias, it's me Gooden. Uncle, I've come home."

For the first time since arriving in America, Clara allowed herself to hope. The fear began to erode, to slough off like an outgrown skin. They had fled as far eastward as people could go to this, the outermost island in a sea of islands, one for each day of the year.

He would never find them, and her children, here.

The windowpanes of Perley's House were opaque with frost. Two feet of dirt had been shoveled all around to the beginning row of shingles, two-horse wagonloads of evergreen brush cut and piled up to the first-story windows. Inside, Gooden's sister, Toss, made them welcome. Clara sat thankfully by the kitchen stove, stretching out her toes stinging with returning blood.

The rest of the house was unheated, one by one its rooms abandoned on the way to the final stronghold—the kitchen stove. On the second floor, Toss had shown Clara the bedroom she and Gooden would use. Clara pulled open the rough pine blanket chest and stared down: stacked to the brim with frozen pies.

But here in the kitchen, in the fellowship of heat, the Glenwood cookstove's cast-iron bulk glowed, in its rolltop cabinet a pie warming. Clara's fingers flew as they knitted the grand pair of cream colored booties for Johann, of wool soft as an eider down chick with flaming red toes and cuffs, the initials "JB" picked out in green thread.

"Such a pretty baby," Toss Beal said. She was forty-one but had never married.

"He is named—"

"Johnny," Gooden said. No one must know their son had been baptized Johann Bertolt Schleicher.

"Such a good baby, too." Johnny slept in his cradle by Clara's foot which rocked him gently, tirelessly. It seemed she never tired of caring for her son.

Willi began to cry again.

Clara felt the floor drafts close in around her ankles.

"Time we stopped going all around Robin Hood's barn," Gooden said. His thick long fingers spread stiff on each knee. "Where is Mother, Father? Evelina? Where might everybody be?"

Uncle Tobias's gaze darted to Toss's face framed in the woolen kerchief, then away. "Couldn't rightly believe you didn't know."

"Know what?"

"They all up and took bad sick, Gooden, long time ago. Was black typhoid, doctor said. After that foreign schooner put in—came in for the time at the cannery, and dancing and all. Weren't you here then? And then the black typhoid, it swept us, Gooden, must've been right after you left. Children, parents, Smiths lost eight of eleven children just in a week."

Gooden remembered lying in bed, hearing the oxen's hooves clattering over the planks where the cart path always flooded, the path that led to the burying ground. After the hooves came the thunder of the cart with its hastily nailed wooden coffin bouncing, the body within contagious, buried at night unheralded, without prayers. The hooves clattered over his heart.

"Mother?"

Tobias nodded.

"Father, Will, and Eben? Sydna Ellen, Alice?" His voice stumbled: "Evelina?" Eating dates and laughing, spitting them out on the plank floor—her face danced before him for the very last time.

And Mary Stella? he wanted to ask.

"Not Alice. She's down to Boston now."

"Boston?"

"And the Archbolds pay their maids good," Toss said. "Alice worked for them at the Point couple summers, and then they took her back with them to Boston, running water in her own room."

Clara looked up from her knitting. They were talking about Seal Point, and Alice had actually worked there. Perhaps she could, too.

"I want to see Mother's grave."

Toss waved goodbye from the kitchen door. Clara, Gooden, and Tobias started up the rutted frozen trail in the twilight. It crooked left into the thick cover of the evergreens. With each step, Clara's boots crunched the whited spears of frozen mud like glass. She looked behind. The snow had swallowed the clearing, harbor, houses. Perhaps they had never been.

She was not yet eighteen and she was frightened. She would have to be everything to Gooden now.

The little Beal burying ground was twenty yards back from the trail, the stones moss-grown and old, white and new.

Tammy dere beste pisoned
17 May 1795 O I greve.

In Memory Of George
son of Eben Beal
who died of the
putrid sore throat
Janry 20th, 1868
Aged 4 years and 6 weeks.

Clara straightened, dusting snow from her hands. She wanted desperately to run home, but where was home? Here?

Gooden stood by an empty stone cenotaph, reading the names chiseled into its side.

The names of his family were there.

His broad shoulders shivered in the tattered coat but there was no sound, nothing at all. Clara stood rooted, filled with the blind urge to break and run down the hill and away from this silent tormented stranger.

"Couldn't bury them," Tobias said. "Doctor said fire them and was done, like he said."

"Gooden," Clara said. "It is the time to go home."

She saw the life come back into his eyes, the flash of fish through blue waters the way they had looked at her in Schleicher's barn. It would be good here on Aguahega. Perhaps she could start a laundry in the abandoned schoolhouse, heaps of crisp white for Seal Point. She must make it good for Johann, Willi, Gooden, for all of them.

She was no longer a woman alone.

"When you say home," Tobias said, "you rightly mean Germany, don't you?"

CHAPTER 5

High above Clara's neatly braided hair the church bell was clanging, but not louder than the thudding of her heart beneath her new white-collared dress. She thought she would burst with excitement right through her skin.

"Now, mind you be neighborly to everybody," Gooden was saying in his tiresome slow-tongued way. "Time we started breaking the ice around here."

"Shhh," Clara motioned impatiently. She was trying to look, smell, hear all the fascinating things around her, especially the gossip of two women just entering the village church in front of her, the church whose foundation bore the words:

JESUS CHRIST
HIMSELF
BEING THE CHIEF
CORNER STONE

She was like a calf let loose in spring. It was the first time Gooden had allowed her away from Toothaker since their arrival four months before. But, "I must to worship," Clara had insisted, watching him out of the corner of her eye. He couldn't refuse that request. And the minister came just in June, July, and August now, Gooden had said—Reverend Witney and his wife, Mary Stella. Gooden's voice had faltered in the strangest manner over her name.

Inside the church the tall windows stood open, the salt breeze stirring the masses of lilac branches in pails around the plain wood altar, lavender and white and deep red lilacs from the bushes growing alone in the woods, over the foundations of burned, tumbled-down deserted farmhouses. There were so many of these now, it seemed.

Reverend Witney's thin hard voice assailed them, starched as his straight back, stiff face, stiff robe. But Clara didn't hear the sermon. The silver cry of the gulls through the windows stirred her blood. Then, with the first hymn, she heard a woman's throaty contralto, strong and sure and true. She stared again over at the forbidden left side of the aisle where the summer people from Seal Point stood.

The hymn ended; the singer closed her hymnbook, sitting upright as a heron among crows. She wore black and white tweed, a fringed yellow cashmere shawl across her arms. One gloved finger impatiently tapped her cheek beneath the black silk of a sailor hat. Now she raised her tan leather gauntlet, stifling a yawn as Witney's voice sawed on.

Did she see Clara staring? She shot a look across the aisle that divided them and then, as if sensing a kindred spirit, her painted mouth broke free in a grin.

Clara smiled back. Why, the woman wasn't much older than herself. Clara wished desperately for a real friend. This woman had no children like Johnny and Willi, either, who were squirming now and mussing the crisp brown of her precious new dress. Perhaps her husband practiced "masculine restraint." Clara wanted no more children, had broached the subject to Gooden who had reacted just about as Schleicher had. Every month she counted the days until "the flowers" appeared....

Perhaps this woman from Seal Point was a "woman alone."

"The *Point*." Gooden had spat at the stove. "Lower than whale's dung, all them up there." The moisture sizzled, danced, was gone.

"Now don't go scowling like that, Gooden," Tobias said. "Got us a new road, like they knew you was coming. And then the schoolhouse up to the village rebuilt."

"But who paid for all that?"

"Summer people. And we tax them, too. Not trapping so many lobsters, maybe, but we're trapping plenty summer complaint."

"It said 'Lorelei'—the school sign."

"Name of that summercator's yacht."

Clara looked across the church aisle again. Perhaps this woman even lived there: the great house on top of the cliffs.

After the service, the pews emptied out into the welcome warmth of the sun. Clara watched the beautiful Seal Point woman walk away.

It was time for the social: just for the year-rounders on the grass outside. The cloth-draped table was burdened with rapidly disappearing doughnuts, cakes, and pies. Amid the talk and laughter Clara stood alone. No one, she saw, cut into her beautiful high yeast bread studded with raisins.

"Want you to meet Mary Stella here." Gooden's fingers closed on Clara's elbow, urging her toward the Reverend and his pretty blonde wife.

Mary Stella let out a squeal, then her fingers flew up to hide her mouth. "Gooden Beal! Can't rightly believe it's you. Why, haven't you gone and finally fleshened up so's I'd hardly recognize you." Her hair was the color of taffy spun out in the sun but it was bound in a tight little knot. She looked up at Gooden from the sides of her eyes that glittered bright and blue.

"You're—" Gooden cleared his throat. "You're just perxactly the same."

"Well, just go right ahead then, insult me, like as not to die right here." Her small fat fingers fluttered down to her collar where they pressed as if to quiet her breath.

"I meant it for good."

Her small lips pursed, tight as an unopened flower.

With just the end of her gloved finger she touched his wrist where it stuck bonily out from his too-short jacket sleeve.

Clara stared. Gooden's bare skin jumped like a horse registering a fly.

"This here's my wife Clara. Know you two girls'll soon be fast friends."

"Of course we will." Mary Stella pressed Clara's sweating ungloved hand. "Why, Clara, you're ever so much nicer than I thought you'd be."

Mary Stella moved back to the minister's tall black-clothed side. "Why, good day to you, too, Mrs. Smallidge." She reached out her hand to the fat matron. "Now how's your youngest's cough—Jack, isn't it, dear?"

Everyone was either a Vannah or a Smallidge, and either a "good" Smallidge, Gooden had warned in a whisper, or a "bad" Smallidge, with whom you had to take care.

All she saw were the backs of heads.

When she moved near a little knot of people, all conversation stopped dead. When she moved away, she heard it spring back up behind her again like a flattened mushroom.

Some people just at sight of her approach were edging away.

Clara stood in her pinching high-buttoned black shoes, in an ache of shyness and unease before the faces that shattered every time she stepped near into a kaleidoscope of bits and flying pieces. The browns and grays and blacks of their Sunday best flooded outward, coalesced to the frightened pounding of her heart.

The table was a litter of empty cake plates, scattered crumbs—except for the screaming circle of her untouched yeast bread.

She could hear the surf that advanced upon her but just as rhythmically ebbed away.

Mary Stella's face was a pale disk suspended in the middle of the people, the flashing hands and skirts that moved around her in a dancelike circle. Gooden was there on the edge of the circle, his face turned toward Mary Stella too.

"Gooden." Clara's hand clutched his arm. "My bread no one has eaten. Why will they not eat my bread?"

He looked around at the table. "Why, so you're right. Now whyever can that be?" He bent over the cloth and hacked out a huge slab. Clara watched his strong white teeth bite into it. "Glory," he said loudly, "Clara, that's some good."

A silence had fallen.

"Best cake believe I ever ate."

"Gooden, shh. Please."

"It's just," he whispered, "you're from away."

"Away?"

"Not born on here."

"Oh."

"Everybody's Beals or Vannahs or Smallidges, like I said. Related someway."

"But a Beal I am too, Gooden. Or you think not so?"

His face reddened. They had never married: Clara had not been divorced. "Sure, sure." And then loudly, "Hank Vannah, trot right over here and have some of this'n here. Best cake here, you bet."

"Full near to splitting now."

"Why, you can eat like a house afire."

"Full up to here."

Clara stared around her. She felt everyone looking back, not liking what they saw. She grabbed the yeast cake's plate and held it above her head. "What is it which you believe is in it?" she screamed. "The sauerkraut?"

She threw the plate crashing to the ground. Gooden's body bent away from her, shrinking.

She began to cry in the midst of what she had done and the broken pieces. She turned and her boots thudded away from them toward the thick hidden woods circling Seal Point.

The gravel crunched beneath her black-booted feet, a hard angry sound like the sound of bones breaking, bone-white dust rising tickling to her nose. Through the firs she saw it: the cottage called "Tenhaven" escaping toward her in glimpses of light. Clara stopped and stared. Her burning gaze traveled from the first story of rough-laid local stones, gray mossed and lichened, to the half-timbered second story and on to the third story shingled like the roof. Two rambling wings were fat with sleeping porches, and six gables rose pointy as witches' hats between square mouths of chimneys. At the peak of the roof, a stone cupola consoled a widow's walk. The sun reflected off the polished bronze plaque mortared into the house's southeast corner:

1899

And Thine house and thy kingdom
shall be established forever
before thee: thy throne
shall be established forever.

A hollow baying startled Clara: a Scottish deerhound a yard high at the shoulder raced toward her, trumpeting his discovery of this interloper to anyone who could hear.

"Bizer, down. Get down, you worthless hound."

It was the tall woman who had smiled at Clara in church. Her fingers ungloved now, took hold of the dog's chain-link collar and it lunged against the restraint.

"Hello, dear. Have you lost your way?"

The dog's jaws above a beard of wire-haired gray and rust and silver foamed with eagerness to get at her. Clara burst into tears.

"Oh. He's harmless, really, don't be scared."

Clara cried harder, for everything: the months of toil cutting spruce boughs for lobster pot laths, hauling granite split by frost for ballast, too much work, they all had to help. Gooden returning home from hauling, hands so swollen he could not hold his own wife just when she needed him, needed him most.

"Dear, what's the matter? Come along in, we'll splash some water on your face."

In the Louis XVI sitting room, Clara perched on the edge of the hard gold upholstered chair. "I have now to go. Please. I am sorry, please."

"Nonsense. It's Bizer's fault—I think we bred his manners out. Have a little nip of sherry before you go."

Clara's large red fingers closed fearfully around the tiny crystal glass.

Without the hat, the woman wasn't quite so pretty: bobbed black hair smoothed down with brilliantine, the exaggerated widow's peak touched up with pencil. Clara watched her fit a cigarette in an ebony holder and light the end: a woman who wore paint and smoked cigarettes!

The woman was smiling now as if amused, and Clara felt reassured again. She was more friendly than anyone else on Aguahega had been.

"There now, that's better, isn't it? Go on, have a sip. Tell me, dear, are you European?"

"Germany." Clara gulped from the glass. It warmed down to the pit of her cold clenched stomach. She took another drink, feeling bolder now.

"Isn't that wonderful! Germany! My mother's father was German too."

Clara nodded. Something cricked too loudly in her neck.

"And Goethe is one of my favorite authors—for a man. Do you like to read?"

Again Clara nodded. She drank off the rest of the glass.

"I'm Eleanore Greeley (only). I call myself that because while dear Fairfield is my husband, I do not choose to take the name of Chancellor, but am known as Greeley (only). I'm a Lucy Stoner, you know. Or do you? Do you know of Lucy Stone, dear?"

Clara shook her head. The woman was pouring her another sherry. The liquid looked so beautiful and amber; it clung in oily drops to the side of the glass.

"If you would like, you may take these home to read." Eleanore extended a thick sheaf of pamphlets.

Clara stared down at the title on top:

The Congressional Union for Woman Suffrage,
The Executive Committee Report.

"I particularly recommend the pamphlets by Charlotte Perkins Gilman," Eleanore was saying. "One is called *Are Women Human Beings?* And the other—you'll find it in there—*The Waste of Private Housekeeping.*"

Clara put the pamphlets in her lap, placed her hands one above the other on top. A queer excitement raced through her.

"Now, dear, perhaps you'd like to tell me. Did you come here about a position?"

"A position?"

"A job."

Why did Gooden hate Seal Point so much? She never wanted to leave. Her neck seemed of its own accord to nod.

"Well, we can always use someone else in the kitchen."

"I have so much love to work the laundry."

"Do you have experience?"

Clara nodded her head, firmly now. "No one there is who has better."

"Well. Well, fine, then. You can start tomorrow. Tell me, dear, what's your name?"

Clara hesitated. They would just *say* they were married, Gooden had told her, and who was there to say otherwise? No one would know her real name was Clara Schleicher.

"My name ist Clara Beal."

Eleanore was looking pointedly at Clara's gold "wedding" ring, the ends of her rouged lips quirking up in a smile. "No, no, dear. I meant, of course, your real name. You've got to be quick on the draw around me: I like my girls to be fast. What's the name you were born with?"

Clara pushed the base of the crystal glass toward the leather top that covered the desk. Her hand was no longer steady and a fine hot buzz filled her head.

"Clara Bittens."

"Clara Bittens *(only)*. And the remuneration is one dollar a week, dear."

Clara nodded. She was a woman (only) now. "I will take it—for a dollar and a half."

It was August 4, and in Eleanore Greeley (only)'s bedroom Clara threw open the tall French windows that gave onto a balcony. The fresh breeze off the bay stirred through the vases of roses, perfuming the air. It was Clara's favorite room in Tenhaven: its walls painted with a fresco of pink with pastel traceries of birds, animals, plants. The pink marble fireplace faced two couches heaped with lace-edged pillows.

Clara had just stripped the circular canopied bed. She thrust the sheets in the dirty clothes closet: ventilated with an exhaust pipe that extended upward to the highest point of the roof. Now she tied back the gold-embroidered lilac bed draperies and put her fresh ironed-crisp sheets on the bed. It was so strange, Clara was thinking, as she considered the fact that Fairfield Chancellor's bedroom was far down the hall. These people who had everything didn't seem to want each other.

She was thinking what Gooden would do if she suggested *he* take a separate bedroom. She didn't worry about more children now: it was wonderful. Eleanore had sent Clara to one of the Seal Pointers who was a "modern" doctor, and she had worn the new thing called a diaphragm home. They could love each other as often as they wanted to now, and Gooden wanted to all the time.

Yet when she had told him about working for Mrs. Chancellor, he had forbidden her to return. "You cannot be stopping me. You must go out to go fishing. I will go to the Seal Point then." Gooden had stayed out all night that night. When he returned, he wouldn't tell her where he'd been. He was dead drunk and there was blood on his hands.

Clara began to make Mrs. Chancellor's bed.

"Oh. Now Clara, dear, don't you stop and let us bother you for one minute. Just pretend we're not here."

Eleanore and her friend, Kitty Archambault, stood there, Eleanore's tennis outfit, a black and white checked tunic over a white skirt, stopping several inches short of her ankles, the most shocking skirt Clara had ever seen. She looked down in confusion, stretching taut the bottom sheet.

"Want to play again tomorrow?" Kitty said.

Eleanore flopped down into one of the overstuffed chairs. "We could make it doubles if I could get that stuffed-shirt Fairfield to play. It's just so boring the way he and Fitz sit and talk about Wall Street all the time, even when they're on here."

" 'On here!' Do you hear yourself, El? Starting to sound like one of the natives. Anyway, with men it's all money, money, money, that's what's wrong with them."

"Actually, their brains are between their legs."

"All Fitz can talk about is the new income tax and how J. P. Morgan and Marshall Field had to pay two hundred fifty thousand each. I think it's a new form of competition: who pays the most tax."

"It serves Marshall Field right. Fairfield told me he pays his girls in Chicago a simply grand nine dollars a week, and that's what makes our girls always clamor for raises."

Kitty nudged Eleanore, who glanced in Clara's direction. Then Eleanore suddenly rushed over to the bed. "Oh no, Clara, for goodness' sake, no. I told you about this just yesterday! When you remake the beds, reverse the sheets, put the top on the bottom and the bottom on the top, then turn them endwise each time so the northeast corner becomes the southwest corner, you see?"

Clara nodded.

"I had the last girl mark the north end with red thread, see here? It will remind you to keep rotating them for equal wear. The cost of sheets has gone out of sight."

There was a sound of loud asthmatic breathing, and all three women looked up to see Fairfield Cordell Chancellor, Jr., standing in the doorway attached by the hand to his English nurse.

"Mrs. Chancellor—oh my glory! England declared war on Germany, cook just heard it. And there's a big German liner tied up over in Bar Harbor, loaded with gold. It was on its way to London and turned back. The Mr. Chancellor wants to take the gas boat over and see it and wants to know will you come?"

"Mama, I go too. I go too!"

"Hush, Cordy, dear, you know you'll just go and get all excited and choke up something dreadful. Tell Mr. Chancellor I'll be right down, Miss Hipe, and with Kitty, too."

"Served those rotten huns right," Kitty said, gathering her grosgrain-banded straw hat. "They're going to get it this time."

This time Eleanore nudged her friend, rolling her gaze toward Clara who was staring at them dumbstruck.

Germany? At war with Britain? The flood of emotions drowned out her reaction to the word "huns." There had been rising anti-German feeling all over the States this past year, and Clara knew everyone on Aguahega referred to her behind her back as "the German." Most of the fishermen were undiluted English stock.

Clara thought of bullets, bayonets, dying screams. What would happen now to her family in Schleswig-Holstein? Would she ever see Mama and Papa again?

That evening, Clara, too, saw the ship, the most beautiful ocean liner in the world. Gooden, though not without grumbling after a long day's lobstering, sailed them all the way over to Frenchman Bay. The ship stretched 700 feet long with four bright yellow funnels. Her name was *DER DOPPELSCHRAUSEN SCHNELLDAMPFER KRONPRINZESSIN CECILIE*, but everyone called her Kronprinzessin Cecilie.

At Seal Point, Captain Pollock was welcomed as the social hit of the season. Even the Chancellors had crossed the Atlantic on his German pleasure ship. Clara felt herself bursting with national pride.

"*Pollock!*" Gooden said. "That's not a name, it's a fish. The stupidest fish in the sea. Grab you a bare hook and drop it over the dock, a pollock'll go for it every time."

The people at Seal Point understood: there were many Germans as charming, as distinguished as Captain Pollock in his handsome dress uniform. It was the rest of Aguahega, Gooden's friends, who could not, would not understand.

When she showed up for work at Tenhaven the next day, Fairfield Chancellor called her into his study. "My wife informs me that you are German, Mrs. Beal."

She looked up, proud. "Yes."

"Please do not take this personally. But consider yourself fired."

CHAPTER 6

In 1915, German submarines sank the Lusitania, and 1,198 innocent passengers died. Ernest Muenter, a German instructor at Cornell University, planted a bomb in the U. S. Senate cloakroom.

And on Aguahega, the year-rounders shunned Clara as never before.

In Perley's House at night, Gooden began to talk to Clara of a dream—an ideal boat with plain beauty and simple outfit—a boat to haul lobsters from. And as he talked, he whittled on a block of spruce and the form began to take shape. None of these sails anymore: no, his boat would have an internal combustion engine which would also run a hauling wheel.

With those, he said, he knew he could double the number of pots he hauled.

In 1916, German zeppelins attacked Paris, and German saboteurs exploded a munitions plant at Tom Island, New Jersey. "You never know where these spies may be," Mary Stella Witney said, "even next door." Johnny Beal, visiting at a neighbor's was sent home crying after he was discovered crooning *"Du du, leib mir in hertzen"* to a beat-up tomcat.

Gooden carried his spruce boat model to the builder in Haley's Landing, where they argued endlessly about the design and the price.

On April 6, 1917, the United States declared war on Germany. When Eddie Witney, Mary Stella's son, came down with German measles, she told everyone, "It's liberty measles, thank you." On the island of Great Britain, the Royal Family changed its name from Coburg to Windsor. On the island of Aguahega, Clara Beal had no choice in keeping her name, though she knew nothing of politics: "the German," spoken openly now in her presence with only half-concealed angry looks.

In 1918, Gooden followed the boat builder to the sawyers to pick out the oak for the framestock and the keel. "Has to be pasture oak," Gooden insisted. "Blue as a whetstone and tougher than biled owl."

By March, the builder had scarfed and rabbetted the backbone. By May, he'd put up the forms, wrapped and wired the ribbands, finished the framing. In June, he began the planking.

And then there was the matter of the boat's luck to attend to. Gooden couldn't sleep with anxiety. The keel, never to be laid on a Friday, was laid on a Monday. The boat was painted white and red—no blue anywhere, the sea being jealous of its own hue. A silver dollar was placed beneath the board where once a mast would have stood. A boy was hired to stand all day in the boatyard to prevent birds from lighting on her before she was launched. She would be launched in August on the first eleven o'clock tide.

In July, 1918, German submarines sank more than thirty fishing boats off the New England coast. Gooden thought he saw U-boats in every wave. It had been discovered that sixty miles along the Maine coast provided the best radio conditions in the Western hemisphere for communication with Europe. As if he had an intuition that day before dawn, Gooden longed to roll over and pull Clara closer, hug her warm breath instead of the stiff breeze off the sea. Yet he rose and quickly dressed, took one last look at Clara, and was gone.

He was still fishing when Clara made her way north toward "Amen House," the unpretentious summer cottage of the Cecil Wrights who wintered in New London, Connecticut. She wore her brown and white dress, a pair of cast-off rubber fishing boots with the tops cut off, and a ragged plaid scarf knotted under her chin.

"Clara, dear," the letter had read. "We've changed our mind, we will be coming up after all. Would you be so kind as to open up, air out, and just generally 'red up' Amen House for us?"

The house, once a fisherman's, was white clapboard overlooking a deserted cove, beyond it the archipelago of islets and dry ledges to the east and the sea—unobstructed all the way to Europe.

The quick movement caught Clara's eye. She stared at the white curtain hanging still as a shroud across the winter-locked side window.

Had she really seen it move?

Nonsense.

But the quiver, the tiniest shiver of fabric in motion, danced its imprint behind her eyes.

Squirrels! With a dart of indignation, whipping out the doorkey, she marched around to the porch. Squirrels—the mess they made of a clean, tidied house when they gnawed their way in under the loose eaves or a frost-sprung floorboard: shredding curtains into lace, turning papers into confetti, gnawing chair legs into the shape of hourglasses, their droppings laid out proudly here, there, and everywhere, sunning like raisins on the sill!

Nothing gave her greater peace of mind than cleaning and laundering, unless it was ridding a house of squirrels.

She peeled off the rubber boots and stood on the chill porch floorboards in her wool socks, one foot on top of the other.

The key turned stiffly, loudly, revolving the lock.

The closeness, the smells of the house, breathed around her with animal warmth. Too much warmth for a house carefully locked up behind an unusually cold, late spring.

But still she wasn't afraid. Her mind struggled to resolve the questions, sure the answer lay lightly hid. It was just a matter of....

From the hall, a sudden eddy of coolness brushed up to her bare knees, her curling fingertips. With its passage came the faint acrid scent of doused candle flame.

But the danger came from behind her—something crashing across her windpipe. The room exploded into pain, filling with stars, galaxies, universes of spinning lights. She felt herself dragged backward, her knees buckling, breath gone, soundless, feeling breath hissing hot by her left ear, the smell of sausage.

"Shut up! Shut up or I kill you!"

She lay half-propped against the body behind her, the strength in her legs gone, her mind dully struggling beyond the terrible fiery pain lodged in her throat.

Now there came a new pain, a sharp pointed jab at the side of her neck, a pricking pain hot as the sting of a bee.

"I will kill you!"

It was then she realized he was speaking German.

"*Bitte, bitte, bitte.* Don't. Please."

She felt the breath indrawn behind her ear.

"*Bitte.* Just don't hurt me. Please."

The knife tip wobbled against her skin and she felt a thin hot trickle start down her neck. The knife lowered, and two hands turned her shoulders to face him.

"Sie sprechen Deutsch?"

"Ich bin Deutsch. Please. Please don't hurt me."

The face was young and grimy and desperate beneath a tight wool cap and she thought, he's so young, younger even than me.

The images from the magazine crowded in her brain: bombed-out rubble buildings, a face like her beloved Joerg's just another piece of rubble in a pile of collapsed masonry: plaster, timbers, skull and bones. The Germans were the enemy.

The boy brought the knife up again, its point pressing beneath her chin. "Where are the others? That you bring with you. Hurry, tell me or you will die."

"There are no others. I am alone. Please, put that away."

"I do not believe you. Shut up or I kill you!" His eyes glittered pale blue and bloodshot from within the sooty unwashed face. They stared down into her own face.

She heard the terror even as she tried to cover over it with words: "Where are you from? I am from a little village in Schleswig-Holstein—have you ever been up there?"

His mouth opened, gasping for air, the knife jerking up toward her face again.

"Tell me, how are things back home? I am worried about Mama. Please, let us sit down and talk of home."

Sweat was running, tracing lighter channels in the grime on his forehead. And now she could see he was even younger than she had thought, a teenager from the looks of his wispy beard. He wore a light loose wool jacket that just reached his hip bones above baggy pants, and the jacket had four dulled brass buttons and sleeves much too short. His bony wrists jumped, fingers twitching.

He turned her around, her back to him once again, pulling her with him to the porch window, the fingers of one hand clamped painfully over her mouth. He peered out each window in turn, dragging her in front of him, and at the last window a tiny sound like air from a punctured tire came from his throat.

Suddenly she felt it: his erection pressing against her dress, pressing harder, digging up under her buttocks.

"Please, no. I will not tell anyone I saw you here. Just let me go."

His hands pulled at the buttons of her dress, ripping frantically, and he dragged her down on the board floor. His fingers were cold, pushing up her skirt, raking, yanking down, and suddenly his weight crushed down on her, and she felt the hard cold board beneath the hard round bone at the back of her head. She felt cold wetness up against her bared flesh, against the inside of her thighs as his hand seized limp flesh between his fingers, struggling to stiffen it, to force it in. He wadded himself up against her, then suddenly straightened up and seized the knife, hips bucking uselessly against her as he struck the knife into the floorboard beside her terrified face again and again.

Finally he began to cry.

Clara lay trying to quiet her breathing until the sounds he was making ceased and he sat up finally, away from her. He stared at her face and then pulled the skirt of her dress over her bared thighs. His knuckles rubbed down the cotton-covered length of one thigh, over the rounded hump of her knee, down and then back up, down and back.

Looking at his face, she wondered if he was even younger than he looked. And slowly she lost her fear. Thoughts crowded her mind....

How old are you, oh please tell me what is your name, what town are you from? Do you miss home as much as I do, is your town rubble now, is your mother alive? Do you know how old I am and I have never been back? Do you know if my mother is alive?

Have you ever been with a woman before?

Do you shave yet, do you have wet dreams, do you get up in the middle of the night ashamed, do you wash the sheets clean before your mother sees the stains?

Have you ever been with a woman before?

His throat was pale under the band of dark collar, moving like a frog's as he watched her. She put her hand on it. His throat quivered, hotter than her hand. She could feel the slender bones in his jaw. He was speaking, she could feel the words forming under her fingers before she heard them.

He pressed himself back up against her and now he was hard, as hard as the floorboards back against the hard curve of her skull.

He came almost immediately, and she felt the wet semen tickle as it welled out to the cool outside, trickling down between the crease of her buttocks, soaking up in the dry boards.

His voice was tearing ragged out in harsh gasps, but now she couldn't hear, the room seemed buzzing, full and crowded with bees in that meadow she had run through with Joerg.

His name was Karl Oesten, and he was 22, from Hamburg, he told her. He had small eyes beneath a bulge of high shiny forehead wet now as rained-on glass, the lower half of his face fuzzed with pale beard. Beneath the few wisps of mustache hairs, he sucked in his lower lip as she lay on the floor, telling him everything about Schleswig-Holstein, her mother, father, sisters, brothers (but not Joerg), about the cows and the cow that was born all white but gave no milk, and the cow who calved and then wouldn't eat and died and they cut her open and found a stick that had pierced her heart, pushing to calve she had driven the stick from her stomach into her heart.

He told her about the last time he saw Hamburg, the damp salt smell mixed with tar, the sound of the seagulls especially in winter when the tame birds, drawn to the dock's food, left the coast. Green bananas being unloaded, canisters of tea, sacks of coffee beans and the stench of bundles of pelts. The slapping of waves against gliding metal, ship sirens, people shouting, all intermingling and constant through the day. At night, the toot-toot of the ships' horns, a sound you could hear all over the city, and farther, deeper in the night the soul of Hamburg: St. Pauli, the amusement center of colored lights, foreign restaurants, waxworks, racetracks, and dance halls, the sweet eel soup cooked with dried fruit, pears, and bacon...

"The *aalsuppe! Ach*, Karl, what I would not give for just a little *aalsuppe*, right now."

He rolled over on his back and she saw the grimace,the tense, angry look on his face again. Fear seized her again. Would he still kill her?

"Karl—what is it? Why do you look that way?"

"They are late, coming for me. I was to meet them and now they are late, perhaps they have left me here to die."

"What do you mean?"

"Yes, two nights ago they were to come for me. My work here is complete, and they were to come in the motor launch and I was to row out in the rubber dinghy, but they did not come. I kept on shining the light out to sea, but nothing, nothing. Then I heard it, the second night, the sound of the motor launch in the middle of the night running past me heading straight out to sea. And then it suddenly stopped, well before it had gone out of earshot."

"Stopped?"

"Taken back aboard the *Unterseeboot*, and now perhaps she is gone. Back to Germany. Gone."

He drank from the bottle of brandy without offering her any.

"The *Unterseeboot*?"

"Black and sleek against the blue sea, and she dove like a whale. But she was all stink and squalor on board. Long and long and long and long and narrow and narrow and narrow. You look up and there is only long and narrow, nothing to see under there and yet you look up. We took her down to two hundred and thirty meters and the metal was groaning, screeching, crying, the rivets popping. The metal cries 'yew-y, yew-y, yew-y' as you go down."

His large hands thrust him up onto his feet and he rocked back and forth, squatting, arms wrapped around his knees. He glanced over toward the window which in the early twilight was already growing dim.

"They have to come back for me. They cannot leave me here to die."

"Where were they supposed to meet you?"

The blue eyes slitted, studying her face. "Why should you want to know?"

"Because...because I want to see you safe, Karl. You are just a boy. I do not know anything of politics, I do not care to know. I am not an American anyway, you know that. We are both German, *wir beide*."

"I should not have told you anything of what I have."

"What have you told me? What harm is there? I will never tell."

He rose heavily, knee joints popping loudly in the silence. He walked unsteadily into the other room. When he came back, he held a pistol in his hand.

Her gaze went to it as if in slow motion, then dragged up to his face.

"I am sorry. The common good above the individual good. I must kill you now."

She stared at his face, the pores, the hairs, the little brown hairs that grew in his nose.

He looked back. She saw his hand shake as it raised the pistol, the sweat again on his high forehead. He made a sound as if struck in the stomach.

"Wait! You do not have to kill me, there is another way. You could take me back with you—ask the others in command. Take me back with you to Germany."

The muzzle of the gun twitched as if unattached to the hand. Then the round mouth pointed down to the floor.

"I believe you," Karl Oesten said. "Run away now, quickly from me, before I change my mind. Do not look back. Go."

Clara waited in the cover of the dense spruces on the hill. When the night was black she heard the rubber dinghy rowing out past the cove, past the islets toward open sea.

The *plash* of oars stopped well before passing out of earshot. She knew the submarine had surfaced and swallowed him again: *yew-y, yew-y, yew-y*.

He was going home. To Germany.

She told no one.

That night, as Gooden made love to her, she looked up at the timbered rafters above her head. She could see Joerg's face and something cold and frightening gripped her heart.

Joerg.

Was it always going to be like this?

The next morning, her citizenship papers arrived. Clara was an American now.

"A hun's a hun," Clara heard Rufe Smallidge say. "Can't change that by giving her a piece of paper, now can you?"

Yet at the launching of Gooden's boat, the entire population of year-rounders remaining—women and children and men younger than 21, older than 30, who had escaped the Selective Service net—turned out, putting their prejudices aside. It was the lucky eleven o'clock tide: the highest running tide of the day. The lobsterboat's name was covered with a crocus sack.

Gooden pulled off the sack. Clara heard the gasps fill her ears. Carefully painted in black letters across the middle strake of her stern was:

KRONPRINZESSIN CLARA

Her eyes filled with tears, Clara picked up the bottle of home-brewed cherry rum. She took aim and drew her weighted arm up and back. As the glass glinted in the sun on its downward arc, she saw her arm shiver with the thought: I hate Aguahega. I want to go home. To Germany.

The glass shattered and the sweet red mist furled back into the faces of the crowd, and everyone but Clara cheered.

"You get a face of the old killdevil back like that," Gooden said, "that's the best lucky sign there is."

His words stopped short. He felt something inside him break. He would never get away from Schleicher. His eyes looked out at Gooden from little Johnny's four-year-old face.

As the drops tickled on his cheeks, Johnny Beal extended his tongue, cautiously licked the moisture, and swallowed. With the complete joy only possible in early childhood, without fear of the future, he laughed.

CHAPTER 7

1930, Aguahega Island, Maine

Standing there in the blue-gold light of a rare clear Aguahega July afternoon, she was the first beautiful girl Johnny Beal, 16, had ever seen.

Well, except for Sears, Roebuck slip and brassiere models, and Greta Garbo in the moving picture sixty miles away in Wardwell, where he sweated over Greta's wet lips and spangly gown while Harry Vannah patronized the whorehouse. The picture was called Flesh and the Devil, which had seemed to encompass both their afternoons.

The girl was leaning against the shingled rear wall of the Konkus Club—Seal Point's yacht club where dried-out captains put in for meals and (it was rumored) illegal liquid refreshment. She wore the yellow waitress uniform of the Smith College girls who were hired every summer, one foot in the thick white-soled shoe propped up against the shingles. She was taking quick, nervous drags on a cigarette, looking out to the horizon, away from him.

Johnny had never seen a woman smoke before.

His blood seemed to swim, struggle upstream, like small cold goldfishes through his veins. He knew she was as out of reach as a star, as exotic, as foreign as a visitor from another planet, would have nothing to do with him. Still, his senses drank her in: her hair fanning out about her shoulders in crinkled waves, gold as the silken flash of goldfish tails in the dimestore tank. Her profile was etched against the sky and then, as if sensing his stare she turned her head, startled. And laughed.

"Jesus, but you didn't go and scare me!" The vividness of her face hit him like a blow—the flushed nose and cheeks and chin and gingery hazel eyes surrounded by the moving bright sun of her hair. "Well, don't just stand there now you've scared me to hell and back. I want a proper apology, it's only fitting. Say, what's the matter, cat got your tongue?"

He had never heard a woman use a four-letter word. "Didn't mean to be rude. Just that—I can't—you're beautiful. You look better than Greta Garbo."

She laughed again. "That and five cents'll get me a ride on the trolley. But I thank you exceedingly and so on, honey. You're really very sweet to say so. Come here, you know I can't hear you when you're not talking. What's your name?"

He walked closer, suddenly conscious of his rough sweated-up work clothes in which he'd been hauling trunks, boxes, even a new Crosley Shelvador refrigerator with built-in radio up from the village dock and into the great "cottages" of Seal Point. He was a porter, filling in when he wasn't out hauling, which he did full time now in the summers: every other day or so the lobsters had time to eat supper in the trap's "kitchen," then stay for a visit through the funnelled inextricable mesh he had knitted himself and into the "parlor," deep within the slatted bars. He had seventy-five traps now of his very own.

"Don't you go portering," Gooden Beal had fumed. "You keep clear of the Point or I'll whup you clear." But everyone knew there had been, long ago in Gooden's youth, an incident. What kind of incident? Just darkly hinted at, the way older people loved to do. What had happened to Gooden, Johnny thought, had nothing to do with himself. Every other guy Johnny's age worked at the Point summers—portering, carpentering, taking out boats, pocketing good money, too. Only a fool sneered at easy money.

"Your *name*," the girl said again, impatient.

"Johnny Beal, at your service, m'am. Tote trunks or whatever you don't want to carry. One of those quaint 'natives' you high class people gabble about."

"Really! So there's life in the old boy yet! You're one of the year-rounders, then, the rubber boot set. I don't know how you people do it. Live on this Godforsaken place even in the winter, and it's bad enough in the summer when all these crazy fools think it's fun to play primitive out here. Well, actually, I think they're kind of sweet. They collect shells, pick berries and—" She shivered with disgust.

Was she making fun of him?

"Now, my idea of fun, Boston, that's what!" she said. "You ever been there? Oh, Boston—you beautiful, lovely, exciting old town. Why did I let myself get shanghaied out here?" Her face had been leaning closer, and now her hazel eyes focused full on him. "Oh! I hope you don't think I'm criticizing your home. That would be so naughty of me, don't you think?"

She *was* making fun of him. It didn't daunt him, it sent a surge of excitement through his head. "Well, there are a few sights to see around these parts. Giant laylock blooming over Rowdy Richardson's burned-out cabin. Don't know about loony old Rowdy, the hermit ghost of Aguahega? Begging you pardon, but that's all so *boring.*"

This time she laughed with her shoulders, the sound pealing out into the air. "I asked for that as clear as a day in June, didn't I? Johnny, your name is? I'm very pleased to meet you, Johnny. I don't think I've laughed all summer. I'm Victorine Reese, it rhymes with please."

The name flashed through him like an electric charge, echoing all one word in his head—victorinereese, a name like black velvet, smooth and taunting. But she looked older than he'd first thought, perhaps even 22. *How* old? Was she too old for him, looking down on him like a kid? Would she laugh at him like a little brother, this sixteen year old kid in laughable stupid gawky clothes and the new stubble he hadn't shaved in two days?

She jammed out her hand and he took it. It was cool and yet perspiring at the palm. He didn't know what to do with it—couldn't pump it like he did Reverend Witney's after the interminable Sunday sermon, so glad to be out. Her hand seemed to pulse madly now where he held it against his own.

"Somebody's heart is sure beating," she said. She squeezed his hand almost to hurting with a powerful athletic grip, then withdrew hers, shaking it up by her ear. "Yipes, that gave me the willies—feeling your pulse going like that."

It was *her* pulse, he thought, but his heart sank. Did he disgust her, then?

"But look here, Mr. Johnny, you fine rustic fellow with bells on. This joint is women and snot-nosed brats and fat nannies and nurses all day long. The daddies aren't due till August, and I do truly get starved for the sight of a redblooded adult male face, know what I mean?"

Adult. Male. Face!

Her mouth looked abnormally small, as if it belonged to a much smaller girl. Now that she'd ceased talking, it looked like a round pursed child's mouth, a closed bud of a flower. Johnny stared at it, his mind thick and desperate, his thighs shaking, the heat of his blood suddenly pouring up into his face—the color of boiled lobster, he was sure. Now, worst of all, his nearly omnipresent erection hammered against its wool prison in exquisite pain. Oh, she must hate him, despise him standing here ugly and tormented and tongue-tied, the hopeless dumb animal that he looked.

"See," she was saying, "the big thing, the really stupendous event around here is on Sunday afternoons we all go hymn singing. Charming. And then there are the tea parties all the other afternoons, don't you know, where everyone tries not to talk about the falling worth of stocks. A little something to drink smuggled up, to take away the pain? Oh, no, of course not. Oh, mercy sakes, nothing like that up here. The old ladies sit in rows on the verandahs like ugly old seagulls catching the sun, just ripping up everyone who walks by, like bitchy old catty old cats—"

"Vicky! Vickeeeee!" The voice, female, came from within the open window of the Club.

"Don't call me Vicky, you stuffed old moosehead!" She said it quietly, grinning at him, wrapping him close in her conspiracy to shut those *others* out. Just the two of them, Johnny thought, laughing at the world.

"Vick-eeeeee. McCullers are ready for dessert."

She mashed the cigarette out with the toe of her white shoe, dropped her empty crumpled pack to the ground. Her legs, he saw, were long and thin and straight, her ankles as light and delicate as bird bones. "Save me, Johnny, oh, save this poor damsel in distress. I get off at nine."

"Victorine."

"Huh? Gotta go. Gotta go."

"I promise to never call you Vicky."

And then she was gone.

He leaned over and picked up the crumpled cigarette pack, olive green with a red circle: Luckies, and that was lucky. The pack looked fragile, demolished in his broad calloused palm. He was suddenly aware of the black line of dirt wedged beneath his blunt ragged fingernails.

Okay, he was no gentleman. Probably not a single one of the thousands of beaux she had in Boston had ever had dirt under their nails—and certainly not when they were meeting Victorine. *Victorinereese*. Yet he was aware enough to guess that it was in part his "oafishness," his "quaintness" that attracted her, that made him different from the thousands of other men she had met. Wasn't that what they always said—opposites attract? But it seemed such a fine line—how to attract when it was your crudeness that attracted; how to be sure it didn't suddenly repel?

His hand crushed the Luckies pack, compressing tighter and tighter until the crackling protest ceased. When he opened his hand, holding the flattened cellophane and paper up to his nose, the rich tobacco scent was fresh and sharp, stinging his eyes. He carefully smoothed the pack out, ironing it against his pant leg and tucking it in his back pocket.

A girl you could keep in your hip pocket—wasn't that what men said was best?

The month of July and then the first week of August flowed past like Persistent Creek after ice out. He leaned over her easel set up above the southern cliffs....

"Oh, Gaaaaahhd," she said, imitating Eleanore Chancellor, "this watercolor is completely ruined." Because if she wasn't working, she said, she was painting, and she was now very excited, having moved from bright enameled colors to soft veils of misty tones, washes of tints, pinpricks of pastels more suited to Aguahega, her favorite subject now. "Impressionism," she said. "Victorine was Manet's wife and model, that's why I took the name."

"You weren't borned with it?"

"What a silly idea! Get back, Johnny. You can't see it all up close."

"But I like to look at things up close. What good's a painting you can't get close to?"

A light flickered in the back of her eyes.

Johnny taught her what he knew: Where the raspberries grew—on the sides of the meadows, in the clearings where firewood had been cut, in dense tangles over fallen trunks of blowdowns. They picked blackberries at the squelching rim of alder bogs where the bushes reached higher than their heads, while higher still the alder leaves blocked the sun. They picked blueberries, once called "plums," Johnny told her, and the first summer visitors who came to raid them were "plummers," laughed at and despised.

He called her "Plummer."

She called him "Native."

And best of all, deep in the meadow grass on Hobbomocca Head above the sea, lying on their bellies they picked wild strawberries whose juice ran hot with sun, staining the white bowl of Victorine's sailor cap, staining her lips.

"Did you ever think of leaving Aguahega? Getting a real job? Making something of yourself?"

"Went to Medon once. So many people. Cars, walls of brick, I was just another brick in the wall. No one knew me, cars going so fast, like to run me down. You live on an island, state pays for you to go to the main for your high schooling. Didn't have beyond eight grades on the island. So I did it, picked the best school, that academy they have there in Medon. Were so many people. I don't know. Just came home again."

She studied the stalks of grass between her stained fingers.

He studied the horizon. "The right person was a-running after me, I might run to the mainland, just for them."

He was glad when night fell and she stopped looking in his face.

He walked her back to the Konkus Club where she was boarding in a cell-like former maid's room, "no male guests allowed." Under the concealing shadow of a clump of spruces, they clung together, their mouths grinding together with the same motion as their hips. His erection strained outward against his pants, the drop of moisture spreading coldly outward too, perhaps it would stain her skirt.

He drew away, reaching for her hand. For a long time now she had broken away first, saying she had to go in, they had to stop, it was late. Now she let him hold, squeeze, caress her breasts through the cotton barrier of her shirt, and she seemed to be waiting for something more.

"I can't stand it, Johnny." She pressed herself back up against him, her hands reaching for his face.

He felt the electric thrill as her tongue pushed inside his mouth again. He ground his mouth with all his force against hers until he heard his jaw pop, the joint sliding looser now from hours of necking without end. And in his mouth and head in the damp night air, he heard an inexplicable sound:

She had groaned.

"*Victorine*. What? What's the matter?"

Her hazel eyes flashed for a moment and then shuttered, and in them he had seen a look almost like contempt.

"Better get you inside there before anyone spies us." He reached to take her hand but she slapped it away.

"I don't *care* about those old mooseheads and what they think—don't you understand?"

"Better go back." He loved her, he respected her, and he didn't understand. His fear, ignorance, and adoration wound them like a chain.

Afterward there was the lonely walk back.

When he had returned by the ridge trail to Toothaker Harbor, he reached for the bottle of lotion hidden beneath his mattress. He rubbed it thickly between his palms, letting it warm to body heat, inhaling the bland almond scent, and then, in a few quick strokes, relieved the long torment of the night.

He lay on his back staring up at the rafters, breath slowing, body at long last relaxing, imagining Victorine beside him in the bed. He was turning to her, felt the warm glide of her silk-hot skin down to the magic curve of waist out onto hip. She was all gleam and glow, shimmer and shine. Every inch of her seemed to radiate moisture, so different from the Aguahega wives who looked, in a fog-wet climate, as crackly-dry as autumn leaves.

Instantly, he was erect again, the urgent throbbing of his flesh pleasurable and yet now painful too, bruised as he was from his frenzied jamming against the zipper all the long hike home—the metal teeth snapping and seizing bare skin as on top of the ridge he'd given up and the pent-up prisoner bolted out to freedom.

Hot in the cool night air. Once up there and once down here and now he had a hard-on again. He contemplated the shape of his erection. How could he feel this much desire again? Surely this wasn't normal; no woman had ever felt like this. Was he a sex maniac? Had anyone else ever felt this constant press of tormenting unrelenting desire?

He pulled the book out from under his mattress where it lived stickily with the lotion, the two polarities: holding out and giving in. Gooden Beal had given it to him two years before, the title *What a Boy Should Know*.

> "Whatever unnatural emissions are produced...the body becomes 'slack.' A boy will not feel so vigorous and springy; he will be more easily tired; he will not have so good 'an eye' for games. He will probably look pale and pasty, and he is lucky if he escapes indigestion and getting his bowels confined, both of which will probably give him spots and pimples on his face...The effect of self-abuse on a boy's character always tends to weaken it, and, in fact, to make him untrustworthy, unreliable, and probably even dishonest."

The book snapped shut with an angry sound. Johnny fingered the red new pimple on his chin. What was he going to do?

He could ask his father (the least sympathetic person he could think of). But who else? He'd already told an awestruck Harry Vannah that he was scoring with Victorine every week.

The next morning as he was hammering nails into the 34-inch red oak lath on the lobster pot, the sunlight from the open fish shack door went suddenly dark.

He looked up to see Gooden Beal in bib overalls looming in the doorway.

"What the hell you making there, son?"

"Hello, Father. Don't look now, but it's a pot."

"Pot, pot. Know it's a damn pot but it's square. Square pots don't fish worth a God damn, Johnny. Any fool knows rounders are better."

Johnny lined up another nail and pounded it in, continuing to hammer until the silvery nailhead sank below the surface of the wood, disappearing from sight. "I like the squares and I want to try 'em out, is all. It's choppy, yours get to seesawing all over and bang up right good. You've said so yourself."

His father grunted. "Independent as a hog on ice, are you? Hah. Haul you some empty pots a few days running and you'll come around."

"Father—"

"Hah."

"I wanted to know, I mean, could I ask you something?"

"You're looking pale as a flaked-out fish belly of a sudden. What in tarnation you gone and done now? You ain't knocked up that prissy missy from the Point, have you?"

Johnny laid down the hammer. He was speechless at how close his father's remark had come. And yet how far. He felt sweat burst out all over his body. He wished he'd said nothing, nothing at all.

"Father—" He forced himself to look at the face of the man who had never been like a father to him, who seemed to have it in for him and Willi since birth. Well, he deserved to get an answer to this question if he got nothing else from Gooden Beal in his life.

"Father—"

"Spit it out before your words goes dry."

"What do you do—I mean, I feel all jumpy and twitchy, can't rightly sleep at night. Think about Victorine all night. And I wanted to know. I mean, what do you do when you feel that way?"

"What do you mean, what do you do?"

"Yeah, that's it. I mean, look, Father. Don't just like her, I love her. See, and she loves me, at least I think she does. And we—I mean, how do I deal with feelings like that. Get some release?"

"Now you listen here, you ignorant young buck, you. Just answer me this one little question. She a decent girl?"

"Of course!"

"Then nothing. You don't do nothing. Simple as that."

"Nothing?"

"She's decent, and you say she is, well, you could ruin her for life. You don't do nothing that way till you're good and married." His father made for the door. "Don't forget now, Johnny. Mark me well. Fool around with a decent girl, she's ruined."

Johnny stared up at him as the tall shape blotted out the sun, stepped through the doorway—and then once again the sunlight came in. An orange hawkweed had been blooming by the door, but his father had crushed it under his boot.

Emotions burned inside Johnny. What was he going to do? It was going wrong somehow, with him and Victorine, and he didn't know why. All of a sudden she was always running to meet the mailboat, and her eyes looked anxious as she sorted through the mail. Once she had run with a letter in her hand, flung herself down under a tree. From a distance, Johnny had watched her profile bent over the mysterious letter, one hand holding back the heavy gold hair from her cheek. His face went sharp, his eyes huge with jealousy.

He would have to marry her, that was all. The sooner the better.

He asked her for the most sophisticated evening he could think of: dinner on the main at the Haley's Landing coffee shop that catered to tourists, then back to Perley's House for coffee and his mother's special cold blueberry soup. He would introduce her to his parents and sister Willi, as a grown man serious about a woman ought to do.

They were all sitting around the cherry table in the kitchen, Johnny next to Victorine on the gray-painted old wagon seat with the yellow stripes. Very gingerly, he pressed the side of his shoe against hers.

"What pretty china," Victorine said into the silence. "Isn't this the pattern they call Blue Willow?"

Johnny dipped his spoon into the blueberry soup, holding a blueberry under until it drowned. "There's a story in the plate, Victorine. Want to hear?"

"Oh, now, Johnny," Clara said. "We do not want to bore—"

"I'd love to hear it, Mrs. Beal. Please let him tell."

Pressure of her shoe back against his.

"See the willow tree?" Johnny's voice was excited at the center of everyone's attention, even his father's. "See, here by the bridge with the three people running across? They're running away from the big house back there because her father wants her to marry some ugly old man. So here's the girl and one she loves, the young one, and that's her father running right after."

From the other end of the table, where Gooden sat, came the loud sucking in of hot coffee.

"Do they get away, Johnny? Get to marry each other, the way they want?"

"Sure, they get away. See, here's the boat, they sail away up here to this little island in the corner, just like Aguahega, right, Mother?"

In the sudden silence, Clara Beal's spoon clattered noisily into her soup bowl.

Victorine drank from her tumbler of water. "And lived happily ever after, Johnny?"

"Of course, there's another story underneath," Willi said.

Johnny looked at her, at her shiny hair, blue-shiny in its deep brown depths. Wet lips, moist skin brimming with promise, no Aguahega dryasdust siphoning-off for her. Comically he lifted his soup plate, peering up at the unadorned white bottom. "Sorry. Nothing's there on it."

"There's *always* another story from a different point of view." Her eyes flashed dangerously toward her mother's face.

What was she talking about, Johnny wondered.

"That's what's important, to try to find out the really true story," Willi said. "For instance, you could tell this same story from the point of view of the deserted rich man, who got his heart broken when the girl ran off."

Gooden slammed his cup on the table. "Tell you, missy, would have been money in your pocket if you'd never been born."

"More coffee?" Clara hastily cleared Blue Willowware away.

"Well, now." Gooden looked at her. "Maybe we could use us a little something to warm up a tot, what do you think, Clara? Well, better ask—not one of those dries now, are you, Miss Vicky?"

"Me, a prohibitionist?" She laughed, and her voice seemed to dart and swoop, as full of color as a cardinal among fish crows. And suddenly Johnny looked at his father and wondered why she didn't stop him from calling her "Vicky," and looking he saw not the father but the man—a well-weathered 44, but as bulkily masculine and good-looking as he had always been.

"Well, now, we got a little nice spruce beer down in a crock in the cellar, and even a little home brew tucked away if you can keep quiet about it. Clara, fetch it for us and we'll have a glass—at least those who are of age, and that doesn't include you, Mr. Fish, my boy. Just kidding. But Miss Vicky here looks like she could stand a shot or two."

Johnny stirred: Gooden hadn't called him Mr. Fish since he was ten years old.

"What I wouldn't give for a beautiful amber glass of good old neat bourbon these days," Victorine was saying. "Just to get lit, and not on rotgut, just once."

"Just tell me what you want," Gooden said. "Old Crow, Old Kentucky, Coon Hollow, Old Colonel, Early Times, Old Log Cabin?"

She laughed. "I'd almost think you meant it if I didn't know better."

"Get you any good bourbon, whisky, scotch you want—fifteen dollars a quart, paid up front on the barrel head, of course."

She straightened up on the wagon seat and her foot drew away from Johnny's. "You know, I almost think you're serious."

Gooden Beal smiled. "Sure I'm serious, girl. Man cannot live by fish alone."

"Are you one of those rum runners—oh, I just can't believe this, it's so exciting! Do you really go out in the dark of the moon, the way people tell about it? Oh, wouldn't I love to go out on a rum runner boat, just once, with racketeers and drops and all that newspaper adventure stuff."

"Course, *I* don't go, naturally. But wouldn't say as I don't know some who do. Some who leave notes in lobster pots, orders like, and runners fill them at night on some lonely little gunkhole of a cove, you wouldn't know where." His square-tipped fingers spread out on the stained oilcloth. "Just tell me what you want."

By the following week, Victorine's time seemed to shrink, the little gaps, the hour in the mornings, the Tuesdays off were suddenly chinked up tight, the way she told it. Finally, when Johnny grew insistent, "Oh, Johnny, Johnny, Johnny. Please don't be angry with me. I don't expect you to understand. When you're older, maybe then you will."

"So that's it! I'm just a stinking kid to you and now you hate me for it."

"You're not a kid, Johnny, but you don't even know that yet, you poor bastard."

Still he didn't understand until one night, unable to sleep, he walked down toward the Toothaker dock in an agonized daze. The August night was cool and dark with a rushing breeze and a tiny sliver of moon, cheerless and dim. As he passed the fish shack with the globe of shark oil hanging above the door, he heard a sound. Then more sounds, strung together one after another like pearls.

It sounded as if someone were in pain. Startled, he approached the side of the fish shack and peered cautiously through the window. The thin moon cast a splash of gray upon the blackness of the floor within, and on the gray lay two lighter gray bodies, a man on top of a woman whose legs were spread, her white-silver-gray hands fluttering up and down, down and up from his shoulders to his buttocks like silver butterflies, and the man's buttocks contracted like clockworks under the skimming hands. The woman's face lay spilled in darkness but there was a glow around the hair, and Johnny could see its blonde gleam now as his eyes adjusted, and suddenly the buttocks clenched together like two fists and the man reared his torso, threw back his head, mouth open in a silent cry. His profile with the familiar roman nose was etched silver against the far black wallboards.

Johnny turned and ran, careless of the ringing of his boots against the stone ground, his heart leaping against his throat like a dog against a barred door. He ran up the path from the waterfront, around the silent dark bulk of Perley's House, back to the well. He yanked off the plank cover and lowered the pail.

Gurgling, it sank and quickly he hauled it back up, cupped his hands and drank—pitchy with a few floating spruce needles. He upended the pail and poured the rest, shockingly cold, over his head. Then, blinking, he stared down the stonework of the shaft, fieldstones pale as quartz under the moon, the walls straight, at the bottom the water moving still with the remembered impact of the pail.

"John, boy." The sound grew softly out of the darkness behind him. The hairs on the back of his neck rose, pricking his shirt.

"Johnny, just tell me—did you see us? Back there?"

Johnny gripped the well's hard stone lip with both hands, staring straight down. His face, like all the Beal faces before him, stared back at him in the dark water under the moon.

"She's no good for you, Johnny. You don't know what kind of girl she be. Man doesn't marry a girl like that. Better you found it out soon as this, you'll be thanking me for it by and by."

Johnny thought of his mother who had grown fat as all the island women seemed to grow fat, while their husbands burned lean right down to the bone. Somehow, this made it worse.

"How could you do that? To Mother?"

"Now listen to me. No one's ever loved more'n I've felt for your mother. Do still. But this here has nothing to do with that there. You get older, get married, you'll maybe see. Not proud of it, but she just up and offered it to me, Johnny, don't you see? Man's not a man refuses a woman when she offers it. No, a right man can't."

"I hate you!" Johnny stared down into the well, his words bouncing back and forth, lost in the stones. "As God hears me, I hate you."

"Told you they were no good up to Seal Point, would come to no good you working up there. But you wouldn't listen, now would you, and I spoke the truth."

Johnny whirled. A look almost of satisfaction was printed on his father's face. "Is *that* why? Just for that you went and killed it—everything I had? *I loved her.*"

"Well, now you know. Every man jack from here to Medon's been loving her."

But Johnny was staring behind Gooden, where suddenly now Victorine stood. On her face was an expression as if she had just been slapped.

Gooden Beal turned around. He wished that his tongue had been torn out before he had ever said what he had. He wanted to beg

Victorine's forgiveness. But then welled up a memory of chanting voices, shrill and fierce: "Reek, rank, runk, all the lobstermen stunk. Runk, rank, reek, their mothers also stink." All the years of Seal Point humiliation were suddenly fresh and new. And deeper still, stronger still pressed the inescapable truth that twisted daily in his gut, the aching, burning pain. His only son, Johnny Beal, looked more like Friedrich Schleicher every day.

Gooden picked up a twig and snapped it. Something was finished, done.

"No one misses a slice from a cut loaf," he said.

It was nearing dawn when Johnny halted in his pacing of the perimeter of the island. He knew he should leave Aguahega, the way Willi talked about leaving, but he felt weak, helpless, trapped. Now he knew he would never get away, not without Victorine's help.

He would live and he would die on Aguahega.

Would he?

Or could he do the one thing that would most hurt Gooden Beal: run away?

He thought suddenly of the letter that girl had sent him, when he was still a child, when things were good.

> "To Johnny Beal
> Aguahega Island Maine
> Dear Johnny,
> Im mad I didnt see White Bird first. Im
> even madder that you did. I am twelve.
> Please tell me everything you saw. Id
> be ever so grateful.
> Loara Louella Pritchard
> Scrag Rock, Maine."

A gull cried suddenly above Johnny's head, the sound lonely and brave.

CHAPTER 8

1931 - Medon, Maine

"If you don't still hate me," Johnny Beal's large, bold, black-inked scrawl had read, "even though I committed the unpardonable sin of seeing White Bird first, maybe we could meet. After all, I'm not 13 years old anymore."

Loara Pritchard felt impossibly bold and daring, staring out her attic window under the eaves. "Dear Mr. Beal," she wrote. "I am no longer twelve years old. I have learned to be very forgiving."

Again he had written, asking when they could meet.

If he saw her at the dime store in her hairnet behind the sandwich counter, or in the dim, faded light of the boarding house sitting room where every Saturday night she headed upstairs to her room, reading Westerns while attempting to digest Mrs. Pfleugel's heart stew which seemed after hours of digesting still to be beating—if he saw her like that, he would never want her.

No one else had.

Sure to be a spinster, relatives said.

Dry as a prune even at 16, unwanted, hung out to dry. She hung her underwear under pillow slips on Mrs. Pfleugel's backyard line.

Ah, but if Johnny Beal saw her helmeted and goggled, swooping in from the clouds to the small dusty airfield's runway, alighting like the pilot Ruth Elder, unsnapping her helmet beneath which her wispy light brown hair was snugged back with a bright blue "Ruth" ribbon to bring out the blue of her eyes—then everything might be different. Loara tried to smile like the picture of Ruth smiling still up at the wooden ceiling of her cheese box, where she had kept all her special things. Loara remembered working the points of her scissors around the snapshot, lifting it from the frame of newsprint. If only she could be daring and beautiful and accomplished like Ruth Elder. Loara had stared at Ruth's wavy dark hair, big eyes and dimples, her pale knickers and plaid sweater with golf stockings to match. A broad band of silk held back her hair: this day's version of what had come to be known as "Ruth ribbons," which, the paper reported, all the young girls across the nation adopted as the latest fad.

In 1927, Ruth and her co-pilot had at last departed for Europe—the first woman to cross the Atlantic—in American Girl, her yellow Stinson monoplane. Loara had sat camped by the Magnavox radio's horn, waiting for news. "It seems to me," Mrs. Franklin D. Roosevelt said, "unquestionably foolish for a young woman to fly alone, with only a pilot, over such a long distance."

Ruth Elder crashed only 520 miles west of Portugal. Ruth was saved, but American Girl drowned.

Now, at the tiny airport in Medon, Maine, "Remember, Loara, think ahead of your ship, always think ahead," Al Christy in the cockpit behind her said. "She wants to fly. Just give her her head and why, she'll do what comes natural."

It was her first time at the controls. She watched Sam Sonneborn, the pot-bellied mechanic, seize the propeller in his hands, crank it three times. The early morning dew of the mainland city of Medon had seeped into the polished wood blade, weighted the porous right side heavier than the left. With a violent kick and swing, Sam pulled the prop through and the OX5 army surplus engine, which had cost just $50 and wasn't worth any more, coughed and clattered into a roar.

The powerful thrum of the engine's vibration entered Loara, filling her body and mind. She tugged her leather helmet and goggles tight around her face, waved her hand back toward Sam and started to taxi down the short runway which was perched on a wide ridge above Medon, fifty miles north of Scrag Rock, where she'd been born. There was no flat land at either end as a margin for error. Her hands were cold with fear. She sat in the front of the two open cockpits, both with controls, one set for the instructor and one for the student. But before Loara could nose up or make any real effort the small blue Waco Nine biplane, pronounced whok-co, Al Christy, the airfield owner had said impatiently, broke ground for no reason at all. It flew like a dry leaf in a puff of air. Loara banked out over the patchwork of fields below, the undersurface of the top left wing showing her its layers of bugs splattered upward by the prop blade's twisting column of air. Hot rusty water sprinkled her face, leaking from the exposed engine radiator under the top wing. Her startled lungs awoke and gasped in air.

She, Loara Pritchard, had leaped free of Scrag Rock. She had made it all come true.

A broad, plowed field swept beneath them, its flat dirt surface absorbing the early sun faster than the surrounding trees. The heated air expanded, becoming lighter, and rose, and the plane bucketed upward in the thermal, floating higher and higher. Loara's hands were wet on the controls, her heart jerking with nerves and delight. The flying itself, she thought, was simple, the navigation purely visual: by a river, a lake, a highway, a shoreline, a sign on the roof of a building. The most difficult part was judging the height and distance from the runway when landing, which was what they were practicing today.

She could see the blue tile roof of Mrs. Pfleugel's boarding house, where she collapsed after working six days a week in the five-and-ten cent store. She had managed to save enough money to pay for four flying lessons, but it took ten hours to qualify to solo. It would take a long time to save that much more.

The Waco swept in low over the little airfield and Loara saw a strange open-model Franklin car parked by the hangar, and a young man with his foot up on the running board. Was he Johnny Beal? The man waved his hand and terrified, she took the Waco up again.

"You're smart as a whip," Al Christy was always telling her, "for a girl." But she wasn't a pilot. Or a girl. She was a freak. She had always known it. The painful thing was that now, unmarried, others seemed to know it, too.

The roar of the Waco's engine filled Loara's ears like a crowd's cheers, urging her terror away. She glanced back at Al Christy and her arm swept in a circle outside the cockpit, calling for a "circus," a loop.

Al's hands came up, waved emphatically No. His finger pointed at the low indication of the fuel gauge and then his arm pointed straight down: meaning set down on the runway.

Loara felt the blood roar in her ears. She dropped the nose abruptly, then dragged the throttle to full gun and brought the Waco around and up. She knew Al was helpless: if he touched the controls now, he might turn the plane into a power dive. She could hear him bellowing above the engine's roar.

The Waco climbed where she took it, up the side of the loop, and the world swung upside down. She sagged in her safety belt and the engine battled, but she felt the plane turn soft, loggy, the back pull of gravity too strong. Just at the pinnacle of the great upswinging curve she felt the plane hesitate, inert. A wing fell sideways. They were about to slip off the top of the loop.

Loara hung on the controls, hands frozen in a convulsive grip. The tail started to circle just as the nose dropped, and she felt the crazed shudder as the plane fell into a power spin.

With a sideways jiggle of the stick, Al Christy shook the plane and caught her attention. She elevated both hands beside her head: "take control." Christy let the pull of gravity bring on a dive, then gently drew the stick back until the nose came up.

Around and back toward the runway and she burned with shame, her hands stilled in her lap, helpless as any ignorant tourist with five dollars for a ride.

When she climbed out onto the wing in her baggy flyfront trousers, she saw Johnny Beal standing in the shadow by the hangar door. As he walked out into the clear bright sunlight where she could get a good look at him, she went numb with fear. He was impossibly handsome. He looked younger than 17, with dark curly hair clipped flat above his ears and waving high off his forehead, with a long face and a flat long body and wide shoulders in his loose new seersucker suit.

"Only a girl could pull a fool stunt like that," Al Christy was bellowing loud enough for Johnny to hear. "You near to got us killed!"

Johnny seized her hand, which looking down she saw to her embarrassment was mottled bluish and reddish from the chill of the upper air. He clasped her cold hand between both of his big rough warm ones. "Hello, Loara Louella Pritchard."

Ordinarily she had to trudge the five miles from airfield to town, but now Johnny whipped open the battered Franklin's door with a flourish.

She settled around a sprung spring and stared at the instrument panel.

"Air-cooled engine," Johnny said, dropping into the seat beside her, and she was assaulted by the raw spice of Bay Rum. He smelled like Easter Sunday ham. She wondered if Al would ever let her fly again.

"It's air-cooled just like an airplane's got," Johnny said. "And goes fifty miles an hour. Not bad for down here on the ground."

"Is it yours, Johnny?"

"Well'm—" he coughed.

The car rolled forward, wind pressed her flushed cheeks, and a loud knocking noise gyrated up from beneath the hood.

"Johnny," she shouted, "what's that noise?"

He smiled, teeth large and white, happy as a puppy. "Noise? What noise?" He threw his head back and at the top of his lungs, drowning out the knocking, he began to sing. To her astonishment, she heard herself giggle. He drove recklessly down the road, one hand on the wheel. "You sure look pretty," he said, "with that ribbon in your hair."

Al Christy forgave her. But as the weeks passed, Loara shook out the few coins and bills that were her flying fund from the red-and-white baking soda can. She bought a dress, a soft yellow dress, and then some perfume.

She had taken apart the Franklin's motor, and when Johnny introduced her to his uncle and aunt he said, "Here's that smart girl fixed that knock in your car."

And parked in the car, she told him how, after she soloed and got her pilot's license, she was going to go to college and major in mechanical engineering—she had it all planned—and then transfer after two years to a school that offered aeronautical engineering.

"You're some girl," he said, and leaned across the gear shift and kissed her.

The kisses went on and on but this time her dress was pulled up to her waist and her white cotton pants gone as if they had never been and her knees catapulted skyward in the cramped Franklin seat and suddenly she felt a pushing pressure into her that was entirely new and frightening but not painful. It was totally without pleasure. She was suddenly very wet and she thought it must be blood, but it wasn't.

After you did it once, of course, you really couldn't say No.

Suddenly the world was changed.

A new terrible feeling of vulnerability seized her. She bought a bottle of Lysol and douched with it every time afterwards because sometimes he forgot the "safe," or it broke, or he used the only one he had and then wanted to do it again. Every month she waited frantically as the number of days mounted inexorably and grew day by day too high and then were suddenly released in a flow of bright blood.

Soloing was a long way away, and today there was only her fingers, cutting out not Ruth Elder's picture but the Silent Purchase coupon from the magazine:

"To Sales Person—
One box of Modess, please."

Suddenly all her confidence, that she could do anything, even aeronautical engineering, was gone. Every day she examined Johnny's face, his words, his manner. If she were pregnant, would he abandon her? Did he like her as much as the day before?

She was only a girl who kicked her own ankles as she walked, who had a small store of jokes which she had memorized and used over and over because she could not originate them in her own private emergencies. She wore the wedding ring of her grandmother on her right hand, and inside the band was inscribed "chum, sweetheart, wife," and "9/17/66", and when asked, she would say "those are my statistics," and that was one of the jokes.

With Al Christy and Sam Sonneborn she was bold, daring, raucous, one of the boys.

Now she was someone else entirely—a girl.

"Don't tell me you love me because I don't want to hear it," Johnny said. "Want to see it—know you're sweet on me. You never show a blessed thing." And other mornings he had been inarticulate with grief and anger and leaned across her knees and gently touched her lips. "Loara, we don't have a thing going for us, do we, excepting we're 'in love.' Don't you see? You got to do more."

"What?"

"I can't be just part of the scenery."

There existed between them a tacit assumption of marriage, and without it the relationship couldn't have survived the constant arguments. Always Johnny began them, inflicted them on her and she could never understand. In the end it was her passive ignorance that kept him from leaving. She was, he knew, quite helpless in her ignorance, and might never be loved again by someone else because of her great lack. What it was he had never fully known, but characterized as "that consarned female irrelevance." He was quite aware, though, that she wasn't like other women. Her peculiarities were hers alone. Her mind was never captured for long, and hovered momentarily over bright shiny surfaces and fragile colors and sounds struck sharply from common objects. These objects themselves, he himself, and concerns thought important by his parents she quite subtly ignored. Her opaque eyes showed him nothing, and she could not talk of war or death or money, or even the vagaries of their feelings. She said she loved him, and then moved on to watch the glitter of an oil smear winking upward from the rainy pavement. He was shut out, and if he spoke to her, her eyes lighted on him briefly and then passed to his side where he watched their slow, reluctant focus.

After a while she realized that he knew, too: she was a freak.

Something tightened within her into a sudden apprehension. She saw his lips move, and not to kiss her, and even as she leaned forward to hear him his words dissolved away before she could catch his meaning. "I been pushing you in the corner and forcing you and trying with everything I have to get into you—to make you care, feel. And seems you do. But how'll I ever know if I pushed or you wanted me in the end?"

She decided to let her body decide for her: was she a woman or a freak? She stopped douching with Lysol, stopped asking him if he had a safe.

She was a woman: she was pregnant.

She opened the envelope Johnny gave her. On the folded piece of paper he had drawn, with considerable skill, a wedding ring on which perched six black crows. She looked her question up at him.

"It's that old nursery rhyme," he said.

> " 'One crow sorrow, two crow joy,
> three crow letter, four crow boy,
> five crow silver, six crow gold,
> seven crow secret never to be told.' "

Loara looked at him and she thought she wanted to die before she ever hurt him. But marrying him, she knew she would hurt him too.

"You know I want to hitch up with you, Loara. We can settle down on Aguahega. Sooner the better now, don't you think?"

He was still looking at her. One crow sorrow, two crow joy...

"Maybe I should have made it four crows," Johnny said, " 'four crow boy.' "

He was still waiting, impatient bridegroom, for her answer.

In her room that night she sat under the lamplight of Mrs. Pfleugel's boarding house and looked through her pile of newspaper clippings in the old cheese box. Pilots old and bold waiting for her. She began to tear them up one by one. Suddenly she wondered what it said about Amelia Earhart, and her fingers kept on tearing until Amelia Earhart was gone and she thought: there, I've killed Amelia Earhart.

Finally nothing was left but a wastebasket full of scraps.

Into the room the phone rang. It was Al Christy: "When can we expect to see you back, kid?"

"I can't, Al."

"Why not?"

"I tore up all my clippings."

She put down the phone. Again she unfolded the sketch Johnny had drawn.

Six crow gold...It seemed she could still hear the birds now, those other birds, the medricks far out to sea in the overcast distance, bumbling murmurous hum swelling louder, nearer. But that was on Scrag Rock when she was five years old. Whatever had made her a freak had started in magic, had started there....

CHAPTER 9

1920-1927, Scrag Rock, Maine

In Loara's beginning was the Rock and the birds. They overshadowed everything else, even her parents, in Loara's world. All winter on the Rock the colony of medricks had been gone, but now it was May 10th, it was spring. Loara could hear the birds now, the first few scouts swooping above the five year old's head, but they were still nervous, bouncy, their cries tearing rents in the cold wall of wind. Loara could see it now, the cloud of the colony boiling nearer, white and pulsing, lifting and falling, the far-off hum disintegrating into individual arrows of shrieks.

And suddenly the world filled with 8000 pairs of beating pale gray wings, with black-capped heads and blood-red beaks. Loara reached up with both small smudged hands, laughing, ears ringing with the deafening sound, head dizzy in the whirling wheels of flight.

Loara leaped, arms upstretched to greet them.

But the bite of rope beneath her arms jerked her down.

She was firmly tied to the Rock, and that was how the two elements differed. The Rock was sturdy and steady, rooted and still.

The birds were light as summer air, blew in when the winter vapor left the water and then were gone.

The birds were free.

The Rock was Scrag Rock—a half mile of isolated ledge on which no trees or even grasses grew, its granite walls fifty feet above the surf. It was twenty-four miles to the mainland, and the only reason people lived here, as they had since 1827, was to tend the lighthouse.

Loara's father, Ridley Pritchard, was the keeper.

Now her heart was breaking. Fingers outstretched, she strained against the leather harness and its ropes that kept her from falling into the sea. Her face was bent skyward and tears blinded her eyes. The dreads: the outflight had begun. The medrick cloud gathered its white-bodied wisps and turned once more toward the horizon.

Days might pass before the colony settled back on Scrag Rock to nest and breed.

They were gone, and her child's heart knew only today.

Her sobs thundered, as loud in her ears as the fog horn when it blew, vibration screeching ten seconds every minute, rhythmic as the waves. It could be heard twenty miles away if the seas were calm, seven if storm. The copper-domed top of the lighthouse, circled with a white-painted catwalk, stood 137 feet above Loara, its curtained windows shielding the hyper-radial lenses, 6,720 pounds of glass. The walls, gray granite blocks six and a half feet thick at the base, narrowed to five feet at the top, where Loara had never been.

The cathedral-thick wooden door led to an unimaginable, vertical world where children—herself and the four sons of Assistant Keeper Malpede—were forbidden to go. Her father took off his shoes before stepping on the gleaming waxed floor of the lamproom. He braced himself with a hand against the dripping rock wall on his way down the spiral steps, rather than smudge the polished perfection of the brass railing. Ridley Pritchard rubbed everything to reflect his obsession with order and detail. And children, a detail one could easily dismiss, were just not orderly.

For that reason they had had only one.

Loara jumped forward as hard as she could against her tether, again and again.

But her mother took no notice.

Beyond the neat cluster of freshly painted buildings, red roofs the only smudge of color, Josephine Pritchard was on her knees patting earth into the depressions and fissures of the granite ground, planting the seeds she had stirred all together in the big green mixing bowl: dahlias and geraniums, pansies and petunias, marigolds. With every trip to the main for mail and supplies in the spring, Ridley brought back a bushel basket of earth. Soon, fertilized with iodine-rich rockweed, the seeds blossomed around the dwelling houses and the engine house, oil house, tower, walks, and sheds. Then when the first storms of winter boiled across the Rock, spray dashing over the rooftops and draining the bite of salt down into the cistern's water, the sea searched out every last crevice of earth and swept it away.

But now a mysterious sound crept into the air.

The sound swelled louder all around her—buzzing like the largest yellow jacket that ever lived, buzzing louder and louder. What direction was it coming from?

Loara looked up, head straining back, tugging out against her harness to see over the eaves of the house, eyes squinted against the white glare of the sky.

"Aeroplane! Aeroplane!"

Josephine Pritchard came running, her yellow apron flapping in the wind that poured unceasingly over the Rock. "Loarie, look. Up there, that's an aeroplane. Oh, don't I just wish. There's a man up there, Loarie. He's flying."

Loara stared as the sound swelled slowly nearer, the vibration filling her chest and her head until suddenly: *there*. She saw its rounded tan-colored nose and two long beautiful tan-colored wings, one above the body, one below, and the wings wiggled at her now as if in greeting.

She saw the shape of a man's head, a long white scarf.

They could fly, then.

People could fly.

Into her heart came an exhilaration as wild as the birds. And a determination, hard as the Rock.

Someday she too, Loara Pritchard, would leap free of the Rock and fly.

1926

"Loarie."

Charles Malpede's high-pitched ten-year-old voice pierced the air above the hard-packed sand with the sound of scandalized outrage. "Loarie, what're you doing? Come on back. Your father *said*."

But how did you leave heaven?

After a two-hour wait, Loara Pritchard, eleven years old, was standing only three people from the front in the long line of vacationers, some in long, still-wet wool bathing suits, who pushed and jostled and laughed and ate and stared anxiously up at the sky. But they weren't as anxious as she was now that Charles had found her in the forbidden line, waiting for the airplane ride.

Loara tried to disappear, edging to the far side of the fat man behind her, striving to stare with unconcern down the gentle arc of three-mile-long Old Orchard Beach, whose two and a half miles of unobstructed sand was at low tide the finest runway in America.

"You've got no money," Charles shrieked.

People were looking at her now.

What was the matter with him? For years they had been involved in one escapade after another on the Rock, although the worst was when Ridley Pritchard discovered the parade of parts that was one of the fog-signal engines spread across the engine house floor. *"Is that my fog signal motor?"*

Ridley Pritchard towered above her, his bony shoulders erect in the navy blue serge coat with its double row of three 3/4-inch triple-gilt-on-brass buttons, each emblazoned with a tiny lighthouse that stared right in her face. His blue eyes glared at her from beneath the black patent leather visor of his navy blue cap. On each lapel of his jacket glittered an embroidered gold loop 2-1/2 inches long with the letter "K" for keeper within. The loops shook now as he pointed at her, index finger rigid. "Answer me!"

"Yes, Father. It's your motor."

"Then perhaps you can tell me why you have *wrecked* it?"

She opened her mouth but her throat was so dry no sound emerged. She swallowed frantically.

"You see, Mr. Pritchard," Charles said, "this here is our machine shop we set up. Loarie and me, see, and—"

"We did it because it's fun, Father. We're fixing up—"

"Overhauling," Charles said.

"All the motors around here and—"

"*Fun!*"

"I can put it all back together again by myself, Father." She stared boldly up at him.

"And I'm going to stand here until you do."

"Come on, Loarie. Let's us get started." Charles squatted in his knickers by the parts.

"She *said* all by herself, Mr. Malpede, if I heard rightly."

Loara knelt by the carburetor, gaskets, pistons, piston rings, valves, the ball bearings winking in their rainbow bath of oil. As she worked she began to hum. It was how all the parts fitted together that fascinated her, like a jigsaw puzzle that you cleaned, adjusted, scraped replaced, drilled, ground, and finally assembled, all lubricated and ready for a test run.

When at last she finished tightening the final bolt she sprawled backward to rest her spine against the welcome coolness of the wall and looked up at her father.

A slow flush was rising above his stiff blue collar.

"*Tarnation!*" was all he said.

And so Loara had no intention of abandoning the airplane line, even though she sneaked a glance back at Charles and saw—horrors! traitor!—he was running back toward adult authority and the small town near the beach where they had arrived to visit her grandmother. Loara wiped her sticky palms down the front of her oxford trousers with the fly front. Hah! Let Charles run! It was five long miles back to Biddeford where her grandmother had expressed the thought that if people were meant to fly, God preserve us, then He surely would have given them wings. By the time he could make it back, even with her parents in Grandmother's car, it would be too late.

By then, she, Loara Pritchard, would be up in the air.

"Don't you worry, honey," the potbellied man in front of Loara was saying to a young woman with an impossible shade of blond hair. "It's got a great little OX5 engine that pulls a hundred horses, so it sure oughta be able to handle us."

"Ninety," Loara said.

"Beg pardon?"

"It's ninety horsepower and it's been called 'a failure looking for somewhere to happen.' "

"What?" the woman said.

"Yeah. Last year there were a hundred seventy-nine accidents barnstorming, and eighty-five killed."

The woman bolted from the line, dragging the man along with her. Loara was only one person from the front of the line. Grinning, she stepped forward.

And then the murmurous hum began, swelling louder overhead as the double khaki-colored wings of the biplane *Jenny*, officially the Curtiss JN4D, a tattered army surplus relic patched with canvas, soared into view. It banked over Prout's Neck and Pine Point at the northern end of the beach and then with an easy wiggle of the long wings touched down lightly on the sand.

Red, white, and blue stripes were painted on the tail and the struts between the wings were bright red. Loara pushed with the others ahead as the line moved, trying not to stare at the skinny man in the peeling leather jacket who jumped out onto the wing and then to the ground. She waited in an agony of expectation, resignation, and hope as the pilot helped the teenage boy, the only person ahead of her, to put his foot up on the wing, grab hold of the strut, and haul himself over the rim into the front cockpit.

Five dollars for five minutes: it might just as well been five hundred when you had none. She looked up at the pilot, her wild yearning in her clear blue eyes.

"This your little sister?" he asked the boy.

"Nah."

"Got five dollars, kid?"

Loara shook her head. Her agony was beyond tears as she stared up at him, hardly more that a kid himself. He made a little sucking noise between his teeth, and then she felt his arms lift her up, boost her over the padded rim into the narrow cockpit beside the boy. A webbed belt cinched her tight and an oily smell surrounded her as a mechanic cranked the starter, the engine kicking and clattering into a roar, whirling a sandstorm of grit past the tail. The seat vibrated, her toes vibrated, the air vibrated. The beach lurched and jounced and then suddenly didn't. She was climbing the blue hill of sky.

The houses back of the line of sand, the pier, the rollercoaster and rides, the dance pavilion shrank away. Fields flowed into forests green. The slipstream thundered against her face with its smell of exhaust and oil and the boy beside her shrieked his fear.

Loara laughed as the elevators bore her higher, the sun so close on her hair. And then too soon the fragile birdcage of fabric and spruce-capped ply tipped and turned, the cat's-cradle wings of struts and wires began to descend toward the blue lobe of sea resting so gently against the white sand.

Now someone else was pushing ahead to take her place. Her legs shook as she stared like someone who had seen a vision up at the pilot's eyes.

"Well," he said, "how'd y'all like it?"

"I'm going to be a pilot too."

He patted her head as if she were a puppy. "Sure you will."

1927

News drifted so maddeningly slowly out to the Rock. Loara waited impatiently at the end of the long slip for the boat's infrequent return from the mainland, then ran up the slippery boardwalk with the newspapers clutched under one arm. Carefully she worked the dull points of her scissors around the articles, the photographs, storing them in her wooden cheese box.

Now she picked up her favorite picture: the grainy pose of the two French pilots. Which was handsomer, which one would she marry: the blond Nungesser, or Coli: ten years older, short and dark with a black mustache, and a rakish patch over his right eye?

"I like Coli better," Josephine Pritchard said.

Loara decided she would marry Nungesser after all. Here was the photo of *Oiseau Blanc*, their plane, painted on the fuselage with the emblem of Nungesser's wartime regiment: the Hussars of Death, a black coffin, candles, and skull and crossbones.

Every pilot alive wanted to be first to cross the Atlantic. Pilots were literally dying to do it. Three American contenders had already crashed, one paper said, including Commander Byrd who had flown over the North Pole, and one had died. Another American, an obscure "Captain Charles Lindbergh," the paper said, was planning in July to fly from New York to Paris, and mechanics in San Diego were racing to finish his Ryan aircraft in time.

Too bad for Captain Lindbergh. Because by then, of course, the prize would already be won. For it was already happening, the most exciting event of the century, the most important thing that would ever happen.

It was 1:30 in the afternoon of May 9, 1927.

Loara's heart thudded against the unyielding surface of the rectangular hooked rug, her chin propped on the backs of her hands. Her blue eyes were fixed on the wireless receiving set in its mahogany case, on the black enamel depths within the horn. She wanted to crawl into the horn's eighteen-inch throat and haul out its knowledge faster than it spoke. She listened to the almost palpable sounds.

"Is this the day that two new heroes of the world will descend among us from the skies, the first to fly the Atlantic non-stop? It's raining here in Manhattan and the crowd is silent, and everyone looks up into the forbidding skies.

"Yesterday, at five-seventeen A.M. Paris time, the third leading French war ace Charles Nungesser and his navigator, Captain Francois Coli, left Le Bourget airfield in their white biplane *Oiseau Blanc*. They are expected to land right here near the Battery, from which this broadcast is coming to you, and set down in the Hudson River in just twenty-one more minutes, at two P.M. Why not dry land? They were so heavily loaded with fuel at takeoff they had to jettison their landing gear.

"But can they withstand the icing, the fogs, the whipping winds across the Atlantic? Every field and wireless station, every ship, every lighthouse keeper on the Atlantic coast has been put on the alert: watch for a small white plane with no wheels...."

Loara Pritchard sat up cross-legged, heart jerking. Her father had stood the 6 to 10 A.M. watch in the tower, and he had seen nothing passing under the clouds, above the water, nothing at all. Charles's father was on the 10 to 2 P.M. watch, ready to sound the bell if he saw any flash of white, even if it should prove to be just a gull. Heavy northwest winds had been reported from Cape Race,

Newfoundland, with flurries of snow. And no bell had rung.

Oiseau Blanc: white bird lost in the sky.

The cards made neat, small ticking sounds as Charles spelled them off the deck, then an angry whoosh as he swept them together again. Loara's mother was knitting, her father constructing a ship in a bottle, and all the Malpedes were there, waiting too.

And then the Magnavox boomed suddenly louder in their midst. "Ladies and gentlemen, do you hear that? Handclapping and cheers! A report just handed to me says that *Oiseau Blanc* was sighted over St. Pierre-Miquelon, an island off the southwestern coast of Newfoundland at 9 this morning by an American destroyer. She's made it across. And now here's another bulletin, the first report of an American sighting. At 12:24 P.M., in Abnaki Bay, Maine, north of Portland—"

"Mother!" Loara shrieked.

"Hush!"

"—an unconfirmed report that *Oiseau Blanc* was seen off Aguahega Island by a resident, Johnny Beal, a thirteen year old boy. I repeat, this sighting is unconfirmed."

Loara grabbed a pad of paper and moistened her pencil lead with her tongue. She carefully printed:

> "To Johnny Beal
> Aguahega Island, Maine
> Dear Johnny,
> Im mad I didnt see White Bird first. Im
> even madder you did. I am twelve.
> Please tell me everything you saw. Id
> be ever so grateful.
> Loara Louella Pritchard
> Scrag Rock, Maine."

She folded it three times, ready to mail.

But now it was 9:30 at night and Loara's eyelids grew heavier and heavier, the voice on the radio a soft sweet indistinguishable blur. She felt herself lifted in her mother's arms. She struggled in her sack of sleep.

"Mother, are they here?"

"I promise you. When we hear anything, anything at all, I'll come right in and wake you up and tell you. Now, how does that sound to my little sleepyhead?"

The blur of her mother's face sharpened into focus, the lines standing clear. "You mean, White Bird hasn't got here yet?"

There was a sudden silence. Loara saw the eyes of the grownups, how they sought each other out and then turned away. Ridley Pritchard was still working on his ship in a bottle. He was trying to pull the miniature rigging up with cotton. Suddenly the whole thing gave way—the end of three weeks of painstaking work. He picked up the bottle and smashed it against the wall.

He put on his keeper's jacket, buttoned all the buttons, swept a scrap of lint off one shoulder, adjusted the cap to the correct angle on his head and strode out to take the 10 to 2 A.M. watch.

"Father." Loara ran after him. "Can't I come up with you, just this once? Maybe White Bird will still pass by."

Ridley Pritchard didn't even look back, he just kept walking. "I am going to work. This flying is madness. Madness! For playboys."

"There're old pilots," Charles said, "and bold pilots. But no *old* bold pilots."

Loara ran clattering through the parlor and down the whirling snake of a hall to the bathroom. She lifted the whitewashed seat. Down at the bottom of the Rock, near the sea, the fierce wind was blowing straight into the end of the toilet outlet pipe.

Loara stared down at the swell of the water in the bowl.

She tried to imagine riding in a tiny airplane through the night, sealed between an invisible sky and reaching sea.

Some reporter had asked Nungesser why he painted his airplane with the Hussars of Death. "A strong heart," the newspaper quoted him, "doesn't fear death even in its most morbid aspects."

If you fly, you die.

I'd rather die than not learn to fly.

Are you still going to learn to fly?

And then the tight pent-up nausea in her stomach came pouring out.

CHAPTER 10

1931-1943 Aguahega Island, Maine

Loara married Johnny Beal in the church on Aguahega Island. They lived in Perley's House with Gooden and Clara. Three miscarriages followed, and after each, in her sorrow Loara blamed herself: unwoman, freak.

Finally on Labor Day Weekend 1937, their first child, Johnny's longed-for son, Torbert Beal, was born. Two months had passed since Amelia Earhart's plane disappeared somewhere between New Guinea and Howland Island while attempting to fly around the world. It was official, the radio said: she was given up for lost.

Deep in winter and on the island still the cold continued. Lobstermen pushed their skiffs over the ice to their frozen-in boats farther and farther out. And always, always, the nearly solid shine of ice clogged the eye wherever Loara turned. The beelike hum of a plane made her look up: a National Guard plane dropping its missile—a message asking how they were.

Johnny tied their reply on the middle of a warp stretched between Gooden's clam rake and Beck Vannah's long wooden gaff.

The plane dived low and hooked the message, waving good-bye now in the window after they read it: "Supplies holding, no one sick, bless the Lord."

It was the next morning that the new baby, Torby, began to frown. The frown went away but the next time Loara glanced over, it was there again, tiny lines like premature age signs furrowing his smooth pink brow.

From the northwest, winds blew savagely now at gale force strength and temperatures plunged to minus 25 degrees at night.

Torby had a permanent frown and began to cry: it was a fretful wailing sound. It only stopped when he yawned, not a restful yawn but a weak, giving up yawn followed by a hard direct look and a yawn again. His temperature was 105°.

At dawn the next morning a group of three volunteers led by Johnny Beal, with a pick pole to test the gray stains that peered from the white, set out across the islet-studded frozen expanse for Haley's Landing sixteen miles away. Loara walked on the salt water ice that was tough but giving underfoot, Torby heavily bundled, his mouth breathing heat against the back of her neck where he was slung like a papoose in a folded blanket woven to her chest with lengths of knotted union suits. She heard only the sound of her ragged breath heaving out into the glare of sun on ice, struggling to listen, hairs prickling, for the sound and feel of the small breath behind her.

Six days later, in Wardwell Hospital thirty miles up the coast, without ever smiling again, Torby Beal died.

"Doctor," Loara said. "Was it the delay getting him here that tipped the scales on him? Would he have made it if we'd been right here, close to town?"

"Now, now, Mrs. Beal, there's no sense going looking for blame where none exists. These things happen. Infants are really fragile little packages altogether, you know, and boy infants for some reason in particular. Why, the little Carpenter boy was put to bed right here in town and the next morning he was found dead—and we don't even know why. He hadn't acute bilobar pneumonia like your child."

Johnny seized hold of Loara's sleeve. "You see, Loara, what'd I tell you? No help for it. Couldn't have done more to help him if 'twas pneumonia like it was. God's will."

Loara was on her feet. "*Tell* him, doctor." If he did, perhaps Johnny would let them all leave....

"Tell him the island killed my child."

1943

Their second daughter (after Victorine) was called the "furlough baby," conceived during Johnny Beal's recuperation from the 1st Infantry, 18th Regiment, Company D, after the invasion of Tunisia in 1942 when he took a load of shrapnel in his knee. He had returned home to Loara and two-year-old Victorine with an enormous cast inscribed with signatures, cartoons, and:

I jump with glee
I jump with joy
For I was here
Before Kilroy.

Kezia Beal was born with a strawberry birthmark on her cheek, the slightly raised surface velvet hot to the touch. Five months before, Loara had been down on her knees scrubbing the kitchen floor, pushing the lobes of soapy water out into the dark corners. A mouse, surprised, blinded with fear, jumped into the air and struck her cheek. Her scream brought Gooden Beal to the doorway. She stared up at him, her hand, her cheek bloody where she had flailed at it, accidently crushing it.

Newborn, Kezia lay unwrapped on the kitchen table where the midwife had laid her down. Gooden's eyes stared as Kezia kicked rosy soles up to the light, all perfectly pink and white—except for one red spill.

"Dear God, what is that—it's the *mouse*."

"Don't be foolish, Gooden," Loara said.

"It's marked her for something. But what?"

Quickly Loara rewrapped Kezia, jiggling her close as she lay back on the warm cot by the stove, eyes fierce over the back of the small bald head. "Let's hear no more of that superstitious kind of talk."

But once spoken, it lived.

CHAPTER 11

1952 - Aguahega Island, Maine

Trouble.

It had started some two months before. There had been talk, Kezia Beal remembered, and men meeting in their kitchen, talking about the off-islanders invading their lobstering territories, talking late into the night, she had heard them on and on over coffee and her mother's blueberry pie. She had wanted to know what it all meant, but no one would take the time to tell a nine year old child. Because now there was Trouble, the talk had got louder, angrier, until Clara, Kezia's Grandm'am, had shushed them and then come upstairs where Kezia pretended sleep—"playing possum" Grandm'am called it—always seeming to know.

Then the Trouble got worse, some equipment stolen, there were threats in the air. And more men coming to the kitchen, more pie, more coffee, the talk got louder and louder still. Kezia crept to the windowsill, climbing on the stove-in lobster pot and peering in. The kitchen was full of smoke and noise—but everyone was sitting and there was her father, Johnny Beal, standing, hands gripping the back of a chair.

All eyes, even the reluctant ones of Gran'sir, were focused on her father.

"Chair talk's cheap!" His voice was louder, lower than Kezia had ever heard, filled with a sudden sureness it had never had. "We all know what this is so let's call it what it is: another Cut War. So all of you. We going to sit here on our duffs while these off-islanders goffle up our territories one by one? Are we?"

"No!"

"We going to sit here while they steal everything from us, the bread right out of our families' mouths, so we can't make it through the winter, climb March hill?"

"No!"

"We just going to keep on sitting here and taking it and get et up like a black wing goffling up a little sea duck?"

"Hell no!" He had brought them to their feet. There were wild cheers, a rush of talk.

Johnny Beal's face was red, his forehead knotted, the vein on the side of his neck swollen and pounding. He felt their eyes on him and realized how much he was enjoying this and what they were waiting for—his command.

He smiled.

Under cover of fog he led them out to the bay, where they tied a half hitch around each spindle of the invading buoys until their fingers ached.

They cut off the last lobster pot on each string. Still the strangers hauled. They sharpened their knives and sawed all the grassed-over warps through. Pots, lobsters, warps all swam to the rocky bottom, bounced once, and were gone.

But within a week new foreign pots appeared, their marker buoys blossoming on the waves like a plague of wildflowers: red, yellow, blue, green, and every shade between—striped, whorled, triangled, spiraled with identifying patterns, colors: *my* buoys, *my* pots, *my* territory. Not yours.

Then came the sudden clanging of the church bell across Aguahega from the village, tolling the fire alarm islandwide. There was the roar that was the Beal's dock, orange against the night sky and black water that held them there: pinned to the island, pinned to the fire, the fire fear of people on a pine island trapped between the heat of flames and the cold of water, like living on a torch, white grubs on a burning log.

Kezia had watched her father shouting with the others over the pumping noise of the salt-water fire engine, his face running with sweat, blackened with smoke. She remembered the stories—of the fire that took out the east side just thirteen years before, of the first fire before the turn of the century when the hermit Rowdy Richardson's cabin burned down, that threatened them all for two months, spreading underground, smoldering among the pine roots until the first snows.

But finally this fire, on the Beal's dock, was out. Kezia had inched closer to stand beside the new strength of her father, the bold leader of the Cut War.

He had a strange dead look in his eyes. She started to reach for his hand and then stopped. His hand quivered at his side, fingers twitching like the rabbit Gran'sir caught in a snare.

Trouble....

Now Kezia felt her father's hand at her elbow as they passed the blackened remains of their dock, planks spotted white with the tombs of cone-shaped barnacles.

"Hurry up, girl."

Kezia kept her gaze straight ahead. She had learned it from her father: never show fear. Ahead, on the calm surface of Toothaker Harbor, *Loara B.* bobbed her high wide Noviboat bow in greeting, so sprightly she made you forget the Folger's coffee can patch on the exhaust pipe, the twenty-eight feet of wave-battered wooden dilapidation. And then at last Kezia was there: the vibration of the cedar-planked deck thrumming through her feet up into her bones, the acrid cloud of exhaust billowing backward from the pipe, the Jeep engine's voice—its cough, its hesitation that she would have known blindfolded from any other's—battering again at her ears. She stood beside her father in the three-sided wheelhouse: what Gran'sir disparaged as "that lemonade stand." The blue Tinkerbell lights of the Puruno depth finder danced and crackled across the paper strip and she wanted to laugh aloud because she was back, she was here.

It was when they were hauling the eleventh string of ten pots, two pots to each glass bobber and buoy, that the first pots came up empty.

They were completely empty.

No lobsters or even the thumping of a trash fish like an old toad sculpin, no hermit crabs scared out of their shells, scrabbling in panic, clinging to the dripping laths, falling on the deck and getting crushed underfoot. Not even any "whore's eggs": the round, green-spined sea urchins who ate trap heads and bait and bait bags and even the laths right down to the nails.

The pots sat there on the washrail while Johnny and Kezia stared at them.

His gloved finger traced below the short wood "button" of a door latch. "Took a spool of black thread out here last time, Kezia. Wrapped it around this here lath so if you opened the door, break the thread. Thread's gone."

"You mean, someone's been taking our lobsters? *Stole* them?" The happiness of last year was entirely gone. Fear stood hard in her stomach. It was the Lobster War.

He stared out at the southern horizon and his face sagged bleak and barren, an unfamiliar terrain. Kezia looked where he did. All she could see was the reefing breeze that blew up around noon—a line of deepest blue straight as if ruled on the sea. Even as she watched, it moved toward her, sparkles of sunlight, sharp peaks of waves. She could feel it now, chill as if fresh over a snowbank. A heavy cross chop was running, and the whistle buoy's moaning quickened to short anxious bleats.

Kezia opened her mouth and gulped the breeze down as it lifted her hair.

The rising stench from the bait box where she stood for the first time made her feel sick. The tremendous heat of the exhaust pipe flared near her face. She pushed the pointed spudge iron through a filled bait bag's loops, then scooped up four redfish from the open barrel, threading them, too, on the "spudgin" through the path of least resistance—the eyes. She had forgotten her gloves and her hands were raw and bleeding from the lobsters' thorns as she pegged them, dodging their rip claws and the jets of smelly fluid they shot at her from under their feelers. Now the abrasions smarted in the bait juice "pickle" in the four-legged bait box mounted on the deck. Forgetting the gloves made her feel like a fool.

The wind was cold but she felt the sun burning through her hair into her brain, spinning her thoughts out into the crystal air, dizzy and lurching as her feet. Her arms moved, her fingers followed but all without feeling in the bait box, with what seemed no effect at all. Her nose was burning but she wouldn't put her hat on. She let it flood down and cover her with its blinding warmth.

She rebaited the two empty pots, wiped off the seaweed, latched the doors and watched as her father expertly dropped them so they'd land right side up on the sea bottom again. *Loara B.* surged ahead toward the next buoy, and with his left hand Johnny Beal shut the throttle and slammed the wheel over. Automatically Kezia's knees bent as the boat leaned into its hauling circle. The painted cedar buoy floated close to Lurcher Ledge, a half-tide ledge that only warned you of its buried knives when the tide was far on the ebb.

Heart like a half-tide ledge.

"Daddy." She called louder over the engine: "Be careful."

He threw the potwarp three times around the bronze winch head and 20 fathoms of slimy, spray-flinging rope ground upward.

Now why had she called out—just like a scaredy girl. But what if, what if the propeller tangled in the potwarp and *Loara B.*, helpless, crashed up on a swell into the ledge, and what if, what if the straining potwarp rushing up caught her father's arm, yanked him overboard and held him under until he drowned? Could she act fast enough, cut the warp, save him before he sank? There was no knife except the one that he wore, nothing to cut with, never had been, but why? It had always seemed too scaredy-girl to ask.

There was no doubt now; all the pots on the string were empty. Kezia watched as the last pair sank, the white fractured surface healing slowly back to green.

When she looked up again, the white blur of canvas sails was suddenly there; a sloop running before the wind with its mainsail jutting out at right angles, careening down on them from around Zeb's Head, a boat from Seal Point.

Loara B. stood directly in its path.

Shouts from the sloop: "Right rudder, Tony. *Right.*"

Leaning hard to starboard, following its swordfish beak of bowsprit, the twenty-eight foot boat, silent except for the clink of halyards and the gurgle of bow wave, swept grandly through their buoys and bobbers, snarling the lines.

"Hey!" Johnny Beal's voice sounded small as it passed, a maroon and yellow buoy snagged like a boutonniere against the hull. "Hey, you punks. You God damn—*God damn it.*"

Shrieks from the sloop, and then came more commands: "Strike the jib! Stand by to round up. Tony, you're supposed to be helping with this. Helm's alee!"

In a long wobbly arc, the sloop shot past *Loara B.*, attempting to round back and brake into the wind. Kezia stared at the flash of colors: the golden wood of the mast rising 22 feet, the long wide curve of the hull painted a glistening purple banded with a narrow stripe of white, then gold. On her bow, above a spray of carved ivy were the words:

WILBER A MORSE BUILDER
FRIENDSHIP ME

On her stern her name glided by in white and gold flourishes:

PYED COW.

Johnny Beal shouted, unbelieving: "Kids."

On the *Pyed Cow* four teenagers stared back at them, two boys and two girls, one a pretty blond jouncing far out on the bowsprit hanging onto the rigging with one hand, while with the other she snatched off a white sailor cap and waved it at them like a semaphore, laughing.

More shouts from the boy at the wheel: "Stand by to anchor. Lower away! Pooh, grab it there, douse that mains'l." The anchor tore a hole in the water and sank, and the sloop tested its tether, pulling slowly around to face bare-poled into the wind.

"You kids—you gormy kids'll pay for this mess you made now, by God!" Potwarp stood on the surface like a tangled ball of twine.

Johnny Beal cut their engine and over the anchor went. The slap of water on two hulls was suddenly loud.

A boy of thirteen clambered out from behind the protection of the wheel and peered across at them.

Kezia stared back. Summer mahogany: yachters from Seal Point were thick as spatters from June through Labor Day. But this was the first time she had been this close. The boy's face, long and narrow as a thoroughbred, was almost as white as his sweater. His eyes, so dark between the pale planes of his face, looked at Kezia like a child peering between two boards.

Feelings rushed her: the storm of envy that she always felt for Seal Point and its people, fascination and longing, and yet anger twisted as snakes. Her heart beat fast and pain darted through her, a chill stony feeling that left fear in its trace. "You see that, Keezie?" Gran'sir had once said, pointing at the huge boll that bent, distorted a tree. "The Point's like that, killing off the island, maybe it's already dead. Don't you never let me catch you fooling around up there." So of course she did, drawn to the shingled and stone estates on whose deserted verandahs you could sit cross-legged in autumn, brooding over the bay dark with islands like gumdrops on cake.

She could look for hours in at deserted rooms, up at turrets and towers, across the spreading lawns and naked statues in withering gardens. And sometimes even in summer she had looked out at them from the trees, staring in the wide windows at children with stuffed animals bigger than they were, at uniformed maids glimpsed through curtains blowing sheer as mist. And it followed her home across the ridge trail to Toothaker Harbor where they were jolted every summer's twilight, some arthritic Seal Pointer firing off the sunset gun.

"Sir," said the boy with the white skin and dark eyes. He seemed to be in charge. "I'm real sorry we nearly sideswiped you like that. It's my fault entirely, sir. But everything's all right now, isn't it?"

His voice was calm and confident; it seemed to swoop at them like birds. "I'm Chance Chancellor, sir, and my family owns Tenhaven up at the Point."

"It ain't all right! And I'm John Henry Beal and I own this lobsterboat."

The blond girl giggled. "Oh, mister fisherman. Would you sell us some of your nice lobsters for a lobster bake on the beach, pretty please? Stop it, Chance. I want to get some we know are fresh, now we've got the opportunity. There's nothing more ugh-making than day-old fish."

"Two things that smell like fish," Tony said. "One is fish."

"Shut *up*." The one called Chance bent his upper body at his friends, hands balled in fists. "Let me handle this."

"Want to know how to handle it? I'll tell you how to handle it." Her father stood with hands on hips in the center of *Loara B.*'s deck. He rubbed his nose, always a bad sign. "You can kiss my balls under three shady trees!"

For the first time Kezia saw her father through a stranger's eyes. Something gripped her heart, a chill sensation down her back, a heavy sinking feeling. Silver spangles of herring glittered in the hair on his arms, even in his eyebrows. His glasses were salt encrusted, bent uneven on a face burned harsh and lined with sun. He was stooped and dirty, gurry smeared.

The rich boy looked at her father, seeing everything she saw. "Look, sir, we'll pay for any damage we've caused."

"Money!" Johnny spat into the waves. "What are you lamebrains going to do about the mess you made of my pots?"

"What pots?" the other boy said. He was older than Chance and he stood with his legs braced far apart. "Chance, you see any pots hereabouts anywheres? All we saw, pop, were some of those, you know, little tide sticks floating around."

Tide sticks!

"Those were spindles! As in spindles on buoys. Buoys, as in lobster pots, as in gear, private property, you cheesehead."

The sound of metal clanked on metal, and Kezia saw the rude boy tugging at the anchor chain, hand over hand on the grassed-up links until the anchor heaved clear. The sloop shuddered once and shifted, moving free.

"Tony, what in hell are you doing?"

Kezia saw the two boys scuffling, but the rude boy was not only older but much larger. Now the sloop's inboard engine coughed once, twice, roared powerfully to life.

Kezia blinked, the sudden stinging pain in her right hand burning like fire. She looked down. Her sunburned, abraded hand was thrust deep in the salt pickle in the bait box and as she watched, her fingers closed around a huge glob of chopped herring. She threw the dripping mess toward the moving stern of *Pyed Cow*. It splattered guts-gray across the shining purple paint.

He was looking at what she had done and then staring at her–the thin boy with the high domed forehead, the one who lived in Tenhaven. The sloop was rapidly pulling away but Kezia could hear him trying to call something to her. All in white he stood looking back from the sloop's deck, his words lost in the wind. He turned his palms up and out.

Johnny Beal made a sound like a leaking gasket. "Steers like a toad in a bucket of tar. Steers like a royal hencoop." He tipped his head with contempt toward the sloop. "Well, Kezia, going to give us a bit of a break on your first day out."

She was shocked. They never stopped for breaks before, just a quick swig from the thermos, a grab at a sandwich while racing full throttle to the next buoy. And the lobsters in the tank, sea water kept circulating with a hose–you had to hurry them back fresh and alive.

Johnny Beal looked down at her and smiled, but his smile seemed to decay as she watched. Suddenly she was frightened. The sun burned down between her shoulder blades, soaking into the flat space between, the chill breeze hard against her face. "Daddy, I'm not tired. We don't have to stop."

His face looked grim and yet there was a confused hesitancy about his eyes. "No, let's just call a halt for a time. I need a break, take our nooning now, I guess, just a little spell to just sit. All these things happening out here today."

Crotch Harbor was glassy smooth and tranquil as they nosed straight in, disturbed only by a flock of goldeneyes and buffleheads—diving ducks that splashed noisily into the air.

But there was a boat tied to a fallen tree already there.

"What do you make of that outboard, Kezia? Never saw that one around before. Wonder who she belongs to?"

"Plummers down from Seal Point?"

"Not the rotten shape this poor baby's in. It's new or nothing up at the Point." He sent the muddy anchor back over the side again, and Kezia scrubbed her hands together in the salt water, the cold numbing her fish-smelling fingers. She slapped the surface and the spray leaped against her palm, tickling and falling back in ribbons of droplets. She wanted to forget the moment when Chance stared at her father: seeing herself.

Johnny unzipped the striped bag, taking out Loara's thick oatmeal cookies wrapped in wax paper and the thermos of hot black tea. He poured the round cup full for them to share, handed it steaming and laced with sugar to Kezia. "Remember now, lovey, swallow those bubbles on top and you'll have money."

"You sound like Gran'sir."

"Don't wish that on me. Swallow! Way things are going these days, we may need it."

She laughed, the sound high and clear over the water, carrying back into the listening woods.

From the thick forest of pines and spruces on the hill came a sighing, ghostlike sound of wind on needles, bringing with it an evergreen tang. She sucked in a hot mouthful, bubbles and all. She pirouetted between the stinking bait barrels, around the scarred wood bait box, arms reaching high over her head. "Rich, Daddy! I'm going to be rich, rich, rich. Have real butter every night."

"Not richer than me. Watch this!" He grabbed the cup and took an enormous swallow. His eyes squeezed shut, adam's apple jumped up then down, and he laughed—a small, guarded chuckle with worry still behind it.

He picked up the binoculars and scanned the horizon: an archipelago of islets and dry ledges. Kezia looked where he was looking, north to Sheep Island. A figure topped the hill. Against the sky it looked like an insect creeping up a wall of blue.

"Just your grandmother."

The glasses were heavy, cold against her face. Kezia saw green and buff-dead grasses, rocks embroidered with mustard and orange lichens. There was the old hut from the turn of the century when 500 sheep had grazed there, and the driftwood sheep pen. The scaregull rowed his dry-land stove-in rowboat, a strawman to keep the gulls away. They would attack lambs and even sick old ewes. And there was Grandm'am, eyes translucent, quartz pale beneath straight black brows pinched together under the etch of sun.

You've got the German's eyes. Kezia pulled the glasses away.

"Don't know why she bought those old pelters. Half didn't make it through to spring."

"She paid two dollars a head," Kezia said, proud of her knowledge. Grandm'am had talked to her of little else. "Said pelts'd bring a dollar fifty, and then there's the new lambs." Kezia looked through the binoculars again.

Clara Beal was holding out a fistful of turnip greens. The dirty white-gray bodies hurtled to get away, and then, just out of reach, turned laconically to stare. Now one old ewe reached out its neck, straining for the greens but unwilling to commit itself to a forward step. Its nose wrinkled, lower lip gaping. Finally it began to nibble from Clara's hand. Kezia watched as her grandmother's other hand came up slowly, fingers splaying out to pat the dense spongy wool between the burrs. The ewe jackknifed sideways, away. The dark sheep eyes went white-edged, watching. Clara grabbed the potgutted ewe by the wool at the base of its neck. The ewe ducked, backed away, and Clara flung herself onto its shoulders, arms reaching around. She buried her face in the gobs of matted wool.

"Why's Grandm'am crying?"

Her father looked through, then put the glasses decisively away. "Simpler with an animal, your feelings, I guess."

"I know there's Trouble and this War thing and everything. But we're happy, aren't we, Daddy? We're still happy. In spite of it?"

"Don't never let anything spoil you, Kezia."

"But aren't you? Happy, I mean?"

"You mean the War? Or the arguments with your grandfather?"

"Both, I guess. Well, no, maybe the arguing more." She felt his broad, black-nailed hand reach across, the heavy weight warming her upper back as he squeezed her shoulder. He always touched her; it was what she loved.

"I love your grandfather, and you, very much."

"Does he love you?"

He hesitated just a moment. He was 38, but there were so many lines on his face. She'd never noticed them there before: lines that crisscrossed like a bait bag on his skin.

"I hope he does, yes."

"But then, why do you fight like that in the cellar? Is it because I'm bad?"

"What? Bosh tommyrot! Keezie, whatever gave you that idea? Nothing to do with you, Lord knows. And anyway, you're not bad, not even a little tad."

"Well, what about when I got Nate to steal that pound of bacon and we cooked it in the garbage can lid and ate the whole thing? And, and..." Her voice came faster. "What about when Grandm'am told me not to say BM in front of neighbors and I ran all over yelling BR, and BS, and BT, and she got madder and madder!"

This time Johnny Beal threw his head back and really laughed. The worry was gone. "Keezie, if the whole world was bad as you, why, it'd be a beautiful little place to live in. And anyway, you don't know what a little devil your old pa was. Tied a barrel on this rope and put a cat in, spun it up tight and let her rip! That poor old whiskers had the staggers for days. Then I tried a rooster, then this little neighbor boy, Corydon. Couldn't sit on my backside for weeks after Father got through whaling me. So I put physic in his beer bottles, that spruce beer he was always cooking up down cellar. For days he was trotting to 'Aunt Sally' like a house afire."

Kezia's face brightened. "Daddy, you were really bad."

"Had fun then. Those were the times I liked."

"Why do you and Gran'sir fight?"

He frowned, eating another cookie. "I had a chance once, move away from Aguahega. Looked up, turned around, it was gone."

Kezia looked at her father, startled. A cricking sound ticked in her neck. It was incomprehensible, as if trees could walk. Her father, move away?

His eyes were distant, remembering the name, it flashed through him now like an electric charge after all these years—victorinereese, it rhymes with please. His blood seemed to swim, struggle upstream like small cold goldfishes through his veins. He looked at Kezia, wondering for just a second full of betrayal what she would have looked like if the first Victorine had been her mother—prettier, of course, as pretty and feminine and delicate as victorinereese. He watched her holding the cookie bag with a sunbrowned hand, already hard as a salt herring. Maybe his mother was right. Now that would be funny after all this time, all those fights. Maybe lobstering really was the wrong way for a girl.

He fished a large lobster from the tank and with his penknife began idly scratching his hail: name and address on the crusher claw. Like sending a note out in a bottle, you never knew who would reply, from where.

"When you're young, you always want to be leaving where you grew up. Don't you know that, pudden stick? Natural. More being trapped here than lobsters. It's a sign of old age, you stay for good. Then you know for sure you're buttsprung."

Leave? Leave Aguahega? It was like rocks flowing like water.

"I try so hard to make things as good for you girls as on the main. How can I justify it—living on here if you're going to suffer? That money we sunk in the new well, seven gallons a minute coming up. Then they had to go and hit that iron ledge. Everyone else got good clear water. Ours—like drinking rust. Was going to put in a generator out back so we could finally have a bathroom. Good as they got on the main."

"Who needs a bathroom?" Kezia didn't really understand what he was saying, but she felt angry, betrayed. Aguahega was her. Aguahega was the whole world. She had climbed the Witness Tree: through leafy shade the top flared white with sun, bare heat that plastered her hair. She laughed, wet arms clinging to the heights that swayed and swayed. She leaned her head back to let the Indian Summer sun dry the tears of fright still on her face. And then blinking she stared for the first time at the world: past treetops, shoreline, far out to sea where green gumdrops floated on a plain of blue. She didn't really believe other little girls lived on those islands. She had never been off-island in her life. She was the last child born on Aguahega. Aguahega was the whole world. Daddy said so: it belonged to her. Below the Witness Tree Johnny Beal hollered witness: "Girl, you beat the pants off any boy."

"Even Gran'sir left Aguahega," her father said. "You know that, Kezia? Was eighteen, and he up and sold a hundred acres, too. Sold to the Chancellors at Tenhaven. Hell, we'd still have some land, some money if it weren't for him. Now we've got a couple acres. Firewood rights, we got, in their woods."

Kezia sat immobile on the boat's washrail. "But why? Why would Gran'sir move away?"

"Old wounds there, pudden stick, from Seal Point, where else? Old wounds that just shouldn't be picked over again. He left, met your grandmother, brought her back. And we should head on back ourselves before it gets dark under the table. Haul our poverty boxes, what say?"

The engine coughed, wheezed, died, coughed again.

"Daddy, what about those ten new pots. Where're we going to set them?" The pile of dry traps, each pair with its buoy and coiled warp inside a trap head, were stacked in a neat row on the planked-over afterdeck.

"Oh, thought anyone so important as to be sternman might need little extra cash to impress her friends."

"They're mine?"

"Any bucks they haul, yours free and clear."

"It's more than even Nate Vannah's got!" Blood burned into the birthmark on her cheek with a sudden fierce pride. She looked out at the fenceless corral that was Sheep Island. She could see only the sheep now, vague shapes of white wandering down into the tidal zone after sea kelp and rockweed. Grandm'am was gone.

A white haze had come in on the wind. All things offshore looked dim and far. It wasn't fog, the day was still sunny, but she felt cut off from that distant shrouded horizon. It could still be good, she thought. It wasn't like last year, but to want it so was greedy. Gray eyes meant greedy, Gran'sir said. Big head, a lot of wit; little head, not a bit. Kezia, then, was not only greedy but dumb, her older sister Victorine had taunted.

The wind was still steady but the afternoon was starting to wane. It was colder and Kezia rolled her sleeves down.

The next string of traps was two hundred yards from shore. *Loara B.* punched forward at three knots, Johnny singing over the engine, a rollicking "Life is Like a Mountain Railroad" in his strong deep voice. The first gaily painted buoy appeared, bucketing from the trough to the crest of each wave. When it was eighteen inches away Johnny swung the bow around and leaned far out with the hook-tipped wooden gaff, snaring the potwarp just below the buoy, catching with his other hand the stoppered glass bobber to keep it from breaking.

He fell before Kezia heard the sound—a flat crack like a stick breaking. It was a sound she couldn't identify and didn't try. Her attention was on her father. He appeared to be diving headfirst into the water. Why would he dive into the water when he didn't know how to swim?

His body completed its beginning arc into the waves, his visored cap slipping loose and skipping like a flung stone over the surging crests.

Loara B. turned in her hauling circle, and Kezia's father was cut from sight. She stood with her back flattened against the sharp knobs of the wheel, eyes staring, her throat dry and stiff and refusing to form a scream. She felt the knobs press into her back, harder and harder until it felt as though they would pierce all the way through.

Loara B., heedless, started around once again.

Her father's face appeared, white in the waves.

Kezia rushed out on the open deck, struggling to push one of the new dry traps over. Her arms wrestled with 85 pounds of granite-ballasted piss oak, she felt something give in her back and she pushed, pushed. The trap slipped over the side and catapulted far out of her father's reach.

The boat went around and then her father's face appeared. The boat again, his face.

"*Kezia*. Get back inside. The cuddy. Get inside!"

The air whined around her, the expectation of another sound. The boat came around again but Johnny Beal was gone. The waves tumbled and folded, reknitting the churning surface as if he had never been.

Kezia crawled into the cuddy, closing the light out with the door. In the gasoline fumes, on the pile of dirty rags and spare gear she struggled to comprehend.

The sound—it was a rifle she had heard. A rifle that someone had fired, at her father.

But that couldn't be true.

Because that meant her father was dead.

She had been sick many times.

The boat turned with the world, too fast. She wasn't aware of the engine's roar until suddenly it was gone. The silence roared like a shell held to your ear. The turning motion ceased. The boat rose on a larger swell, and she heard a clattering roar as something rolled outside on the deck, crashing against the opposite planking.

Hooo. Hooo.

The sound came like lips pursed over a half-filled soda bottle, the sound of a whistle buoy, now loud and insistent, now frail and tentative with the shifting wind. Water slapped, slapped against the hull. But that—something else. Another sound. What was that?

The sound lay on the air, a faint whimpering like a puppy. Where was it coming from? Kezia sat listening, body rigid with effort.

Her throat hurt, and she realized the sounds were coming from herself.

The panel door of the cuddy yanked across. Fresh air and light poured in, hitting her like a blow. She curled reflexively, like a touched caterpillar, tried to wedge herself in the dark farther back.

"Please come out."

Her eyes looked at the dark sphere haloed by light that was a face, as if at the end of a long tunnel.

"You can come out, it's all right. I'm Chance—from the sloop—this afternoon."

The voice waited a long time. Finally it reached in and fingers closed around her hot damp skin.

In the fading afternoon light she stood on the deck, stinking, oilclothes covered with vomit. She stared at the voice.

Her eyes were so pale it gave Chance an uneasy feeling to look within, as if he fell forward, as if they weren't there. "Are you all right? Where's your father? What happened here?"

She opened her mouth and a kind of croak came out.

Chance picked up the thermos that had rolled across the deck. He poured a cup of tea that had gone cold.

Her throat labored to swallow.

"Where's your father?" Chance said, looking at a bullet with a flattened, mushroom-shaped tip clearly visible on the deck.

Very softly Kezia began to sing.

" 'One day I was eating an oyster stew,
alone, tee-hee, alone,
And one lonely oyster hove in view,
alone, tee-hee—' "

Her voice stumbled, hesitated. She looked up at the other voice, squinting in the sunset.

"Come on, Daddy. You sing too."

CHAPTER 12

For three days Kezia stood with the others on the southern cliffs looking out to sea. The dry easterly battered at her head.

Two Coast Guard boats and nine Aguahega boats and eighteen more from the main were searching for her father. She watched as Beck and Nate Vannah hauled her father's remaining traps down to the end buoy, looking for a body tangled in the warp.

Behind her she could hear the other men crashing through the puckerbrush and alder bogs of Aguahega, looking for something dropped, someone who might be hiding, a stranger who didn't belong.

Back out to sea, divers from the oceanography school sank and then surfaced, blowing like shiny black seals. Overhead two Piper Cubs buzzed criss-crossing squares over the waves, hunting like the fish hawk for prey.

Four boats converged and circled, and on the cliffs above them Kezia's breath stopped and the blood pressed through her head. And then the boats moved outward again, a false alarm, resuming their patrol.

At twilight of the third day Johnny Beal's faded red visor cap was plucked from the water, black-wet and sopping, and carried to Loara Beal.

And then the darkness came.

But the unspeakable thing—it loomed blacker than the dark corners of the bedroom, more terrible than the dark under the bed.

She had caused her father's death.

The sound of a boat's motor ripping clear, then dulled through shifting fog. She had heard it the very morning he'd been killed.

Too early: no boat should be there...

It had been drawing closer. She should have told.

Kezia sat up in bed, the mouse on her cheek burning like a hot coal. Her fingertips probed its too smooth surface, different from the rest of her skin.

Now the mouse burned like the drop of magic black mud the story's humpbacked dwarf, Rumpty-Dudget, threw on Princess Hilda's forehead. And all the scrubbing in the world wouldn't wash Princess Hilda's spot away....

> And when the wind blew from the north,
> where Rumpty-Dudget's tower stood,
> the spot became blacker and blacker,
> and hotter and hotter, until she
> was ready to cry from pain and vexation.

A cry, stormy, full of water and rage rose from the floor below. Kezia stepped down on the pumpkin pine floorboards that creaked alarmingly and opened the bedroom door. The voice was her grandmother's from the kitchen. Kezia crept out onto the landing, fingers closing around a carved squirrel's back. Now came the soft low voice of her mother that she had to strain to hear. She leaned her head closer between the railings.

"I was going to go down to the shore Monday and meet him when he and Kezia got back. It's been I don't know how many years since I did that. Used to do it when we were first married—put on some lipstick, comb my hair, run down to the dock and look out for him coming home. For no reason I thought of doing it Monday, and then I didn't. Years since I thought of it and then Monday. And then I didn't."

"Loary, you rest yourself now." It was the familiar rasp of Beck Vannah's voice: he wasn't family, didn't belong in Perley's House. "People always think on what they *didn't* do. I did the same when my Velda passed away. Have to remember the good things you did."

Kezia's feet moved toward the rectangular light of the kitchen door. From the darkness of the hall she peered in. Everyone but Grandm'am was sitting around the pine breakfast table. On the wall above, the clown in the painting studied the tablecloth with downcast gaze, his red and yellow ruff blotched with a ball of blue. "It is a tear; he is crying," Grandm'am had once explained. But everyone knew tears weren't blue.

Kezia hesitated, standing with right toes clenched on top of the left. She couldn't go in. It was as if she were a stranger. These faces were familiar but she didn't belong, as if it were something she'd always known.

"Well now, Loara," came Great-aunt Toss's voice. She lived down the coast on the main. "You'll be staying with us in Medon from now on, so you can stop worrying. Clem's going to board in the porch real snug, we'll make us another bedroom out of that, and—"

"You mean leave here? Leave Aguahega?"

Boiling water splashed noisily into the washing machine. Grandm'am pushed the lever to and fro. She fed the steaming wads through the rolling jaws of the Acme Star wringer, rinsed them in the tub of water at her feet, hauled them dripping back to the boiler on the stove where they would cook in the lye soap again. Her face gleamed as red as her hands.

"Well," Toss continued, "it'd be cheapest all around. Gooden and Clara and I have been turning it all over betwixt ourselves. Costs so much to heat this big old place. And you've got to think about the little one on his way. We've got a nice modern bathroom for you, and it's no place out here, no phones, no electricity, no place for a new little one."

"I've got to find some way to get on my own. It's wonderful of you and Clem. But I've been thinking. Maybe a job at one of the canneries on the main."

Steam whooshed from the lifted lid on the iron boiler. Tendrils of hair loosened and curled from Clara's braid.

"Sure, you'll do all right," Gran'sir said. "We'll see you do. Only female I ever met had the sense of a man, excepting Clara, of course. Being gimped up with this arthritis and all, just one way now to take care of you and the girls. And that's selling what we got here."

"But I couldn't. You can't sell here."

"Money in the pocket, Loara. It's what we need."

"But Beals've been here forever. You know it'd break your heart."

"Beals would still be here. Make 'em let me and Clara keep a room long as we live, and why, if they were nice folks, and we wouldn't sell if they wasn't, and if we took a liking to them, and Clara could cook and wash up for them, and I could keep the keys when they're gone come winter, handyman about, well, that might work."

Beck Vannah's voice was stiff. "You mean, sell to *summer* people?"

"Who else's going to buy out here?"

Grandm'am hauled all the clothes back to the wringer, rinsed them again, and through the wringer again. Her fists were raw and furious.

"But I'd want you both to come live with us," Loara said. "On the main."

"I'm on the down side of the mountain, but there's only one mountain for me, Loara. And winter, hell, I like winter best of all. Best fishing, ducks, best little view right smack here out my own window. Might as well be dead as go anywhere else. But if you should drop a son, now, that Torby you want to name him, he might be wanting this old place to do his hauling from, some day he's a man. Maybe then we should think again. But it's another girl, we'll sell."

Grandm'am cleared her throat.

Kezia stood in her nightgown in the doorway, right hand gripping the white-painted frame.

"Kezia," her mother said. "You're supposed to be up in bed."

"Couldn't sleep." Kezia searched her mother's face but Loara wouldn't meet her gaze. She was so different from Johnny. Shame had tightened her mother's eyes, shuttered her face—the shame of emotion, the embarrassment of feeling. It was more frightening than Grandm'am's rage.

"You can't sell Perley's House!" Kezia said. You might as well sell a person, sell the world. It was like herself running, running on too short legs after Victorine up the hill: "Wait, wait for me." Victorine couldn't just run away, abandon her no matter how much she wanted to pretend Kezia wasn't there, connected to her, tied to her, always, always part of her. Victorine had always waited for her.

Loara pushed herself away from the table and in one quick motion Beck Vannah was beside her, his arm steadying around her. "You'll be all tired out tomorrow, Kezia," her mother said. "Come, I'll tuck you back in."

Desperately Kezia scratched and sifted the air for relief, a fierce scavenger saying whatever words came into her head. "But we have to stay, Mother, we can't sell. Got it all planned. Nate Vannah and me, we're going to take Daddy's place. Haul all summer and fall, just like Daddy. I know where all the pots are. And then all winter we'll mend gear and I'll knit the bait bags and you should see the beautiful pots Nate makes, Mother! We can stay right here and never never have to leave, Mother!"

Loara's large square hand, the fingernails ragged with cuticle, pressed the side of Kezia's face close against her swollen abdomen. Kezia tried to burrow closer across the bulge of the unborn Torby who seemed unfairly to come between. The skin-warmed circle of her mother's watch burned hot against Kezia's ear. It ticked like a heartbeat on and on.

Kezia opened her eyes. She was looking into Gran'sir's blue eyes. They squinted and then welled with tears.

"Kezia," Beck Vannah said. His hand was on her mother's arm. "Sometimes we have a little dream we like to dream about. But then we wake up. We have to go on about our life. Go to school. You know you and Nate have to go to school."

"How about if I read you a story?" Loara said. "Would you like that?"

"Yes."

"Which one?"

"Rumpty-Dudget's Tower."

Beck Vannah's thick-fingered hand pulled out his chair again, the one at the head of the table. Kezia's voice was harsh: "You can't sit there."

Beck looked at her, and the silence pressed thick as fog.

"Daddy's sitting there."

A month later Emmadene Beal was born: a red mouth screaming in a blue-painted cradle. Blue was for boys. Already they were calling her Deenie and making kissy noises.

She was a girl. Perley's House would be sold.

CHAPTER 13

"It's the oldest house on the island. Authentic Maine cape-style farmhouse built in Eighteen-Fifteen. Perfect for family or retirement. Complete with Nineteen Forty-Six Chevy pick-up truck."

Kezia's thighs were wet with sweat, so wet she wondered if she had wet her pants. She stood with her face butted insistently against the wind, watching the real estate salesman, dark with hair-centered moles, and the man and the woman: summer complaint.

"Why, I don't believe I've ever seen a lilac so tall."

"It was planted at the turn of the century," Loara Beal said. "A great-aunt brought it back from her honeymoon, planted it in lieu of the Bridal Tree."

"Bridal tree?" the summer woman said.

"You leave your parents but you leave them a tree. The Bridal Laylock this was called."

"Isn't that just charming!"

The man with the moles steepled his fingers. "And look at that view. A living mural of a real Maine coastal scene. Twenty-three-inch wide floorboards, twelve-inch handhewn rafters. Now where are you going to find that in this day and age?"

The air warmed around Kezia, swelled with the nearness of her mother's presence. Her mother's blue dress was so new it still smelled of sizing and store shelves. She'd been going to the main the way Daddy would never let her. She and Beck Vannah. She'd been buying lots of pretty clothes.

" 'Summer people, and some are not.' " Kezia's voice sailed loud. The couple and the salesman turned to look at her and Kezia looked up at her mother and grinned.

Loara's hand pressed hard on Kezia's shoulder, a vise closing her down into the earth. Suddenly Kezia pushed it away, she had screamed something but she didn't know what. Its imprint lay smashed on Loara Beal's face.

Kezia ran toward the safe net of the evergreens. The trail was eroded and muddy underfoot but as she climbed higher it sprang beneath her bare feet like a mattress—a thick, spongy weave of sphagnum moss and gray reindeer lichen and fallen needles decomposing into black humus. She climbed through the wet evergreens up to the molded pink granite and the stunted lone pitch pine at the very top of the ridge.

She felt the resin sticky under her fingers as she struggled up in the pitch pine, its spindly frame bending as she climbed higher, its branches pointing down. The tree buckled, swayed, finally steadied, and Kezia's breath slowed from its fierce harsh gasps and she pressed her hot cheek against the cool bark. She could feel her pulse jump against the tree.

Sell Perley's House? Go to the main? She would never do that. She could hear Daddy's voice: "Things go from bad to worse, and from worse to Medon."

Her big toe kicked at a cone, loosened its attaching fibers. A clear gummy liquid bled out. The dried pitch on the cone's edges glittered white as frost. Nobody knew who had killed her father. But the Lobster War was over, the invading buoys pulled and gone. People acted as if her father had never been.

But not her. She could knit and knit a bait bag for hours, and she could look and look and look. She would look in many faces. She would know him when she saw him, the man who shot her father. No one else would. But *she* would know. She would start knitting another bait bag. And when she finished it, she would find him. It was as simple as that.

Her bare toe dug at the cone's root fiercely, until the cone fell away.

It would be a calling. She had read it in a book in the one-room schoolhouse. She wasn't sure what it meant, but it meant you called and called for what you wanted, and then it would come.

There was a fresh scar where the pinecone had grown: her witness mark, her Witness Tree. Kezia felt a stinging pain, opened her hands. Her fingers were brown with resin and clinging dead needles, red with blood.

A booming drone flared like small faraway thunder down the sweep of the mountain ridge. It was coming from the northwest. She swung to face it, felt the afternoon sun fall like a blessing on her face. Now a distant piping tinkled over the droning, like spring rain on Alewife Pond. It was a bagpipe but she had never heard one. The strange nasal sounds flowed from the place where no one ever had to sell their home, where people were safe. Where no one ever died.

If only she lived at Seal Point.

PRIVATE GROUNDS
NO CARS JULY 4 THROUGH LABOR DAY
NO TRESPASSING
WATCHMAN ON DUTY

From her hiding place in the spruces, Kezia stared out at the great white iron gates of Seal Point. Not a single summer person was in sight. She tried to stifle her panic, breathless pain. The boardwalks crisscrossed like a maze, linking the 26 shingled "cottages" on their clipped lawns fenced with firs to the shingled boathouses, the nine-hole golf course, the red clay tennis courts, and the striped-awning-hung windows of the Konkus Club, all stained shingles above and trimmed ivy below, with a fat tower's clockface peering down into an open central court.

Tenhaven rose straight ahead, a wooden castle on its rock base, gables pointed as the firs. The rough wild music that shook her heart was coming from the rear.

The crumbling wall that protected the famous Tenhaven gardens was mauve with flowers: flanks of heliotrope, delphiniums taller than Kezia's head, clematis flourishing from every crack and overhanging the Moon Gate. Kezia peered through the round doorway, the mouse beating against her cheek, its feet wanting to run away.

Even the light was different at Tenhaven. A smoky sou'wester had blown in, a haze blocking off the sun. All was ghosted, silver...wroght-iron tables lost in summer: lavender undercloths with antique linen laid on top, milk jugs of roses, and on one chairback a great wheel of straw hat.

Kezia crept inside the wall, climbed up through the skirts of a tall red spruce to get a better view.

Gods lived here, they must be, to create the beauty that she saw. At the distant end the Kitchen Garden's vegetables flourished beside eighty rosebushes to cut and mass indoors. Strawberries grew red as the roses, gooseberries named Early Green Hairy, Hue and Cry, Green Snake grew green as the leaves. Then came the Scented Garden with herbs and honeysuckle trained high over the benches. And closest to Kezia *The* Garden was bordered on four sides by the shaded canopies of pleached lime walks. Its beds were cut into the grass, spilling flowers lush and overgrown; 300 different kinds of iris, 150 daylilies, 50 peonies, 50 kinds of ferns. The central green-sward held a fountain whose bottom winked with colored pebbles, sea shells, gilded leaves. As Kezia stared she saw a golden carp rise in bubbles to the top.

Lost in dapple and languor, their pale clothes glowing paler still, all whites and pastels were more people than Kezia had ever seen. They spilled from garden to garden, drinks in hand, listening to the music hidden somewhere in their midst. On the edges there was din and chatter, pictures of children extracted between numbing fingers, love innuendoes, and the splashing of the surf.

A party was family and relatives.

A party was only at night.

Women wore aprons.

You ate in the kitchen.

You wore brown or green clothes.

The crowd shifted and now Kezia could glimpse the piper, traceries of gold braid on his jacket, a white fur sporran hanging down to where his legs met, its black tassels twitching like horses' tails with every step. He wore a tartan kilt—a boy in a skirt!—for he was still a boy, perhaps thirteen. He was all long arms with no shoulders, long bare calves that ended in sockless battered sneakers windowed with tears at the toes. His head was bent over the too-short blowpipe, black beret with a red pompom, cheeks puffed beneath.

Surprise darted through her, leaving fear in its wake. The piper was Chance.

He pumped the bagpipe tucked like a long-necked goose under his left arm. The three drones rose behind his head, red tassels blowing in the wind. Kezia watched him march slowly before the crowd, right foot heel down first in front of the left, then toe down, cautious, then weight gliding forward. His feet were his eyes as he focused inward on the tune, fingers intent on the ivory-mouthed chanter. He played "Lament for Red Hector of the Battles," a waterfall of sound, the most beautiful song Kezia had ever heard.

Kezia clung to the tree. She never wanted to leave.

Now it was ended and he looked up, flushed, as the crowd applauded.

"Well done, Chance. A bit flat at the end."

As if glad to be free of them, Chance snatched off the beret and kilt. He stood in nothing but too-large faded madras shorts that hung seat-empty over his hips.

The speaker clapped a large hand possessively on Chance's bare shoulder. He was tall and thin with the face of a hawk, a bald head with ears like handles on a jug. His other hand remained deep in his pocket, bunching up his pin-striped vest and jacket that sported a white gull's feather instead of a rose. He was widest at the belly, which was covered in white duck, and he wore white deck shoes.

"For those of you who don't know," the man said, "our fine piper is my grandson, Fairfield the Third. Know around here as Fairfield the Next."

Chance was pouring moisture out of his black-velvet covered pipe bag. He stooped to lay it back in the wood pipe case. As his hands flattened it it rudely burped.

A titter ran through the crowd.

"A hundred seventy years ago today," Fairfield Chancellor began...

Another burp.

"The government of Great Britain repealed the act which forbad the wearing of Highland Dress and the playing of bagpipes. The repeal symbolized this: a reawakening to a golden age. Edinburgh became 'the Athens of the North.' Why do I bring all this up today?"

Two more burps, louder still.

Fairfield's face kept its half-smile but his eyes swept to Chance, deep-sunk and forbidding. "Because today we look ahead to the end of summer when we dedicate our very own, our Norumbega National Park. Our reawakening to Aguahega's golden age!"

Through the applause Kezia stared at the old man. She had heard Gran'sir talk about the park, but she didn't really know what it meant.

"Now back at the turn of the century timbering interests took an interest in our own fair isle and lo, the natives lined up to sell. With a few other pirates like myself, we obtained a charter for the Norumbega Land and Improvement Company of New York—"

"Which was not, incidentally," someone called, "tax free."

"...whose purpose was to acquire for public reservation all land on Aguahega—except for our own cottages here, of course. Dear friends, the eastern half of America, Chester Bowles told us, 'offers no suggestion of its western half.' 'The Atlantic Coast,' James Fenimore Cooper told us is 'low, monotonous, tame. It wants Alpine rocks, bold promontories...' But neither had seen Aguahega! Here we stand in a St. Peter's of America, a temple of Nature in all her primeval beauty, looking much as she did when first seen by the questing eyes of Verrazzano."

"What about that last in-holding?" someone said. "What's it called?"

"I'm sorry to report that Toothaker Harbor isn't yet ours. There are two holdout families ensconced there, Vannah and Beal, and they're still holding out."

"Out to squeeze you for every last *sou*."

"No." Fairfield Chancellor's dotted bow tie jumped with his adam's apple. His voice was sharp, querulous, "You just have to understand the native mind. This 'in-holding' matter, now, we're speaking of his home. His family has lived here for hundreds of years. This is the mind of a 'failure,' this one who, while the ambitious left, has remained. 'Fixed like a plant on his peculiar spot; to draw nutrition, propagate, and rot.' This one can't succeed in the outside world. Aguahega is his womb—there is no price on that. Some method very subtle is needed to part him from the womb."

"Well, it isn't like *they* care if Aguahega goes to ruin," Chance's sister said. The third in a line of Annes, she was called Tertia. "It was the natives wanted to sell it all off to the timber people back—when was it, Grandfather? And all there'd be left now if it weren't for us would be"—she hesitated over the embarrassing word, "*denuded* mountains."

"Eighteen ninety-four."

"Toothaker can stay there till kingdom come, in my opinion," Eleanore Chancellor said. Chance's grandmother looked eternally startled: protuberant brown eyes above an anxious gash of mouth. "I always thought those little white lobsterboats picturesque."

"We've got a situation down there." Fairifield's voice was heated. "It's nothing but a rural slum. Is that the sight to greet the eyes of park visitors? Toothaker is the"—he hesitated—"*backside* of Aguahega, a swamp of privies and discarded automobiles."

His words were beginning to deflect off the drink-stiffened adult hillside. The party had relaxed into a soporific state, drinks were let slide, and there was a general migration down the giant's steps toward the bay, granite walls separating the elevations that swept down to a screen of ancient firs protecting from idle boaters' eyes. Beyond spread the best view on Aguahega.

Kezia looked at the endless blue sea and sky, the island hills on a plain of blue. In her head was the feeling of mid-somersault, everything upside down. Frightening and sickening, the world gone wrong. Only this time the world didn't turn back right.

Oblivious to his shrinking listeners, Fairfield took his glasses off, polished them, put them back on. His eyes shone through, bitter blue. "And personally, I don't want that southern view spoiled. Some people say ours is best, but I fancy the one from Mitten Mountain overlooking Toothaker Harbor and the cliffs. It is not too accessible. I was considering...perhaps we might donate a road to the park, an ocean view road."

"For what?" Tertia said. "No pizza, no phones, no movies, no restaurants, it's always fog, the natives are surly, nothing to do. Seal Point is Point No Point, as far as I can see." Her gaze slid to Chance, who sat cross-legged on the grass by his closed pipecase. "Of course, *some* of us find plenty to do all over the village."

Chance kept looking at his ankles which he held with both hands.

"What do you mean, Tertia?" Eleanore Chancellor said.

"You should have *seen* him. Paintbrush in hand, making a perfect fool of himself."

They were arguing in front of others as if they were alone, as if what others thought didn't matter at all. Kezia had never seen grownups like this. Perhaps Tenhaven had no cellar.

"There were signs all over," Chance said. " 'Help Paint The Schoolhouse.' It needed it, so I did. It was fun. The ladies painted the lower half and then we men—"

"Men!" Tertia laughed.

"—got up on ladders and we got it done and it looked really good, you know? And then we had like a picnic under the trees with all kinds of great food, I don't know how many kinds of pie."

The family group stood alone now.

"Chance." One handed, Fairfield was flipping the silver dollar between his knuckles. It was a bad sign. Years ago it was his talisman on Wall Street, where during the Crash of '29 Fairfield, too, experienced a turn of fortune. His fortune had been freed of stocks months before. On Black Thursday alone he made $100,000.

Was it guilt, too much of a good thing? At 43 he sold his seat on the Stock Exchange, spent more and more time on Aguahega, privately publishing his book on philosophy and nature: *Within Whose Walls*.

"Chance, I forbid you, I absolutely forbid you hanging around the natives. I will not be embarrassed by my grandson, particularly with this sensitive in-holding matter going on, I will not be embarrassed by my grandchild patronizing these good people."

"Patronizing!" Chance stood up, hands in fists.

His grandmother's voice was soft. "You meant well, but it's none of your business what goes on in the village, that's all Grandfather meant. We don't live here, not really. We've just borrowed some time here. The year-rounders can take care of things themselves, that's what they want. They don't want us interfering, just like we don't want them interfering with us. We leave in the fall, and I sometimes think of them here in the middle of February, an ancient stalwart race. And then I just try not to."

Ancient stalwart race? *You. Wretched. Native.*

"No. I'll do anything I want to. You can't stop me."

Fairfield Chancellor's eyes were cold above the pale blue of his collar. "Chance, pull yourself together. You've got to learn to control that temper of yours one of these days. Today might be an excellent time to start."

"You make everything ugly and I won't listen to you!"

"That's enough!"

It had been enough. He ran toward the Moon Gate in the garden wall, anger fueled by the fear that his grandfather might be right.

Chance passed so close to the hidden Kezia that she could hear the air fighting out of his lungs. He continued on, through the hedges of boxwood and Blackthorn to where the deserted pool shimmered, opal beneath the rapidly graying sky.

How much allowance did *he* get? Hers was a nickel a week, and no matter how hard she tried to save, even conquering the seduction of chocolate ice cream cones, it was never enough, never would be enough for the pink bath set in the store on the main: with the bottles and canisters printed with roses, all maddeningly sealed where you couldn't touch them under cellophane. And in the store Kezia's father had led her firmly past the magic counter of pink to the shoe section in the back—littered with shoe boxes, steel foot forms, the smell of dirty feet. He picked out a clumpy pair of oxfords for her: the ones she hated most, with the hard brown smelly leather, the rawhide laces so stiff they wouldn't stay tied. "Daddy, I've got shoes. Couldn't I get the bath set instead?"

"We haven't got a bathroom." And then, perhaps to make up for it, he bought her an army surplus can of athlete's foot powder which stood on her dresser now, in olive-drab tin. While at Seal Point, probably every single dresser top sparkled, glittered with the magic of pretty bottles, like the glass cosmetic shelf in the store. Probably every little girl had her own cellophane-wrapped bath set waiting to be used.

Because at Seal Point everyone had bathrooms. Everyone had everything.

Kezia knew she should leave. She didn't belong here.

Instead she followed Chance through the tall hedges. The sounds of the party faded in the afternoon.

Chance was completely naked. He bent to dive in the pool, light gleaming over the tensed arch of his back, long toes gripping the pool edge: the first male without clothes Kezia had ever seen.

Shock cold as flung water; Chance stood there in the mystery of adulthood, a mystery not dispelled by his nakedness but only deepened. Impossible, something she could never plumb. His hairless chest was tanned now, all of him otter sleek—except there. Seeming to hang to his knees, a translucent white column of flesh arced proudly out, then down from a jungly root.

Kezia stared in fright, in awe.

But boys didn't grow hairs-down-there. Only girls did.

"Do you got any hairs-down-there yet?" Vangie Carter had whispered at school.

She didn't. She was embarrassed. She played dumb.

"What do you mean, 'hairs-down-there.' "

"If you don't know"—triumphant—"you don't got 'em!"

Now Chance exploded the myth along with him into the pool. He gasped at the cold water, then breast-stroked frantically until his reaching fingertips brushed the white marble at the end of the pool. With a kick he flipped his body over and pounded back, over the merman and fishes on the pool's bottom—lapis lazuli mosaics that winked up at him like old friends.

He hauled himself out, shivering in the cool breeze.

From her hiding place Kezia's eyes widened.

Frightened gulls boomed upward as Chance chased them in zigzag flight around the pool, back bent, face skyward to watch their wheeling wings. He didn't spare a glance at Tenhaven's frowning dark windows.

Kezia knew she shouldn't be here, staring.

He was drying himself now with the madras shorts, running the cloth under his arms, down his belly, down over his legs.

Kezia's mouse had a life of its own: it beat now hotter than the rest of her. It seemed to be taking up all her air.

As if he heard something Chance's motions suddenly ceased, his head turned to the side, listening.

Kezia darted back, farther, and then ahead loomed yet another wall. It was yellow stucco, again with a round doorway, but this one was blocked by a white wood door.

Looking back she saw Chance stepping into the shorts again.

In full panic Kezia jerked the door open and hurtled through. Inside the grasses bent all lush and overgrown, not neatly mowed like the rest of the lawn. Tangled flowers gone wild, locked mongrel heads. At one end a rotting pergola sagged, latticed timbers open to the damp. At the other end stood a tiny thatched roof cottage with a miniature window and door. And now, too late, Kezia saw that the walls met, encircled, held her. She was in the Secret Garden and there was only one exit, back through the entrance gate. She whirled, heart beating faster, and as she stepped out of cover into the center of the garden Chance bulked large in the middle of the gate.

"I *knew* I saw someone go in here. Okay, I give. Who the blazes are you?"

"Kezia."

"Kezia? What kind of a name is that?"

Her tongue stiffened, a glacier blocking words. Now he would see, she didn't belong. She would crash into things. In her pockets her hands made fists. She stared up at him, dirty, tattered, covered with needles and smears of blood. Her feet were brown with dirt and there were holes among the bold-colored patches on her slacks. Not even clean slacks. Victorine was always accusing her of putting her dirty clothes back in her drawers.

He stood too close. He didn't smell fishy like all the men she knew. She breathed in the sharp clean of chlorine.

Their eyes met, lingering a fraction of a second longer than they should have. Kezia was puzzled; what did it mean?

Recognition dawned across his face.

"Kezia lived on Nantucket, during the Revolution," she heard herself recite. "Was a smuggler, Kezia Coffin was her name."

"Are you related to her?"

"No." She felt like a milk bucket under a bull. Would he never stop staring at her?

"You're the little girl, aren't you? The one on the lobster boat that day."

No, she wanted to scream. She felt tears well in her eyes. As if in response, she heard his voice. "D'you want to see the pet cemetery then?"

She followed him to the front corner of the garden, near the fissured wall. There stood miniature headstones in rows: Bizer and Duke and Boots. Silence surrounded the buzzing of a bee. She watched it land on an urn sculptured of privet with roses.

"I liked your music."

"You like bagpipes?" His face blazed in a smile. "What I played, it's peach bread—what I call it. Spelled p-i-o-b-a-i-r-e-a-c-h-d. It's the classical music of the bagpipe. Most people don't even know you can play a bagpipe slow." He took a reed out of his pocket and blew. Up close he looked different: high forehead that seemed to take up half his face, full lips with four lines bisecting the bottom lip, two close together, two far apart. His eyes were narrow, deepset, overhung by brows. "You're the one I found on the boat, right? Did they find out who killed your dad?"

She shook her head. Her toes dug at the dirt. "He doesn't even have a grave marker."

"Why not?"

"Didn't find him."

"Maybe he's not dead. Maybe he'll come back."

"Fortune teller said that about Nate Vannah's uncle. Uncle Clyde. He came home but he was wrapped up in kelp. The tide brought him in."

"You didn't have any funeral at all?"

"Gran'sir rowed out to where he went over, took his Bible and his old pair of slippers. Was supposed to take his cat in a sack. He didn't have a cat. Gran'sir threw it all in."

"I'd like to throw the R.O.M. in."

"The R.O.M.?"

"My grandfather. My father's the Old Man. Grandfather's the Really Old Man. Hey, you want to see my shell collection? I've got a really neat bunch of things."

She grinned up at him.

Tenhaven looked almost friendly now with its shingled, three-storied, many-chimneyed Victorian rambles. The windows of its 38 rooms were thrown open to the breeze, and mud was tracked on the threadbare Oriental carpet. There were spots on the floor where the Scottish deerhounds had scratched and piddled on the waxed boards. The first floor core of the house was empty and silent, four rooms strung lengthwise in an 80-foot chain whose rear windows kept watch on the sea. Kezia stepped forward, stumbling over nothing. She felt sweat crawl down her spine. Ascending above the massive fireplace were, in order: a portrait in oil, a five-foot spread of some animal's horns, and a faded tapestry.

It wasn't too late: she could always turn and run.

"Look at this." Chance was bending in front of the shimmer of a glass cabinet. Now he inched its door creakingly open.

Kezia breathed the musty, organic strangeness that wafted from hundreds of eggs: cream, pink-cinnamon, fawn spotted with chestnut, and deep sienna brown, the brighter colors paled with age. Each egg stood mounted on a labeled three-legged ebony stand.

"These are osprey eggs. They're my favorite birds. They're so gentle they let sparrows rent out a basement flat in the bottom of their own nest. And they mate for life."

"What's an osprey?"

"Those big brown and white hawks. There's a nest of them down at Toothaker Harbor."

"Fish hawks."

"Yeah. They're the same."

"R.O.M., peach bread, osprey. I have to remember all these names. Grandm'am sends me over to Great Egg Rock and I pick up the gulls' eggs there."

"You eat gulls' eggs?"

"The yolks're orange. They turn scrambled eggs pink."

"The R.O.M.'s a manic birder. Got a Life List this long. He's the one got this egg collection together. Ospreys are his favorite birds."

"Then why does he steal their eggs?"

"It's like the park. To study them, to preserve. I mean, they're still here, the eggs. If they'd hatched, the ospreys'd all be dead by now, right?"

Unconvinced, Kezia nodded anyway.

Chance opened the adjoining cabinet. It was filled with sand dollars and starfish and jingle shells threaded on strings, sand dollars and dead sailor's toenails and mermaid's purses. "I find if you park them under the kitchen stove overnight," Chance said, "they dry out really good."

Kezia nodded. She was looking at a map tacked to the wall. It was the first map of Aguahega she had ever seen. Only one white blotch marred the field of green plainly labeled Norumbega National Park. It was the only inholding left: Toothaker Harbor.

Sweat stood on Chance's forehead and his eyes evaded hers. "Hey, it's stuffy in here. Let's go outside."

Why did Gran'sir and Daddy hate Seal Point so much? Kezia never wanted to leave.

"Last night"—Chance spread his arms wide—"the whole lawn was nothing but fireflies."

"Lightning bugs. I know a secret about lightning bugs."

"I'll bite. What?"

"Know where they hide, come thick-a-fog." It was thick-a-fog now bringing an early evening in.

"Yeah?"

"It's a real special secret."

"I won't tell."

"Took my hand once, brushed it across the Bridal Laylock. Grandm'am said was just like playing a harp, only silent."

"What did it do?"

"Burst out in gold."

He turned; he was looking at her intently, a way he hadn't looked at her before. As if surprised...Now his arms swooped wide and he dive-bombed at her, suddenly a child again. Laughing, she turned and pursued. The hill was dark with massed fronds, and Chance ran ahead of her and then he was rolling faster and faster down through the snap of dead brown fern to the buoyant green of new fern beneath. And Kezia followed, the ferns cushioning her from the rocks as she turned, spilling out at the bottom ecstatic and dizzy under a reeling sky.

They stood up, looking at each other, wet with dew and fog. The hill bulked black behind them, shutting out Tenhaven and its lights. It was as if they were two children, both of whom belonged.

"I'm going to call you Red."

R.O.M., peach bread, osprey, Red.

"Ever been exploring in Digby's Den, Red?"

"What's Digby's Den?"

"The cave! The one in the southern cliffs."

"There's no cave there."

"It's on all the maps. It's labeled: Digby's Den. And inside there's a whole colony of hidden white birds in a hidden green room. You want to go see it sometime?"

Her eyes widened, burned into the night. "Sure!"

In her pupils he thought he saw himself, a tiny harlequin only comical in its dance. But she was looking up at him as if he were a god. "Maybe tomorrow, huh? Deal?"

"Deal."

"Chance."

They both looked up to see a tall figure on top of the hill. "Have you someone down there with you?"

"Yes, Grandfather."

They waited as Fairfield Chancellor made his stiff-legged way down the hill. "Well, what have we here, now?"

"This is Kezia, Grandfather."

"Somehow you don't look like you're summering at Watersmeet."

"Not the Adams' girl. Kezia Beal."

"Beal. Oh. From Toothaker Harbor?"

His eyes, twin stars of light behind their glasses, glittered frostily down at her. "Well, now little Miss Beal. Your grandfather made my acquaintance once. Sold me rare pollocks for one dollar each. Then I discovered they schooled around the village pier."

"Grandfather—" Chance protested.

"You'll have to be trotting along home. Parker will take you. You don't belong here."

The silence ballooned around them, stretching tighter and tighter. And then, to her amazement, Kezia heard it punctured by her own thin voice. "My Gran'sir says the park's like a snake. If you step on its tail, it'll turn right 'round and bite you. You have to kill it at its head."

CHAPTER 14

Tomorrow was the dedication of Norumbega Park.

Tonight Kezia felt only her father's absence washing in like a wave that never went back out. Down by the water of Toothaker Harbor she saw movement, a darker shadow among the shadows. Small, round, it crossed the silvered granite in the moonlight, starting, stopping, then vanished in the woods. Kezia's wide-braced feet moved lower, carrying her down into the old well until the world outside its stone rim vanished.

She never wanted to climb out again.

She felt the loss of everything loose and rattling, something broken inside.

In the well the air smelled like raw fiddleheads: earthy and damp in their brown ostrich-plume covering. Her fingers and toes grasped the cold of the walls, followed their nub and jut farther down the ancient jigsaw puzzle of the unmortared stones. The stones were grown together, mossy solid with age.

Kezia stood at last up to her knees in cold.

This was her secret place, when you had to cry.

Her neck bent her heavy head back. The stars were so far away. Everything was where she wanted it, far away.

But the man who had killed her father was from away. Farther even than Medon, she guessed. She would have to go wherever he was to look for him. When she was grown, she could go. How could she go before then?

The answer arrived early the next day.

Perfume curled through Kezia's open bedroom door, heavy as lilacs but not lilac sweet. Only one woman in the family wore perfume: her aunt, Wilhelmina Beal.

Kezia crept across the hall, peered into the other bedroom: peeling white paint of the iron bedstead, the edge of an unraveling rag rug, colors faded on the plank floor. Wilhelmina Beal, 40, was bending toward the bureau mirror in only a black lace-covered slip.

"Kezia! Quite all right. Come on in."

She was unembarrassed in her undress, not like Mother or Grandm'am. The long red nails reached for deodorant, rubbing creamy white smears under her arms. She was small and girlish looking, fascinating in the mystery of adult rituals, humming just the way Daddy always did. Now she frowned into the mirror.

"Eggwhite, dammit."

"Eggwhite?"

"Right here, pat it on the corners of your eyes every night. It prevents laugh lines, you know." Willi swooped the puff into a powder box and white scent precipitated through the air. "The past is a buried city. Your face is a relic of wrong streets, mistaken rooms. Just don't forget that."

"No, ma'm." Kezia glided nearer the bureau. Its scarred top was bright with crinolines rolled up in torn stockings, sheer blue stockings, and green and gray ones, even red ones as red as Aunt Willi's fingernails. She sniffed at the crystal bottles glittering like the ones in the store on the main. She imagined pink perfume, piles, poufs, billows of pink bath bubbles, pink lotions, none of which her mother used. Loara Beal's one cosmetic was Albolene cream: unscented, white, greasy as lard.

"So. What does one natter about to one's niece? How ancient are you now?"

"Nine, ma'm."

"Don't call me ma'm!"

Static crackled form the brush to her hair which was long and the color of mink dirt, Kezia decided, the dark rich soil on islands where mink used to live. The large square head, square jaw were oversized on her body like a sunflower on a stalk. Willi shook her hair back and Kezia saw the lumpiness like unstirred batter beneath her skin.

Aunt Willi put down her brush, looked full at her niece, and laughed. It was Daddy's laugh: it sailed out like a bird and flew around the room. It didn't hang back in the trees.

"Didn't anyone teach you not to stare?"

Kezia lay down in the middle of the spool bed, on the green and red zigzags of the Drunkard's Path quilt. "Used to lie down on Daddy's and Mother's bed. Could tell, just by the smell, which one was on which side."

"It was terrible. About Johnny. That you were there, had to see it."

"No one's looking for the man as did it. They've give up already."

"*Given.* Johnny was your father, I know. But he was my only brother, too. Do you see? I feel just the way you do. He was the only one I was close to, the only real family I had left. Do you understand? I never got married, had my own family, you know. And now Johnny's gone, it's all just wiped out and finished. I've tried to make it part of me, to accept everything that's happened. But I was old when I was five. I'm a child now. I'm a forty year old child."

Kezia didn't really understand what she was saying but fierce pride burned into her earlobes. Aunt Willi was talking to her as if she mattered, as if she were a grownup.

"Why couldn't they *find* Johnny?" Aunt Willi said.

"They trawled the bottom with fish nets. Said he might take ten, fourteen days to come up. Could be anywhere."

"Christ! How do you know such things. That's what I always hated about Aguahega, all the time there was this other—dying, things dying all the time. You could smell it in the flats at low tide—all the crab legs and belly-up fish, all the parts and skeletons. God, I hated that smell. You couldn't walk the shore after a storm. You never knew what would wash in."

Kezia sat up in the bed. "I'll hurt him the way he hurt me. The one who did it. He'll pay for what he did."

Willi Beal was staring as if taking her measure, the way Daddy always did with each new trap lath. "That's right. Get mad, Kezia. Let it out."

She would keep the hatred, make sure it didn't go out. Hatred would be her one known point. Kezia could see it now, its light was hot and angry, the way the mouse was on her cheek. She would burn and burn with it, her tears were scalding her now. She would never forget. She would dream of the killer.

Kezia got up and ran to her room. When she returned she held a scrapbook in her hand. Aunt Willi sat down beside her and together they turned the pages. Black paper with snapshots of men and men's faces: men in billed caps and plaid shirts and heavy jackets and sleeveless T-shirts, leaving the general store, a porch, entering a mud-spotted car. None were looking at her Brownie camera. The pages collapsed as Aunt Willi turned them, stiff and weighted with the mounted photographs.

Aunt Willi's finger stopped, held down the next page.

"Who are these people, Kezia?"

"Haley's Landing. Incomers. Maybe killed Daddy. Every time I snuck over, took my Brownie along."

"You know, Kezia, I think we could make something out of you."

Kezia's hands closed the scrapbook. "Am I pretty? As Victorine?"

"You need clothes and a haircut, dear." Willi opened the lid of a florist's box and folded back the crisp green tissues, drawing out the gardenia whose musky sweetness exploded into the room. She brushed her dark hair smooth and flat, coiling it all to the side at her right ear, and sticking pins through the chignon. Above her bare left ear she pinned the gardenia, leaning close to the mirror now, intent on not browning the creamy petals with the touch of her fingernails. She was humming again. "Now what's this I hear about you hobnobbing with the Chancellors, with that grande dame Eleanore of Aquiline? And their chauffeur brought you home—just too chic!—in a horse and cart?"

"Don't allow cars at The Point."

"Oh, so now it's the Point! You know, I used to think the only way you could joint the Point was to be born a Chancellor, a Pinchot, or a Scottish deerhound. But there is another way. If you play your cards right you could end up as Mrs. Chancellor. Now that would be something, wouldn't it?"

"What would it be?" Kezia felt something turn in her stomach, like a chrysallis trying to open its wings.

Willi talked on, into the mirror. "Chancellors were pulling on riding boots while Beals were still pushing plows. Too bad you're not my daughter. I could beat your little plowshares into boots." She turned around now, and under the intensity of her gaze Kezia looked down. "You're a very lively little girl. No wonder the Chancellors like you. So tell your old aunt, just how often do you get off this benighted place?"

"Been nine times, one for every year how old I am. Gran'sir doesn't know. I snuck over on the mailboat."

"We'll start on your grammar. Sneaked, not snuck." Willi's hand gripped Kezia's arm, her fingers sudden and pointed and avaricious. "Kezia, is Gran'sir ever cruel to you? Has he ever mistreated you?"

Kezia was shocked. She shook her head.

"Well, he made life a perfect hell for your father and me. The ugly old coot. I ran away as soon as I could. We were all out gathering flowers—it was going to be an 'island wedding,' you see. The groom was Beck Vannah. I went up over the hill, arms full of flowers, and I just kept traveling on."

"Who was the bride?"

"The bride was me."

Kezia stared at her face, its emotion so like her father's, so distant from her mother's reserve.

"Kezia, you should think about growing up and getting off island before too long. If you stay, you'll get old and fat and stupid before your time. You'll never find out about the world, and after a while you won't care anymore, just like Johnny. I grew up here just like you and I know. It was like being asleep all the time. When I left I woke up for the first time."

"Like Sleeping Beauty?"

Her aunt laughed and her face dipped near: small hazel eyes shadowed blue, skin whitened with powder, lipstick red. "No, like Wilhelmina Beal."

Kezia looked down at the three matching suitcases on the floor. A luggage tag read: "Wilhelmina Beale."

"Look. Beal's spelled wrong."

"In New York wrong is right, niece. That's what's so marvelous there. Anything you're not allowed to do on here you can do there."

Kezia was thinking of Medon and the rented second floor of the house there. They were moving next week, Mother starting at the sardine cannery too. Medon was all cars, noise, walls of brick. Her father used to say it: "In Medon, a man's just another brick in the wall."

It was then the thought came: Aunt Willi had run away. She knew all about it, where to go. There, where the man who killed Johnny had run. If she stayed on Aguahega all her life she would never find him. She had to move away.

"Aunt Willi?"

"Yes?"

"Could I go back with you?"

"To see me off?"

"Live with you. New York."

A look of flattered pleasure was almost instantly there, followed by a frown. "I don't like children. I still don't. But I do like you."

"Could I?"

"Your mother would never agree to it. Splitting up the family that way."

"We're already split up."

"Your mother told me she thought a party would help, since you'd be moving to Medon, a party for your friends. She said she had a treasure hunt, hid a roll of dimes and the kids're running all over the house. And all of a sudden the little Smallidge kid says, 'Hey, where's Keezie?' And you're nowhere to be seen."

Kezia looked down.

"So somebody said, 'Let's make Keezie It, hunt for her.' And finally they found you. On the floor of the outhouse curled up behind the door in a little ball."

"I don't like it here anymore."

"Of course, perhaps just for the school year, in New York. Then in the summers you could come home again. That would really set Father on his ear."

"Could I?"

"What about Victorine?"

"She *wants* to move to Medon. There's more boys there."

Willi laughed.

"Then you'll ask Mother?"

"My, you want things so terribly, don't you? Don't you want to grow up to be a lobsterman's wife?"

Kezia stood absolutely still, afraid to breathe. The scales were going back and forth, just as they did at weigh-in down at the lobster pound.

Willi finished dressing: black leotards and ballet flats, a Guatemalan skirt hand-loomed in charcoal gray. Kezia was disappointed. She wasn't going to wear any of the rainbow of colors that spilled from the open suitcases.

"We're going to be late for the gas of the year, this Park dedication thing."

"So you'll ask Mother?"

"Yes, Kezia. I will ask."

"New York—is it far from Haley's Landing?"

"A little way."

Kezia squirmed on the unyielding wood of the folding chair, staring up at the Governor, the most famous person she had ever seen. Beyond the red, white, and blue bunting-draped platform the southern cliffs fell 1,000 feet to Grumpy Shoals and the expanse of sea below. She tried to bite back the grin that kept grabbing her face. She knew what mischief Gran'sir was brewing, though no one else did. She watched the Governor's shoes as they clicked across to the microphone. She didn't dare raise her eyes: she was afraid she would laugh out loud.

"Ladies and gentlemen—" The breeze swept back the Governor's white hair. "Mr. Justice Howells, Senator Anson, Representative Marshall, State Senator Crowninshield, Mr. Fairfield Chancellor, distinguished guests. We are met here on glorious Aguahega Island for a momentous occasion. Here today we dedicate our own, our long-fought-for Norumbega National Park! It's not the biggest—it's the best!"

The applause came from the left side of the aisle of wooden chairs. Just as in church, the Seal Point contingent sat apart, rows of whites and pastels. Across from them sat the few year-rounders who hadn't boycotted the dedication, their hands staying stubbornly in their laps.

Kezia felt uncomfortably out of place. Aunt Willi had seated them deliberately here, on the Seal Point side. She could see Chance and his family just two rows in the front.

Should she applaud? Everyone around her was. Kezia's fingers knotted together in her lap, strangling each other like vines. But still the Governor's voice pried through.

"As someone once put it, who also labored under the scurrilous badge of politician as he gazed over Gettysburg Cemetery: it is not for us to dedicate this great park. No, rather it is for us here to be dedicated to its preservation, for now and all time."

Kezia sneaked a look behind her, tense with anticipation. She could see Gran'sir's panel truck slowly backing toward the line of parked cars. She squirmed on the unforgiving seat.

"But why, some of you may ask, name our park with these strange syllables: Norumbega? What means this: Norumbega? Along our Maine coast many a sailor in the swirl of fog just like today has glimpsed it, the crenellated castles of a fabled city, and he gives voice to what he has seen: 'Norumbega!' It is a lost city whose citizenry wear gold armor, and their houses are built with gold, silver, and crystal. Verrazzano first spied it, and put it on his map just north of here."

Kezia glanced back at the truck again. Gran'sir was clambering with difficulty down from the truck's front seat, Grandm'am emerging from the driver's side. She stood behind by the back of the truck, watching as he made his halting way alone, toward the crowd.

"Fabulous creatures were seen in Norumbega. A tusked beast as large as a horse chased men up trees. And another beast was bigger than an ox with ears floppy as a bloodhound. And I ask you, was this not our very own beloved Maine moose?"

Laughter rippled through the knot of year-rounders.

"What in blue devil you folks laughing at?"

Kezia turned around with the others to stare.

"That Aroostook farmer up there," Gran'sir was bellowing, "wouldn't tell you if he spied your hat on fire. Just stand and watch your eyes melt!"

"Oh my god," Aunt Willi said.

Kezia wanted desperately to feel proud. But at first there was nothing but shame. Gran'sir looked so small and bent standing there. His gray hat sported a jaunty feather but the felt was stained. His hands and face were ginger spotted, his gray socks had a hole and runs. Even his fly was at half mast.

The Governor's voice swelled louder, drowning Gran'sir out. "For a hundred years every explorer sought Norumbega. Finally came one Samuel de Champlain. But at the site of the lost city he found only this: a Norman's humble grave with its weatherbeaten cross. There was, he said, no Norumbega after all."

The Governor stretched his arms wide. "My dear friends, where Champlain failed, we have not. We have found lost Norumbega—in our own back yard!"

Whistles, stomps, cheers. Just when the noise began to die back down, Kezia heard Gran'sir's familiar gravelly voice. "Not *your* back yard, it ain't."

This time there was a chorus of "Shhhhh." A few children laughed. "I have never been so embarrassed," Aunt Willi hissed.

Kezia tried to swallow. It was almost time....

The Governor faltered, a line of red flushing up above his stiff white collar. "Now, then, this handsome bronze plaque you see to your left gives witness to one who needs no introduction: a devoted humanitarian, an apostle of nature, who for the past more than half a century has worked without surcease, giving selflessly of his time and money to make the marvels of Aguahega available to all. Let me present the father of Norumbega National Park: Fairfield Cordell Chancellor."

Amid the applause Kezia stared at the now familiar tall figure on the podium. His eyes peered out over the crowd, distant as ever.

"Sheepherders. Sheepherders!" Gran'sir was shaking his fist in the air. "Think to pull the wool over our eyes? Chancellor sold us out, lied to us, goffled up all our land when we didn't know what he was fixing to do."

"Did you *ever*?" someone said into the air.

A ranger in a uniform and another man in a neat dark suit were suddenly there on Gran'sir's either side. He swatted at them: "Lay off me now."

"Wait." The voice of Fairfield Chancellor boomed through the microphone. "Tarry a moment there, let that man be. I bear him no rancor. Let us listen to what our neighbor here has to say. Just who are you, sir?"

"Gooden Beal. My people homed here since Canada was called the English Dominion, and was no such thing yet as the States. We was here when Maine was just a parcel of Massachusetts. My family came to America to be free. We got rights, same as anybody else. The whole island, by rights it belongs to me."

Fairfield Chancellor stood straighter. "That is all quite interesting, to be sure, friend Beal. But—"

"Got a copy of the deed right here, the first deed, just lief me read." The paper rattled in his hands.

> " 'Consigned to Amariah Beal...a parcel of land commonly called by ye name of Aguahega, lying and being a Island in ye Sea, bounded with Duck Isld on ye West, Burnt Isld and Great Egg Isld to ye East, Cape Andrews on ye north.
>
> By the Hand of Joseph Quaduaquid, Sagamore.' "

"Thank you, friend Beal. It's all quite interesting but we haven't now the time to—"

"You lied to us! Sent your agent, calling himself Altoona Land Company, him in spats and checkered pants. Said he spoke for a logging firm. 'Mr. Beal, sir' he said to my father. 'May I call you Perley, sir? Your neighbor Haskins sold to us already and now he's bought a fine house for the wife over in Wardwell and what he had was just a alder bog. Next week may be too late,' he was saying. 'Train's leaving the station, Perley, sir.' "

"Now hold on there!"

"You lied to us, all you basters up to the Point. Stole all the land."

"My dear friend Beal. Wasn't it a fact that back then most of your esteemed neighbors were ready, nay, eager to sell to a timbering corporation?"

Gooden Beal stood silent.

The voice boomed out again, so much louder through the public address system than her grandfather's piping voice. "Isn't it a fact that all this verdure of trees we are blessed to see around us would have been cut down had not Altoona Land Company offered two dollars an acre, and the timber company a dollar fifty? Isn't it a fact that you yourself took advantage of this financial remuneration and sold a hundred acres yourself?"

Just when Kezia was ready to burst with pride for him, she saw Gran'sir's expression falter. A look of confusion whitened his face. All around Kezia the Seal Point people were sniffing as if they could smell the old man's smell on him: sweat and pee stain, staring as if he were a strange marine fossil washed up from the sea. Answer him, Kezia thought, *answer him.*

"Oh my god," Aunt Willi said.

"Mr. Beal, my neighbor and colleague, this land was not stolen, no, but acquired. Yes, and now it has been *given* as a gift, a free and clear gift to all the American people, and that includes you. From the strife of cities men and women will come here to repair themselves, here at the fount of all that is fair. It will flower as God intended, unspoiled by petty greed."

"You fooled us!" Gran'sir's voice was high and tight, unmagnified and small. "Don't that mean nothing? Like we was garbage or nothing or worse!"

Kezia felt tears sting her eyes. He had lost the argument. In the silver flow of Fairfield Chancellor's words, Kezia realized that somehow Gran'sir had drowned. She felt herself on her feet, standing up the way she wasn't supposed to; and yelling, instead of Gran'sir, the code words she'd been waiting all afternoon to hear. *"B-a-a-a-a. B-a-a-a-a. Pull the wool over our eyes."*

The panel truck's rear doors burst open and sheep boiled down the ramp, Grandm'am whacking with a stick behind them. She drove them straight on toward the prim rows of chairs. Seal Point dowagers screamed, children erupted into the aisle as chairs knocked over under flailing hooves. In the mass confusion people and sheep fought for space. The sheep bleated in terror, milling through the chairs.

Abruptly Kezia felt herself running after the feet of Gran'sir which were not touching ground but treading water somewhere up in the air. The park ranger and the dark-suited man were carrying him.

But it was the ranger she focused on: arrogant authority in his stiff new dark green uniform with its brass badge, the Smokey Bear plate of a hat. The brown bulge of a scuffed leather holster held his gun. With all her outrage Kezia grabbed his arm.

Muscle leaped beneath her fingers, unforgiving as rock. She felt, not saw, his other hand flash back for the gun. The gray brim of the Stetson tilted down at her. His head turned on a thick powerful neck and broad shoulders. The face was aggressive, leading with its Roman nose, curving back like a strung bow at forehead and chin. Kezia stared at his eyes. They had no eyelashes. She saw the dark flecks in the pale green flash wider, darker until his gaze stabbed at her stony and black.

Then his eyes registered her: a harmless girl. The dark entity behind his gaze, the flash of violence drew away. He blinked and his eyes went green again.

"Let my Gran'sir go!"

Gran'sir stumbled free, rubbing his thin arms where their force had gripped him.

The ranger was laughing down at Kezia. "What have we here? The junior black sheep of the family?"

Gooden Beal nodded. "Whole family's meaner'n turkey-turd beer."

The ranger's face went gentle. "You all right, sir? Didn't mean to rough you up any there."

"Why don't you arrest them?" Gran'sir said. "Those basters high and mighty on that fool box up there."

Again the gentleness was in the ranger's voice. "Look sir. Why don't you come along and pay a visit to my trailer. It's not far. I'll spring for a Pabst and you can tell me all about it."

Kezia had never seen skin the color of the ranger's. It was the color of a pelt, not skin: palomino gold or the gold of a puppy's coat, deep and fresh, animal gold in which his creaseless lids sank half-lowered, lazy, the pale green of his eyes winking light from beneath. He was young, only eighteen. His namepin read Reo Macrae.

Beyond, near the truck Grandm'am was sitting cross-legged, as undisturbed as a china figurine. Grandm'am looked up at Kezia and smiled. "You are full of the vinegar, both of you. I always like the vinegar with my onions."

Kezia saw Chance in a white shirt, khaki shorts. He was walking their way.

Gran'sir's voice was strong. "Years ago I told everyone. No one would listen! The Chancellors *are* the park. The park is them."

Chance's face went red. He turned away, back toward the whites and pastels.

"Kezia, listen smart to me. You're never to see that rich pup again!"

CHAPTER 15

Moving Day was here.

The scene in front of Kezia bit deep with pain. She sat cradled in the Witness Tree's tire swing, its rubber still warm from the heat of the sun. She pushed off with one foot and then tucked her legs up in the black circle, swinging in a long low arc over the ground, sweeping out toward the slanting rays of the lowering sun.

The ladder still leaned up against the shingled siding, ready in case of chimney fire. White still shone in the kitchen window, the sheet protecting the table's butter and sugar. Johnny-Ride-The-Sky still rode the rooftop—the jockey weathervane of ancient wood and iron, not splendid in red like the jockey at Seal Point. Johnny pointed south out to sea where her father had gone.

But in the doorway of Perley's House two men struggled to remove Daddy's tall cherry secretary with all the cubbyholes behind the fold-down lid, with the scrolled pigeonhole brackets hiding six secret drawers. In one he had kept the whalebone stamp that had gone around the world on Asa Beal's whaling ship. It was carved from white bone with a little knob on top to hold it with, and a raised whale's flukes like Toothaker Harbor on the bottom. The firm architecture of Daddy's knees supported her as she stamped it down on his blue ink pad, pounding its message all over the paper: "Lost Whale, Lost."

The Chancellors had bought the secretary, but Mother saved her the whalebone stamp, found while cleaning out all the papers and bills. No insurance papers; many bills. But the Chancellors had bought a lot of things—a copper warming pan, six ladderback chairs, the mahogany grandfather clock with the broken fretwork, a checkerboard candle stand, three Victorian spool beds and every hooked rug except the one in the outhouse.

The DiBlasi boys' shouts sounded now from inside the house where they were exploring—running up and down, up and down the stairs. Summer people had bought Perley's House. Even though the Chancellors offered twice as much, still Gran'sir had refused. Even though the DiBlasis' offer was far less than he'd been counting on, far less than it should have been worth...

Toothaker was a depressed market, the real estate man kept saying. It was the park. Buyers were saying the park was an octopus, one arm already everywhere else. What was to stop it from grabbing Toothaker as well?

But he was willing to take the uncertain future as it came, Professor DiBlasi said: a short fat spider of a man with a wife and two spiderlike sons. They would be glad to have Gooden and Clara stay all winter, count it lucky, even provide a little caretaker's wage.

The screech from the front door made Kezia look up. The workmen pulled the Christian door off its hinges, were carrying the corpse out to their truck. The crucifix of panels moved sideways, the hand-forged iron latches thrusting above. What did the Chancellors want with their door, anyway?

You couldn't have a home without a door. All the devils would get in.

Kezia stared at the empty socket of Perley's House.

"Eight-Twenty isn't home," Chance had said.

"Eight-Twenty?"

"Eight-Twenty Fifth Avenue. Just where we live in the winter. Maybe you can visit. We could go ice skating in Central Park, Red."

"A pond like Alewife? In New York?"

"I used to think it was one word—summersend. Hated to hear that one. Trunks being packed. Mothballs. White furniture throws. I thought there was just a summer Aguahega then. Vanished on the horizon when we'd leave, swallowed up out on the edge. Like those old maps where they'd letter in the unknown spaces: 'Here there be dragons.' "

And just as Chance had promised there it was where he pointed, the dark mouth of the cave Kezia had never noticed in the sheer diorite rise of the cliffs. The lip of rock swallowed them into dim gray cold. Seaweed dripped down the walls, the water beneath whispering with the suck and push of tide. And then the oars propelled them into the hidden pool and the light that flickered green all around. Kezia's eyes looked at Chance, reflecting green.

"It's crumb-of-bread sponge gives it this color—" The air was full of screech and wings. They ducked and flattened themselves as hundreds of cliff swallows battled to escape. Chance pointed up at the adobe nests on the upper ledges, round mud balls hardened one on top of another like Medon, like bricks in a wall. "Tide fills all the way to the top of the entrance. The birds have to wait in an air pocket up here until low tide. They're trapped, but protected too." He smiled at her, teeth not white but green. He was beautiful with green teeth.

She could visit him in New York.

Kezia looked up at the Witness Tree above her. She had climbed it so long ago. It was terrifying then. Maybe going to New York would be like that, climbing the tallest tree in the world, finding out you could do it after all.

Her fingers reached for the bait bag in her lap, the one she'd been knitting ever since her father died. She hadn't found his killer; she couldn't seem to tie off its end. She ripped the loose end, unraveled it again—a snowflake in reverse. Now it was just a heap of patternless white.

She put one leg out of the tire. She was ready to go.

With her bare dirt-stained foot she pushed off.

The voices of people were coming up from the waterfront: Gran'sir and Grandm'am, Beck and Nate Vannah, even Aunt Willi, and...

"This right here's the fella, Loara," Gran'sir called. "One's been leaving the lobsters in our car."

Kezia ran to see. Every other night—they hadn't been able to catch him at it—someone had been giving them part of his catch, in the 10 by 15 slatted wood box in the water where lobsters were stored until sold. She was disappointed: he was ordinary, short. His freckles converged, collided into torn islands, continents of brown.

"Milo Gilley," he said, one hand removing his cap. He looked at Kezia Beal and unwillingly saw himself, the crooked-tooth boy living with his family in the abandoned wooden potato house built into the side of a hill. School was closed, it was mid-September and time for "pickin'." The digger man had torn free the rows of potatoes, his own small hands grimed black shaking the potatoes from the tops, watching the earthworms clench and unclench across his toes, like the uneasy feeling in the pit of his stomach when the farmer's bus brought him home again.

His flat pale blue eyes glittered like glass at the bottom of a stream.

"Well," Loara Beal said. "Can't but up and thank you. Why'd you go and give us your lobsters like that?"

Kezia saw Gilley looking at her and his face went white behind the freckles. She saw a kind of urgency behind his eyes. There was a message there but what kind of message, what did it mean? He looked like a dried crabapple—small red, puckered at eyes and mouth, a worm at the core.

"M'am, we're not all like that one that— Look, was trouble before, sure, but nothing like that. Nothing justifies killing a man, now do it? If we ever find out who, well, m'am, you can bet he won't come to no easy end. Maybe a part-timer, drifter, probably. Maybe a thousand miles gone by now."

"You mean," Gran'sir said,"you were in on the Cut War?"

"It's over. Everyone's gear's hauled and gone. The park's the thing now. I'm going to get me a job with the park."

Gran'sir stood stiffly. "Have not a thing to thank you for."

"Father," Willi said. "Is your brain so reptilian small you can't understand what this gentleman is trying to do? Can't you see an olive branch?"

"He's from the main. Not one of us."

Loara Beal stepped forward, extending her hand. "I am thankful, Mr. Gilley. Thanks to you for coming here and telling us."

"You can call me Milo, m'am."

In Victorine's arms Deenie fussed, small red fists striking the air. Taped to the crown of her bald head was a festive pink bow. Expertly Victorine inserted the tip of her little finger into Deenie's rosebud mouth. The mouth stopped hollering and began to suck. "Want to hold her, Keezie?"

"I hate babies. They're all girls."

Victorine recrossed the blanket, chaining the fists down inside. "Well, I want lots of babies. All girls."

"Nobody wants a girl."

"Kezia's right," Aunt Willi said.

"Wilhelmina."

Gilley turned to stare at Grandm'am, at her accent, flying wedges of sound, long thin strings of vowels.

Beck Vannah put his hand on Loara's arm. She looked unusually pretty in her new yellow polka dot dress. Kezia saw the look he turned on her mother, the kind Vangie gave Nate Vannah, the kind grownups gave when they were sweet.

"Beck and I have something to tell you all," Loara said. "We have—Beck and I have, well, we've decided to marry. Yes, I know it's a surprise." Her face turned to Beck, bright and animated, worried and flushed. It had never looked that way around Johnny Beal.

"So," Beck said. "Nobody's moving to Medon after all. We'll keep on living here, right here. In my house."

Kezia heard her own voice. "I'm going to New York."

"I'll be back."

Nate Vannah, 13 years old, was standing with the others on the village dock. "No, you won't. Dad said you probably won't."

"Liar! He's a liar."

Aunt Willi's hand was on her shoulder. The long pointed fingernails owned her now.

It was low tide. Kezia climbed down to the little dory, the leather mail bag at her feet. The mailboat captain was a stranger: he didn't ask who she was and Aunt Willi didn't volunteer. He rowed them away from the long-legged dock whose barnacle-white pilings rose fifteen feet above the water, thin as stilts.

The fog mulls of summer were gone. The day was blue and gold and bright with a light that filled sky and sea, glinting through air clear as glass. The suicide days, some called them. September brought the days of the Northwest wind, for some bringing only despair. It was too generous, too good, only serving to remind that soon the dark close of island winter would press down.

The mailboat was pulling away. The village houses were shrinking, white and gray. Voices seemed to crowd out at her from shore: her father's, her mother's, Gran'sir and Grandm'am, her own voice, high with joy. There was the village: a grocery, post office, schoolhouse, church, the gray of granite stretching behind them on the ground. To the south the frowning bare walls of the old quarry gaped between the trees.

Aunt Willi's finger tapped on Kezia's shoulder like a schoolmarm with a lesson. Now it was pointing north up the Seal Point cliffs where a house stood, its many panes of glass staring over a columned piazza out to sea. No lights shone in the waning afternoon: Tenhaven was closed for the season.

"I always did hanker to see what that hovel looked like inside." Aunt Willi's eyes looked into hers.

She was "going to America."

"Isn't that what you people call it?" Chance had said. "Going to the mainland?"

"No."

"I read it somewhere."

The mailboat thudded oblivious through the waves.

Kezia felt a heaviness in her chest. Whenever she came down with a cough and congestion Grandm'am filled the jar with violets, covered them with water where they brewed on the windowsill. She sweetened it with two cups of sugar, dosing Kezia every hour with violet liquid on the big tarnished spoon.

Kezia pulled her jacket tighter.

It seemed she could taste violets now, in the prick of salt wind on her tongue.

All the time I'm gone it'll be here, just the same. I can always come back.

Kezia raised her hand, and on the dock the tiny figures waved, all except Nate Vannah standing off by himself, arms at his side.

Wrong was right, in New York. She, Kezia, was wrong. But when she came back she would be right, she would belong at Tenhaven.

CHAPTER 16

1958 - Aguahega Island, Maine

It was here, Loara Beal Vannah thought, the morning she had been waiting for all through the dark winter, brief disappointing spring—the most important day of the year. She leaned far out of her second story window in the unpainted Vannah house at Toothaker Harbor. The smell of clamflats and rockweed rushed sharp to the bottom of her lungs. There were the two white lobsterboats in the harbor where they belonged, bobbing their tethered heads like Clara's sheep. Already the fog was drifting away and oysterlight paled the sky, the sheen that came before dawn. It was June 1st, the day the boats were finally launched. And something for herself, too.

A shrill rising whistle pierced the chill air. The fish hawk hunted 100 feet above the harbor, white belly flashing. With the sound now of ripped canvas it dropped, at the last second its legs flinging forward, talons in front of its beak. The water sprang up to swallow it, a white circle closing over turbulence, ripples spreading out.

Loara held her breath, fingers numb on the windowsill half an inch deep in dew. She was 43, but still she believed. If she breathed, the hawk too would gasp for air but take in water and drown. If she blinked, he was blind. If scared, he too would freeze forever on "the edge of the bottom," fifty fathoms out where the floor of the sea fell away. It was her magic. It had always worked.

Her breath fought to burst from her lungs. She heard her heart and beyond it, all around her, the tricklings of moisture off leaf, branch, eaves. Once her father had caught a codfish at Scrag Rock. Attached to its back, talons so tightly locked Ridley Pritchard had had to cut them away, was the skeleton of a fish hawk.

Now Toothaker Harbor fractured upward in glassy sheets of spray. The great wings of the hawk climbed the hill of air, shaking free of the silver cords of droplets, a pollock tail-flipping in the black talons. Loara's lungs grabbed air.

From the floor below Beck Vannah's voice, pungent and clear, came hollering good-naturedly up at her. Loara sprinted through the bedroom door to the center hall stairs, her hand suddenly wet on the railing. The kitchen door stood open, the space beyond warm and inviting with light. Then she heard Beck's voice again.

"Don't think you'd better haul with me after all, honey. Your place's rightly at home."

The hall was dark and cold. Not go! Her heart thudded into her ears. All the sounds and smells and bustle braiding together into boats and bait and getting ready and going at last "outside"—everything that was the waterfront at dawn.

She walked into the kitchen. Warmth swept her flushed face—radiance from the huge black cookstove whose nickel-bright piewarmer swelled buxom as Clara Beal. For an instant the propane lantern's glare blinded her, scouring all shadows from white walls thick with old paint, gray moldings, low wood-pegged rafters that creaked like a ship during storms.

"Well, honey." She heard his hooting laugh and her heart took hope. "Finally up early now there's a chance you can go?" Beck scraped back the chief's chair, his old ladderback rocker by the stove, painted red from the ocher where once an Indian had been buried.

"You said June first," Loara said. "You promised, remember?"

"Come dogfish and summercators, first of June." His face leaned toward her, narrow, long chinned between parentheses of lines. She saw the hesitation printed there, stopped as a clock.

"Did you remember?" she insisted. "I'm your sternman. Going out with you."

"Why do you want to go anyway? Boat stinks like rotten fish and the paint's gone all funny and flaky."

But he hadn't said No, had he?

"Women rule the house," he said. "Men rule the sea."

Loara jerked open the icebox door, rummaged inside among the clink of bottles. She imagined the block of ice they had cut from Alewife Pond last winter, sleeping inside. Everything had been happy then. Now the ice was dead, dull, slushy, like the frozen pond after an afternoon's sun.

As she began to fix breakfast she looked desperately at Beck. But he stared pointedly at his outstretched boots rippled with soaked, then stove-dried wear. His right toe rubbed the left, trying to peel off a splotch of green mold.

"Know what Corley said last fall, when he seen you and me coming in to the dock? He said, Seeing a girl haul's like seeing a white blackbird."

The oven damper was open to a "summer" fire: hot and fast, but Loara's hands were still. She felt the linoleum chill her feet, cold with the cellar hole beneath. Her bare right toes crept for comfort on top of the left. Beck dared a look at her face. Loara was looking back at him, and now she screwed up her face and then dropped it, mouth open. It was like a visible sigh.

"Honey," Beck said. "You're always taking these fancies—for months on end nothing else, thinking of nothing else. And now this."

Loara's eyes had lost their usual faraway look. She tugged her short light brown hair behind her ears, where it frizzed errantly forward.

"You mean," Loara said, "you grow up, like the Bible says, put away foolish things, childish dreams. Better not to let your hopes build for something you can't have. Better not to be disappointed, ridiculed."

"You don't want to be like Willi Beal, do you? Frustrated as a cut cat and neither hay nor grass, if you know what I mean."

"At least Willi was smart enough to clear out, leave Aguahega, wasn't she?"

Beck bent over his thick white cup draped with the tags of eight used, clothesline-dried teabags. He poured the tea into his saucer, fingered his upper dentures loose and let the tea swish back over his gums, teeth floating free. "Tea nowadays got no taste at all to it."

The fullness in Loara's chest seemed to hang mistlike in front of her eyes. In it she seemed to see the whole summer vanish. Off-island was called "away," the sea beyond their harbor "outside," and the 50-fathom curve "the edge of the bottom." She wanted to go where the men and the boats went: away, outside, to the edge of the bottom. Nothing would stop her, nothing could. She looked at Beck with all her desperation in her face. Now he would say it: Yes, she could go.

Beck's lips quirked down, released, quirked again. It was a look that never failed to fill Loara with dread. But still she said, "Some person has to make the decisions around here, Beck. Assume the responsibility. It's not that I ever wanted to be that one."

"What in hell's that mean?"

"I have to watch out for us, worry about the money and how we are going to eat all winter. I am tired. Tired to death of it, Beck, of all of it. With me as sternman you can double your haul."

"You're always raising a ruction. Pink stink."

Loara was standing, heavy and inert, but her eyes were desperate to escape. She looked through the rear window that framed spruces and a decaying car.

"Then why can't you get a real job?" she said.

"I don't want to hear another God damn—"

Loara seemed to swell as tall as the cookstove. "Beck, keep your voice down. Let's go down cellar."

"Nothing to say I can't say it right out front of God's green everything!"

Loara pulled the cellar door open and started down the stairs. The pounded dirt walls exuded 137 years of stored crabapples around her head. She could see the shelves of her home-canned mackerel: tinkers and smaller tholepins, sweet and sour in spices, sugar, vinegar. Jars upon jars of her piccalilli, dilly beans, chili sauce, and preserves glittered behind neat white labels. Behind her the cellar door shut. There was the silence, and then their two voices, rising and falling, shaking the floor, the timbers, the roof, making the rock world flow like water under her feet. When they came back upstairs, Loara ran out through the back door.

Instead of flowers, shrubs, pebble-bordered paths, the Vannah house stood among its own history: piles of semicircular slatted-wood lobster pots damaged in past storms, old rubber tires, a baby carriage with a broken axle, a car engine bled dry into the tarry earth beneath.

The dim refuge of the "little house" closed safely around Loara. It had a small square window high up, a door sagging on its hinges, an old rag rug on the floor. She sat on the edge of the whitewashed seat hunched over, hugging her cold knees. She watched a small red spider traverse the moldy paper roll. Tears were blinding her eyes.

After a time she turned around, scrambling up to balance precariously on the rim of the wooden seat, reaching far up above her head into the dark cobwebby eaves. At first her fingers groped in cold empty air. Then she felt the reassuring crackle and pulled it down. With trembling fingers she opened the paper bag. Inside lay a little pile of knitted white twine, looped and lacy, intricately patterned as a snowflake. Her hands ached with the remembered labor over the six-inch wooden needle, struggling to tie the knot for the first loop.

"Hold your fingers crooked just so, Loara," old Mary Stella, the preacher's wife, had long ago taught her. "Or it'll slip away. No no no. Not *that* way. Now here, try it again." Loara kept on looping and knotting each loop, baggy and loose and over when it was supposed to be under and then unraveling, starting again until her fingers were senseless and swollen numb as wooden pegs, and frustration smarted in her eyes. It had taken two months to learn it and then do it until she had fifteen rows of knots across and ten rows of knots down and she had threaded the needle through the final loop that secured the bottom of the bag. Then she had burned off the remainder of the twine so it wouldn't ravel.

"Loara, burn the *twine*, not your finger," Mary Stella said. "Now don't you go and make that face again. 'Tain't Christian." And then Loara had turned the bag inside out and there it was, a beautiful bait bag, all done.

Now in its brown paper wrapping Loara held the gift she had made for Beck on this, the first day, the launching of his boat, the

April Day. She held it poised over the outhouse hole. She ripped off the top of the paper sack.

"Like a white blackbird." Tatters of paper one after the other fluttered down.

"Women rule the kitchen, men rule the sea." The brown sack vanished into the outhouse hole, but still she gripped the bait bag. She had decided, she thought. She would tell Beck, the sooner the better. He was right, everyone was right: hauling wasn't for her.

The bait bag dropped of its own accord white into the darkness below.

"Honey!" The careless exuberance that was Beck Vannah's voice was calling her from outside. "You going to run get dressed or what? Fall out or I'll leave you quicker'n scat."

Blinking, she emerged into the thin first light of dawn. Beck's huge head looked even larger under the sealskin cap that he had shot and tanned himself. "I'm going?" she said.

"Promised, didn't I?"

She could hear him and then she couldn't.

"What you wanted, isn't it?" Beck was impatient now.

For the first time Loara saw Beck through a stranger's eyes. She saw his smile, the joy that he always gave himself up to. Everything was right in his world.

"Get a move on, lazybones," he said. "Late as it is."

Still in her nightgown and robe, Loara went inside to dress.

But something had changed. She pulled on her green corduroy pants. One knee felt the chill of the air. Looking down she saw that one knee had unwoven itself in the dark like a bait bag in reverse.

CHAPTER 17

Kezia Beal, 15, put down her pen and leaned her forehead cold against the window, watching the fields pass between the smudges. The train clicked and swayed its way north to Aguahega. Nearer and nearer it carried her to Chance who would be waiting for her all in white, his narrow dark eyes watching her the way they used to, like a child peering between two boards.

Of course, Chance didn't exactly know that she was coming yet.

But for one like herself, she thought, who made things happen, who wasn't afraid to open Pandora's boxes wherever she found them—for her it was just a matter of time.

She picked up her pen again, gnawed the end, then scratched its scented lavender ink in great looping swirls across her diary page:

> "I will make Chance fall in love with me.
> And because I want him I shall have him,
> and that is my power, I will be wild and
> ruthless and female and mysterious because
> I am a woman. Life demands me to be alive,
> to feel, to be female and a woman, to sense

> and to enjoy, to be anything but small, to
> be glorious, to be loved warmly, hotly,
> fiercely, and to know that what I feel is
> life and I have not missed nor bystepped
> because I was afraid."

She snapped the diary shut, blotting the ink. If only, she thought, I were pretty, too.

As pretty as Lady Flora in the photography book, described as "untarnishable, the loveliest young Englishwoman of her generation."

How safe, how absolutely powerful, invulnerable Lady Flora must feel.

Kezia's eyes caught sight of the chewed fingernails on her always red, too large hands. Her fingers curled tightly inward, her hands balling into fists. She wanted to be untarnishable too. Of course, she was stuck with a coarse common simpleton of a last name. But already she had picked out a new name: Wilde, Kezia Wilde. For Oscar Wilde, of course. She imagined Chance acknowledging the introduction, his lower lip brushing the back of her tiny white hand. "Ah, Kezia...Wilde. And *are* you my dear?" She would laugh, throwing back her long, ivory column of a neck (as Cholly Knickerbocker would report), while her lips bubbled with some shocking, bold reply. Behind her, murmurs: "Not just a beauty, but a wit!"

After all, she was from New York, where she could ceaselessly become someone else—whoever she wanted. New York was a place of infinite possibilities, of swarming exuberance, of freedom from Aguahega gossip, morality, little minds. She *had* become someone else, someone worthy of even a Chancellor's love, someone other than, "Hellion! Hellion-hearted girl!" as Aunt Willi was in the habit of shouting.

No one would dare call Lady Flora a hellion.

And it was good Aunt Willi was always working late at the advertising agency or out with men—she let Kezia run wild. Kezia was the local leader at Stanhope School, the one with all the good ideas: mixing chopped up flies in their mothers' oatmeal batter, stretching waxed paper under the school toilet seats, practicing total abstinence from soap and water to see whose gym socks would stand up all by themselves first.

Once she had turned thirteen she had grown more sophisticated: smoking, swearing, and shoplifting every trip to Saks Fifth Avenue, carrying out lingerie clutched precariously between her thighs.

"Do you wish your berth made up now, miss?"

It was the train porter in his splendid brass-buttoned uniform, only a little frayed around the cuffs.

She wished he had said "madam." She was certain she looked 21. "Why, yes. I thank you."

The train grumbled through the night while Kezia lay on her side in the top berth, staring out at the little trackside towns, the lonely houses blossoming and fading in seconds. It was hot behind the dusty curtain; she was wide awake. She struggled up in the darned sheets, the top of her head grazing the low ceiling. She was careful not to muss her traveling outfit hanging beside her, the only grownup outfit she owned. She pulled her cardboard suitcase across and from its depths, in which rolled two apples, a bottle of gin, and a stack of waxpaper-wrapped brownies, she drew out a battered Raggedy Ann doll.

She opened the gin, took a deep swallow, coughed, and felt her eyes water.

They kept on watering.

Kezia had never felt sorry for herself. She liked who she liked and hated all others. Certainly she hated Aunt Willi, but everyone hated their parents, didn't they? She had known for as long as she could remember that Aunt Willi didn't love her. Last Christmas Kezia had given her the pretty rayon nightdress. "I don't like sleeves," Aunt Willi said, grabbing up a pair of scissors. The metal jaws snatched, wadded, sawed off the fluttery butterfly sleeves.

In the train compartment Kezia hugged the doll. Inside its red and green dress the stitched heart bore the message: "I love you."

It was ridiculous, she thought, Lady Flora with a Raggedy Ann doll. Kezia felt the observer in her steal forward as it always did, slowly displacing the hot fierce hurting emotions, commenting on the scene in raucous, earthy tones.

Aguahega.

Had it waited for her, never changing, just the same?

She took another slug of gin.

Kezia stood on the open deck as the mailboat returned to Aguahega. High on the northern cliffs above her soared the steep-roofed gables, the broad chimneys of Tenhaven. The wind pressed like hands around her face. The widow's walk with its stone cupola rose above the firs like an old friend. Was Chance even now looking out a window at her?

"There's your folks now, waiting on you." The mailboat captain pointed toward the village up ahead.

Kezia stared at the crazy quilt of colors, seven people huddled on the dock in a tight close group. The colors misted, drizzled together into incomprehensible shapes.

She didn't belong with them; she belonged at Seal Point.

Kezia stared at the man her mother had married. "Beck Vannah is not my folks."

Slats nailed to two planks made a walkway up to the dock. It was low tide; the incline stood at 50 degrees. Kezia's high heels caught, she stumbled in the fur of dark green kelp that splotched the planks and everything else that touched the sea: doughnuts of kelp that were bumper tires mounted on the dock, reeking columns and vines of kelp that were pilings and warp. Aguahega was kelp glue, no getting away from it.

They were all there: Beck and Loara, Gran'sir and Grandm'am, Nate and Victorine and Deenie. No one embraced; they didn't do that anymore now that Johnny—the one to whom it came easily—was gone.

"Beck's got a little something for you, Kezia," Loara said. "Just to welcome you home. Well, now, go on, Beck. She's dying to see it."

"Not much, hon. Thought with this, see, you could show all your sophisticated New Yorky friends just what your real home looks like."

Kezia's fingers were nerveless, the package she held infinitely distant, as if seen from the wrong end of a telescope. She watched her fingers come together and tear the bright tinsel-and-purple paper. Inside, like a shag chick in corrugated packing lay a black camera.

"Isn't that nice?" Loara's hands were behind her back.

"Yes. Thanks, Mr. Vannah."

"Well, now. Why don't you just call me Dad?"

"I'm scared of her." Mouth open, Deenie Beal stared at Kezia with all the unabashed directness of six.

"It's just you're wearing black, is all," Victorine said. "Wish I had a suit like that."

"For the sake of heaven, Kezia," Grandm'am said, leaning close to inspect the camera. Her hair, still long and braided around her head, was now dyed chestnut. "Go on. We loaded it with the film for you. Take a photograph of us, of all the family together."

Kezia shielded her burning face behind the camera. Through the eyepiece the seven were small. Everyone was smiling except for Gran'sir. Kezia moved the frame until Beck Vannah stood outside. The shutter whirred.

Gran'sir was walking toward her, head bent forward almost at right angles now. His face had a thin questing look as if he were scenting the wind. He stared into his granddaughter's face. For a minute she thought he didn't recognize her. His voice stumbled on the words:

" 'The man in the wilderness asked me,
How many strawberries grow in the sea?' "

It was the nursery rhyme, their old familiar game. Kezia heard her voice, too high:

" 'I answered him as I thought good,
As many as red herrings grow in the wood.' "

He was still staring at her, on his face the question: did she still belong?

CHAPTER 18

Toothaker Harbor lay like a tarnished bowl of silver at the bend in the road. It smelled of gasoline. Beside the water the rusting split-pine clapboards of the tall, anemic Vannah house stood in yellow grass, an icebox and broken chairs on the porch. Within, Lady Flora observed the dinner tableau as if from a million miles away.

She had never belonged here.

On the wall hung a painting inspired by a giveaway insurance-company calendar cover: a stag pausing in mid-glen, one hoof raised. Two ducks, orange rampant, flew wings outstretched above.

She had done her own painting. She sat here now in camouflage, birthmark gone. Aunt Willi had bought her the Lydia O'Leary covermark, a thick pastelike substance you dug with a miniature spatula from the jar. Patted, not rubbed with the fourth finger of your hand, and then the setting powder, talc based, and then you layered base and powder again.

On Aguahega the mouse was magic, demonic. In New York it was common, labeled, safe. "Just a little port wine stain, dear," the doctor had said.

"But what is that?"

"A benign blood vessel tumor beneath the skin."

There were reasons for being disfigured, stewed in superstition thick as any Gran'sir had had. They were all about your pregnant mother's sin: while carrying you she ate too many Harvard beets, she drank too much wine, she angered your father and he beat her. Sins of gluttony, drunkenness, marital discord.

Worse than that was the "just world" theory. No innocent victims, they bring it on themselves. You're blemished because you deserve it. There was an experiment on the New York subways, Kezia had read it in the Sunday *Times*. Actors pretended to collapse, some made up to look as if they were victims of port wine stain (hereinafter referred to in the *Times* as "PWS"). Help was offered "significantly less" for those marked like Cain with stain.

In a just world she had been punished, and yet the unblemished people were just as bad.

"Just so," Kipling said.

Carrying a platter, Loara Vannah drew out the chair at the table's end. "Aguahega 'turkey,' " she announced, "is Beck's favorite thing."

The visit doesn't revolve around the visitor.

Beck sat hands in lap while Loara heaped his plate. "Tell Kezia what's been happening on here, Beck. I know she's dying to hear."

"Oh, the usual." He passed the platter down. "Cold to beat the band. End of October, George Smallidge, his boat exploded, burned like a flaming firecracker, I tell you, George with third degree burns. Was Thanksgiving then."

Lady Flora's fork shredded her "turkey": salt fish boiled in a cloth bag in a potato filled pot. She poured the gravy of hot pork scraps and grease over fish and potatoes, the way Kezia Beal had always done. But Lady Flora's throat dried up, refused to swallow.

"Not two days after," Beck continued, "but Charlie Boyce's running a crane off the dock at Haley's, and it fell plumb off, nearly took him too, totaled the crane but that Boyce, he's still cooking. Was Christmas then...."

Christmas, Lady Flora remembered. Christmas Eve, in New York. It was magic, stepping through the ornate glass doors of Luchows, the German restaurant where Lillian Russell had refused to marry

Diamond Jim Brady on bended knee. A horde of anxious humans thronged the anteroom, pressing against the velvet cord barrier strung between gold posts. Ahead, through the tall doorway, Kezia could see the dining room that sat one thousand, with imperious waiters gliding about balancing overloaded silver trays. "By the tree, please," Aunt Willi said, looking the maitre d' in the eye. Kezia watched his hand engulf the offering without a trace, his eye not wavering downward. Could he tell how much it was, just by the feel?

Willi, her lover Ben, Kezia, and her best friend Brantley were whisked to a table near the huge Christmas tree whose topmost star reached the ceiling. It was hung with gold and silver ornaments but the strings of lights were dark.

"Girls," Ben said, "(and I include you in that nomenclature, Wilhelmina), wait until you taste! In all the world Luchows is my second favorite thing."

"Then what's the first?" Brantley said.

Kezia stared at Ben with a certain dark fear, since Aunt Willi had informed her that having graduated from writing for true detective magazines he now wrote "erotic literature." She had had a secret crush on him ever since. He looked much younger even than he was, 38 to Aunt Willi's 46, skinny with wide shoulders, a pale face dominated by deepset dark eyes, old eyes in a young face, and teeth that snaggled over each other when he grinned. "What's the thing I like best?" he repeated.

"Ben."

"Hah!" Kezia said. "We know just what you're hinting at."

"Then if we're all so sophisticated—waiter! We want *Berliner Weisse!* Four glasses, *schnell!*"

"Ben please. They're too young."

"Too young?" Kezia grimaced. "I *may* vomit."

"I and Kezia," Brantley said, "are amazingly mature for our age."

"At your age, kiddoes, I was ordering martinis served in soup bowls. Oh, waiter, what a delicious cold soup. Why, fancy that, I've found an olive!"

"Ben."

"Waiter, four *Berliner Weisse!*" Ben repeated, eyes meeting Kezia's in a look of such conspiracy she felt a burst of love. "The madame and myself are unexpectedly thirsty tonight."

This brought more giggles which Kezia sought to stifle as the tall balding waiter, lips pursed as if on a sourball, poured a dollop of raspberry syrup into each large stemmed glass, following with golden German beer.

Kezia seized her cold glass and drank. It was bitter and sweet, icy and fiery, and bubbling endlessly up into the back of her nose, out her eyes tearing as she laughed. She took another drink, marveling at the fierce burn of its coldness deep down in her throat and farther, into the pit of her stomach and farther, tingling into her toes and fingertips. She drained her glass.

"Can I have another?"

"May I," Aunt Willi said.

"...and after Christmas," Beck Vannah continued, "it was cold as all cold, snowed and stuck plenty too. Then Bill Smallidge's out scalloping, told him he's a blamed fool in that kind of weather and don't you know, ram what controls the boom, what the drags hang on tore clean out the deck. Boom swung right out, turned whole damn boat over. But Bill got hauled out by Jimmy Todd...."

In New York Ben was looking at Kezia again. "So, Kezia, my pet. Willi tells me you're from an island in Maine. How romantic can you get? Or was it? Why'd you leave?"

"*Ben.* Brantley, that's the prettiest dress."

"This is an island too," Kezia said. "Manhattan, I mean. I love it here."

"So did I. Once. But it ain't dog eat dog anymore. It's piranha eat piranha."

Kezia felt Willi's fingers press her arm. She sank her fork into the appetizer, *Schwarzwalder Pfifferlinge*, Black Forest mushrooms in dill sauce. She had thought she hated mushrooms, but these touched her tongue with a pungent fairy wildness, the way she had always imagined those others would taste, the forbidden puffballs and neon-colored fungi in Aguahega's woods. "Eat Me," they whispered, "Eat Me and you'll grow tall."

"You see, Ben, Kezia would have been utterly wasted there. On Aguahega, I mean. Of course one can be contemplative there. But there's nothing to contemplate—an empty room."

"We didn't even get any newspapers, daily or Sunday," Kezia said.

Brantley's fork scraped her plate as she flattened the last of her mushrooms into broth. "The Latin for island is *insula* and that means insulation, we had it in class."

"And they had no bathrooms, can you imagine it? No electricity, no telephones."

Kezia stared down at her mushrooms. Actually they didn't look anything like puffballs. She wished, just as she had in Tenhaven's front hall, that these were the ones that when eaten made you small.

"Anyway"—Aunt Willi was smiling at her—"I tell Kezia, for God's sake don't grow up to be just a wife and mother. It's bad enough in the city. But in rural Maine!"

"Ralph Waldo Emerson called New York City 'a sucked orange,' " Brantley said as bowls of *Pfirsichkaltschale*, cold peach soup were placed before them. "We had it in class."

"More like the City of Brotherly Shove," Ben said.

"But if Kezia had stayed on Aguahega, she would just have ended up a lobsterman's wife. Am I wrong, Kezia?"

Kezia carefully laid her spoon in her bowl.

"And now she's at Stanhope getting all A's, and chosen to give a sermon on Youth Day at the school assembly. I think, just between us, we're going to hear from Kezia someday."

Kezia felt hot pride move up her body.

"Sermon?" Ben said. "And soda water? What was the sermon called?"

Kezia cleared her throat. " 'Man, the Future, and Optimism: Does Ultra-Optimism Hamper the Realism with Which It Is Necessary to Regard the Future.' "

"I see."

They were starting on the third bottle of wine when the main course arrived—roast goose with *apfel* dressing and saddle of venison with chestnut puree. And suddenly the room was plunged into darkness, the sob of the Victor Herbert strings was silenced, and Kezia peered about in alarm.

"Ahhhhhhhh." The air swelled with a thousand voices as in their midst the Christmas tree sprang shimmering to life, glowing like a dragon's treasure—gold, silver, emerald, sapphire, ruby. And now a starry diamond blazed on the topmost spire. "Ohhhhhhhhhhhhh."

"...And then was Town Meeting," Beck Vannah continued, "everyone up in arms over this new park road and all, after which we had us a Robin Storm. That don't sound any too exciting, I wager, after all the flashy goings on down to New York."

She was back on Aguahega, inescapable now. Under the table Kezia's stockinged feet kicked out of her high heels, right toes creeping onto the left. "Ralph Waldo Emerson called New York 'a sucked orange.' We had it in class."

Deenie dipped her chin in her glass of milk and then raised it, grinning.

Kezia studied her napkin as if cramming for an exam.

"Beck, what's the matter now—fish isn't right?" Loara's face dipped near.

"Well, sure. Well, cooled off a bit. Could be a tad hotter."

"Oh, oh I'm sorry. Just put the heat on under it for you." Without asking if anyone else's were cold Loara scraped Beck's plate back into the pot.

Grandm'am was looking at Kezia again.

Their faces were different, not like New York.

Here where the world was wet, the air saturated with dew, fog, dew again in endless cycle, women's faces were dry. Tinder dry as the toadstools in Gran'sir's pocket, ever ready to crumble into powder and ignite the stove. Dry hair, dry skin, dry-as-dust, ready to blow away at a breath of air, prematurely aged, lines around mouths bracketing the sorrow.

Deenie covered her cheeks with her fingers, yanked the skin down, exposing red-rimmed brown irises looking around.

Nate was looking at Kezia again. She snatched a glance. His hesitant grin broke the sunburnt varnish of his rough grainy skin. His powerful chest stretched a white t-shirt with hacked off sleeves. She watched him interlace his broad fingers—raspy, sandpaper sound—behind his lank brown hair and lean back into the cradle of his hands, rocking on his chair. From his underarms dark threads woven in the center with dampness tufted bold as pubic hair.

At 19 he was a man earning his living. He had bought the *Loara B.*, now renamed *Loara V.*, combining lobstering with a toolbox-for-hire. Parts of a car engine were spread on the livingroom floor. His hands were grimed with oil.

Kezia looked down into congealing grease on her plate. Last Christmas he'd sent flowers to her in New York and she opened the green tissue-lined box, fingers trembling as she unwrapped her first flowers. Inside, nestling together in floral nightmare were five roses, red, and five carnations dyed St. Patrick's Day green. Aunt Willi laughed. But Lady Flora made not a sound.

Now, on Aguahega, Nate tipped his chair forward again, hands coming down on either side of his plate. "Launched our boats last week, Keezie. But you'll not be believing it—Bill Smallidge's thrown in the towel. Sold to the park and he's moving to the main."

"Oh Nate. Why? Money's that bad?"

"Well, we're pulling in a red-hot twenty-five hundred bucks a year now, and that's just gross. Lucky to find one keeper a pot, you know."

"But you'd never leave Aguahega, would you, Nate?"

"You did."

Water dripped from the hand pump into the slate sink.

"Keezie," Victorine said. "You haven't sprung a word about my ring yet and you have to have noticed, right?" She brought her left hand up and kissed the ring. It was red glass, a class ring secured around her finger in clouds of puffy blue angora.

" 'A woman without a man,' " Lady Flora said, " 'is like a garden without a fence.' " She grinned wickedly. "We had it in class."

Victorine had grown unaccountably pretty, that is, if you liked dishwater blondes. She sat with elbows bent inward at the waist, hands on knees, as if gathering her body in for protection. Her hair ruffled out, fanlike, and her blue gaze was as clear and cool-eyed as her mother's. She still had that look of crisp self-containment, the faint air of aloofness that had been so maddening when she was so tall and so twelve and Kezia, nine. Now Victorine was eighteen.

"It's a tragedy of true love already." Nate sawed away at an imaginary violin.

"Just hush up, Nate." Unperturbed, Victorine petted the angora. "But it's true, Keezie. Hank and I are in love—"

"Looooove," Deenie crooned.

"He gave me my ring twenty-eight and a half days ago, and he's so cute, tall, in sports, and we have a lot of fun together. But we almost lost each other because there was this other guy, Lee, and he started talking to me a lot and so like a silly kid I left Hank, who I knew liked me, for Lee, who I thought liked me. Lee came over a lot and all but somehow we never actually went out. I thought the grass was greener over the fence but it was brown and the side I was on was the greenest grass I ever saw. Because then Hank asked me to the Haley's Landing prom."

"What's it called?" Lady Flora said. "April in Kabul? Rhapsody in Puce?"

"Anyway, Hank's folks are moving to Portland in September, but we've pledged to be true to each other. And you know the best thing of all?"

Kezia forced her gaze up to her sister's eyes. They looked heavenward, a saint hung in a museum.

"The best thing is it will never end."

"Love begins with a prince kissing an angel. It ends with a baldheaded man looking across the table at a fat woman."

"Kezia." Grandm'am's z's were liquid, so full you were afraid spit would land on your face.

"Can I be 'scused?" Deenie said. Forbidden, she lowered herself to nose-level with the tablecloth.

"Mom says you write," Nate said, looking at Kezia.

It took her a full beat to realize he meant Loara Vannah.

"How can you find time for it, you New York a-cris-to-rat, what with all the boys buzzing around?"

Kezia examined the frayed darn on the tablecloth. Its threads wove up down, in out, intricate as a bait bag. *Boys.* Of course he didn't mean it; it was just a polite thing to say. She looked sensible, Aunt Willi said, had a short straight body interrupted by the embarrassment of breasts. And this year she had lost the Stanhope School poetry contest to Sylvie, who *was* pretty, which had meant she wasn't to be taken seriously, that she was writing for vanity or show or some such reason. That she couldn't win.

Kezia watched her after the awards ceremony, alone as she always was. Kezia knew what lay behind Sylvie's opaque eyes, what she clutched so desperately around her. "Listen!" Lady Flora screamed. "You think it doesn't matter now that you're alone, because you have something. And you think, 'what a victory!' that no one will touch you still. But now it's awe and fear that keeps boys away. But it isn't. They just don't care—there's your victory! They don't care what you won."

But Kezia hadn't screamed or moved or made any sound at all. The year before, she too had clutched the fragile warmth, walking trembling thin-kneed up to the platform to receive her certificate and the inscribed fountain pen and come back down alone, but warmer. And she thought there was envy, and awe, and respect, and a hesitant boy-shy eagerness to know what she might be like.

But Stanhope's boys only came to stare at her, furrowed back somewhere in her decorated poetry mazes, looking back at them with desperate eyes.

Kezia looked across the tablecloth at Nate Vannah. "I think love is dumb, and disgusting. And I'm never, never going to fall in love!"

The grownups' laughter seemed to soar up around the soot-blackened ceiling, and then shatter down around her ears.

A long whistle wailed from somewhere to the west.

Kezia waited, but no one said anything.

Two more whistles. Then an explosion rocked the air, rumble of vibration under the linoleum, turning the air hard as stone around Kezia's face.

Still no one reacted.

Three long whistles blasted now.

"What in God's name is that?"

"It is himself, the Earl of Hell!" Gran'sir sucked in a raw onion slice large around as a tennis ball.

"Just the park," Loara said. "It's here, nothing we can do. But I never thought they'd build a road—"

"Around smack where we are?" Beck interrupted.

Loara paused. "Well, no, I meant a road just to look from, and I–"

"You mean come right on past us here?"

Loara paused, much longer now. "Well, I just thought tourists wouldn't—"

"Well, you can't say such if you don't know, honey. You studied up on what tour-asts do?"

Loara's pause dragged endlessly. "No."

Beck smiled, looked around the table. "Honey, sure could use dessert now."

Kezia looked at her mother, and for the first time she saw her not as "Mother," but as a person, another woman. Anger stood dark in her eyes. Beck didn't belong—his sharp acrid aftershave among the crystal bottles she had brought from New York. His ugly fake-gold watch, his square hands moving among the gauzy white curtains fluttering in the kitchen window.

"Going to bring the hordes on here, overrun the whole falutin' place and us be damned." The old fire was in Gran'sir's voice. But the sealskin cap he always wore was gone. The top of his head looked strangely vulnerable, blue and pink beneath the few white hairs. His scalp looked at her with its blank face.

"It's money in the pocket," Nate Vannah said. "We'll put us up a few souvenir stands, right? Sell them all our overripe bait clams, our scuzzy softshells."

"That's scuz *talk*," his father said. "Shut your flap now."

"Cravat emptor," Nate said.

Kezia laughed. No one else did. The sound hung frozen in the air. She felt her stomach stretch rigid.

"The park wrote to the professor a letter," Clara said. "To Mr. DiBlasi, sir, it said."

"Clara." Loara stiffened. Her hands stopped dishing out the "ice cream," sea moss pudding creamy white in the small glass bowls. "I asked you, don't bring that up on Kezia's first day back."

"The park wishes to purchase Perley's House, and all that surrounds."

"*Our* house?" Kezia said.

"This is our house right here," Loara said.

Kezia's frightened eyes sought help. But Gran'sir had gone piebald since she last saw him. Once he had hair brown as walnuts and apple-ruddy skin. Now both were dappled brown and white, age spotted, livered, and silvered around wire glasses bandaged with dirty adhesive tape across the bridge. It was as if the solid colors had been his strength. The whitened dapples had broken it, drained him weak.

"Then this appraiser came," Grandm'am said. "He was one of theirs, the park, and with him a private appraiser. They said, yes, I could accompany them, yes, and they looked all around."

"But the DiBlasis aren't interested," Kezia said. "Are they? It's just the park is asking the price, isn't that it? Anyone can ask."

"Have you ever heard of this—it is Eminent Domain? I am trying to understand it. It means they take what they want, the law says."

Deenie straightened up, walked her knife and fork across her plate.

"Well," Lady Flora said, "Perley's House is what? Just shingles and wood."

She couldn't eat her ice cream. She remembered long ago mossing for it in late October after the heavy storms ripped the rust-brown plants free of rocks, tossed them up on shore. The last time: just before the Vannahs' dock was torched. And all along it wasn't Vannahs they wanted to kill....

She started. She felt someone's knee pressed solidly, bone to bone, to hers. Now it dipped a little, moved back, like a caress. Openmouthed she stared at Nate. His gaze flicked over her like a thrown net.

"Well," Lady Flora said, "wonder what the ritchbitches and Point No Pointers are up to this summer." The mouse burned on her cheek, eating through skin and flesh, branding itself on her bones.

"Saturday before the fourth—July Fourth—they're having some big wingding at Tenhaven," Loara said.

"A party?"

"Flowers on the tables, they'll even eat outside on the grass."

"Oh, I wish I could go." The words flew swift as birds out of Kezia's mouth. She only wanted to shoo them back in.

"They don't want our kind up there," Nate said. His voice was loose and easy as ever, fitting itself in like a well-sized lath. "Mr. Beal, been meaning to tell you about the pile of net I found. In a locker at the Currys'. You could use it in your weir."

"Net! Useless as tits on a boar. Cut the brush from new birch, I do, hang them in the ribbands. Used to be three hundred weirs hereabouts, built like that."

"Ninety feet of net and good condition, too."

"Seals, sharks, dogfish'll tear holes in net soon as look at it. Have to sell your damn net to someone else."

"It's not for sale."

Gran'sir looked up.

"Was planning on *giving* it to you."

"Why didn't you say so! Haul it right over tomorrow before ten."

Gales of laughter. Even Lady Flora joined in.

"You cannot sneeze that away, you old crock."

"Ye gods, Clara."

More laughter, loud enough to drown out a park blast. Kezia felt a glow in her stomach. Perhaps she fitted in: a foundling could find her way home again.

"Remember," Victorine said, "when Reverend Witney gave that Easter sermon, and Gran'sir called out—" hiccuping with laughter.

Nate pounded on the tablecloth, red eyed.

"And Mrs. Betts got all ticked off and she—"

"That was the best one yet!"

And so it went.

Tear-eyed gusts of laughter, references, all references to things Kezia didn't understand.

In her corner she grew quieter and quieter still.

Now they were looking at her; they understood that she felt left out but they were helpless to stop now, reluctant to explain. The sounds of laughter shut her out as surely as the sounds of arguing from the cellar long ago. Were there always the subterranean tunnels of fear, rage, loss, abandonment? Would her foot always keep breaking through a thin floor?

Kezia felt her shoeless feet press her upward.

"Going somewheres, Aunt Keezie?" her little sister said.

Silence washed outward like ripples from a stone. Kezia waited to hear them fracture on the shore.

"Of a sudden," Lady Flora said in her broadest, down-Eastest Maine accent, "I got me the down-river cant."

Like her mother years before her, she ran out the door.

Something was wrong with the horizon.

Perley's House was still there. Kezia knew it would look small. You grew from childhood while your memories shrank. What was big now is diminished, small. Perley's House stood humped as a lunchbox, cramped, smudged, melting gray into the gray scrabble rock around. The DiBlasis' zoo of cement and plastic animals cavorted around it like Snow White's cottage. Kezia walked closer; Snow White didn't seem to be home. It was still there: the lost-luck horseshoe embedded the wrong way, mouth down in the oak-ribbed fan above the replaced door.

Shingles and wood.

Her nose pressed the iron-smelling rust of a wire screen. All was dark and still in the hall, nine feet across, its length disappearing into deeper dark. Drafts moved heavy with mystery: a stranger's house.

Was it better never to go back, to find everything changed?

Kezia turned around, saw what was wrong with the horizon. The Witness Tree was gone.

The wind poured cold over her body—solid wind. It dried the words from her throat, thoughts from her head. It stripped her dim and dumb, left her barely holding on, like the year-rounders here. Kezia tried to gather moisture enough to swallow. In Maine was poverty of mouth: lipless lines that clamped on words as if words were gold.

She walked over to where the great oak had stood.

There was a new Witness Mark now, the DiBlasis' own.

She stared at a low cement marker with an X red-painted on top.

"Crash the Chancellors' party in disguise," Lady Flora instructed. "They'll never know you're a Beal if you're me."

CHAPTER 19

The little outboard, battered, paint peeling, nosed straight in toward the granite stanchions of the Seal Point dock.

PRIVATE
NO DOCKING
NO GAS OR WATER
GUARD ON DUTY

All was deserted. Kezia tied up amid a fleet of moored yachts, sails neatly furled in navy blue canvas covers. The American flag on its flagpole whipped in the wind, cracking its warning. But she clambered up on the dock anyway and then stood there absolutely still.

She felt the water running out of her tennis shoes.

On her face she assembled Aunt Willi's expression: hauteur and (though she didn't know it) fear.

She was no longer nine years old in green pants with holes in the knees.

She was tough as bullbeef, cold as a welldigger's (not "elbows," as Gran'sir said when children were around) arse. She would argue with the Devil or a lamppost. She was ready to become somebody—herself.

Hugging her package of finery she hurried into the woods to change.

She emerged in her new white organdy, the most beautiful dress in the world. Her damp hands crunched the starched layers beneath ("Unbelievable! Now 28 Yards Wide Nylon Net Petticoat $3.99!"). She blinked, armored with eyebrow pencil, liner, mascara, blue eyeshadow, on her lips Cherries In The Snow.

She had transformed herself into the person Chance would love.

The twilight under the overarching trees was pierced by the bright round doorway in Tenhaven's garden wall. Beyond stretched the summer afternoon: dapple and languor, sun-sifted flowers. The great rectangle of central greensward was crowded with people, in their hands drinks and winking arcs of cigarettes. Others strolled the flagstone paths, legs brushing the spilling beds of peonies, astrantias, monardas, phloxes, polemoniums, soapworts. The air was rich with a thousand scents.

Kezia tried to stifle her panic. It was too far gone to be excitement; it stifled, breathless pain.

Every girl is beautiful in white.

She stumbled forward, threading her way among deserted flowery tablecloths to the edge of the grass.

Dozens of eyes turned toward her: she wanted to drop through the earth. Dozens of people stared at her, all wearing clothes fit for a hot-dog roast. Not one other woman wore a dress, let alone high heels. Kezia felt hers sink in the lawn.

Her chin stabbed higher. She stepped forward out of her heels, left them standing, twin white sentinels behind. It was like getting out of her girdle and having a scratch. Her bare toes wriggled in the cool grass.

Where was Chance? After an hour she had drunk four Champagne Carltons, but every group of people she tried to approach fell silent as she drew near, as if she were an eclipse come to stay.

"Woodcock go by some other name on Aguahega," a woman in slacks and waist-knotted blouse was saying. "But what? I can't think what it is."

"They're the only game bird you can serve rare. I split them and wrap with bacon, grill just till the bacon chars."

"But what are they called on here?"

"Timberdoodle, I believe," Kezia said.

A small knot of people looked at Kezia. Her eyebrow arched. "You know the natives. Have a dadburned native-sounding name for ever por critter you kin name."

They laughed at her rendition of the Maine accent. A man laughed, his face burning warm and steady as the sun. "I don't think we've been introduced."

Kezia looked into a blond-framed face. He was incredibly handsome but old, perhaps even twenty-five. His teeth were white in a slow grin.

"Tommy Griswold," he said.

To her horror she felt Tommy take her hand, draw it toward his mouth. There were her fingernails, ten ragged, bitten raw squares. His lips pressed warm on the backs of her fingers, his moustache tickling. His eyes looked up at hers.

"Finally a girl who's not afraid to *look* like a girl. And what's your name?"

"Kezia. Kezia Wilde."

"Allow me to present my credentials. Rhodes scholar, Russian lit major, currently correspondent for *Time*."

"Then how do you find it?"

"What?"

"The time."

"For what?"

"Your indefatigable pursuit of the next conquest?"

"Kezia, allow me to refill your so very empty looking glass."

"He's married!" the woodcock-recipe woman warned.

"I'm not married. My wife is."

Desperately Kezia tried to think of sophisticated comments, like "paté makes your breath smell bad." But it didn't seem to fit here.

"Red?"

Chance stood quite still, staring at her, and now he was walking her way.

Twin thunders filled her ears. Chance was six feet two now, all length and bones and nose, shoulders wide in the navy cotton sweater with a single white stripe threaded through the crew neck. Below chinos unraveled above sockless shoes. He seemed to swim toward her through her thick cold fear.

His arms would go out, she could feel them already closing around...

He held two drinks, one in each hand. "Red?" as if not sure.

"Actually, the long-lost Russian princess Anastasia. But I'm glad you didn't recognize me. I'd rather have you like me for myself."

His deepset eyes seemed to swarm from their sockets, a rim of white beneath the irises. The horse she rented in Central Park had eyes like that, spooked. But when, scared herself, she held the sugar lump on a palm whose hummocks strained to lie flat, his lips nuzzled velvet through green foam dried to glass.

"Is one of those drinks," she said, "for me?"

"I wouldn't have recognized you, Red."

"But you did." She smiled and reached for the glass but there was already another hand there. It had five long polished pink nails.

"Who's your little friend, Chance?" The black haired girl tucked her other hand cozily through his arm.

"This is my friend Kezia—"

"Wilde." Kezia thrust out her too-big, farmer-red hand. "Pleased to meet you."

"How do you do."

"I'm from New York."

Kezia tried to sit very still in her green cushioned white wicker chair. At every move it talked beneath her bottom, went on whispering about her even after she was still. Her left hand crept up from the napkin in her lap, touched the rosy ribs of the shell beside her plate, one of thousands of seashells embedded in the garden's round concrete table whose center was a pool. Lily pads and candles in holders floated on its surface and she asked again, "Would you pass the salt, please?" just to watch it pushed across to her, dipping and bobbing in its little boat from the far shore.

Here she sat at the honored table, the sea breeze fresh through her hair, Chance's family all around her (and the black-haired girl, whose name was Helen Hanft).

Kezia looked from Helen to Tommy Griswold, giving him her widest smile.

"That's what I like," Tommy said, eyeing Kezia's heaped plate, "a girl as uninhibited as her appetite."

Her body made noise: growling now, giving voice as it always seemed to at the wrong time. There were lobsters and steamers from the seaweed-covered pit by the sea. There was corn on the cob and tomatoes layered with basil leaves and fresh mozzarella, sprinkled with deep green olive oil and a grind of fresh pepper. Reed slim raw asparagus stood in hollowed out red peppers. Kezia plucked one free, dabbled it in the little pot of sea salt, looked at Chance and bit off the end. "Uninhibited? I don't know. But I always do just as I please."

"And what pleases you about men?" Tommy Griswold said.

Kezia heard herself giggling. There was the Calloway white wine and Mouton Cadet. She had already tasted both. Chance's face, watching hers, was turning as red as the lobsters.

"All I will say is that Stanhope, my school, proudly proclaims its Latin legend to the world: *Puellae venerunt, Abigrunt Mulieres."*

"Which is?" Tommy said.

"Girls they enter, women they leave."

"L'erotisme du Sixth Form?" Helen Hanft said.

Chance's grandfather looked across with displeasure, a swipe of grease across his chin.

"Tell us, Miss Wilde," Bettina, Chance's mother said. "What does your father do?"

"I'm an orphan. I live with my aunt in New York. She works on Ulcer Gulch."

"Isn't that fascinating."

"Madison Avenue, I mean. It's an advertising agency."

"Isn't that wonderful? I know someone—don't I, Chance?—at Benton and Bowles. And just let me assure you I don't for a minute think advertising is full of hucksters like that novel said."

"Oh, but it is," Kezia said.

"It is?"

"My aunt can sell you a widgit even if you don't want a widgit. She calls it Motivation Research. For example, take germ-fighting soap. Many young girls wash like Mrs. Macbeth herself: they feel dirtied by these brand-new sexual desires."

Tertia Chancellor sat forward with interest. She had full petulant lips, and though her body was slim, already the beginnings of a double chin. She was 17, and her interests thus far had been limited to a campaign for "girl who lost her virginity the most times," at Miss Porter's School in Farmington, Connecticut. Tertia, who enjoyed sex very much, felt obligated by social constraint to convince each succeeding man that upon entering, he was the first. Men had been easily convinced by her performance, rich as it was in obligatos of sobs.

Fairfield Chancellor leaned forward, his knit shirt tightly buttoned to the throat. "Well, Miss Wilde, I for one think your remarks most apropos. I want to know how you plan to sell me that widgit."

Kezia forced her lungs to expand. "Okay, we have the market, right? Young girls afire with desires. When even they approach saturation, my aunt gets the company to lower its price and widgits continue to sell. When they can't reduce prices any more, she introduces a campaign for the new improved widgit with TR-948, E-Z-grip handle, decorator colors, and a button that lights up red when it's on."

"You see, Bettina," Fairfield said, "she is making a joke."

"Oh, *Gaaaahd,*" Chance's grandmother said. "I don't see what's so funny. *Christ!* It adds to the cost of everything. That's why everything is so expensive these days."

In the uncomfortable silence Helen put her fingers on Chance's arm. "Wasn't there a lobster cannery right here on Aguahega once? I'm interested in all these old island tales."

Kezia wished for a ceiling: she would flip the butter curl up with her napkin. The butter would melt, dripping down on Helen's gleaming self-satisfied black bangs.

"Yes," Chance said. "It opened in the mid-eighteen hundreds sometime—"

"Eighteen sixty-two," Fairfield said.

"I stand corrected. Anyway, Helen, by all accounts it did very well. So well the catch was seriously diminished for the first time. A minimum size limit was set. And soon there weren't enough legal-size lobsters left to make it profitable. Government interference makes it inevitable."

"What?" Tommy Griswold said.

"It closed down."

"In eighteen seventy-nine." Fairfield lay down his fork. "Aguahega is a veritable laboratory of failed industries, Helen, my dear. By eighteen ninety-four the stone quarry became defunct. People didn't want buildings of stone anymore. And such fine, true, clean-grained granite Aguahega's was. Some of it was used to construct the Cathedral of St. John the Divine."

Kezia tried to imagine a church built from the giant's tumbled blocks, the sheared-off cliff, the vast giraffe neck of wooden crane that remained, an eyesore on the western shore.

"And of course," Fairfield went on, "there was commercial ice harvesting on Aguahega. One person alone could cut and store three thousand tons—workers were industrious in those days. But by the late nineties an entrepreneur appeared who formed the American Ice Company, with assets something over twenty-one million dollars, I recall. And Maine ice was simply too distant, too difficult, too expensive altogether to compete. Its assets—"

Chance cut in. "Melted, shall we say?"

"You're very fond of Aguahega, aren't you?" Helen said to the old man.

"It is my home."

"Someone told me years ago," Chance said, "that lobsters *didn't* die out back then. Their relative used to see thousands of full-sizers schooling at the surface."

"Quite impossible," Fairfield said. "I wouldn't want you to be misinformed. Lobsters simply do not school."

"He *saw* it."

"But scientists have verified that such talk is simply myth, old-wives' tales, quite impossible."

"Sure, Grandfather. Just like the 'scientist' who proved that aerodynamically bees can't fly."

Kezia looked across at Chance and grinned. "Who was it that told you that, about the lobsters, I mean?"

An absolute deviltry was spreading across his face. "It was you."

She wanted to sink through the floor. Sweat stood above her lip, a platter of nerves they couldn't fail to see.

"Grandfather, now who were those first people to settle Aguahega? I keep forgetting their name," Chance said.

"Beal. The first was just a poor salt-water farmer, Amariah Beal, who purchased the whole of Aguahega from an Indian chief for three gallons of cherry rum. He had two wives, did old Amariah, the first died in childbirth, and he married her sister and produced sixteen heirs, although only eight lived beyond childhood, such were conditions then."

"A regular Robinson Crusoe to come way out here," Tommy said.

"As Trollope said, 'though the life of a Robinson Crusoe may be very picturesque, humanity will always desire to restore a Robinson Crusoe back to the community of the world.' "

Kezia stared across at Fairfield Chancellor. Who was this crotchety old man to tell them about her own family, as if they were a lesson in a schoolbook.

"Grandfather," Chance said, "they'll think you are a know-it-all."

"History belongs to all, and it must be preserved. When it's gone, it's gone. Life runs in cycles, such is what I believe. Life flourishes, then life wanes, just as Aguahega's population has. There will be new industry on the island now. Evolution occurs among man's institutions, just as among species, of course. The old Aguahega, which we all love, may have exhausted its resources. So the new Aguahega must burst forth and take its place. I'm referring, of course"—he smiled all around—"to Norumbega National Park."

Bettina Chancellor stifled a yawn, her other hand reaching for the bell.

The serving woman appeared. "Hi!"

"No no no. Not 'hi,' dear, for heaven's sake. She's in training, of course. We are ready for dessert and coffee now."

Kezia stared aghast.

In black fronted with a silly white doily of an apron stood the big-boned frame of Loara Vannah, who was staring at Kezia as hard as Kezia stared at her.

Why hadn't she *asked* how her mother knew when the Tenhaven party was? Why hadn't she told someone she was going?

"The coffee. Christ!" Chance's grandmother said.

Chance was leaning back, the same devilish grin on his face. "Well, I hope the park doesn't interfere with another institution here. I believe in local custom. Now what do the natives call it? Oh, yes, the Duck Drive. Kezia, you're our expert on the arcana of Maine. Tell us all about it."

Kezia stared at the retreating form of her mother, burdened with a tray.

"Yes, tell us," Tommy Griswold said.

Kezia shook her head.

"Summer hunting of eiders is verboten legally, has been for years," Chance said. "But that's on the mainland. Pretty much anything goes on here: the islanders police themselves."

Chance winked at her but she kept her gaze on her plate. The Duck Drive: no outsider was supposed to know. The Duck Drive: exciting as the Fourth of July yet spoiled by the anguish of envy. It was a daylong celebration of hunting (for that staple of winters past—salted eiders, and eiderdown), a celebration of the communal spirit (platters of fried duck, endless kinds of pie), and of beauty, the main event: the reign of the newest Queen of Aguahega (and comparison with all the other girls who only stood and watched). The Duck Drive: it was blood and feathers plucked free on the air and the Queen in the traditional water lilies in her hair and wearing a white dress.

Every girl is beautiful in white.

"They elect a queen for the Duck Drive," Chance said. "You know, you should be Queen of Aguahega, Red."

Now they knew: she wasn't from the Point. The bright fantasy of the day burst.

"A queen can't be short."

"Don't tease us, Red. We want to hear about the Duck Drive."

Bettina Chancellor looked confused. "You're just here for the season, aren't you, dear? Aren't you the ones renting 'Elsinore'?"

Kezia felt Chance's gaze on her. Something moved in his eyes, quick and glinting as the carp in the garden's fountain. It took her place at his table and threw it away. She knew what he wanted: it was an inverse form of snobbery. He wanted her to tell them he was a "real" Aguahegan, what his grandfather tried to be. A game you played in summer, abandoned in fall.

He would never marry a native like her.

Her trembling legs pushed her up from the chair.

"We're summering at Bleak House, didn't you know?"

The grass slipped damp and fresh-mown under her bare soles, across the endless garden to the Moon Gate, the forest dark and swallowing her beyond.

CHAPTER 20

The twilight that had been just a pool under the trees was now everywhere.

Kezia shivered in her grass-stained bare feet and thin dress.

The colors that were land and sky were now just different shades of gray.

"*Red*. Wait up."

The air was heavy with iodine from the sea below. She ran on along the path that took you out to the edge of Seal Point's cliffs. Fear opened her and she was falling through space. "Dare you," Nate had taunted her when she was eight. Nothing was more forbidden than going near cliffs, but "Double daffy down dare you, Keez. Go on, look over the edge." On bellies they had snaked over sandpaper ground, closer, her stomach hollow, shaping itself around the rocks. Blood pinged in her ears.

Down is falling. Down is nightmare. Down is dead.

Crawling on anyway, fingertips white on the giant's fissured building blocks, finding a crack, something growing there, green in a stone garden of death.

The bitter wild tang of open ocean scoured her nose. You could smell the drop-off before you saw it, the great face of the southern cliffs thrusting sheer, darker than the surrounding pink granite, 1000 feet into the air. Breath held, the child she had been peered over the edge.

Miniature dizzy breakers deep down rock tunnel, sea crashing, tide that sucked not in and out but up, down. "Bold shore" it was called, sea so deep so close-in that an ocean liner could anchor there where the cliffs went on straight down drowning under water to the center of the earth.

"Nate," she'd said. "Can the cliffs come for you in the night?"

"Kezia." She heard Chance's breathing jagged from running behind her.

These weren't the great southern cliffs. These were just the Seal Point cliffs, 145 feet down.

"Leave me alone! I hate you."

"Hey, I was just teasing you back there. Okay, it went too far. I didn't realize till right then how young you still are."

"In front of my mother!"

"Your mother?"

" 'Hi!' 'No no no, not hi, dear, for goodness sake.' "

"Oh. Christ, I'm sorry. I've never met your mother. I didn't know."

Did he feel anything at all of the way she felt for him? She dared a glance up at him. Something leaked for expression through his eyes. She looked at the face that was the dearest thing in the world to her.

Warm fingertips touched her chin.

"Come on, smile. With the teeth."

"When we were younger, it was so easy." She looked away from him. "Being together. Now something's coming between us."

"We're growing up is all."

"Don't feel grown up."

"Look at yourself. I thought old Griswold was going to have at you right on the lawn."

This was better. He was jealous, that was all. "Just where is old Griswold correspondent? Outer Ruritania?"

"He's a permanent graduate student, so they say."

"So he's just a farrago of crapola, as Aunt Willi would say?"

"That's right."

"Which one? Orville or Wilbur?" It was like juggling. You could only keep the jokes in the air so long. She shivered in the cooling air.

"Hey, you're cold." He pulled off the navy sweater with the too-short sleeves. His chest was bare beneath.

The warmth was dense, comforting as Kezia pulled his sweater over her head. Chance's scent wafted up to her from it: a fibrous haysweet smell like the saddle blanket from the Central Park horse's back, a clean green animal smell.

"I was never that enamored of growing up." Chance's thin arms crossed, hugging his chest. Straight hairs marched in ranks from the concavity of his breast bone, like salt grass harped in one direction by the wind. "I used to watch the St. Patrick's Day Parade right from my window at Eight-Twenty. Even then I knew."

"What brings this on?"

"I mean, the greatest outpost to see it from, right? But the window was always kept locked with this double paned glass, I was seven and the bands went by on Fifth Avenue like a phonograph turned down too low. And this little messy street kid was down there laughing and pounding his heels and dribbling mustard all the way down his shirt, sitting on top of this stone wall out in front. Until Gerry, he was the doorman, made him get off. As he was scrambling down this kid looked up at me, gawked like I was the biggest freak in the world. And I was just a little kid like him. And I knew something."

"What, Chance?"

"Everything was going to be like that. A phonograph turned down too low."

His words frightened Kezia. She made her funny face, the one he called "squirrel." But still he looked sad.

"How about you Red? How were things at school?"

She remembered the first terrible fall in Manhattan. Outside the temperature was in the low twenties and the wind raw and blustering off the East River. Even here there were the poor and the rich. Herself in her school uniform of pleated black-watch skirt, navy blazer with the Stanhope crest, trudging the long way from the bus stop to the Gothic stone pile of the school, her exposed knees burning fiery as tomatoes. While the other girls stepped from the greenhouse of chauffeured limousines, knees white roses.

"Not chauffeur, *driver*," Brantley had said.

Now Kezia looked at Chance and grinned. "I got suspended for 'roofering' this term."

"Roofering?"

"I invented it—a sport. Got a bunch of the kids to follow me up and over the Stanhope roof at night. In the dark it's a whole other world. Avoid the dragon: Jimmy, the watchman. But then he's always in the basement, drunk. Climbed out to the edge of the auditorium, which not incidentally has a glass roof. I was the first to put my heel through the panes."

He laughed. "You'd be a hit at Dartmouth. It's all hell night, Ping-Pong in the buff, meeting the—excuse me—'fucking trucks' in front of the Hanover Inn on Friday afternoons."

Kezia examined the speckly bluish red mottles on the backs of her chilled hands. Translucent hands, too thin, she'd inherited them from her mother. She pushed them into the pockets of her skirt.

"Sorry. The Marlboro men of the east ain't exactly known for euphemisms, you know. The buses of women from Colby-Sawyer or whatever."

So. He had done It.

Even Brantley had done It.

She had walked toward Kezia from far away down the school's green tile hallway, her face with its strange, taut, Cheshire cat, frightened, stunned, clubbed look: "Well. I did It."

Everyone knew everything about life, Kezia thought, except me.

"But SAE isn't so bad," Chance continued, "as frats go. We took turns visiting these fragile old people in the nursing home. Hair like cotton candy, some of them even strapped to their chairs."

"Are you still in pre-law?"

"Offeree, offeror, nisi quash 'em, Harvard Law!"

"Wild-eyed enthusiasm, huh?"

"Let's put it this way. It'll be a miracle if I get in. I'm having a lot of fun at Dartmouth. Getting good grades isn't fun."

"Cole Porter went to Harvard Law."

He looked at her. "How'd he do?"

"Dropped out."

"Then there's hope for me yet."

"You're brilliant, Chance. You have nothing to worry about."

"Except what I'm doing it for."

"To be a lawyer, aren't you?"

"As the saying goes, 'If the facts are ag'in you, argue the law. If the law is ag'in you, argue the facts. If both are ag'in you, use the rules of procedure to delay and force a settlement.' "

"That's the law, isn't it?"

"Not justice. I want to be of some good in the world."

"So what are you going to do?"

"I was thinking of pointing things toward Legal Aid. Dad and Mom will be fit to be tied."

"Not exactly riven with filial grief, are you?"

"They teach you words like that at Stanhope School? The OM's such a hypocrite. 'All people are equally good in God's eyes,' he says. 'Whomsoever much is given, of him shall be much required.' " Good works, of course. So he says. What he *wants* is for me to be the captain of industry."

"What about your grandfather?"

"A robber baron would suit him fine."

"Chance, you should just do what you want."

"No. I'll do what they *say* I should. Hoist them by their own petards. What the hell is a petard, I never did know. That and a lot of other things."

"I'm not too hot on parents myself these days. Mother told me to think of Beck Vannah as my friend."

"So?"

"He's my friend all right. And I hate him!"

She was glad to talk about herself. Talking with Chance wasn't a fair match. She rarely got to lob even one ball back. Instead she just ran after his ball and told him what a great shot, or how sorry she was he didn't hit it with top spin.

"Well, maybe your mother's happier now, anyway."

"No, she's not."

"How do you know?"

"She's not! She never has been!" Kezia was surprised to hear herself say this.

"Why?"

"Mother has only three books, Chance. She owns three books: *The Trail of the Lonesome Pine, The Scottish Chiefs,* and *Being Born."*

She heard his laughter. "What's funny about it? But you wouldn't know." She saw the impact of her words. "You don't know what it's like to live here and never have anything and never know anything and end up here always a stupid fisherman's wife, trapped on here. That's what it's like being poor. Wanting, all the time wanting. Things you can't have. Things you can never be."

"I can't believe you said that. I can't believe it. New York's ruining you."

Pain bit like a fish hook in her mind. The only way to get it out was to push it straight on through: "Ruin!"

She felt the warmth of his breath burst suddenly close. She felt the beginning pressure of his arms around her and her mouth opened. Wonderful hot naked skin against her, she felt the desperate desire to wrap herself around him. She pushed blindly toward his warmth, but it was already as close as it could get. She could feel a pulse beat warm and flushed and she needed it closer, warmer—

Her eyes opened. He had taken a step back, was smiling crookedly down at her. He hadn't even kissed her.

"Oh Red. I wish—"

What?

She put her arms back around his neck.

The shallow dark spaces of Chance's pupils seemed to widen, deepen as she looked. Their gazes held, a beat past whatever Kezia knew to be normal. Who had started the looking—was it her, or him?

Had he finally discovered her? Was she *seen?* Was it happening, was it real?

She forgot to wonder if her covermark looked okay or if there was a "corner": mucous in her eye. Her blood rushed through her body.

"You could sell me widgits any day," he said.

Why didn't he kiss her?

"If you could see yourself now. All the blood's up in your cheeks, your color, all ginger and smoke."

But he was disentangling her fingers that clutched so desperately around the back of his neck. "Red, do you ever? Think about the way it was before?"

"Before what?" She hated this in him, turning everything over and over, searching for the slug beneath the stone. She was losing him, she could feel the coldness deep down in her bones.

Chance's arms hugged his bare chest again, feeling the taut sensitivity from that morning's sunburn, and over it the dark lowering cloak of loneliness. "When we were kids. Remember Digby's Den?"

She had stared where he'd pointed, the dark mouth of cave in the sheer granite rise of the cliffs, the cave she hadn't known was there. She was of it and didn't know it. He knew it but wasn't of it. He'd put his hands on her to tickle her. Her skin seemed to leap, warm and lithe beneath his fingers. Her pants were rolled up, and struggling, she kicked up her legs. They were roughened and scarred, all bones thinly covered, socks falling down. But there was the long lean muscle curving beautifully at the calf. He saw the downy red-blonde hairs growing there, as if she were a woman grown. He had felt dizzy, suddenly sick with excitement.

She was only a little girl, wasn't she?

He'd sat up, arms dangling over his knees, afraid his erection would show. The oars propelled them into the hidden pool and the light that flickered green all around.

"Want to live here," Kezia had said. "Stay here always and always, just you and me."

He was like one of the poachers who sold their venison at the "meat market" on the mainland. Like a snake in Eden after the beautiful, gentle little deer here who ventured cautiously out of the woods in late August, rearing after the siren call of crabapples on their toothpick hindlegs. And one had even been bold enough to wander past Tenhaven in the middle of the afternoon.

He only wanted to get her home, and safe.

"You going to marry me when we grow up?" Kezia had asked him then.

After that trip he began to avoid her. He saw the betrayal accusing him in her eyes.

That night he had a dream he was swinging in darkness. He fell off but felt nothing. Nothing at all.

Now, on Seal Point's cliffs, Kezia felt Chance's hand reaching for her own. "I want to take you somewhere."

"Where?"

"You'll see."

Ahead, hidden in the trees, a log cabin bulked a blacker dark. She felt the wildest exhilaration, fear. "Chance?"

"There's no one there."

So it would happen. She would finally know what love really meant. Oh, please please let me make Chance happy. Please please let me be able to love, to truly love, to give, to lose thought of myself, to love and love and love.

Inside was the smell of mildew, dampness and then Kezia's nostrils prickled with the scent of the struck matchhead. Chance's face gleamed white as he bent over the kerosene lamp's tiny yellow-blue flare, white hands cupping its growth. He lit three lamps and Kezia stared around. She bumped down on the edge of a daybed couch. It was higher than she had thought. A handwoven Navajo blanket thrown over it scratched the backs of her calves. She pulled her skirt down over his knees.

He seemed to be waiting for her to ask why they were there. But she didn't ask. A sophisticated person is never surprised.

"No plaster or paint anywhere," Chance was saying. "Just stone and wood, local stone and wood."

Kezia tried to fix each detail in her mind: the big stone fireplace, walls hung with curls of loosening bark, another Navajo blanket bright on a bench, a brass tray on legs for a coffee table. Up a few steps was a platform that was the kitchen with upended sawed-off logs around a table for chairs. That was where they'd sit tomorrow morning. Leaning heads together over a cup of coffee. She would *know*: what everyone else knew.

"This is Grandfather's retreat. Only he hasn't retreated here in years. Irony, huh? First they build Tenhaven as a retreat. Then they had to build a retreat from the retreat!"

Her heart thudded wildly. "What's this carved lamp?"

"Kashmiri. It's one of the pieces that holds up the roof on pagodas."

She tried to sound casual: she'd done this many times. "What about the head on the wall?"

"The Mask of Kali, I think from Calcutta. The Great White Wasp went wild buying things so he could rough it. I think he got took on this one. Kali's the Goddess of Destruction."

He turned toward her and every cell in her body jumped. "I want to show you something upstairs."

He led the way up the stairs: floating trapezoids of wood hanging from metal rods, twining in a circle around a great spruce trunk. She stared upward, unable to make out the top.

"Hey," she had whispered to Brantley as they walked toward Luchows, Ben and Aunt Willi ahead. "Do you think they *do* It?"

"Shhh," Brantley had said.

Willi tilted her face up to Ben, the hood of her dark seal coat slipping back, snowflakes lighting like sparklers on the coiled chignon of her hair.

"Doesn't she look just like Anna Karenina?" Brantley said.

"She looks cow-eyed, if you ask me. Anyway, now I'm sure of it."

"What?"

"They *do* do It!"

"Come on," Chance said above her on the stairs.

Aunt Willi had been a clerk at a tuna fish importer when she met the man who slew her virginity. He was a Greenwich Village radical who took her on the floor beside a pedestaled bust of Trotsky. He gave her a poem and the clap, she'd said.

Kezia hiccuped, all her passion suddenly in her diaphragm.

She stared up at Chance, hiccuping like a fiend.

He was very slowly opening the bedroom door.

Kezia's nostrils widened: the ineradicable smell of memory—rotting fish.

Chance struck a match to a fat white candle in a saucer, lit the wick. The black walls receded: a floor gleaming white with three inches of sand, a sagging overstuffed chair covered with a patched canvas sail, windows covered with vertical wooden bars.

"Chance—" And then she saw it: a fish hawk in all its extravagant beauty, head and chest white, buff-tipped brown feathered cloak over shoulders and tail, eyes framed by a Lone Ranger mask of darkest feathers staring at Kezia in solar gold.

In the instant that she saw it it gathered itself atop the screen perch, a green-striped deck chair cover tacked in a hanging loop over a frame of boards.

"Get back!"

The five-foot wings mantled then whipped apart, the crest of white feathers on the back of its head fanning erect with angry little ticks. With a shriek the fish hawk rose, wings beating great gusts of air.

The candle flame snuffed out. In the complete blackness the air was crowded with frantic wingbeats, strange piercing calls that rose higher and higher. Kezia heard a thump as the leashed bird on its way up to the rafters fell back against the hanging screen of the perch.

The bird's scream was the worst sound she had ever heard. "Chance, stop it, please. Let it go."

The candle flame winked under his face, and in the sudden light she saw the hurt look on his face. "Hey, give it a moment, will you? You'll see."

The fish hawk hung by its feet, swinging by its jesses and the leather leash, head down.

"You can help me. She's fine. We'll set her back up okay."

His hands closed on hers, pressing her thumbs together, lowering them onto the fish hawk's back. His fingers spread hers, holding the wings beneath flat while lifting the heavy hawk up and out by the powerful bunched muscles of its thighs.

Hot. The body pulsed so madly hot through the cool firm depth of feathers, like a coal in a featherbed, while something racketed up near Kezia's index fingers. It was a heart, she realized, a heart jerking in panic, so close to her holding fingers, like a live creature running in fear.

It hissed suddenly, beak open, tongue panting, feathers flattening into a bullet shape that shook with rage and fear. Behind Kezia, Chance quickly held the hawk up against her chest, its feathered breeches thrusting out in front, ebony talons clutching harmlessly like grappling hooks at air.

Tiny brass bells were ringing, one on each narrow leg band. Chance was tightening the jesses through one loop of the metal swivel, the other holding a two-foot leash.

"Doing great, Red. Now we'll carry her, tail to the perch. Turn, slowly! Lower a little. Her instinct is to step *up*. Now lift her up until her talons brush the carpet on top and she should grab for it. Great!"

"Now what?"

"Get back!"

The hawk hunched once more on top of the perch, the golden eyes sunken and glaring, beak wide as a glistening blue-red flower, tongue pink and pointed. The eyes blinked. It swiveled its head, looking at them upside down.

Chance was looking at her; she couldn't keep back the laugh.

"You are a princess," he said, voice soft. But he was looking at the hawk again. "You are a beautiful, beautiful princess that an evil witch turned into a raptor. But someday I'll break the spell, princess."

He didn't know, she thought. He must never know how she had misinterpreted the evening, what she had hoped for.

She would rather die than have him know.

She had made a love potion last winter: a snowflake caught in midair, three teaspoons of snow gathered on a silver star-spangled night, an icicle on a black night in the shadow of a tree, a pine needle, a holly berry, dash of red wine. It had sat in its jar on Aunt Willi's apartment windowsill. Nothing had come from it but mold.

"Nobody else knows about this but you." He was looking at her. "It's a secret. Her name's Bandit."

She sighed an exaggerated sigh, arms crossed across her chest. "Okay, Chancellor, out with it. Tell me about your latest prehominid-brained scheme."

"Falconry!" He thrust his fingers into the stiff buffalo hide tunnels of a gauntlet glove, opened a half-size teak-topped refrigerator and took a fish out of a pail. "You've heard of falconry, right?"

The hawk ignored the fish offered on his palm as if it weren't there.

"You mean training a dadburned fish hawk—"

"Osprey!"

"to jump hisself through a barrel hoop? Well'm, you know summer folk. Make some big, high-falutin' sport of everything."

"That sounds like the Red I used to know."

"The indigenous life form?"

He was stroking the fish head along the gray-blue toes now. "I always wanted to live in the Middle Ages. Knights in armor, jousting, hunting on horseback with dogs and falcons, roaming the moors. Falconry's from the Latin *falx*, curved, sickle-shape like her beak. The main diversion back then. The only way you could catch much of anything, rabbits, quail, before guns. Now I'm going to make it real."

"What?"

"Make the fantasy real."

"Isn't that an oxymoron?"

At his laugh Bandit swiveled her head, eyes unblinking, staring up into the dark corner of the ceiling.

"A falcon on a knight's fist, a merlin for you on milady's glove...."

"All right, Chancellor. Give. What's a merlin?"

"Small hawk, size of a thrush. And you know, the Chinese hawked butterflies two thousand years ago. Khubla Khan had five hundred falcons and ten thousand serfs to beat the bush—"

"And I'm the serf? But you said rabbits. Bandit eats fish."

"James the First had a royal mews, place for falcons where the National Gallery is now, facing Trafalgar Square. And the book said he hunted fish in the Thames with ospreys."

"Fish hawks."

Bandit leaned forward, rocking on her talons and pecked at the mackerel's eye. She jerked her head backward, tossed, caught, swallowed it whole.

Kezia saw Chance looking at her, eyes overweighted by brows. At the excitement, inner absorption she saw there she felt diminished, afraid. Unless she joined him in his game.

Bandit tore off long strips of flesh now.

"Need an accomplice?"

"The conditions of employment will be no doubt appalling. Long hours, tedious labor, no pay."

"Oh well. Nothing better to do."

"You'll be Anne Boleyn, her crest was a falcon, you know. I'll be—"

"Not Henry the Eighth. I never lose my head."

His fingertips brushed the bare skin of her arm. " 'I do invite you tomorrow morning to my house to breakfast; after, we'll a-birding together. I have a fine hawk for the bush.' "

Bandit's beak rested on her filled crop now, a fat man's belly.

"Shakespeare, for sure, I know that. But which one?"

"Got me," the scion of the Chancellor family said.

The brass bells rang with a half-note dissonance. Bandit pulled at the leather binding of her jesses, first the right bell, then the left, then the right, the left.

"I think we'd better be getting you home to bed."

"At the time of falconry, did they have *droit de seigneur?*"

"What is it?"

"The lord's right to rape the peasants."

"You have Tommy Griswold in mind?"

The hawk made a shallow small sound, a comic peep.

Bandit would bring them together. Surely she would.

The hawk's eyes were shut. They opened now, glinting gold as if to wink at Kezia, then sank back closed.

CHAPTER 21

Sky and sea had vanished.

The black above was pricked with cold hard stars, the black below with dancing reflections as phosphorescent creatures swam down the paths of light.

Kezia stared out into the dark of the moon.

She and Chance were heading back for Toothaker Harbor in the Chancellors' inboard cruiser, towing her little outboard skiff behind. Bandit was safe, the madwoman in the attic locked away in the middle of the woods. Kezia wanted to ride like this, close and warm, forever.

"I hope we don't run aground," Chance said.

He was standing too close to her. His arm brushed her shoulder, brushing its warmth onto her. He seemed too hot, or maybe it was her, the close denseness of the wheelhouse. The tip of her tongue tasted salt—droplets of sweat in the cleft above her upper lip. She knuckled them off and Chance brushed her again. The salt beads formed again.

"Worried?" Her eyes ached from staring into the dark ahead. She glanced from the swells at him. In the flickering blue light of the fathometer his silk-straight hair lay soft above the bony prominence of his face.

"Who, me worried?"

"I'll get you there."

Even as he said it: "Forget it," she was pushing him aside and darting behind the wheel, hungry hands reaching for the Morse levers, fingers closing hard over the white knob. The 120-horsepower Alaska diesel engine surged with power. She thrust the knob forward and hit the throttle hard.

"Get away from those controls."

The boat leaped from the trough of the wave and away. Kezia sucked in the exhilarating ocean tang. She was back where she belonged. The boat responded and she had not forgotten.

She reset their course: past the silhouette of Mistake Ledge, the bulky shoulder of Popplestone Island, the good hard sound of the bell buoy rocking away. That was all navigation was: leaving one known place for the next, and then the next. She hadn't forgotten. And Aguahega had not betrayed her and changed.

"I have to pay you a compliment," he said. "We haven't hit anything yet."

"Oh, I can keep us on the road, all right. There's a road through the water, you know. Of course if we miss the turn here we'll hit Gormy Ledge. Tomorrow the natives'll row out and pick the wreck clean."

"If it's a road, dammit, give me road signs, street lamps—"

"Stop worrying! I'll steer you 'dead rabbit,' as the natives say. Night, day: the island makes its own weather, have you noticed that? Nothing like the mainland. It's so high, so far out, I guess."

His arm brushed her shoulder again.

She stiffened. It had passed within a hairsbreadth of her breast.

She concentrated out the windshield. Waves ceaselessly reared and toppled toward them, fracturing at their crests into lines of phosphorescence, cold leaps of fire.

"You miss all this, don't you?" Chance said. "Lobstering, I mean."

"Hell, I'm no lobsterman. Can't get up at dawn, break your back, storm comes along and smashes every pot you've got. Spend your whole damn life at sea."

She hummed.

"Why are you humming, then?"

She felt a sudden overwhelming feeling of rightness and belonging. The familiar sounds, smells, vibrations of a boat lulled her and she forgot that if you cared, it could be wrenched away from you, murdered. If you cared, you could die of grief and fear.

"Sure, I miss it. Aguahega's a good place to be from. Not a place you'd want to live."

"But you want to."

"What?"

"Want to live here. You think I don't know anything about you, but I do. Your face never hides anything."

"Wish to God I had me some gin." Her hand reached for the security of the Morse levers. She felt the sudden heat of his fingers on her stiff cold fingers. Why were they cold when she felt so hot? His hand was long and slender, with tapering fingers. She watched his fingers press her hand, warming the chill.

She struggled to draw her hand away, slipped it through his grasp.

"Oh, no, you can't get me that easily."

"Can't I?" he said.

Lobstering—she hadn't thought of it in years.

He was half-slumped like a lazy bear against the counter, looking back at her.

"Guess you rich boys think you can get anything you want."

"Yeah? What I want is a beer."

"Put a lid on your cave, wog!"

He squared his jaw, hooked thumbs in pockets, quick drew an invisible gun. "It was Tuesday, January eleven. It was cool in Los Angeles. We were working the Day Watch out of Forgery. My partner's Frank Smith. The boss is Captain Welsh. My name's—"

"Friday!"

"Frank, where'd you hide that beer?"

It was darker now, as if the stars had dimmed.

"Can I ask you a question, legal eagle?"

"Shoot."

"Don't care myself. Just asking for Gran'sir and Grandm'am."

"Shoot."

"They got a letter from the park."

Chance straightened from his half-hunched lean.

"It said they're interested in buying what they call the 'inholding': Perley's House."

"Who was the letter addressed to, Red?"

"The DiBlasis. But Grandm'am and Gran'sir live there. It's their home."

"But legally it's not anymore is it? What does it say on the deed of sale? Whose name is there?"

Kezia felt her head fill: behind her eyes a buzzing pressure built. "Well, they—it says DiBlasi, I guess. But they said my grandparents could live there as long as they liked."

"But was it on paper?"

Kezia stared at the cuticle on her bitten-raw nail. It was angry and red. "I think it was just verbal. I don't know. No one would have thought to ask for it in writing. A man's word is his word, and Mr. DiBlasi *said*—"

"What if he decided to sell?"

A word was not a word. In New York people knew all about things like this, streetwise like Aunt Willi. You asked for it in writing, asked your lawyer, young Mr. Chancellor here, cravat emptor, as Nate would say. On Aguahega your word was immutable, fixed as rock, not shifting like the shore. But DiBlasi was not one of them. He was a summer person. He had deliberately not put it in writing.

"But it's Gran'sir's house."

"Not in the eyes of the law."

Kezia looked at him. She saw the picture of him that she had always held in her mind blur and slide out of focus. When she snapped it back, it wasn't perfect the way it had been before.

"Well, what can they do?"

"DiBlasi should just refuse the price the park offers. In these kinds of things they prefer a willing seller, a negotiated purchase."

"Prefer. But would that really end it there?"

Chance stared through the windshield into dark.

"What is this Eminent Domain thing?" Kezia asked. "Could the park just take the house?"

"Not take. Eminent Domain isn't take. It would be paid for in any case, a fair and just price. 'Just compensation'—it's in the Fifth

Amendment, I think. Eminent Domain is a legit governmental power, often necessary, you know. Goes back to Virginia, seventeen hundreds. One Jethro Summer found his fifty acres condemned to make way for a town."

"But that's not right. It was Jethro's land."

"Needed for public purposes, and that's a greater good. The good of the many versus the good of just one. Look, this all sounds bad, I know, but we don't really know anything will happen. I'm sure the DiBlasis will refuse the offer and keep the house. It's a great house."

"It's only shingles. And wood."

He blinked rapidly, the whole side of his face near his eye joining in. "Of course, if the park still wants it, a nonemergency situation, they could use a 'Complaint in Condemnation.' Involves courtroom litigation and a judge decides who's got authority and just reimbursement. There's always a shortage of condemnation funds though. Takes years."

"You think it should just go to the park, don't you?"

"That's not for me to say, Red. I didn't grow up at Toothaker. It's not my home."

"But you think like your grandfather, don't you—it spoils the view? A blot on the pristine scenery that you all want preserved forever, like fish hawk eggs under glass."

"I never said that."

Kezia probed the raw edge of her cuticle where dead white was attached, rooted in pink. She suddenly ripped the hangnail off. Blood pulsed, a tiny bubble of red. "But who has the right? We were here first."

"I think," Chance said, "the trees were here first. That's what I think."

She tried to unclench her stiff shoulders. "You're really full of konkus these days, Chancellor."

"That's the Point. The Club."

"It means dry rot, a lumberjack term."

"Dry rot?"

"As in, prohibition caused the dry rot of the Konkus Club."

She was relieved to hear him chuckle under his breath. She thought about Nate, how she would have to tell him. They couldn't keep pretending there was something between them anymore.

She loved someone else.

"Want to join us natives at the Duck Drive this year?"

She was close enough to see the gold flecks in his dark eyes expand.

She made the black and white barrel on a pipe that marked Chebacco Rocks, worked her way around west of the jumble until, if it had been day, she could have seen right into the welcoming arms of Toothaker Harbor.

She heard the sad marine lullaby of the buoy at Drown Boys Ledge, rocking away.

And then she started, unsure.

A light was shining where no light should be.

She reviewed her navigation, she was sure she had found the safe passage. But then what was this light doing there?

Kezia throttled down, cautiously felt their way forward among the rocks. Suddenly she remembered. She knew who had always done that when you were late getting back, after dark or in a storm.

"She put a lantern out on the end of the dock."

"Who?" Chance said.

"Grandm'am."

Chance was looking at her but she couldn't stop it. The sight of the light haloed by darkness sent tears streaking down her face.

CHAPTER 22

The rest of the night Kezia sat on the hill above Toothaker Harbor, thoughts racing too fast to sleep. She still wore Chance's sweater, whitening now under the spreading embroidery of moisture beads. Even the salt grass was silver with dew. She bent her head to peer up.

Bright particular star, not so far above her. She would wed it someday soon.

The silence shattered: the hum of the electric generator in its shed beside the Vannahs' porch. Kezia stiffened. They were up, then. Her mother's hand, Mrs. Vannah's hand with the broad gold ring, would be reaching for the spattered-blue metal coffee pot.

But Kezia couldn't go in.

She stared at the Vannah house, where a faded American flag, not crisp with authority like the one at Seal Point, bellied from a post. She could almost smell the mildew from the old auto's backseat that sagged in parody of a porch swing.

She didn't belong there, never did.

But there was the circle of the harbor and *her* house—gray-shingled as the overlapping clam shell pile the Indians had long ago left. It had not really been that long. You could almost believe everything was the same.

Her heart roared in her ears, and behind the roar she thought she heard a voice—small, high-pitched—ask, "Where do the lightning bugs go come thick-a-fog?"

But whose voice was it?

And then she remembered it was hers.

The noise of a second generator switched on.

Her feet began walking, carrying her closer, as if against her will, to Perley's House. She pressed her nose against the chill window glass. The wind played bass to the generator's tenor. Someone was getting up here as well. The motor pumped below the loose windowpane which vibrated in time.

She opened the back door.

Inside, the walls pressed close: the air different, smells of strange cooking, damp in the dark hall. But the familiar painted-on carpet unrolled beneath her soundless feet, the broad rows of maroon and brown diamonds bordered with blue bands, unchanged since that time when it was common to hide with stencils the lack of money for carpeting.

She knew her grandparents still used the front room on the right for their bedroom. Softly she opened the door.

So small.

The space, in Kezia's memory a ballroom of farway walls, had crept close. There stood Gran'sir's hand-carved armchair that no one ever sat in: crude and splintery, bluntly hewn from a whole oak trunk. On the wall hung Grandm'am's hooked rug: a horse, dogs, a cross, heart, shoes, looped wool on burlap that looked back at her like a reclaimed pet. In the sagging double bed, barely mounding the covers, lay a single inert form.

Under the eaves the barn swallows twittered with the first lightening of dawn.

The old yellow floorboards creaked under her weight. "Gran'sir? Grandm'am?"

A sprig of yellow-white hair stirred under her breath. She could see Gran'sir's big hooked nose now. But there was no response, no sound of breathing. Kezia touched his shoulder—would it be stiff, gone cold?

"Whozher?" The covers struggled upright. An empty whiskey bottle rolled out and crashed to the floor.

"It's me, Gran'sir. Kezia. I've come home."

The sheet dropped from his naked hairless chest. Clumsily, slow blinking as a tortoise he wrapped the sheet around his wasted naked legs. His breath came to her dense and sweet with the smell of alcohol. He put his bent, gnarled finger up to his lips.

"Shh. Have to keep trap shut these days. Mrs. DiBlasi is choiced of sleeping late."

A large red hand, fingers wrinkly water-ended, puckered with damp seized the bottle, held it by the neck as if it carried typhus. Clara Beal had come in so quietly they hadn't heard her.

"I see. I cannot leave you for one minute only, now can I?"

Gooden's face took on a crafty look.

Only his eyes still seemed alive, Kezia thought. His brows gone white had shed their life but his eyes, even if faded, were still blue. Like a brilliant shell picked up wet and bright, but when you got home it was dull and pale.

The bottle crashed into the wastebasket.

"Ye gods, Clara." The covers fell away from his waist.

"Gran'sir, don't you wear pajamas to bed?"

"Oh, don't you pay no never mind what an old man wears. Hah. Skinny dipping. They used to do that up to the Point."

"How do you know, Gran'sir?"

"Night has eyes."

"It has whiskey too." Grandm'am looked at Kezia. "Everything, is it all right over at the Vannahs'?"

"Yes."

"Then let us all get moving. A rolling stone gathers no mud."

Kezia followed her grandfather out the door to check on his weir. The path led past the old Beal graveyard, in more ruination than ever, and skirted in and out along the deserted shore to Goosegrass Cove. In the early light Kezia looked down at his weir, 25-foot spruce stakes interwoven with smaller stakes and birch brush enclosing 80 feet of cove. The long fence of the "leader" was an arrow piercing the twin bulges of the pocket.

"Looks like a heart," she said.

"Someday that cursed weir'll pay off. The big score, I'm about due." He stared into the weir: no gleam of silver herring was there.

He rotated the balsam tip between his front teeth. "Don't comb your hair come dark. Don't cut new door in an old house. Don't watch a man go till he disappears."

"What's that, Gran'sir?"

"Keeps bad luck away."

"I need some luck. All I hoped for was a good summer, but it's horrible in that house. Mother acts like a stranger since she went and married Beck."

"Well, you know Loary had to make ends meet."

"But she acts like a teenager around him, like a fool. And she ignores all the rest of us like he's the only one she cares about anymore."

Gooden stood listening to the rushing gurgle of water over Lazy Gut Ledge. "Well, now. Don't take on too hard what she does. Told me she didn't want to get hitched up again."

"What?"

"Couldn't make ends meet alone."

Kezia struggled to digest this, suddenly ashamed.

"Suppose I shouldn't've spilled that. But thought you were growed enough for some home truths. Let's take the skiff out, what say? Row us out to Massacre, have a picnic for our nooning."

"But we've brought no food."

"City girl."

The clear sky of morning had vanished and as the land heated up, small puffy clouds drifted shadows over Aguahega's hills. Kezia watched the sea darken with the wind, watched the small shape of a seal floating on its back, paws folded blissfully on its stomach like a fat old gentleman after dessert.

" 'Eat it up,' " Gran'sir urged, " 'wear it out. Make it do, do without.' "

Kezia scooped together the last few raw beach peas between her fingers, popping them into her mouth. At their feet lay the broken red carapaces of the two lobsters they had steamed under rockweed. She held up the frond of sea lettuce, looking through its translucent green into the sky.

"Can't we just stay here like this, forever?"

She lay back on the sun-warmed white quartz that streamed through the granite of Massacre Island. Her finger traced the red streaks in the quartz: blood, people used to say. It was a favorite story to tell to children, how the settlers had fled there to escape the Indians who paddled out and murdered them all anyway. Its shivering scariness was fun on a warm summer day. But today, she thought, even the ghosts of Massacre Island seemed sated, asleep in the sun.

Her fingers were sticky from raspberries. She sat up, dabbling them in the shallow water of the tide pool.

"Shore hereabouts used to wash up every fool kind of plank lumber a body could want," Gran'sir said. "Go down to the shore, pick up what you'd need, build a table or a bed. All that wood, marked with the saw from the mill on the main. Were building so many then, Kezia, a hundred-maybe sailing boats. All sails, then."

Kezia felt impatient; old people always wanted to talk about the old days. "But sails were slow, weren't they?"

"Didn't bring us a passel, but we sure had a heap. Free lumber, free food from the sea. Didn't want anything we didn't have. Didn't know about combustion engines. These hands right here rowed to the main and back, sixteen miles each way just to make egg money. Hauled all those pots with nothing but back bent and elbow grease. And know what? People were happier then."

"I don't believe that. Maybe for men. It's one thing for a man to live on here. Another for a woman."

He sat up, face the color of boiled ham. "They pushed us out, the rich did. Too many people run away. I ran away, worked in a little circus, handy boy. World's fattest girl was there, six hundred pounds. Holy smoke she's fat, she's awful fat."

"But if you hadn't left, you never would have met Grandm'am."

In the silence Kezia turned to look at him. His bent frame was leaning against an overturned sawhorse, its battered legs thrusting into the air. No one lived on Massacre anymore. His gaze followed the low stone fence that wandered and curved and went nowhere.

"Are you happy now, Gran'sir?"

The wind sucked and poured over the little island, chill in the shadows away from the sun. He picked up a dripping Deadman's Fingers, a sponge with long fingerlike branches. He turned it in the sun: all the fingers were unbroken. He laid it on the granite to dry.

"That wave passed over me, honey bun, come out on the other side. Relief, what it is, but you miss the excitement of all that."

What was he saying: it was a relief not to be happy? You might as well be dead. "Do you love Grandm'am?"

"Surely do." His pink scalp shone through the sparse white hairs like a rabbit skin.

"Does she love you?"

His watery eyes rested on the Deadman's Fingers. "Have to trust that somebody loves you, honey bun. Can never know for sure. Remember you and Victorine, fool game you got up about blindfolds and messes of food all over your grandmother's kitchen?"

Kezia laughed. She remembered the tight black blindfold creasing her eyes, the helpless feeling that made your spine go soft, your mouth tremble as you held it ready, open with the greatest effort of will. Victorine standing ready with a tablespoon, some vile concoction lumpy and liquid and stirred up in secret.

"You wouldn't put anything *nasty* in it, would you, Victorine?"

"Nah." Horseradish and peanut butter and coffee and cabbage and mashed carrots and turnips and milk. "Come on, Keezie, eat it!"

"You wouldn't, really. Would you?"

"Eat it!"

Holding her breath, taking it in trust but ever ready to vomit Kezia had always taken it dead-center on her tongue.

"But, Gran'sir, what if you loved someone from a different world? Someone who doesn't love you but you love him still?"

"Who-eee. Waves have some mercy but the rocks got no mercy at all. This somebody. Is it a boy?"

Kezia looked down, hands clenched between her knees.

"Do you mean, you and Nate?"

Through her shock came a stab of pleasure. So she had made it, free of Toothaker Harbor after all.

"Well, now. Let me think." He smoothed a space in the sand by his knee. "Take myself, only lesson I can draw from is me. Others be what they be. But I never loved Clara just because she loved me. Hadn't to do with whether she loved me back. Loved her just because she was Clara. Didn't matter who she was, from where. Could have been a stone, and loved her still."

"You mean, like the way I loved the Witness Tree? It didn't love me back, it was just there. But I loved it and now it's gone."

"Something like that. So you see—do you? Wouldn't matter where they were from." His split, blackened fingernail traced a circle in the sand.

"Gran'sir..." Her voice stole forward, shy. "Did you ever love someone—from the Point?"

"Nope. But your father did. And that's all I'm going to say about that there." His hands were deep in his pants pockets. Kezia could see the fists round and taut through gray wool.

She felt a deep elation inside. Something rose up in her, ready to take off against the wind.

"Feel that wind," Gran'sir said. "Huh. Don't get a moment's peace. Wind's howling and tearing and never letting up: spring, summer, fall, winter."

"Wind? That's Aguahega." *Island wind*, unlike any other kind. Not something that came and went but a continuous presence, a permanent force. "You've been listening to it for a lot of years."

"That's it. Too long maybe. I think the wind's got into my head."

It was late afternoon when they returned, Kezia streaked with mud and lobster juice. As they passed the old fish shack, its globe of shark oil still hanging above the door, Gran'sir hesitated. "You trot on. I'll catch up. Work to do."

Work? But he didn't seem to do any work anymore.

Kezia sat by the water, arms around her knees, waiting for him to emerge.

She watched the two strangers who were her sisters beyond the Vannah house. Deenie was running zig-zag along the shore, darker than the other Beals, brown hair and eyes snapping hazel light. Suddenly digging her toes into warm-wet tidal mud she arched her back, shouting at the passing day. She saw Kezia watching her. Embarrassed, she threw a shell into the air. A curtain of gulls rose as Victorine, arms wide in mock menace, pursued Deenie, long beautiful legs flashing under khaki cuffs of bermuda shorts. Kezia watched their back-and-forth flight, all carefully away from her, around the shore.

Now Kezia was alone.

Deenie seemed to know nothing of the bite and hurt of being a child. Her world was blue sky cupped close, her happiness the water lapping on sun-dried sea legs, her eye finding a coral glint within a shell.

Kezia felt the observer in her push forward.

Sea, sun, salt, wind—as though that were enough to fill a world. She who builds sandcastles all day would live to see them crumble and empty of her crab friends.

The fish shack door was still closed.

Kezia walked over and peered through one of the two high small windows, cloudy with dirt.

Gooden Beal was listening for the wind.

His hand went to the back of his weathered neck, rubbing the loose folds. He crossed to the cabinet, stopped abruptly in front of it.

His hand went out, feeling for the fallen knothole, great splayed fingers searching for the stray bit of damp sea air.

He stuffed a rag in the knothole, removed a half-empty bottle from the cabinet. With a grunt he sat down on the single wooden chair, tilting the bottle in the crook of his elbow. The pops and gurgles of the liquid were the only sound except for the wind.

Gooden wiped his lips on his sleeve. He pulled the rickety little table, the chair to the middle of the room, meticulously positioning, repositioning them into the exact center of the space. His hand reached out for the bottle again.

Wind, wind. Always wind.

He listened now, eyes straining to pierce the gloom of the unlighted shack. He felt the silvery bristly hairs on the back of his neck rise. His lungs labored for breath.

There it was again. The wind. Stronger now. He felt it swooping down from the silence where it had swirled without direction, could sense it settling about the shack. It set its shoulder to the wood frame, testing the strength of the boards. The whiskey bottles rattled in their jerrybuilt cabinet.

He cringed, hands balling with fright.

But the shack was strong. He listened to the wind slack off again, breath trembling out into the air. His hand reached again for the bottle.

The wind howled suddenly, furiously—a tattering sound. He drew his hand back from the bottle as if stung.

Into bits. That was the kind of sound it had been. Into bits. Then they began to come into the shack. A crack. A knothole. Crumbling clamshell mortar he had never repaired. Little writhing lines of wind curling about the floor, spiraling toward the ceiling to die in stilled movement there.

But more waited to replace them, crowding outside.

He felt the chill of their breath. He drew up his legs as a cold draft brushed his feet. Behind him was a clicking sound.

A jagged crack in the wall let the wind through. The clicking sound rose higher, to desperation as he watched what the wind was doing. Set precariously on the windowsill Clara Beal's picture danced in its frame.

Rocking, teetering, the wind had set her to jigging as she had never done in life.

Don't dream about cabbages. Don't wash new clothes before you wear them. Never, never kill a toad.

The tarnished gilt frame tapped against the wood. His breath sighed out in little gasps. Why didn't the picture fall over? The grim-faced lady jigged defiantly on and on.

Suddenly he rose, looking wildly about. He pulled at his clothes, the old gray sweater, patched shirt beneath. He clawed, ripped them, stuffing the shreds into the cracks. He lined the door and the jagged window crack, he filled the knotholes and the unmet corners.

The picture had stilled, Clara ceased to dance.

The wind had stilled.

Gooden Beal sat down in his chair, trembling. He reached out for the bottle but his hand felt all pins and needles, the whole of his left side as if encased in an elastic bandage. The bottle knocked over, lay balanced on its side on the edge of the table.

He listened to the spatter of whiskey falling to the floor, then the gentle drip, drip.

He put his head down on the table, on the fish oil and the gray tufts of mold that grew there.

He hadn't killed a toad: still things had happened as they had.

He listened to his tears dripping with the whiskey.

"Kezia." It was Nate's voice. "What're you doing?"

She turned away from the window, trying to hide the fear on her face. It was the park, she thought, threatening Gran'sir's home, the park that was ruining everything.

"We got to plan what we're doing on the Fourth."

She looked up at Nate as his arm went around her. "I plan to kill the park," she said.

CHAPTER 23

In the clear windy space of the lambkill-grown Commons, Kezia and Nate Vannah lay flat on their bellies, fingers searching for the tiny tart-sweet strawberries among the grass and granite. Clinging flecks of earth fell warm and sweet, indistinguishable from the fruit on Kezia's tongue.

The Fourth of July had arrived, continued all night long. Of all the holidays Aguahega made a specialty of celebrating the Fourth. Kezia had stuffed herself at the church pancake breakfast, watched the parade of "horribles" through the village, around the schoolhouse at noon. She had overeaten again at the traditional dinner: a thirty pound salmon pink among the green peas, the yellow-white of egg gravy served in the Vannahs' house.

Kezia hated to break the silence. It would only mean she would now have to tell Nate. She couldn't continue to be with him as if there were an understanding, as if they were in love. She loved somebody else.

The full white moonlight winked up at her from below, where it reflected a vein of quartz among the chunks of granite blasted free the day before. Kezia stared down the slope at the roughed-in stretch of what would become the park's ocean view road. The smoothed earth was raw and black in the moonlight, stitched on each side with surveyed-straight white stakes. The backhoe sat abandoned on its three-foot-high tires, the jaws of its scoop laid on the earth like a sleeping dog.

"Give a listen to that racket, willya?" Nate rolled on his back, wriggling his knotty body down among the tussocks of grass. "Keep those Seal Point basters up and blear eyed all night. Go to it, gun it, guys!" From Aguahega's northern end the wilder locals hotrodded up and down the one-lane road, dragging behind their bumpers the exploding music of corroded boilers, a hayrake, a bathtub. Car radios blared, and every five minutes someone paused to yank the church bell.

Now, louder than a hundred sunset guns the "shriekers" went off, and the rockets: angry sizzlings of suspense followed by *whumps* that vibrated inside her chest. Chrysanthemums of yellow, white, red blossomed across the night sky.

Beside her Nate sat up, wiping his sticky fingers down the legs of his pants. "Let's get us to the fun. See any guard down there—nope? Neither do I."

Later, Kezia thought. She could always tell him she loved someone else, later. Tell him she still liked him as a friend, that he meant more to her than anyone else but it just wasn't love. She could always tell him that—later.

"Do you think we really should?"

"What? Give over. You saying that and yesterday it was 'let's heist the peapod to the schoolhouse roof.' You going chicken on me?" His blue eyes, pale beneath half-lowered lids, looked out at her from the sun-burned dark of his face. "Hell's bells, this is what the Fourth's for."

"Not scared! It's just—Chance would kill me if he knew about this. Last year someone actually, he said, did something, *you* know, in their well."

The rough burst of Nate's laughter was warm near her cheek. "No kidding? Dumped a load?"

She nodded.

"Well, Chance ain't here. And all I hear you yammer about these days is that bird-brained business and that summercator."

Kezia saw his mouth fumbling through the air toward hers. She struggled to her feet and his broad hot hand dragged reluctantly down off her arm.

"You still care for me, don't you, Keezie?"

She looked away, felt her head nod. "Last one down the hill's a rotten bum!" She ran through the wind, stumbling and jumping over rocks down to the raw slash of the park's new road. She bent over and began yanking at the first of the survey stakes.

It resisted her, rooted as a carrot, pointed and long, and then suddenly heaved free—black earth staining the white paint—and she toppled over backward. She shrieked and then laughed, staring up at the cupping night sky, and felt something surge wild and free and exhilarated within her. "Come on, Nate! It's the Fourth! The Fourth of July."

As he pulled her up her arms went around his waist squeezing as hard as she could, and then she leaped away, arms out as she whirled dizzily around. His face flashed, still and watching, each time she turned.

"Come on!" She heard her voice high and shivery. "Are you scared? Scared of Seal Point? Let's tear up the whole darn park."

"Yee-haw." Nate bent over the next stake, tugging with both hands, working his way down the row like a gardener gone mad. He straightened, flinging the stakes into the dense spruce woods, and saw what she was doing. "Keezie. Better not."

Her body moved nimbly up into the cab of the backhoe. The motor coughed, died, then ignited like an awakening giant, shattering the air.

"Keezie—" She saw the fear move over his face like a shadow in the moonlight, then vanish as he blinked.

"A machine's got no feelings," she said. "Come on. It's okay to kill a machine."

"What are you fixing to do?"

"If you don't kill one of theirs, they'll kill both of yours."

His weight sagged the cracked leather of the seat beside her. She released the clutch, driving the backhoe over the line of stakes. Down to the end and back up again, smashing the wooden markers, and then the drop-off, just a few feet deep but black with shadow, was suddenly there.

"Nate, jump!"

They leaped free, one from each side. Kezia felt her breath slammed out of her as the ground came up to meet her. She stared. The backhoe's giant wheels were upending, grinding forward, and then the front hood slipped down in the depression and struck. The sound was like an explosion. The backhoe quivered like a gut-shot deer and toppled over on its side. The giant tires spun.

The engine roared.

She felt the same constricting terror, the aching paralysis that had seized her in the Stanhope restroom where all the girls were playing cards. Her fingers, organisms on their own, engulfed the forbidden Pall Mall that thrust at her like a question mark from the circling pack.

The backhoe screamed, a dinosaur mired in tar. Nate slowly got to his knees, then his feet. He limped over to the backhoe and Kezia heard the engine suddenly die.

At Stanhope, afterward, Dean Flacke discovered the mayonnaise lid among the damp paper towels in the trashcan. She had counted the number of cigarette burns to see how many criminals had participated—brandishing the black-pocked lid in the auditorium (glass roof repaired), while lecturing on values and character, obedience and sin. But no one broke; no one told. Nothing had happened then. Nothing would now.

Kezia saw the axe some workman had left lying in the dirt. She hefted its weight by the handle, then started up the hill where the bronze-fronted wooden plaque loomed a black rectangle above the overgrown grass.

"Keezie—you're not!"

"I am."

"Don't believe it, I don't."

"You soon will." She walked around to face the sign whose incised letters in the shine of moonlight on metal read:

> IN HONOR OF
> FAIRFIELD C. CHANCELLOR
> father of Norumbega National Park
> who labored half a century to

> protect and preserve the wonders of
> this unique geological area for all time.
> Dedicated September 4, 1952.

The weight of the hatchet lifted, suddenly soared high past her head. The jar of metal against wood shook upward through her palms to her shoulders and the sound was a thunderclap, splitting the sky. Shocked, Kezia saw the chipped blade buried deep in the sign's round wood base. She lugged it back out and began chopping, widening the pale triangular gash.

"Chop that devil down," Nate encouraged. "Oh baby, sweet baby, chop it down."

Her foot came up on the side of the plaque, pushing to break through the last half-inch of wood. With a splitting, protesting creak it sagged over and Nate's hands tore it loose.

"What stinks and's got one eye?" Kezia shrieked.

Down the hill was an outhouse, a sieve of knothole-fallen boards silver gray with age. It stood near a lilac filled depression where once a farmhouse had stood. Holding the prize aloft, Nate and Kezia ran down the hill. In the outhouse Kezia pulled up the lid of the seat and shone her flashlight down. Horrifying depths, unimaginable browns dotted with toilet paper grays.

She hesitated a minute. And then she pressed the plaque sideways through the hole. There was a second of silence, and then a flat, very final receiving *slap*.

They burst back out from the cover of the trees, began running along the smoothed dirt of the road. Suddenly Kezia froze.

Silhouetted in utter blackness on the top of the hill stood a man and woman, peering down.

The sound of a voice cut into her: "Kezia? Is that you?"

Chance came slowly down the hill, his face dark, a blur. And then she felt his long fingers, and pain, as he seized her by the wrist. The axe dropped from her grip. She looked back up the hill. The girl had come partway down. It was Helen Hanft.

Chance's hand held her arm as tightly as a leather jess. "You were going to stay with Bandit tonight. Or so you said."

Shame burned through her head. "I hooded her. She went right off to sleep. So I thought I'd just—"

"Just what? Destroy Grandfather's plaque?"

"I just—"

"I heard you chopping it down."

"We cannot tell a lie," Nate said. "If you're referring to a certain cherry tree, why, yessir, we chopped it down."

Chance turned to stare at Nate and then Kezia felt his gaze, leaden, walled from feeling, back on her face.

Nate stirred. "Leggo of her arm, you don't mind."

"It's all right, Nate."

The girl on the hill was silent. Her tanned face blazed blue and then green as the rocket flared.

"What did you two do with that plaque? It's government property, you know."

Now he was talking like a lawyer. Kezia turned, looking back toward the outhouse half-hidden in the woods.

"In the woods? Maybe we can put it back up again."

"Not actually *in* the woods," Kezia began.

"Down the toidy!" Nate said. "Down the tube, the rabbit hole, down the ole outhouse drain. Kerplunk. But hey, we didn't mean to scrape your scab. No getting that thing back out now anyway. What's done's done, right? It's the Fourth of July."

Chance looked at Kezia "I thought I could trust you."

Tears stung in her eyes and suddenly she twisted her arm up, hurtingly around in his grip, and then jerked free. The air between them was harsh and angry. "Leave me alone, Fairfield the Next. Go on. She's waiting up there."

Chance turned away from her and started slowly back up the hill.

"It's the Fourth of July!" Her voice was thorns in her throat. "This is Aguahega, not New York!"

Why had she said it? The words rang in her ears. You never think, you just do. She would say she was sorry, she would—

"Chance!"

Without turning to look at her he walked faster. He raised his hand, its back to her, fingers spread as if to ward her off.

In the silence it seemed she could hear Dean Flacke's voice: " 'For one sweet grape, who will the vine destroy?' "

After a time Nate reached for Kezia's hand. He drew her over toward the edge of the strawberry patch where they had lain before, within the welcoming shadow of the trees. "Think we need a drink. How about it?"

She sank to her knees and took the washed-clean Clorox jug. She chugged down a mouthful of vodka and grape juice and lemonade. She grimaced. "Well. It's not Champagne Carlton."

"What's that?"

"Sparkling wine and raspberry puree. Do you think we'll be arrested?"

"Naw. You kidding? That turkey's so special noble he'd kiss a robber—thank you!—on the lips. Probably go for it, too. Not quite straight, I heard. Anyway, he's gone now, left awful quick, you notice? Like he got the trots. Tell you, it doesn't make any odds. No one looks rich with their ass stretched over the hole."

Had Nate always talked like this? The jug leaked, dripping over her chin, but the pit of her stomach felt warm and safe now. They were hidden in the black spill of the shadows where no one could see. She remembered that she had planned to tell Nate tonight they couldn't see each other anymore.

Now Nate was all she had.

She lay on her back amid the strawberries, searching for a feeling of romance.

"He has the rag on. That's all. Permanent case. All the summercators do."

She sat up on her elbows. "Nate Vannah, can't you say anything nice for a change?"

"Like what?"

"Everybody has some good in him. I saw that movie *The Razor's Edge*. The man was in the Swiss Alps, inspired by the sunrise and his closeness to God. And there're all the kind people and the great—Buddha, Christ, Abraham Lincoln. Where does that come from? Is it just because we're smart? Yet how did it develop along the evolutionary scale? There's nothing like it anywhere else, except small dabs in some pets."

"What are you talking about?"

"Do we have some sort of intrinsic response to basic truths like Beauty, Truth, and Goodness? How did it get there?"

"You're crazy as a fly in a bass drum."

Kezia was silent. She was remembering in class at Stanhope, leaning across the aisle, trying to make friends:

"Do you like that writer, ah, Kay-mus?"

"Whaaat? Boy, you talk funny! Where are you from?"

"Maine. But do you like him. Kay-mus?"

"Who?"

"Kay-mus. The writer of that book you've got there."

"Do you mean...Albare Ca-moo?"

Now, in the meadow, Kezia hated herself. Now she was like that ritchbitch, snobbery looking out of her eyes. "I didn't mean to sound pretentious, Nate. I was just wondering about things. I mean, you believe in a basic truth about something, don't you?"

"At Thanksgiving Reverend Witney said, 'The greatest thing upon earth is man's love for woman.' That's what I think."

"The greatest thing is to forgive someone. That's why I don't like dogs. Dogs don't forgive. If you accidentally step on their tail they're pissed for hours. But cats don't blame you. They know you didn't mean it personally."

"Yeah, they're too dumb."

"That's not it. At all."

He rolled nearer her, on his stomach. "I want to kiss you, Keez. But I've got a cold."

She laughed, drank again long and hard from the jug. "Well, if you've got a cold...." She watched his face sag.

"Dad's got it too, he got it first. Mom's been sleeping in the spare room—did you notice?—for a week now."

"They're not in love then."

"Says who?"

"Love means a great possessive affection for the idea of catching someone's cold."

Misunderstanding, his breath burst out in a rush of relief. Quickly he was on top of her, his mouth hard and familiar on hers. She felt the quick surge of passion, the desperate rush of her blood. Closeness, pressure, warmth: last summer it had almost been enough, grinding around, against each other, mouths starved and seeking, his fingers moving only so far as to unbutton her blouse.

Now it was no longer enough.

She burrowed her head under his chin. The warmth cupped the top of her head, her back and shoulders, pressed her arms and legs. A heart thundered down on hers. He smelled of gasoline and fish and she pulled each breath in, holding it hard and soft, sweet and sour, tasting it on her tongue, as happy as she had ever been.

She felt something hot and rigid spear against her belly.

She turned her face to meet him, drove her mouth up to the wet hotness of his mouth.

He pulled back. His eyes swam into focus. They were pale, washed-out denim blue eyes.

The warmth. She wanted the blood warmth again. She felt as if she were underwater–her arms and legs of their own accord floated out.

She could see the question, anxious and insistent, afraid to take advantage on his face. She felt as safe as she had ever felt.

"You look like a little girl that wants to get ravished."

Nate lay between her legs which were spread apart in bermuda shorts. When she felt his erection through his pants, when it probed for the first time against her shorts-covered crotch she thought she was going to faint.

Suddenly he pulled himself up, away from her. "Kezia." He never called her Kezia.

The silence circled around them.

"Kezia, please. Let me take off your clothes."

She lay as if frozen. She and Brantley had read *Peyton Place* aloud to each other, giggling wildly. "Anything," Constance kept saying in the book. "Anything. Anything." Kezia remembered her own voice, afraid to know (and to not know) in the dark: "Brantley? Just what do you think she meant by 'anything'?"

"*Anything.* He could do anything to her and she would like it."

"Yeah, but what anything? What exactly?"

"If you don't know, I'm not telling!"

Even then Brantley knew.

Aunt Willi knew. Everyone in the world knew, except her.

Nate's fingers undid the buttons on her blouse, unsnapping the white cotton bra, and as her breasts moved into his palms, he groaned.

She lay still and realized she had to do nothing, nothing at all. It would happen to her, all of it and she would have no responsibility in any of it. It was almost as if she wasn't here.

Nate's fingers moved trembling down onto the back of her shorts, searching, fumbling for the closure, then around to the side where the zipper still wasn't, then to the other side, yes, it was *there*.

Suddenly she lay in the too cool air wearing nothing but her white cotton underpants. All passion had vanished: she felt far away, removed from herself. She remembered reading the magazine in Stanhope's library, looking at the Keepsake diamond ad: a boy and girl lying in a field of flowers. Someone had drawn above the girl's mouth a balloon. "Fuck me, baby," it read.

"Kezia, please," Nate said. "Take them off."

Her white cotton underpants that still, humiliatingly, said "Carters 12-year-old" on the faded label.

Struggling, she half sat up. "I don't want to take them off."

"Why not?"

"Not unless we're going to do It." But why? she thought. Why that? Because she didn't want to reveal herself in all her swampy nakedness? Because he would find her repulsive and hate her? But if they were going to do It you had to take off your clothes.

"Please, Keez. Take them off. Let me take them off." His blunt-fingered hands were on her abdomen now and she felt the quivering of his fingers, his knee pressed into her side. "Oh God Keez please."

"I can't! Not unless we're going to, Nate."

He sat up huddling away in an arc from her body, his hands over his head, head bending down into the grass. His voice pumped out, "I. Don't. Want. To have. A child."

She knew her body would not betray her. It would know that it must not get pregnant and ruin its own life, and therefore she placed her trust in her own body, her mind armored by fear. The egg in her body was like a dodgem car. It could dodge the invading sperm.

"It's just before my period, Nate. It's safe."

"It's never completely safe."

She sat up, embarrassment drowning her, fingers feeling nervelessly for her bermuda shorts. She struggled into them, then the blouse. His eyes wouldn't meet hers. He lay on his back in the grass. She could see the bulge of his erection through his pants. He was afraid, she thought. He didn't dare. She hated the fear in him. He was supposed to take care of her, know what to do, ease *her* fear. Or perhaps he just didn't find her attractive.

"You know, Keez. There's more to it. I think the man should be pure on his wedding night, just like the wife."

"Too bad. The color of your hair just matches my Aston Martin."

He sat up, a frown on his face. "You're full of weasel juice tonight."

"Well. I don't think that. What you said."

"What do you think?"

"If I finish college without meeting anyone I love, then I'll go to Europe. After that, I'll come back to the U.S. and become the mistress of some comfortably well-off man."

"I've got to ask you something." Nate's voice was high.

Kezia felt a sinking nauseous drop, without gravity.

"You've been acting all summer like maybe you don't want to go out with me anymore."

"You know I care. You're the only one who knows how much you've meant to me. But I've, I guess I have always considered you more like a friend."

His eyes beneath the foldless lids stared at her. Tears formed at the edges of his lids. "Well, I've always considered you a friend. More, too, but against my principles to get serious. Remember I asked you last summer if you believed in going steady. I said then I didn't, if you remember."

"I remember."

"Is it someone else? Is it—"

"*No.* Please Nate. I feel sick all of a sudden. And anyway, I don't know what love is."

"I know what it is."

"What, then?"

"Like what my grandparents had. Married fifty years, and they were sitting playing Clue when Grandpop had a heart attack and just fell over dead on the table. Grandmom told me about it. She said to him, 'Earl, is you a-dyin'?' On their fiftieth anniversary they both said would've done it over again."

"Maybe they were secretly unhappy." Kezia ate a tiny strawberry, cutting it with her teeth into many even tinier parts.

"Maybe they weren't."

"What is love?"

"Asked Grandpop once what love was really all about. He said 'Love is sacrificing. You get to love a person, you know you love them because of what you have sacrificed for them.' That's what he said."

"That doesn't sound like a very good answer."

"Someday you'll know, Keez. And maybe it could have been like my grandparents, you and me, if we hadn't felt more like we were friends."

Someone yanked the church bell's rope.

"We're missing Pogo," Kezia said. "Up in lights on a frame, Pogo playing in the 'World Serious,' that was the end of the fireworks show."

"You've grown right away from us," Nate said.

"I didn't want to."

"But where do you feel at home?"

"Nowhere anymore."

"Do you like that—Chance?"

The name spoken by someone else thrilled her, danced in her head like the blooms of the fireworks, hot and loud.

"Of course not, Nate."

He reached for her hands and she felt their warm rough surfaces, and suddenly she was crying.

"Just remember, Keez. What I told you last year. About the atomic war. If there is one, you stay put in New York, okay? We've got to get this straight. I'll come to get you. But you've got to stay there so I can find you."

"Oh Nate. There's no one like you." The tears ran over her cheeks, dripped off her jaw. His thumbs wiped clumsily under her eyes.

"And anyway," she said, "there's not going to be an atomic war."

"You just stay put in New Yorky York and wait for me. You acris-to-rat, you. Okay?"

"Okay, Nate."

She was looking up at the blank space between two stars. Was it true—there were dark stars? Could a person really be born under a dark star?

That night she dreamed of ice.

She was kneeling before the huge block of Alewife Pond ice, staring into its radiance, breathing in its cold. She looked for her face in the ice.

But it was ash, slate, varicose vein gray. Eyes bulged in clear blisters on either side. Rubbery lips grinned wide, a cave of teeth live as fire and black beyond.

The wolffish frozen in the ice stared back at her.

CHAPTER 24

Kezia's bare feet moved on the path that twisted away from the Vannahs' house, away from Toothaker Harbor, down the shore out of sight to Plummers Cove. It was nearly bottom of the tide: weed-mossed rocks and an old lobster pot lay exposed on the cove's mud floor.

Suddenly she wanted to slide into the water. She had never swum here, not knowing how to as a child. But she had learned in Manhattan's YWCA pool, counting laps down white-buoyed lanes through green chlorine that stung her eyes. When you sat up streaming and dangled your legs, chlorine mist settled on your shoulders, a strange warm dew. It was a good place to go when you had to cry.

Chlorine made your eyes red anyway.

Kezia looked south, counting the tide clock in her mind. There was still time for the tide to take her to Great Egg Rock, the steep hill of grasses and gulls from whom she'd once stolen eggs. When the tide turned she could follow it back in. She looked up at the sky: slow gathering clouds beyond the mountain ridge.

"Short warning, soon past,
long foretelling, long last."

But she'd be back safe on Aguahega by then.

She stripped off all her clothes. Her feet picked their way on the mudflat, the stones and shells sharp, and then she lowered herself into the bathwater-deep cove.

Cold. The water was never more than in the fifties, Chance had said. *Chance:* she didn't want to think about him again. She hadn't more than half a mile to swim.

The afternoon sun was good on her face as she moved into deeper water, settling into the only stroke she knew: sidestroke. The icy water hardened the points of her breasts, flowed between her scissoring legs. She felt her hair float behind her gauzy and free, her scalp tingling with salt. There was the tiniest thrill of fear: just enough to give it all an edge.

She could see a closed anemone like a fat orange attached to a blue mussel in the shallows nearer shore. The pointed beaks of the white barnacles were also closed, but they would part and the anemone too would bloom in welcome like an orange flower when the tide brought her back in.

She felt warmer now with the exercise. The shore widened, deepened, folded back into itself into Toothaker Harbor. Dark harbor, sailors called it. You could sail right by it and never see. It was what she wanted to do now. Within, she saw the white of Nate's moored lobsterboat, *her* lobsterboat, its name painted over from *Loara B.* to *Loara V.*

It was bad luck to change a boat's name.

In the sloping seaward side of Drown Boys Ledge, standing tall above the water now, she could see the black dike fissuring the granite, pointing its long finger in warning out to sea. The black was once-molten diabase, Chance had said.

It was bad luck to burn apple branches for firewood, she thought, just like Gran'sir. Bad luck to count the stars.

She could see the sign Beck Vannah had put up on his clam flats: YOU STAY OFF. But everything below the high water mark belonged to the government, Chance had said.

Never, never kill a toad.

She could see the osprey nest big as a boat in the dead spruce. Chance had caught Bandit there, soaked a rag in sulphur, dried it and lit it in a bee-smoker. It knocked her right out, he'd said. Then was the Wake: staying up three days and nights with Bandit on his arm until she gave up and went to sleep, accepting him, his arm as her perch. The idea is you both suffer, man and bird alike, he'd said.

Kezia straightened, trying to see higher from the water. She couldn't see any ospreys warming eggs above the nest.

She saw one flying and she turned in the water trying to follow the path of its flight. It veered and listed, a foundering sailboat in a storm.

Something was wrong; it was sick.

The hawk flew on, heading for the gray curtain of the sheer diorite cliffs fronting the southwestern shore. Kezia watched, waited for the turn that never came.

The osprey hit the cliff—a small brown and white object tumbling down to the surf-tossed rocks below. The wave rushed in; the hawk was gone.

Kezia's hand flailed back, reaching for something that wasn't there, striking something in the water where nothing should have been. She splashed, struggled half up. Through the brown blades of kelp buoyed up by their gas-filled bladders, she could see the sharp warning of the ledge. The water poured streaming over its mossy head, sucking her toward its teeth, churning the forest of kelp that tangled around her legs, wrapped her arms, struck her face.

No ledge should be there.

A dogfish darted and then another–dead eyes on her as they passed–and then another. They were small sharks, two and three feet long. She had always been afraid of them. They were harmless to humans, or was that wrong? She tried to remember. The waves were much higher now: how had they gotten so high?

She sank both hands into the furry brown-green slime to the rock beneath. She gulped a breath, her face plunged under and she heaved herself off and away. Her heart thundered in her ears as she stroked again and again, trying to keep her breaths deep and even until the kelp's brown glue grew thinner, a pale stain against the blue.

She tried to struggle higher, tried to see. Where was she? She was so tired. Shouldn't she be at Great Egg Rock by now?

She treaded water but the waves were higher, crashing again and again on top of her head.

But there it was: the familiar outline of Great Egg Rock, solid and safe, not so very far away.

But something had gone wrong, wrong.

She was looking at its eastern slope—a flat bulging boomerang shape. Not the high hill on the west that overlooked Aguahega, so near you could almost touch.

She had been swept around somehow to its far seaward side.

Another wave crashed down on her head. Kezia tried to raise her torso higher up in the water, to shake clear. She felt her lungs open, gasp like a beached fish in the wrong element for air.

Beyond the seaward edge was open sea, all the way to Portugal.

You've got to stay calm.

She choked, spitting water, hands clawing.

Please God you've got to stay calm.

She turned back on her side and swam as hard as she could, punishing long pulls with arms and legs. After a few minutes she raised her head: Great Egg Rock loomed closer, but she was farther still along its deadly eastern shore. A current, a tide rip—she didn't even know exactly what they were—some force stronger than she was pulling her inexorably east.

She swam now in full panic, flailing, thrashing. When she again raised her head she saw the jagged edge of Great Egg Rock, and beyond it framed between a lone pillar and the rock itself—the open sea.

The rock's safety was there, so close. She could almost touch the nesting gulls; she could smell the fishrot and painted rivulets of birdlime.

And still the water pulled her around, and away.

She rolled over and tried to pull directly across the current, her breath screaming in her lungs. But her legs felt weighted, clumsy, slow. She paused for a second and felt the current take her, sucking her away.

One moment her body had been hers, it had worked. Like clockwork, pulleys, spun wheels. Now it was gone, stopped, out of control. It would not answer her. She felt its center fade, pass from her into the sea.

The wind poured cold around her head.

The water was thick and cold, wrapping her, tugging her like kelp from a rock. It pulled her around—she stared up at the lone pillar—and past Great Egg Rock and out to sea.

Her head struck something. The sound shattered endless as a bell's vibration down through her legs. She blinked: behind her now danced the paint-faded colors of a wooden lobster buoy bobbing safe, impervious above the waterline.

Her hands lunged for it, a cry tore from her mouth.

The slime of kelp and algae wiped onto her fingers struggling to clutch the straining potwarp beneath. The tension of the ballasted trap far below vibrated up into her palms. Her weight submerged the buoy and she sank on top of it completely beneath the water, struggled up again gasping, feeling it slip from her grasp as she rose.

The potwarp was held up from tangling by a bobber, a corked dark green bottle buoyant by her face. She grabbed for the buoy again, pulled it to her; she had it, safe. But her feet were swinging around with the current and she felt its mouth along her body, eager for the open sea.

She looked: there was nothing that way to stop her. The waves were already higher than her head. She hugged the buoy's cedar block beneath her chin. It smelled wonderfully of land, splintery and woody. She tasted it: it tasted of the sea.

She put her head back and screamed for help, again and again.

Far away on the black rampart of Aguahega she thought she saw a figure in the bright yellow of oilclothes. Did it wave back? See her? Hear her cry?

Fast-gathering clouds were massing, yellow-streaked and gray, above the mountain.

Rain began to fall, each drop striking her with a separate hammer of cold. She squinted up at the cliffs.

After a time she felt the cold sink in. She was shivering, shivering. Her teeth chattered, her muscles tensed and hard. Her throat was raw from screaming but no one cared. She concentrated on her fingers wrapped one by one around the buoy. They must not let go. But they looked like sticks, purple, unattached, unresponsive to her will.

The thick cold climbed her legs. Her feet had disappeared. She felt all of her a hollow tunnel up which the cold grew. Her thoughts, then her fear began to slow. She felt almost warm now, comforted. She could just let go.

It was so simple. It would be too bad not to do the things she had wanted to. She should have told her mother she loved her when she had the chance.

But now that was all past, a distant graveyard, requiem of the winds.

The stiffening in her neck loosened. Her head sagged forward soft as a scaregull, and down.

Water poured in at her nose.

Coughing she fought her head higher, felt the stomach acids rise bitter in the salt water in her mouth.

I don't want to die.

But it would be so easy. Let her fingers pick themselves up one by one off the buoy, just let go.

Her head was solid, a stone. Around it dragged an irritating sound: *swish, swish,* like "mares tails" through the sky, the thin streaky clouds foretelling storm. *Swish, swish*—the "white horses," Gran'sir called them, of the waves. It wasn't until New York and books that Kezia knew it was from a poem by Shelley: "Now the wild white horses play, champ and chafe and toss in the spray..."

Water swished in her ears with the sound of hairs, dragging now harshly like the sound of the tide on a smooth beach; a sound like brushed hair, full of static and cling. And when the waves washed back out you could see them there: brushed marks in the mud, imprint of a giant's broomstraws on the beach....

The roar that was the lobsterboat was almost on her before she saw it.

Was it him, coming to kill her father again?

Her lips puffed but were unable to make a sound.

Hands anchored in her armpits, dragging her up. Hooked but not caught, she felt herself slipping back in.

Now she was grabbed anew, dragged higher, the coaming scrape-bump-scrape on her chest, rain falling on her back. With a heave the coaming passed her thighs, knees, finally toes.

She was born again, slipping out of the envelope of the water.

Somehow she lay on the vibrating heartbeat of a boat's damp deck.

She heard her own cry.

The dark within closed on the dim gray daylight like a shutting mouth. She breathed a rush of gasoline smell. She felt the pile of rags under her and the hands—wonderful hot heavy hands—touched her cold face and her ice shoulders, rubbed her hands. A rag, oily smelling, was scrubbing futilely against her cold wet body, a body that belonged to someone else. The rag's hard tight-woven surface couldn't make her warm or dry.

"Keezie! Snap out of it!"

She was in the cramped cuddy of a lobsterboat. She heard a zipper and the crash of a belt buckle, a curse and the thud of boots: one, two. And then wonderful hot naked skin as bare arms and legs wrapped around her. A thin rough covering lay over them both. She crawled blindly toward the warm belly, felt the hot solar plexus beating its warmth into her. She needed it closer, warmer—

"Keezie, stop struggling. Lay still now. Like a damn fish on a hook."

The warmth beneath the blanket bloomed.

After a long time her squeezed shut eyes opened.

They looked into the narrow blue eyes, bright beneath the sunburnt/white lines on his forehead, of Nate Vannah.

Her eyes asked the question.

"Going to be okay, Keezie. Just lay there now. Lay and get warm. Christ but you had me scared."

She didn't know she had slept until she woke.

A wedge of light in the cuddy door told her it was late afternoon. She turned her face: Nate was looking at her. His crewcut, clipped too short, seemed to draw all his features up in a question mark. In that long moment she felt something draw up in her, out to meet his eyes.

Something hard jutted between them, against her navel. A drop of moisture cooled against her skin.

"What were you about in that damfool water?" His voice was gruff.

"I was swimming."

"Swimming!"

As if tied to the rise in his voice, the thing against her belly grew longer, concertinaed out.

"I like to swim."

"Now where did you go and learn yourself to swim?"

"New York."

"They swim buck-naked in New York?"

Her eyes sank back closed and she giggled. She was so happy—being warm was everything.

She felt his lips graze—an accident?—against her cheek. She turned her face to meet him, her mouth hungry against his. A flash of desire passed through her.

The warmth. She wanted the blood heat again.

He pulled back, his eyes swimming into focus. She could see the question again, anxious and insistent, afraid to take advantage on his face.

But where her legs joined was a magnet, a heavy force that for the past few years had sent out invisible rays that grabbed her fingers, the heel of her foot, the book laid on her abdomen, the bicycle seat, the upward flare of the English saddle while cantering the Central Park trails. Pressure, heat, friction sweeping her into passion, a well that never ran dry. Every morning her body woke and seized her, first with pleasurable tension, tiny bursts of feeling that nibbled at the hollow ache, the torment to be pushed into, the ache to be filled.

"You look like a little girl that wants to get ravished." It was his joke; usually he smiled.

In her silence she saw the pupils flood his eyes into black. He looked like a stranger looking at her.

Last fall she and Brantley had written it down, a solemn pledge:

"I will not have intercourse for

a. fear of strangeness

b. fear of pregnancy

c. fear of change in me."

Brantley had done It anyway.

Kezia tried to struggle half up. She felt so weak she could hardly move. "I haven't...I never have."

His expression shattered into feeling, a rock in a pond.

"Lift up. Hitch your butt up there."

Obediently she raised and felt a hill of wadding, rags bunched up underneath from her waist to her hips. Was he expecting blood?

His face was clenched, eyes shut. His hand came up, groping blindly for her face. The ends of his fingers were rough and warm against her cheek.

Kezia felt the round hard smoothness press between her legs. She gasped. Her mouth opened, her legs opened, and the smell of gasoline stung in her nose and her mouth.

Brantley had looked at her tensely, confessing, "I did It."

Just as suddenly now she had done It too.

Nate's cry was still loud beside her ear.

She lay on her back, trying to still the gasping of her lungs. It was embarrassing now that he was through. He lay limp as if jointless beside her, eyes closed, moisture drying in those lines on his forehead. Lines? He was only 19. She stared with frank curiosity at the meeting of his furred thighs with the line of hairs down from his belly.

Nate was hard again, on top of her again, his thighs were between hers pressing hers apart. He was in her again. Afterward his face lay cradled against the side of her neck. She felt their fluids mingle, begin to flow.

She squirmed sideways to look: couldn't see any blood.

He was kissing her and nudging hard once more between her thighs. She looked up and he grinned, a simple sweet look full of pride.

"Not many as can do it three times, huh?"

The sum was three times already.

She imagined a future heavy with numbers, round with strings of zeroes; she imagined counting the number of times like this forever.

She felt tender and raw and like crying but she was afraid if she started she would never stop. Nate's mouth sagged open and he began to snore.

His body trembled. She watched it pass like a wave down his naked body, out to his twitching fingertips. Timidly she brought her palm up, stroked his back. It was rough, hilly with moles. The twitching strengthened under her fingers. Beneath the closed lids his eyes raced to follow an invisible tennis match back and forth, shuttling left, right. She rubbed his back harder, hoping to wake him, afraid to disturb him, this stranger whom she had known all her life.

His cry was loud—louder even than before. His head jerked, eyes opened, blinking at her through the run of sweat. His eyes stared in fear.

"Nate, what is it? A dream?"

His hand scraped across his eyes.

"Was it a nightmare?"

"They were after me, I was running. Up to the top of the mountain ridge. They kept on climbing and I couldn't get away. Trapped on here." His face flattened down against the dirty blue rag of a workshirt.

More than lobsters trapped on here. It was as clear as if her father had just spoken. "Nate, it's just a dream. Everyone gets them—bad dreams, nightmares. I have one, about a wolffish in Alewife."

"Apple-crapple. No wolffish in Alewife. Never was." He sat up, face calmer now. "We have a child, let's name it Torby. Okay?"

"We're not having a child."

"Well, just in case." His gaze traveled with shy, eager possessiveness over her naked body.

The covermark was all washed away. She turned her suddenly flaming face to the side, staring at the cobwebbed gray of the boards. She felt his fingers pry her own away, felt his fingertip touch where no one ever had, tracing the outline of the birthmark. It was harder to lose this virginity than the other.

"Damned if it doesn't look like a tattoo."

She looked at him, afraid.

"Like a tattoo of a beautiful rose."

Her fingers touched the white of his pulse under his sunburned chin, touched and held.

"You know, you raised quite a ruction," he said. "Out on the water, I mean."

"Did you hear me yelling?"

When he wasn't talking he let his mouth hang slightly open and he sucked in his lower lip now. "Was looking for you everywhere, trying to find you. You could of died, you know."

She kissed him.

"Trying to find you. You kept me busier than a one-armed paper-hanger with the hives."

She kissed him but this time he frowned.

"It's against the damn law, isn't it?"

"What?"

"Us. Brother and sis now."

Did that mean they would never do this again? She was startled to realize how much she wanted it again—now, tonight, tomorrow, always. But she didn't love Nate, except as a brother, did she?

It was Chance she loved.

Was she a tramp, then? Or did she just have normal animalistic tendencies? What would Brantley say?

"It's not," she heard herself blurt out. "Illegal. I don't think it is. You're only my stepbrother, right?"

"Dad said it would be against the law, you and me."

The noise of his bare feet struck the steps and he was out on deck, hauling up a bucket of water, spilling half of it, hauling again. She heard his knuckles bang against the tin. A grunt, tormented, angry as the water sluiced down his front.

It seemed she could hear Aunt Willi's voice. "You don't know your own wealth, niece of mine. You'll allow it. The all unraveling of your young grace. Just to please the moment and love. You won't even cry at the pain."

"Pain?"

"Of birthing a woman."

Kezia stared up at the planks above her head.

She could see his face now and something cold and frightening gripped her heart.

Chance.

Was it always going to be like this?

CHAPTER 25

"Never loved Clara just because she loved me. Hadn't to do with whether she loved me back. Could have been a stone, and loved her still."

So there should be nothing to forgive Chance for.

Kezia's feet slowed, then stopped. At the upper end of the Commons, the stony meadow where once all of Aguahega's sheep had grazed, she saw Chance standing with Bandit on his fist. Just in the past week Bandit had been climbing regularly to the glove, allowing herself to be carried outside four hours a day. She accepted Kezia's fingers stroking gently down her back, sliding over her breast between the powerful upper parts of her legs, where Kezia held the thudding heart as if in her hand, felt it slow and calm under her touch.

"I thought I could trust you," Chance had said.

Bandit hadn't belonged to both of them, Kezia thought. It was Chance who owned her just like the Chancellors owned Aguahega, gave it away so they could have their park.

Together she and Chance had weighed Bandit daily on the converted baby scales, his face grinning across at hers. She had written down the nearest quarter ounce in the tooled leather logbook, as well as the state of eyes and feathers, consistency and color of droppings while he consulted the experts in crumbling books of lore:

If your Hawk should be bit by a Mad Dog,
presently clip away the Feathers where
the wound is; and piss therein.

Now Chance thought *her* the Mad Dog. Uncontested cruelty, no visiting rights ever.

Chance set Bandit on a spruce stump and walked slowly away, paying out the fifty yards of *creance* as he went. Before he had a chance to turn, to try to get her to fly to him, she hopped down and with a ducklike sideways gait waddled after him.

Back on the stump; duck walking again.

Kezia heard the uncontrolled hoot of her laugh come pouring out.

Chance turned in her direction, watching as she trudged the long way across the grass. The familiar features of his face were stony, askew, different on the left than on the right.

"Hey, you guys," Kezia said. "Need an assistant?"

"We're looking for one named Red."

"Oh I know just the one. Devoted, professional, experienced even."

"But does she do windows?"

"If you promote her to friend."

"She's already a friend. The best of friends. You tell her that for me, okay?"

"Well—"

"She might not believe it if she heard it from me. See, I know that girl pretty well."

"But what about the Fourth?" She heard the tension stretch her voice.

"It didn't happen. It's forgotten."

"But—" She looked up into his face. She was relieved at what he said, and yet she knew deep inside that it could never be buried. "I want us to make it right."

"Today is today; we go on from here. Unless you're going to be too busy now, spending all your time with that boyfriend of yours."

She felt his gaze probe through her, the one person to whom she wanted to look good. He saw her lies, her birthmark, he saw her destroying the backhoe, he saw everything she wanted to hide. "What boyfriend?"

"That so-called member of the male species in whose company I found you two nights ago."

"That? That was just Nate."

"Funny, he speaks well of you." Chance lifted Bandit onto the buffalo glove, his arm stiff in an L-shape, and swung her around close to his face. "What do you think, bird? Is it Kezia loves Nate?"

Kezia held her breath. He reached his face toward Bandit's dark-masked head. His lips pressed against the muscular bulge of her chest, his nose fitting close in the curve of her throat, her sharp beak poised between his eyes which were closed.

"Just so afraid I'll lose her. She'll get loose somehow, after all our work, I'll leave the mews door open and her leash'll pull free. Or just at that moment, transferring her from perch to fist she'll pull away, get the jesses out of my hand. Sometimes I can't sleep at night thinking about it. How can they do that—I mean, after years of a hawk working with its partner? Do you think Bandit loves us, Red? Even a little?"

Like a stone, she thought, like the Witness Tree. Suddenly she felt older than Chance because she knew he didn't want to hear the truth.

"Of course she loves you." There was too much in her voice: she drowned it out with words. "Bandit didn't leave any chicks behind, did she? I mean, she doesn't have a mate?"

"You shouldn't have to ask a thing like that. I checked all that out. She's a passager, hatched last summer, hasn't moulted yet."

"There aren't any ospreys on the nest this year."

"Grandfather once told me he counted eighty-one nests."

"Where've they gone?"

"There was an eel grass plague in the twenties, left the bays bare of that green grass. The flounders vanished with the eel grass, and that was supposed to be the ospreys' main food. But I don't know. Neither does Grandfather."

"I saw one osprey, but it was sick. It died."

"Nobody knows."

Chance walked away and then turned, crying the falconer's call, waving a fish in the air.

On the stump Bandit paced back and forth and then was suddenly airborne, neck held low, boring in on Chance like a bomb to a target. Kezia saw Chance's look of elation wipe to fear. He suddenly broke, ducking as she dived at him, snatching the fish from his fingers as she passed. She flew over his sprawling form on the ground, and for one moment Kezia saw Bandit rise, gold eyes fixed on the horizon, her wings oaring their way toward freedom until the *creance* brought her down.

She fell, a brown and white struggle in the patchy hackmatack.

When they ran over Bandit was lying still, unhurt, a dazed look in her eyes. Kezia held her gently up against her chest. Sweat was running on her face and down clung to her hair, itching as it fell against her lips. "I didn't realize, not till right this minute, how much I love her."

Bandit's head cocked sideways, her eye observing the moon face of the human, her flat eardrum absorbing the sounds. Her beak opened and out came her unhawklike tiny chicken's chirp.

Chance was grinning wickedly down at her. "As much as you love Nate?"

She handed Bandit back to him. "I'm never going to fall in love. It's the worst thing in the world, Aunt Willi says. You want *him* to fall in love with you. Then you can wrap him around your finger. Otherwise he wraps you around his finger and he's just after sex, after all. If they're going to play, Aunt Willi says, make them pay. I'm not just saying this because it's the big, sophisticated act or anything. A sophisticated person doesn't fall in love." Her voice was too high, tremulous. "But I fall in love. I just don't want to get hurt."

"Are you free for dinner in Paris tomorrow? You and Nate, I mean?"

For the next four weeks they concentrated on Bandit's training, but for every step forward it seemed there were eight back. Entire days went by when Bandit appeared to forget not only her training but even the fact that these humans, boy and girl, were her friends. Once more, for Kezia the first time, they had to resort to the Wake.

The Wake was now two days old.

Kezia felt a hundred years old: tiredness had softened her spine, thickened her tongue. She didn't care about the goals of falconry anymore. The only thing left was not to admit defeat.

"Just a fast minute there, young lady."

It was her mother's voice in the Vannahs' kitchen, honed with its disciplinary edge. Kezia's hands froze over the thick layers of peanut butter she had just spread on eight slices of bread. The knife clattered back into the depths of the economy sized jar.

"I'm just fixing some breakfast—for Chance and me."

"At three A.M.?"

"We're hungry now."

"Kezia, don't lie to me. You didn't sleep in your bed last night."

Kezia turned to look at her mother. Why wasn't she feminine, like Aunt Willi? Why didn't she care about clothes? "I didn't *sleep* anywhere." Kezia opened the grape jelly jar. "That's the point of the Wake."

"What Wake?"

"The trainers stay up; the hawk stays up until he accepts your arm as his natural perch and so sleeps. And from your mutual suffering, a bond grows."

"Well, I thought you were going to spell each other off—you'd be sleeping in your room while he stayed awake. I thought that's what you said."

"No." Kezia spooned great gobs of purple jelly onto the peanut butter, the nauseous sinking feeling inside her spreading with every push of her knife.

"You mean you and Chance were up all last night in that cabin up there—alone together?"

"Mother, what are you getting so excited about?"

"You're fifteen. He's nineteen."

"So what?"

"You know what."

"How can you say that? How dare you say that! This has nothing to do with that!"

"Kezia, it only takes once, you know."

“What are you talking about?” Knowing full well, playing dumb, stalling for time. Could her mother have found out about her and Nate?

“Consequences, that’s what. It only takes once to get pregnant.”

Kezia stared at her, eyes dark with fear.

“I wasn’t going to mention this,” her mother said, “but now I think I better had. Your teacher at school sent me a letter.”

“A letter?”

“Miss Zielsdorf. She’s concerned about you, said perhaps a doctor’s visit was in order.”

“For what?”

“To test for pregnancy.”

Kezia felt all her thoughts fly out of her head.

“You wrote a story for class, she said, about a girl up a sycamore tree. She thinks about the thing growing inside her, whether she should just jump off.”

“Oh. Oh, that.”

“*That?* Are you worried, is uh, something on your mind?”

“That was the *point*. Of the story. It’s really a cancerous tumor but it’s described in such a way the reader can’t tell if it’s pregnancy or what. Aunt Willi says with either one you might as well be dead.”

Her mother’s fingers examined each of her knuckles as if to see whether they were still there. “Oh.”

Kezia piled lids on the four sandwiches, cut them hard, swiftly, slicing down to the board beneath.

“Well, I don’t want you spending another night out there with Chance, you hear?”

“You haven’t any right to tell me that!”

“I have a right to govern your behavior as long as you’re still living with me, Kezia Dorothy Beal. I don’t mean to sound harsh. You may have learned a different behavior in New York, but when you’re on here, what I say goes.”

It was unthinkable, it was monstrous, maybe other people but not her mother. And yet it had been true. “You and Beck Vannah! You were together and you weren’t married yet.”

“What are you talking about? Keep your voice down.”

“You did. I saw you, taking all those packages from Sears up to your room, never showing us what they were. I looked in your dresser drawer. They were under the big white underpants, the ones you used to wear. A black lace bra, thirty-six A, black bikini underpants."

Her mother's face softened; she almost smiled. "We were going to be married..."

"Why did you have to marry him?"

"Do you know what it's like to work in a cannery? Three kids to support. Even in your sleep hear the trucks going past bellies full of herring. Stand there all day while the belt rushes you, cut the fish in half, pack them in tins. Heads and guts back on the belt. Look down, see your face in the steel chop tray running with oil and blood."

"So it's true. You *did* sleep with him." Kezia looked at the kitchen doorway just as Beck Vannah walked through. She looked back at her mother: "You're not even blood kin."

"Of course I am." Loara's face was white.

"You're not. You only *married* into the Beals. You *remarried*."

"Kezia, your father died. Till death us do part."

"Daddy didn't die. To me."

"You can't get blood out of a turnip," Beck Vannah said, suddenly standing there. "And I think Kezia feels like a turnip right now."

Kezia picked up the sandwiches and bolted to freedom through the door.

Like a phantom in the cabin's candlelight, Kezia peered in at Chance and Bandit in the chair, its lap and broad armrests protected by a patched canvas sail. The thin green scarf was draped over Kezia's head, to keep her inadvertent eye-starings from the newly skittish Bandit to whom a stare was preliminary to attack. Chance's left arm lay on the armrest, the osprey's manacled legs bound in leather fastening it firmly to the human in the chair. Dirty sand crunched under Kezia's feet as she crept nearer, her senses fuzzed with tiredness, the hard stone of her consciousness receding in smaller and smaller circles, like ripples on a pond in reverse. She wondered how much longer she could really stay awake, and Chance, and Bandit too. Her eyes struggled to focus, streaming and smarting as if filled again with the YMCA pool's green chlorine.

Before her in the chair both pairs of eyes, man and hawk, were magically, finally closed.

Bandit slept.

Kezia felt her feet take root in the sand. Bandit had given in to the Wake, had accepted Chance's arm as her natural safe perch and so slept.

Kezia had missed the moment: like a baby's first step.

It was only two weeks later when Chance said, "It's time."

Kezia looked at the two-foot leash dangling free, unattached to Bandit, in his hand. Tears of fright stood in her eyes. "I don't know if Bandit's ready yet."

"She's ready."

"Then I don't know if I'm ready."

"Sure you are. Milestone Four: flying free. It's what we've been working for."

"What if she never comes back?"

"Then we've lost it all."

"How can you be so calm?" Kezia saw the osprey blur, felt the moisture well up just when she really wanted to look, to fix Bandit's image in her eyes.

"Take her up, Red. No different this time than all the others. The *creance*'ll still be there, just invisible this time."

He unsnapped the long line from Bandit's jesses which stirred free, moving in the wind. Kezia felt Chance's gaze on her. She took Bandit gently in her arms. The hawk stretched out the snakelike length of her neck, drew a strand of Kezia's hair like a feather that needed preening through her beak.

"Do something awful like shit on my arm. Why not? You do it every other day." Feathers clung to Kezia's damp hands.

Chance was whirling the lure, a leather pouch stuffed with sand and sewn to a fishtail, attached to a long line. Bandit watched intently: already she had flown to the lure many times.

"Okay, Red."

The gold of the osprey's eyes glared up at the unobstructed sky.

"Let her go, Red."

Kezia squeezed her eyes closed. She turned until she felt her face move squarely into the wind. It pressed her eyelids tighter, drying the tears. It was easier for birds to take off against the wind. Her arms sagged and then tossed the heavy weight upward, felt the wings catch hold, brush back once against her and then the weight was gone.

Kezia opened her eyes to see Bandit's long wings climbing the mountain of air. Behind her she heard the falconer's call as Chance whirled the lure two armslengths above his head.

Against the bright glare of sun the hawk's white belly was lost, outlines fading. Now she was just another small cloud in a sea of clouds. The bells on her legs tinkled faintly down the wind.

Kezia stared in the sky where Bandit had vanished. The loss filled her utterly, too great to comprehend. Her fingers tugged heavier downward by her sides. Every puff of wind teased her ears with a sound so faint, so not there she knew it was imagined, the sound of thinnest beaten metal Indian bells.

"Devoted to you," Chance said. "And then that day, the door left open, and she's just gone."

Kezia couldn't look at him. The grief was too large to share.

The sounds of the Commons, of the island swarmed up about her, drowning the ringing in her ears that mimicked bells. She heard the rote, the *kleew-kleew* of gulls, the sucking whisper of wind combing spruce, pine, balsam, a dog barking far away, a mechanical buzzsaw hum from Beck Vannahs' square white beehive at the far end of tangled grass. At the center boomed a vibration like a drum, and after a time she realized it was her heart.

The ringing in her ears slowly strengthened, competing with the bumble of the bees.

A swarm of bees in May
Is worth a load of hay,
A swarm of bees in June
Is worth a silver spoon,
A swarm of bees in July
Is not worth one bee.

Kezia heard shouting behind her.

Chance was pointing upward, and beyond the end of his finger she saw a distant familiar bent-winged shape, dark brown above and white below, sweeping toward them with the wind from the north. She watched as the ringing slid gradually apart into the sound of twin bells. The jesses on the tucked-up legs flared backward like another tail.

"Bandit."

She didn't know who had said it for at the same instant she and Chance were in each other's arms. His shirt was soaked with sweat, pressing through her own shirt into her skin. She felt his heat, boniness, the jointed length of his legs pressing through the warmth. He had been conditioning the leash with neatsfoot oil and his fingers on her arms were slick as water. His fingers came up, framed her face.

The oil felt hot as tears on her cheeks.

Now he would say it. He loved her; she knew he did.

But he tore free from her arms as Bandit swept closer, still hundreds of feet above their heads. He swung the lure wildly again and again. "She's ignoring it. Come on, Red. Run. She's heading for her old haunts at Toothaker."

Kezia's lungs heaved, unable to pull in breath. But at the sight before her at Toothaker Harbor she couldn't repress a smile. For the first time since Chance had captured her, Bandit was hunting, circling fifty feet above the harbor, studying the blue wash of waves for movement below. Tail spread, wings cupping, she stalled: then dropped like a puppet cut from a string. In a boil of spray the water closed over her, smoothed out.

Now Bandit flung upward from the water, wings pumping, talons gripping the struggling fish. Chance whirled the lure, calling his hoarse cry again and again. But Bandit flew outward, tracing along the shoreline, releasing one foot from the fish and turning it headfirst into the wind. She came to rest high up in a spruce that slanted precariously out over the water's edge, began to eat the fish unconcerned by the two humans who coaxed and swore below.

Finished she glided across to the water and flew low, swinging her legs forward and down, dragging them and the soiled jesses through the waves.

"Chance, we gave her a room. But look: she wanted a room with bath."

"What are you chortling about? We haven't caught up with her yet."

"But she's loving it—don't you see? The freedom—"

"Come on. Let's see if she'll come down to us now."

Bandit had returned to the spruce, sat some twenty feet above their heads. She held the wet laundry of her wings outstretched to sun and wind.

Chance edged nearer until he stood beneath the tree, leash ready in one hand.

Bandit roused her feathers, fluffing them outward with a vigorous shake. As Chance spun the lure below she annointed her beak in the oil gland at the base of her tail, began water-proofing her feathers again. Finally her eyes sank closed and her legs bent, locking the tendons that would hold her to the branch even in sleep.

Chance eased into the lower branches.

Bandit's yellow eyes opened, shut, opened again and peered down.

Chance's hand reached in a clumsy swift pass for the ends of the jesses. Bandit rose, wings spreading, feet pacing nervously back and forth.

Chance grabbed again. Now both jesses were securely threaded through the leash's swivel.

Bandit was strangely passive as Kezia's hands held her warm damp bulk against her stomach. Chance reached up with the hood and the osprey's head popped slyly now first to the left, then right. Then the hood was on, its plume of golden pheasant feathers waving above softest brown leather with two eyepieces of darkest blue, blind as the night.

Knights wooed with their falcons on their hand. The gift of a falcon was a pledge between high-born lovers. Perhaps someday, Kezia thought, Chance would give Bandit to her.

The head weighted by the hood dragged down upon Kezia's arm, the feathered crop bulging hard as stone now against her skin. A soft velvety croak came from the covered head.

"Well, we did it, huh?" Chance said. "She flew free just as we planned, and just for luck we tossed off Milestone Number Five, too. The first kill. We really did it, huh?"

"No. Bandit did it."

"Can't you let me enjoy this? We trained her, it worked. 'And thus I teach my haggard and unreclaimed reason to stoop into the lure of truth.' "

"Chance, I think she trained us." She wished he would tear his eyes from Bandit, look into her own. "Now you look sad."

"It was a dream, wasn't it, to do all this? But now we've done it. It's just that, I don't know, it's not really better or worse than I thought it would be."

"What is it, then?"

"It's just different." Dreaming of falling off into darkness and not feeling anything. "Do you know what I mean?"

She didn't but she said she did.

"Don't forget the Duck Drive," Kezia said. "They've changed the date again: now it's set for August seventh."

"Looking forward to it."

"And you know what? I'm to be Queen of Aguahega, just like you said. Beck Vannah's First Selectman, and Nate asked him to put in my name. Of course it's a primitive native spectacle, guts and gore. But you like slumming, right?"

"Nate again!"

Kezia smiled her Rita Hayworth smile. Sometimes when she lay on her bed in New York she would hold the mirror up like a lover bending over her, to see what it was that he would see and whether it might be acceptable. Something about falling back on the bed, hair spilling wide, mouth falling open, eyes long and mysterious in the half light that made her look almost (if she caked on enough dark red lipstick) like Rita.

"You'll never be hung for your beauty," Aunt Willi said.

Every girl is beautiful in white.

When he saw her, Queen of Aguahega, he would know she was the one.

CHAPTER 26

Eighteen boats waited offshore for the signal: to herd the eider, largest of North American ducks like cattle into the open-mouthed corral of Crotch Harbor. Twenty-eight islanders and their friends and relatives waited at the "crotch," and already the cookfires were glowing.

There were only three or four weeks when the eider were in the critical phase of summer molt, having lost all their black and white tuxedo finery, their flight feathers. Hundreds rafted up on the islets and dry ledges offshore, waiting in hoped-for obscurity: their eclipsed plumage, dusky gray-brown feathers unable to launch them into the air.

"Gooden, have you seen him, yes?" Clara Beal said. Her voice was worried, but everyone shook their heads.

Among the noisy laughing people Kezia stood silent, staring out at the narrow half-mile tongue of blue. It was the same harbor they had pulled out of after their nooning, just before Daddy was shot.

She had laughed, safe on *Loara B.* with her father. It was going to be the most wonderful summer of her life. The sound had carried high and clear over Crotch Harbor, back into the listening trees....

"Where can that old crock have got to?" Clara said.

Now the battered, many times repainted peapod slid its sixteen feet away from the northern bank.

"Hey you dorks," the Queen of Aguahega called from her commanding position on its front plank. "Do we need to bail?"

"Only when it fills with water!"—someone from back in the crowd.

Kezia's right hand held the first two fingers of her left.

Now the Town Clerk bellowed. "Ladeez, please, and gents all: the Queen of Aguahega!"

On the peapod Victorine raised her thin pale arm in a queenly wave.

Jealousy is the sister of love. Kezia felt nothing but keen cruel pain. Beck Vannah had put Kezia's name forward. But there were two other Selectmen, the Town Clerk, Treasurer, Tax Collector, School Board, Constable, Fire Chief, and Secretary of Civil Defense. And the Tax Collector had pointed it out: it wasn't right to have a Queen like Kezia, who was after all only a summer person now.

"Don't she look slick as a squid?" It was Beck Vannah's voice.

"She does." A sound of surprise. "A real 'island maid.' "

From Kezia's other side Chance's voice settled into the air. His words drifted visual as smoke in front of her eyes, the edges dissolving but the centers holding, floating still.

"She looks a lot better," Kezia said, "than she used to look."

The double-ended peapod's wake spread a darker sapphire on the glassy surface of the water as Victorine's two best friends rowed, one on each oar toward the mooring in the harbor's center. At their feet Kezia could see the tied brown heap of the "crocus" sack, within whose burlap prison lay the largest seaduck the men had been able to find.

Victorine lifted the grassed-up painter, tied it to the corroded iron ring. She stood up in the peapod now, balancing unsteadily, and looked back at the confusing mass of people ringing the shore.

Every girl is beautiful in white.

Kezia stared at her precious Saks Fifth Avenue white organdy dress. The wind plucked the skirt, buoyed outward like a sail by the three white crinolines and the wicked red one hidden underneath.

"Please, Keezie," Victorine had begged. "I don't have a white dress, you know that now."

The dress's sophistication was gone. Victorine's neck and wrist were circled with white plastic pop-it beads. On her blonde hair, made blonder by a bottle of peroxide over the kitchen sink, the traditional wreath of water lilies had slipped askew over one ear: creamy white flowers in five inch broad heart shaped leaves.

Victorine parted the neck of the sack and gingerly embraced the prisoner within. She held the four pound duck aloft, one hand at its legs and the other around its neck, holding the large strong bill away from her face. The eider looked comical, a shaved poodle. It had been plucked naked except for its wing and tail feathers: a tradition said to ensure a successful drive.

Victorine lifted the now struggling duck higher.

"Ho ro ru ra ree, 'h-Iar-Tir." Her voice carried thin and reedy on the wind. Where had the words come from, what did they mean? No one remembered anymore, except that the last word was Gaelic for "westland." It referred, some said, to a far-off Hebridean island, as far west as people could then go. Now they were here, at the edge of dawn, as far east as people could go.

The eider flailed against Victorine, slapping its wings, and then came an ugly burping sound. From under its tail flowed a sudden broad river of brown. On the shore Kezia stared in horror as the feces stained the white bodice with all the tiny covered buttons, and down over the billowing skirt.

As if in slow motion Victorine's face bulged in alarm, hands flying out, releasing the seaduck. It splashed into the water and dove, flying beneath the surface toward the far peopleless bank. Now her face contracted into a child's prewail grimace and she looked eighteen, and barely that, not Queen of Aguahega. The sounds, even titters, subsided as the crowd waited to see if she would cry.

"She's going to cry," Kezia said.

Victorine's face was flushed shiny pink, her dress striped brown. And then suddenly she leaped in one motion over the side of the rocking peapod. Kezia heard the dress catch, a long ripping tear. With a clumsy bobbing dogpaddle Victorine splashed toward the shore, her face brilliant red now as if fired by neon, the water lilies floating forgotten in their garland white against the blue.

She stood up on the cobble bottom, dress drenched now and tattered, the brown faded to a streak of yellow. She looked at the wall of faces.

Suddenly she laughed.

The crowd sighed—relief sucked in for a long second of sound.

And then everyone was laughing as Victorine waded ashore. Through the thin soaked organdy her body peered now in peach-colored patched, round windows of flesh. Through her bra her extravagant breasts, nipples large and brown, showed clear.

Feeling their gazes on her she suddenly ran, soaked shoes an impossible harassment and outgrowth of her pale body, flapping as she moved. All summer, Kezia thought, she had scarcely noticed her, this splashing child-woman in the sea. Victorine was older but this summer she had seemed younger, her words only the sketch of a woman, all naivete. New, waterlogged, she looked younger still, drawing away prickly from their adult thoughts. Narrow sparse knees pressed tightly together in agony of modesty as she ran, holding up her drenched skirt, shoes kicked off now and small pointed child-feet flashing.

Kezia felt a sudden chill surround her heart. It was like a tiny draft in a warm room, a movement so evanescent you wonder if it is there at all until suddenly you shiver and reach for a sweater. Now Chance was doing it again, sneaking small quick glances at Victorine.

He was not looking at the child.

He was staring at the dark nipples through soaked white cotton and something drew his nose out to a point. His mouth was cruel now in its line against his face, watching Victorine.

Kezia's face grew sharp, her eyes big. Pain flared in a trembling flush inside her chest. She stared out toward the open sea as if the horizon held some sight fantastic while Victorine scrambled up into Beck Vannah's pick-up truck. Kezia heard its motor start. Somewhere beyond a rifle shot reverberated: the start of the Duck Drive. The fishing boats swept into view in a V-formation toward the islet where the molting eider had been sighted.

"Around about eighteen-ten," Nate Vannah was saying to Chance, "took upwards of two thousand buggers in the Drive. Don't I mean. Back then sold a hundredweight of feathers every year and took what?, some six ducks, give or take two or three to make you a pound of feathers."

"Well, hell, Nate, no wonder there was only one pair of eider anyone could find fifty years ago."

Kezia rolled the sense of betrayal back and forth as if it were a ball.

"Feathers brought fifty cents a pound, back in Boston then. So they'd know if a son'd got serious about getting hitched up when he started saving feathers, like a hope chest." Nate's eyes sought Kezia's but she wouldn't meet his gaze.

" 'Hope is the thing with feathers...' " Chance said.

"What's that you said?"

Her hands were deep in her pockets. She could feel the seams at the bottoms start to give.

The noise of the boats droned closer. Kezia stared at the demilitarized zone between the turmoil of the darker, wind-whipped sea beyond, and the glassy paler surface of the harbor. Now she saw the small brown bodies begin to pop to the surface, dive with a quick neat crystalline splash and surface again farther in, hundreds of seaducks breaking now across Crotch Harbor.

"Hot devil dog," Nate said. "Won't be long now."

The boats plowed closer, an armada beyond the harbor and before their advance the panicked ducks plunged. At the land's end awaiting them the water lay hatched with grassed-up netting, a strange vegetation across the surface. The ducks dove and swam and now Kezia could see the powerful webbed feet and wings oaring like brown gleaming seals beneath the clear water, surfacing beneath the net sky and struggling there, imprisoned, flapping on the water.

Was it loving Bandit that had changed her? The sight brought not the simple anticipation, growling stomach it once had, but only the ache of tears behind her eyes.

Scores of ducks swarmed to the netting and then the nets were gathered, hauled with their pocket of squirming brown bodies up on the hard rock by the shore.

They were swung by the feet until their wild struggles lapsed into dizzy submission, then laid over two huge stumps dark with old blood. The axes fell, and headless the ducks jerked and some ran, blundering near the smallest children who answered with delighted horrified squeals.

Victorine, in dry pants and a shirt, was back.

The wall of corpses grew.

Like a savage, a painted squaw, Victorine sat cross-legged on the ground, plucking feathers two-handed until the air was a snowstorm of dusky brown, the ground heaped with drifts of mottled gray. She was laughing while the blood ran.

Now everyone took a duck, digging for the stiff sharp pin feathers with knives and tweezers, then dunking the whole bird in one of the vats of paraffin melted in boiling water, then in cold water to harden the paraffin. They stripped the wax off, taking with it the fuzz of downy feathers too small to be plucked.

The assembly line of older women removed entrails, quartered the meat, gentled its fishy tang by washing it in bowls of cheapest blue-red wine. Breasts, drumsticks, wings slid smoking across hot cast iron frypans, and soon there were platters of fried duck on the long trestle tables along with bread and butter, homemade pickles, and fifteen varieties of fruit and cream pies.

Victorine held central court under a tree, a paper plate in her lap, flirting with her boyfriend who would be moving away tomorrow, and even Beck Vannah and the other older men.

Kezia stared at the duck breast, bloody at the bone, that lay on her plate. Beside her at the table Chance gnawed at a drumstick, grease shining across his chin. He paused only to empty a glass of lemonade in uninterrupted swallows. He appeared to be having a great time.

"Aren't you hungry, Red? You haven't touched a thing."

"Only a place as benighted as Aguahega would permit something like this. It's cruel, sickening. It's barbarous—killing eider when they can't fly."

"Seaduck." He grinned at her. "Tastes good, though."

"Puts hair on your chest," Nate said.

"It's better in a stew, I think," Loara Vannah said. "Potatoes and onions cut that strong taste."

"Hey, Keezie," Vangie Carter called. "You must be proud, huh? Of your big sister?"

Kezia looked at her. What would Lady Flora say? "What's to be proud of? She'll just end up a bourgeois little housewife on Aguahega, crawling around the floor on all fours with a dustrag between her teeth."

Vangie sucked her protruding teeth with her tongue.

Nate laid down his drumstick. "Keez, what in the hell's got into you?"

They could hear Victorine's laughter sail silver from under the tree. She was looking up at her boyfriend, at something he had said. In her face were centuries of submission, pink tinted as an old photograph.

Chance was doing it again. Not Looking at Victorine, looking everywhere else, north, south, east, west, then a quick look, dead-centered through the heart.

"I just don't go for homecooking." Kezia pushed her plate away. "As Marie Antoinette said, 'Let them eat out.' "

Listening envy drops her snakes.

What was Victorine laughing at now?

Kezia felt her face tremble, as fragile, as little under control as a spilling pool of water.

Victorine's voice rang with triumph: "Get your cooties off of me!"

Kezia kept the surface of her face quiet. She had to.

There was a wolffish within.

The cry lay on the air like a blow. You couldn't remember hearing it start, just hearing it end.

Kezia turned toward it.

Grandm'am was running toward them, her hands reaching out, fingers spread. Her crown of bright dyed hair had slipped askew, her lace-up black shoes with the thick heels flinging mud.

"Gooden." She pointed back the way she had come.

Kezia felt her fingers go cold with dread.

At Goosegrass Cove she was afraid to look, but everything looked reassuringly normal. There on the mudflat lay Gran'sir's boat, name painted black across the stern: *Ye Gods Clara.*

He used it now just to tend his weir: it lay there innocently overturned. It was ten feet long and he had designed it himself before the arthritis got so bad, whittling the plan on countless blocks of cedar. He had built it himself of cedar, oak, and mahogany, drove in the copper screws. Now all he could do with his hands was paint it. Never did a boat see so many coats of paint.

But all was in order: nothing was wrong here. Kezia willed it so. He used the rising tide as they all did, to lift whatever couldn't be lifted: his boat. And then, after the tide had safely retreated he could come out and work on his boat. It lay ready now, bottom up, overturned. Ready to have its barnacles scraped, ready for a new coat of bottom paint.

But where was Gran'sir?

The tide had come back in—washing around the still overturned boat and a paintbrush that floated there.

Beck, Nate, Chance, and the other men were rolling the boat right side up.

Kezia drew in a breath.

But there was nothing underneath.

Except for a gallon can of Woolsey bottom paint and a single black folded-down rubber boot smeared with old paint—her grandfather's boot.

"Must have fallen right over on him," Beck said. "Pinned him." Beck looked back at the waiting crowd of people. "And then the tide come in."

Kezia felt the tears blinding her gaze. But still she stared out at the ocean, as if she could see. It was "lobster bottom," rocky with caves for them to hide in. And farther out was "the edge of the bottom," the fifty fathom curve where the great shelf of the sea fell away.

Gran'sir, are you there?

She'd been eight, nailing old lobster laths into the lowest branches of the Witness Tree. She was a pirate there, a fearless bold captain, and when Gran'sir gave her an abandoned stove-in lobster pot she became overnight the most successful lobsterman on the entire East Coast. She'd climbed up the next morning, stepped aboard to assume command and saw a flash of movement within the lobster pot. She sank to her scabbed-over knees, fingers clutching the bent laths, peering within. A miracle! The pot had caught a lobster. Her legs shook violently as she scrambled down the tire swing to the ground. She had pounded up to Perley's House to her mother, falling twice, voice screeching with excitement and wonder.

Gran'sir was already standing there, rotating a checkerberry leaf between his lips. As his grin widened the leaf fell away, and his deepset, squinted-up blue eye winked.

Now, staring out to sea, Kezia heard a sound beyond the surf chuckle, a sizzle like bacon frying, like rain on Alewife Pond, a turbulence turning like water boiling on the cookstove. She looked toward the weir where the pocket was covered with a rising, falling cloud of gulls. Gran'sir's weir had finally come in. Cormorants stood guard on every post. Through the brush-thick walls studded with seaweed, mussels and kelp she saw the blue and silver boil of the fish racing for an exit that never came.

"Look at that there," Nate said, pointing. "Must be fifty hogsheads of herrin' if it's a one!"

The sea washed in, wetting Kezia's bare feet. The sea beyond the weir as far as you could see gleamed empty, clear. The lobe of wave fizzled, salt-sharp between her toes.

It was a drowning coastline, Chance had once said. The sea had been, still was, rising at the rate of 0.084 inches per year.

Gran'sir, are you there?

CHAPTER 27

Then had come a month of fog mulls, rolling down in gray cold wetness from the "fog factory"—the Bay of Fundy far to the north. For ten days at a time Kezia had looked out the window of Perley's House and seen only the plaid of her shirt and above it her face, frowning gray.

But it was better than looking at Victorine here in the Vannah's living room, her blonde ponytail pinned in a bun at the nape of her neck like her idol Grace Kelly in "The Country Girl."

Because Chance was in love with Victorine.

On the unsteady base of the rag rug, in front of the worshipping eyes of Deenie, Victorine hugged herself with both hands and twirled. "Then we built like a little fire for the lobster bake," she continued, "below the high water mark so it'd be safe, and then Pooh and Tony disappeared into the little shack."

Little. Little. Kezia wanted to scream. Even Victorine's favorite book was *The Little Prince.* And she was huge, galumphing, tall as Grandm'am (with equally large breasts).

"And then Chance said, 'What are they doing in there, do you think?' I mean, it was a long time. And I said, 'staying in there a long time means they're not really doing anything, I can tell you, because there was this girl at school and she smuggled her boyfriend into her room but only for about three minutes her sister said and they were doing something because by the end of the year she was wearing little blazers all the time but it still didn't hide it and bingo—now she's a married lady.' "

Deenie was rubbing her back against the side of the couch; a bearcub against a tree.

So this was what Chance wanted, a girlfriend who had to be rustic, a member of the "natives," a stalwart ancient race. Someone for "squaw winter," cold days in August.

"You don't mind, do you, Keezie?" Victorine was looking at her. "If you'd mind, I wouldn't see him again."

"He's just a friend."

"For sure?"

"Like a brother."

Victorine hugged herself in a happy little dance. "Oh, Keezie, I want, I want, I want! I want to go to New York like you and take the Candy Conover modeling course and wear the little gold coat hangar up the back of my dress like that girl in Life."

Kezia studied her features: the black brows so wrong against the blonde hair, the chin that wasn't quite as firm as it should be. "Your hair's your best asset," Aunt Willi had always told Kezia. "And the way you kind of look up at people from under your brows, that's an asset." "But am I pretty?" "You look sensible, dear."

"I'm bored," Deenie said, tugging on Victorine's skirt.

"And then we all went back to Tenhaven," Victorine said, "and we rode the elevator. Did you ever ride the elevator, Keezie, imagine an elevator in a house!"

"No."

Victorine whirled again, her face gone into shadow and then around again into lamplight, gone and around again. "And you know, Keezie, the best part, the best of all?"

"No."

Still whirling in her bare-armed pink dress (always either pink or powder blue), arms unmercifully haired. "It will never end."

The wind at the top of the mountain ridge punished Kezia's face. On her arm she carried Bandit whose feathers ruffled like beach grass, cool and stirring against the burn of her birthmark. Kezia held the osprey close until it began to struggle, anxious in the emotion of her grip. The two jesses were threaded securely down her left palm between her thumb and forefinger, the leash looped twice around the post of her little finger. She had never held them so tightly as she did now.

Bandit paced on the glove, talons squeezing painfully even through the scratched buffalo hide.

It seemed she could smell it still, curls of smoke rising crisp and fatty with the scent of frying duck. Raucous laughter sounding through the underbrush.

Kezia's arm jerked and Bandit, already nervous bated backward off her arm. Shrilling her alarm call, feathers adrift she swung head downward on her jesses, her tongue panting a red spray of just-eaten fish blood onto the granite ground.

"Damn you." Kezia glared at the hawk who was struggling now to curve, bend, claw her way back up to the perch of Kezia's arm.

For just a second Kezia did it: so swift and so soon over that afterward she couldn't be sure. She twisted her hand and the jesses, deliberately frustrating the osprey's progress back up.

Then, ashamed, her hand slipped under the hawk and lifted her weight, heavy as a Manhattan telephone book, to the glove.

You see? The just world theory of birthmarks: you really are no good.

Bandit's gaze fastened upon the lowbush blueberries one hundred feet away. Her neck arched in complete absorption of attention. Kezia carried her over and set her down, still holding the leash, and Bandit pounced at a tiny patch of earth. But what was there? Kezia knelt, thrust her fingers into the midst of the one-inch square. Damp molding needles and moss were there, scurrying ants and granite. Kezia watched the bit of fragmented life, a jumble of planes and angles and twigs be disarrayed by a scrabbling June bug into a new pattern.

Bandit's beak struck. The June bug was no longer there.

Kezia rubbed gently between the hawk's eyes, felt the tightened feathers loosen, body relax. The golden eyes, with eight times the visual cells of a human, closed. One powerful foot curled toward her breast and Bandit balanced on her other leg—or rather, "arm," Kezia thought.

Chance insisted on proper terminology. The blue-gray fish-gripping scales of Bandit's feet were "hands," her legs "arms," her wings "sails," her talons "pounces," and her toes "petty singles."

Bandit scratched with one petty single behind her head.

But what Chance insisted upon no longer mattered anymore.

In her memory more laughter rose from Crotch Harbor where Victorine was laughing at her over her paper plate heavy with fried duck, laughing thick as fog.

Kezia thought of what she planned to do.

Against the growing reluctance and doubt, she felt her pain push through. Her fingers unhooked the jesses from the leash's swivel and then pulled the band of soft leather from each of Bandit's legs.

"Go on."

Kezia shook her arm and above it the osprey clung, still so tenaciously gripping.

Bandit's black curving talons paced, her head bobbing nervously to the right, then the left. Kezia threw her arm up and surprised, the hawk bounced. And then the five-foot wingspan spread, carried her a few feet above Kezia's head onto the twisted limb of the pitch pine at the top of the ridge.

"Go on, you stupid bird. You don't even know anymore when you're free. Get away. I don't love you anymore. We don't want you. Go on, now. *Go*."

She waved her hands, darting suddenly at the immobile hawk. Bandit fluttered only to a higher branch, settling among the sparse needles, sparing few glances at the human talking below.

Suddenly her eye caught at something in the sky.

Kezia stared upward. The *bawk, bawk* of a fish crow filled her ears, the faroff toy drone of a passing plane. The sky was opaque in its dense fog gray.

Bandit's eyes remained fixed on the sky, body leaning taut as a pointer flushing quail. Something was there. Her wings expanded, experimentally cupping the air.

"Bandit."

The osprey's body gathered, bunched beneath its wings, eyes fixed on the far place in the sky.

"Bandit, wait." But she had left the lure behind, that she could now be whirling above her head to bring Bandit back. "Wait. I changed my mind!"

Kezia tried to call the falconer's call as Chance had done, but a chill stony weight settled in her throat.

Kezia climbed into the pitch pine, but she wasn't nine now but fifteen. The branch buckled under her weight. She yanked the branches, pulling the whole tree toward her while at its peak the osprey calmly adjusted to each swaying move.

Bandit leaned farther into the sky now, drawn there but it was not too late.

Bandit would still respond, still come home.

She was theirs—hers and Chance's.

Her fingers reached in a desperate grabbing lunge and the osprey rose, the wind from the wing beats pushing a last refusal into her face. The hawk rose higher and higher, white beneath and brown above, and then only white visible against the pale white-streaked gray sky.

The wind slapped through the bent-over pitch pine.

Where was it now, what Chance had promised: an invisible *creance* of trust and love?

She could hear his voice now, that long rainy afternoon on Tenhaven's third floor when he had read to her among piles of books smelling of mildew and summer, every reference to falconry in Shakespeare...

> "If I do prove her haggard,
> though that her jesses were my dear heart-strings,
> I'd whistle her off, and let her down the wind
> To prey at fortune."

In that moment she realized she had driven Chance away.

She had made herself like him: the one thing he didn't want.

Kezia wanted to turn and run, below toward the dense spruce cover where the sky was hidden and the wind was still.

But she stood for a long time on the ridge, calling at the place in the sky toward which Bandit had vanished.

She knew this time the hawk wouldn't return.

The leash and jesses swung empty in her hands. She saw the far look endlessly repeated in Bandit's eyes.

Kezia turned away and looked far out on the blank plain of gray water.

"Don't be so excited," the voice of Aunt Willi had once said. "Happiness doesn't last."

Kezia felt something tug loose in her, like a leaf in autumn, and flutter to the ground.

She hated Aguahega and her family. She renounced them all.

Happiness doesn't last.

Then she would set her sights on the North Star of anger. Let it guide her forevermore.

She would have a career, a brilliant career in New York.

Like Aunt Willi going to the expensive photographer, a man in a suit ushering her in. "Engagement pictures?" the photographer said from his high wooden stool. "No, career woman," the man in the suit said.

She would never marry.

She would never come back to Aguahega Island again.

As the osprey flew higher—four-five-six-seven hundred feet, Aguahega Island shrank below, an oblong of gray trees banded with granite gray immersed in gray.

Twenty miles to the west the hawk flew over a much smaller island where a man stood looking down at a body. After the high breakers of the williewaw, the body had nudged ashore wrapped in branches of kelp. The holdfasts were so wedded to skin that when Serenus tugged them loose, part of the flesh tore away.

Serenus sucked his decaying teeth with the front of his tongue. The body wore a pair of men's pants.

There wasn't much left within the pants, having been grazed by the summer herds of scavenging crabs, eels, sea urchins, squid, and lobsters, or course. Man ate lobsters. And when they had the chance to return the favor, lobsters ate man.

Serenus didn't want any visitors, even a dead one.

Once he had lived on another island, with people. They said he was as queer as Dick's hat, queer as a three-dollar bill. Children tested his craziness, made it into a game, holding out a palm with a nickel and dime on it. "Go on, Serenus. Take whichever you want," giggling wildly.

He always picked the nickel.

The children laughed harder and skipped off, satisfied.

"Why don't you take the dime?" Ma said.

"Didn't take the nickel, why they'd stop doing it," Serenus said.

And then Ma died, and his brother, and his brother's wife moved away, and he was alone in the drafty ten room house. He dug clams, picked berries, and when he met someone walking on the road he stepped into the woods so he wouldn't have to say Hello.

But still the people came too close.

In his outboard boat he had come to Thrumcap, named after the little rope-yarn caps sailors used to wear. No one lived here anymore except gulls and shags. The gas was gone now. But there were clams and berries here, too, and gulls' eggs and an occasional gull and an old shack with a stove and a chest of drawers. He turned the bureau face down and slept on its hard back dreamlessly by the stove, burning driftwood.

But now, looking down at the body, Serenus pondered what to do. He had had nothing to ponder for years. Thoughts were unaccustomed, drafty in his head.

He sucked his teeth with his tongue.

There was a gold tooth in the head and one arm was missing.

He took off the pants, spread them on a rock to dry. Then he buried the body, gold tooth and all, where the soil was softest, by the raspberry bushes on the rise above the cove.

Gooden Beal had finally come to rest.

CHAPTER 28

1964 - Aguahega Island, Maine

Fog dripped thick and gray at 4 PM on June first, Chance and Victorine's wedding day.

Bodiless voices of strangers shouted requests for directions, faces appearing and fading in the cold strobe of banked lights. Loch Ness monsters humped in and out of tatters of fog: twisted cables that ran from nowhere to nowhere. An attempt had been made to close the village dock, but an island has many doors.

Kezia, 21, hesitated at the foot of the long boardwalk snaking steeply up the hill to the boxes-on-boxes white steeple of the First Congregational Church. She wondered if the *Women's Wear Daily* photographer were here. FISHERMAN'S DAUGHTER TO WED CHANCELLOR, their story had read. " 'We want a simple island wedding,' the happy couple said."

Chance was in for a surprise, Kezia thought. He wanted a simple island maid; Victorine wanted only his wealth.

"He gave me my ring—emerald with diamonds, Keezie, the most beautiful thing you ever saw. One point two-three carats, the emerald, and it's African, really *dark* green where the Colombian ones are lighter and Chance said I could pick what I wanted so I picked the biggest and the darkest. It cost twenty-three thousand, Keezie."

She was deaf. "What?"

"And six hundred dollars. Do you believe all this?"

"What?"

"Getting hitched up! Me and Chance."

Slowly Kezia climbed the boardwalk, the weathered planks slippery underfoot, one of her hands trailing reluctantly along the flat-topped rail. She felt the splinter go in—sharp and deep—and then the pain.

Through the fog's twilight the church's bright lights poured like sun. The door shut behind her. The first few chords of the wedding march struck with a percussive boom around her head. The inner doors opened: faded red carpet between white painted wooden pews, all filled. All heads turned to gape.

At twelve Deenie was too old, the too gangly flower girl in apricot silk strewing her rose petals from the basket as grudgingly as if they were dollar bills. Kezia walked down the aisle past the pews' armrests scrolled round and tight as fiddleheads (one of them carved with her initials, hers and Nate's). Her apricot bridesmaid's dress scratched uncomfortably at her neck. She looked ahead at the altar and Chance.

He was staring at her: chin down, a black Y of gaze with eyebrows that met in the middle. His lanky body hung from the yoke of wide shoulders straining the charcoal gray cutaway above striped trousers. He twisted his head in a nervous jut of chin as if his stiff-collared shirt were too tight. The dove gray ascot centered with the pearl stickpin rose as he swallowed. Kezia could see the fine film of sweat across his forehead where her fingers longed to brush back the hank of straight hair.

But he wasn't looking at her.

Kezia could hear by the indrawn breaths that down the aisle behind her Victorine stood.

Every girl is beautiful in white.

Her skirt flowed in narrow circling tiers of cream taffeta faille, her blonde hair framed by a palest lemon net veil ringed with fresh orange blossoms. But her cheeks flamed with two spots of red too violent to be rouge.

Beck Vannah was listing leftward, clinging to *her*, his ill-fitting rented cutaway ballooning toward the floor, pearl gray tie yanked loose, white hair shiny streaks plastered hastily with water. His blue eyes struggled to focus like a calf gone down in fright.

"He might not be drunk," someone whispered. "Maybe he's ill?"

The organ crashed louder, drowning out the talk. Kezia glanced to the left of the aisle where the guests from Seal Point sat. Eleanore Chancellor's head was held so high, so far back on her neck it looked ready to fly off.

Closer Victorine came, the bite of mortification on her face as the hedges of hothouse flowers swamped the air with a sickly, too swiftly blooming/dying/rotting tropical scent.

Beck Vannah's fingers spread, his arms flailing outward for balance as he stumbled on a wrinkle in the carpet. There was an audible sigh of relief as Victorine arrived at the altar and Chance took her arm.

"Dearly beloved, we are gathered here together in the sight of God and in the presence of these witnesses..."

Kezia stared up at the huge circle of stained glass above the altar, its colors glowing from an artificial sun. It was like seeing an old friend again: Jesus in red holding the white lamb tucked in his arm, four other sheep paying homage at his feet. Beneath, the inscription read:

IN MEMORY OF MRS. BECK VANNAH
BORN JAN 21 1911 DIED AUG 6 1950
BY THE FAMILY

Kezia felt someone looking at her and she turned her head. Nate Vannah was looking steadily back.

"...to join together Victorine Judith and Fairfield Cordell in holy matrimony; which is an honorable estate..."

Kezia felt a sharp stab of pain, the splinter still in her palm. Her thumb pressed down on it, drove the pain higher, harder. The other pain grew too—like the cut tatters of baitbag twine. The ends would go on unraveling forever unless you burned them off.

Victorine's face burned up at Chance.

The stained glass began to dance before Kezia's eyes. A piece of herself was gone. Victorine had stolen it. Victorine—always in control, calm, efficient, at ease with herself, walking tall. "The sun shines strongest on the tallest tree."

Kezia stared at her shoulderblades zippered in virginal white. Had they done It already? Of course, in the back seat of a car. A life decided in the back seat of a Karma car. How many times then: once, twice, for years? Or would tonight be the very first time? That was all marriage really was about.

It wasn't romantic at all.

It meant what had happened to Vangie Carter (Finlay now), her best friend from before, on Aguahega, who had moved to the main. Vangie so precocious. Kezia saw again the one-room schoolhouse needing paint, the lunch hour desertion of the room, the troop of little boys lining up to gang-rape Vangie's purse. There it sat at the blackboard on the chalk rail. They opened it, sniggering, lining up to peer again. Kezia had pushed her way through them and stared inside: the little rectangle of vinyl, strap torn off at one end, enclosing the Kotex white and blind that shone back at her between navy blue lids.

"...which holy estate Christ adorned and beautified with His presence in Cana of Galilee..."

Kezia had been sixteen when she took the bus out to visit Vangie at Vangie's new home. She was barely twenty, married to Earl Finlay. The trailer was down a dirt road too ashamed to abut the highway, the spruce forest encroaching on the clearing, leaving it sunless and bare. Twin American flags tried and failed to brighten the rusting trailer's door.

Kezia knocked at the door which banged back at her, hinges loose.

"Hi, Keez."

Inside it was dark and cluttered, poverty scaling off the thin metal walls. The two year old ran unheeded across the floor, diapers sagging with an unchanged load. The back of the trailer led off a dark narrow hall. Closed doors and then one opened, a baby with dark hair lay frog-legged in a crib. There was a smell of diapers that needed changing.

> *You you you you*
> *enhh enhh enhh enhh*
> (cough, cough, and repeat)

Waves came in threes; babies cried in fours. Now a pacifier plugged up his mouth.

"He's so cute," Kezia said. "Really."

"Go on. You can hold him."

"No, no, really. He wants to stay there."

Vangie began changing the diaper, and the amazingly large scrotum with its pink nose tumbled out in view. With one hand Vangie brusquely held both feet straight up, jouncing the scrotum around with a wet cotton ball.

"The potty calling the kettle black?" Kezia said.

Her words died in the air.

Out in the living room the two year old squirmed up into Vangie's lap where she held him disinterestedly, loose as a sack of grain. When he squirmed down the imprint of his wet bottom stood dark, ignored on Vangie's dress.

Oh Vangie.

But this wasn't Vangie—something had happened, just getting married had done it. And now there was a stranger that broke your heart in her place.

At six Earl pulled up in his homemade truck, an old sedan with the body hacked off behind the front seat and a truck bed grafted on. He overflowed the tiny dinette in his undershirt, black chest hairs boiling loose, drinking beer after beer—Brador, the brand from Canada and illegal, too potent for the States. He sliced off pats of butter and ate them off his pocketknife. While the television blared he ignored Vangie and Kezia, idly petting the two dogs. Kezia suggested going out for a walk. When they returned the male dog was mounting the female, his claws scratching wildly for purchase on the vinyl floor. Earl, face flushed, eyes bulging, yelled, "Get her, Rusty, get her."

It could have been me, Kezia thought, here in Vangie's place. She had not seen Vangie since.

"...Into this holy estate these two persons come now to be joined. If any man can show just cause why they may not lawfully be joined together, let him now speak or else hereafter forever hold his peace..."

Kezia wanted to stand up and scream. She knew the truth: Marriage was Psyche chained to the mountaintop to await Death. Marriage killed the Psyche in every woman, the one they worshipped from afar. It wouldn't be any different for Victorine than it was for Vangie; one in her trailer, one in Tenhaven. "I can't wait to live in

Tenhaven," Victorine had said. "And then there's 'Eight-Twenty,' that's on Fifth Avenue, twenty-four rooms with butler, cook, kitchen maid, waitress, valet, and chambermaid, and a view of Central Park. And Sky Farm: it's at Southampton on Long Island, and a caretaker keeps it open just for an occasional weekend. You'll have to come out and see us, Keezie, okay?"

"I, Fairfield Cordell the Third, take thee, Victorine Judith, to be my wedded wife, to have and to hold from this day forward, for better or worse, for richer, for poorer, in sickness and in health, to love and to cherish, till death us do part, according to God's holy ordinance; and thereto I pledge thee my faith."

It took so few minutes, Kezia thought, to ruin your life by getting married.

The rings were exchanged and old Reverend Witney smiled his yellow-toothed grin. "I pronounce that they are husband and wife together in the name of the Father, and of the Son, and of the Holy Spirit. Those whom God hath joined together, let no man put asunder."

But perhaps a woman could.

To bring a lover back: stick a needle through a candlewick.

Kezia looked at the wall, into a molded-plastic bas-relief based on Leonardo DaVinci's "Last Supper." Christ had dust in his hair. She looked at Reverend Witney and remembered the sound he made when the water balloon she dropped burst on his head: he had farted, simple and loud and good.

To bring a lover back: don't burn apple branches and don't count the stars. Never, never kill a toad.

The splinter in Kezia's hand sent a sudden imperative message. Opening her palm she saw the bright red patch, within it a tiny black speck and its shadow length deep within the skin.

Deenie was retreating back up the aisle, picking up the rose petals she had scattered from her ribbon-trimmed basket, putting them thriftily back inside. Stubbornly she shook off Kezia's restraining hand.

There was no use trying to pick the splinter out. It had gone too far.

Kezia watched Chance kiss Victorine.

It would have to fester to get free.

CHAPTER 29

"Still stuck on Chance?"

Tenhaven's hand-wrought iron door latches stared back at Kezia, borders of panels forming a crucifix. It was from Perley's House: the Christian door.

"I was a kid then. Kids have crushes. It was just a crush."

Willi Beale stopped to adjust one stocking, heavy on her leg with its blue, red, and gold pailletes. Kezia, an editorial assistant at *Vogue* magazine, had named it "Scheherazaderie" in the two lines allotted to her under its photograph. "Ie" was big this year: already she had used "Turquerie," "fantasie," and "caravanserie.")

"Poor Victorine," Willi said, "lamb to the marital slaughter."

Kezia felt her gloom lighten. "How dare you impugn the sacred institution of marriage."

"Marriage is truly a blessed state—except when it's hell. But then there's nothing wrong with marriage—it's just the people who get married. But who cares? We've got the Chancellor millions in the family now. Wonder how long I have to wait to ask for a loan?"

The sheltering heart of Tenhaven led you straight on through: front porch, center hall, colonnaded rear piazza—between the columns white-linen-draped tables with centerpieces of roses fragrant on the damp fog breeze. Kezia stared at milling guests, at the Barnum-sized yellow and white striped tent spreadeagled on the lawn beyond. Left far behind in another world were the islanders' pick-up trucks and battered cars shedding their rust on the immaculate white gravel of the horseshoe drive. Nate's '38 Chevy sagged trunk door still missing (it had to be bailed out like a dory after rain). *Women's Wear Daily*: " 'Just real folks underneath, the Chancellors,' the lovely bride's stepfather said in his charming Maine accent. Mrs. Cord (Bettina) Chancellor responded equally warmly. 'We're privileged to know the Beals and the Vannahs,' she said."

Kezia and Willi paused, hesitant to enter the fray.

"About marriage. Do you mean you wouldn't have married Ben Hodierne if you'd got the chance?"

Willi flicked her fingernails out beneath her chin, an Italian street urchin being rude. "That idiot? I have enough albacrosses to bear. He always said I was interrupting him because he never stopped talking."

"But then why did you go with him for nine years?"

"He had a bullying manner that I took to be strength."

"But what goes wrong so much of the time?" Kezia said. "Why can't it ever work out?"

"I'm the expert? I don't know. You get married because you want to be together all the time, correct? But once you are, the reason apparently loses its immediacy. You get pregnant and have to give up your job. You have to cook and clean all the time and your husband says you've let yourself go. How could you keep the romantic feeling—dealing with in-laws, seeing him on the toilet. At first intimacy with another person's life is exciting. But then it becomes humdrum."

"Was that what happened with you and Ben?"

Willi exhaled, an impatient sound with open mouth. "With Ben and me. It's beyond all that. I think the seeds that destroy it are planted at the start." She drew herself up, looking ahead at the tumult in the tent. "Of course the fact that he started screwing a nymphet like Brantley had nothing to do with it."

"Brantley!"

"Come, my naïve little Miss Beal. We have a reception to attend."

Inside the tent the gray fog receded before ten varieties of roses in fourteen shades. On the platform two lobstermen and one retired lobsterman jammed with accordion, sax, and a battered wood upright piano fresh from the school: Chance's idea, Kezia guessed. How much more rustic could you get?

You could hardly move for the crowd, faces that were turning to look at her and her unorthodox clothes. If they were going to hang you, it didn't matter how high. Kezia squashed Gran'sir's stained old felt hat with the feather in the brim farther down on her head. She had stripped in the church outhouse, pushed the hated scratching apricot down the hole. Now in her usual jeans, argyles, and tennies, she picked up a plate and approached the buffet: lobster with truffles, fish pate with goose liver, swordfish, crayfish with oysters, angels' hair spaghetti: all just appetizers. Soon they would be served rack of lamb and squab. Dom Perignon stood in iced silver buckets, with five more wines and a paradisiacal 1880 French cognac: Gaston Briand Le Paradis.

Her throat closed. Was she going to be one of those people going through life eternally nostalgic for fiddlehead greens and lobster scouse? She put the plate down, suddenly breathless, and stepped outside. Fog rained like tears against her face.

Through the thin tent wall she could hear voices and music and the clink of ice in hundreds of glasses. Not common ice cubes but it seemed she heard something else: the long glitter-blue prisms hammered off a block of ice from Alewife Pond, tinkling a fairy music all their own. Harvesting, Daddy had called it when the ice was frozen down a foot and a half, the rig sawing the surface of Alewife into squares, a giant's checkerboard. All the neighbors and the Vannahs were there and a bonfire going and hot chocolate to keep you warm. The ice was clean and pure because the pond was pure. Something Gran'sir said—"as cold as pure ice."

No ice since had tasted like that. Would she ever find it again?

She heard islanders' voices now, through the tent, island men and Beck Vannah's half-sotted rasp.

"Insult, I call it, her in that getup on Victorine's marrying day."

"Kezia's from away now. Maybe she don't remember how we do things on here."

"Hah. Thinks she can do whatever she's a mind of. Thinks her shit don't stink."

"How come she's like that, Beck, and Victorine such a right sweet pea?"

"She's put on airs."

The Jam session suddenly ceased. Kezia could hear a far voice cry, "Speech! Let's hear from the groom and the bride."

"SPEECH." "SPEECH." "SPEECH."

Kezia walked back into the humidity and the warmth inside the tent, watched Chance pulling Victorine beside him, the crowd parting around them, giving them room. On Kezia's cheek the mouse battered her with its fists.

"I don't really know what to say. A speech, you say?" Chance looked flushed and very young. "Well, I've been told there's only three ways to become a real Aguahegan—and to those of you who know me, you know I mean a year-rounder, of course. You do it by groom, by womb, or by tomb."

Claps and cheers.

"All I can say is, doing it as a groom sure beats those other two ways."

Ribald laughter.

"And I want to say that my, uh, wife—the sound of that takes getting used to, but she certainly doesn't. My wife here is a real American Venus, homegrown, fits in your pocket. And I'd like to recite a little something for her, if I may. It's real romantic, so get ready.

"The jury is still out on Chancellor *v.* General Fools. Watch him reason as a lawyer; finding reasons that are unreasonable. See him distinguish the identical. See him place the species inside the genus and the particular case inside the species. See him distinguish inherently dangerous from imminently dangerous, and things in their nature dangerous and those which become so by an unknown latent defect."

Into the embarrassed silence came a sound rustling like cornstalks in a breeze, taking Kezia a moment to realize it was only old Fairfield Chancellor laughing. A few others joined in.

"Actually," Chance said, "that one was for my Harvard Law buddies over there by the booze—R-Teep and Bones, the ones who *didn't* flunk out."

A few more embarrassed laughs.

Flunked out? Kezia stared for answer at Chance's face. But everyone knew he was going to be a brilliant lawyer: it was all Victorine talked about.

"Now I've got a real 'recite' for Mrs. Flunkee, er, Chancellor, I mean."

Victorine's face smiled just as adoringly as ever up at his face.

" 'Shall I compare thee to a summer's day?

Thou art more lovely and more temperate,

Rough winds do shake the darling buds of May,

And'...and, uh—"

Kezia heard her own voice saw sharp into the air. " 'And summer's lease hath all too short a date.' "

Necks craned, faces stared at her, a Seal Point matron took out her half-glasses to peer frostily at the button on Kezia's shirt:

J. EDGAR HOOVER
sleeps with a
NIGHT LIGHT.

"Let's us hear from the happy bride," Beck Vannah boomed, words slurred.

A look of panicked confusion darkened Victorine's face. She shook her head. Chance whispered something in her ear and she shook her head harder.

"SPEECH." "SPEECH."

"What goes for the gander goes for the goose!"

"Tell them about the peecan, Victorine. The life and times of the peecan under your bed, now there's a real island tale." Kezia could see her mother staring at her, Beck Vannah starting toward her grim faced. "How you fetched it out full loaded, slipped and spilled it all over the hall stairs."

Silence. Nothing, nothing, and then Beck Vannah gripped her arm.

"I don't know any poems," Victorine said, "At least I can't remember any, ceste la vye. Uh. I want to thank everyone for coming and I'll just say this. They say marriage makes two people into one body. This man is the head and the woman is the heart. That's good because my head was never all that great."

"Smooch her!"

"Kiss the bride."

Kezia flung free of Beck's grip, wound her way closer until she stood one person removed from Victorine's side. Chance leaned formally, bowing to Victorine, fingers sweeping toward the hem of her taffeta skirt. They came up and tangled in her hair. Kezia could hear him whisper, "Do you still love me, Rose Hips?"

As he kissed her the cheers broke sudden and deafening. Kezia turned away, found Aunt Willi by her side. "It's amazing, no?" Kezia said. "A trite example of duo-labial contact and the crowd goes wild."

"That's my girl."

The music of accordion, sax, and piano once again plowed the air. The bride and groom danced around and around in a space that cleared and shaped itself as they whirled. Victorine's flounces trailed brown now at the hem. From the corner of her eye Kezia caught a quick flash of shiny purple dress, a shelf of breasts. She smelled the dense powdery old-woman's scent, couldn't look at her: the one person before whom she felt ashamed.

"Kezia! How could you do that—about the peecan, in front of strangers," Clara Beal, 68, said.

"It was just a joke."

"Do you feel the sadness, now she is married? Well, do not worry. You are next."

"I'm *never* getting married. Marriage is a blessed state except when it's hell."

"What? At your age I had the husband and two children already. People keep asking me when it is you are going to settle down, get married."

"I want to find out who I am."

"Who you are? I did not have the time to ask such. I just did what had to be done."

"But, Grandm'am, you didn't *have* to do anything."

"How can you tell me that, you with never a child in your body. Mrs. Carter is already a grandmother twice, and her Vangie is not much older than you. You and that career. You are going to be the old maid, I do not want a granddaughter who is an old maid."

"Well? You going to introduce us?" The short old man moved stiff-legged between them, nose and chin nearly meeting over absent teeth. His face was as wrinkled as a dried herring.

"Kezia, here is Henry Gathercole."

"So, you and Mr. Gathercole, are you an item, Grandm'am?"

Instead of looking shocked Clara's face broadened, smile full of mischief. "They made him leave the nursing home when they found the two of us in the bed."

"What?"

"So you think the old crocks like we do not feel the same things you feel?" Clara said.

Henry Gathercole was plucking at Kezia's sleeve. His fly was at half mast. "You're from New York? You're the one from New York?"

She focused her eyes on his face. "No. I was born on here. I happen to live in New York, I work in New York at the present time."

"My daughter went down there in forty-eight, worked for Ma Bell. Lice there were in the operators' room, come right out of that equipment, they wouldn't let them wear pants on their legs and bit them up good. Maybe you met her, lived on Seventy-Eighth Street?"

"No. I was here in forty-eight."

His locating mechanism, a faulty antenna, struggled to place her in time and space. "She was a bitty thing, real pale hair? Did you meet her in forty-eight?"

"I'm sorry, Mr. Gathercole, I was five years old then. I lived right here on Aguahega. I was born here."

"So you're the one from New York?"

Kezia turned away, but the only thing to look at was Chance and Victorine circling to the music again. Now Beck Vannah cut in and then Chance danced with his mother and then with Loara Vannah who laughed, protesting.

Victorine stood for a moment alone.

Their eyes met and Kezia stared at her, looking for the child who had shared her double bed, opossum eyes peering out at her from under the covers, furry warmth. "But how does the penis *know* it's going to have intercourse," Kezia had long ago asked her, "so it can know to get hard?" "Oh, you're just so dumb," Victorine said, not knowing either, turning away.

Just as she turned away now.

Kezia stared at the floor.

And then abruptly she saw the gray suede muzzles of a pair of formal men's shoes pointing at the ragged hems of her jeans. Hands at the striped trousers' side tugged upwards and the cuffs rose.

Ankles glowed in fire engine red socks.

Kezia giggled and looked up.

Chance's narrow dark eyes were looking down. "There's nothing on that floor that's that interesting, you know. Care to oscillate on top of it, Miss Beal?"

She heard her breath rush in. She launched herself toward his reaching hand, manacled by the gold ring. Of everyone here, only Chance understood.

She breathed in his scent, the same as it had always been, fresh sweat and sandalwood soap.

"Hey down there. Smile. With the teeth."

She felt her lips stretch back with a rubbery sound.

"Definite improvement. Look, Red, I know we've hardly spoken these last couple of years. I want to amend that now. Wanted to be sure you were all right."

She was furious, that he could think he had had such an effect on her that he might have damaged her. When he had meant nothing, nothing to her at all. She saw Aunt Willi watching from the edge of the crowd, her back turned to the light, face in shadows—she thought her face couldn't stand up to the light.

"You're as politic as a Gaboon viper," Kezia snapped. "Of course I'm all right!"

"All that happened with"—his voice hesitated—"Bandit, that's all forgotten now, Red. It's past."

"Chance, you just don't know. I've regretted it so many times. Over and over, I just wanted to run to you and say—"

He whirled her around. She saw the wall of faces blurring past, eyes watching, dark and light. "There's nothing you need to say. Please believe me."

"So you do forgive me? Chance, it would just mean so much. I mean, if only I could know—"

That you really love me? Kezia saw his eyes focused over her shoulder, saw him wink at someone as they turned. She saw

Victorine's face watching back, turning to keep them in sight as they danced. Smiles flickered, coming and going over her face: a strong smile that didn't last quite long enough, a smile lasting long enough but too weak to be real.

Does she know?

Kezia smiled up at Chance. "Remember when we had all those grass fights, and then you threatened to roll me down the hill if I didn't stop throwing grass at you and—"

But Chance was leading them still dancing closer and closer to Victorine.

"Chance." Kezia's voice was urgent with the need to keep his attention, to remain in his arms as long as she could. "Did you really flunk out of law school?"

"I quit." Voice tense, whispered near her ear.

"What? With how much to go?"

"Don't tell anyone. Three months."

"Check your brainwaves to see if you've got any! That's the most self-destructive thing I've ever heard."

"I'd say it was self-preservation. But I learned something there."

He whirled her around.

"What?"

"I'm not the competitive type. I'm enrolled in the grad program at Indiana University for the fall—speech pathology and audiology. Remember you wondered why it was I stuttered everywhere else, every place but Aguahega? Maybe I'll find out."

"Indiana?" Impossibly far away.

"They have a really good program there in speech therapy. Maybe I can do something of value in the world."

"Be a speech therapist, you mean? But what happened at Harvard Law?"

"Self-knowledge."

He didn't have to support himself. Perhaps that made it all too easy, shedding careers like outgrown lobster shells.

"Self-knowledge? Then tell me, which do you love more, her or the island?"

She saw the truth of it spear between his eyes.

Chance tapped Victorine's partner on his cutaway shoulder. "Hey, Dad, mind if I exercise the prerogatives of the groom?"

"*Droit de seigneur*?" Kezia heard her own voice say. "The Lord's right to rape the peasants?"

"You're starting to sound unpleasantly like your aunt."

He was already looking at Victorine. It was one of those looks—mysterious, full of light, the kind he had never turned on her. She felt the warmth of his left hand let go of her palm. As he moved back toward the bride Kezia could barely hear him say it.

"Thanks for the dance, sister mine."

She turned away, trying to grab the emotions that hurtled across her face. No one must ever guess how she felt.

"Let him go," Willi said. "Give him a nice Congregational handshake and send him on his way."

"You don't understand. You hate men."

"I don't hate men. Men have been the fulcrum of my life, the dark, hairy force at the center, the things that go hump in the night. Why I should find myself dry and stranded at the age of fifty odd is as much a mystery to me as to anyone else. Come along now, let's get some wine."

But someone had looked at Kezia once, the way Chance was looking at Victorine. Kezia forced her eyes to focus, to idly sweep across the noisy antics of the crowd.

But where *was* Nate?

As Willi made her way over to the bar Kezia saw Beck Vannah watching her aunt with the same lightful look Chance turned on Victorine. Everyone was part of a couple, everyone wanted desperately by someone else. Everyone except her.

Knots and tangles of people and then she recognized Nate's broad back: comforting back, the kind you wanted to put your arms around. The seat of his suit pants gleamed with too much wear.

She tapped him on the shoulder: hard reddened weather of the back of his neck, the same blue eyes, something loose about the skin along his jaw. He looked old and he was 25.

"Kezia." The joy was genuine, but the look wasn't there. And then she saw his right hand, how in the press of people crowding near it was joined to the left hand of a woman whose face was pebbled with acne, upper lip darkly haired.

Across the bridge of their hands Nate said, "Kezia, I want you to meet my wife."

CHAPTER 30

1964 - Thrumcap Island, Maine

Twenty miles south on Thrumcap Island Gooden Beal's bones had gone where the sea directed him.

What had been raspberry bushes on a hilly rise six years before was now beach. The waves had bitten away the southern side of the island, built it back up on the western shore.

It was the day after his oldest granddaughter's wedding, still patchy with streamers of fog.

"I can hardly *see* Thrumcap," Willi Beale said, peering ahead, "let alone know if I want to do a goddamn fool thing like buy it."

"Stay another day." Pruitt Hoskins was looking at her legs again.

She was 52, but she thanked God every morning for great legs: they were the last things to go. The word "buy" sent a delicious cold shiver down her spine. If she wanted she had only to scratch her name on a scrap of paper and a place, a live miniature world would be hers. Hers to do with just as she wished: repel all boarders. Not like Aguahega, stonecoast, spoiled with memories at its heart.

She had never owned anything except her advertising agency—she rented apartments and cars. Nothing had ever owned her.

"And then," she said briskly, "there's the matter of that crazed old coot of a squatter living in the shack."

Pruitt sat up as if goosed. "Wherever'd you hear tell about that?" He was Hartville's first selectman, trying to fatten the public coffers with the town's sale of seven islands offshore.

"An informant called 'Buyer Beware.' "

Pruitt eased the boat into the curve of sheltered water, Thrumcap's only point of entry, shallow as it was. The grass-blown hill of Thrumcap, round and bare, bulged above them. The motor died.

"Well, now, could be you're right. Serenus Bartlett is his name. Hermit thirty years so I heard. Harmless. Now take your time, just take a gander around. On a civil day you can sun and fish and swim. Mackerel good hereabouts."

"Five acres is too small. And of course there's not enough trees."

"Small enough to be familiar; trees block the view."

"And all this fog. What use is a view?" Willi turned to look at him: a crusty red-faced man not much older than her brother Johnny would have been. "How long do you think it'll last—what is it you natives call it? The thick-a-fog?"

"Until it clears."

Oh, he thought he was putting one over on her, thought her a naïve summer tour-ast. She gave him her prettiest smile, not too wide, the skin of her face fitted looser, just a little looser, thank God, like a well-loved sweater gone baggy with wear.

She clambered out of the boat in her high heels, felt them sink in the kelp-strewn mud, her skirt hiking up higher on her legs. "So there's no problem with the title or anything, is there?" Her bottom felt wet with condensation from the plank seat on her dress.

"Nope. Went up to Augusta myself. State official said we could get on with the sale."

Willi was looking around, the smell of beach roses and bayberries sweet on the salt-water tang. She took a deep breath and a fresh wild exhilaration filled her head.

And then, "What in the hell is that?"

"What?" His voice broke like a pencil lead.

Ahead on the muddy beach a length of white bone jutted from its shallow grave.

Pruitt dug with his oar until he unearthed the loose pile of bones. Willi leaned over him as he tried to arrange them back into a skeleton, pointing out his anatomical mistakes.

They stood looking down now, discussing what to do.

"Do nothing," Pruitt said. "Been here probably fifty years. Some poor sailor washed overboard, I guess."

"Or Captain Ahab." Willi looked over at the hermit's tumble-down shack. A fresh pile of emptied clam shells lay beside the door, which was silent and closed. "You don't think our antique Mr. Bartlett did someone in, do you?" She was glad now that Pruitt had come here with her.

"No. Lord no, course not. Bet this poor bugger's laid here *sixty* years if he's a day."

"Well, cover it up again, please. Put that skull down. It's got a gold tooth: did dentists do gold teeth sixty years ago?"

"Sure. Leastwise, I think so. Dirt here'll just wash loose again. Let's deep-six it higher up. How about up there, top of the hill?"

Willi turned away, face into the fresh fog breeze. She wanted to recapture the way she had felt before. As Pruitt began upturning the soft mossy soil on top of the hill with a flat rock, she walked all the way around Thrumcap's shore. It was nearly as round as a thrumcap. She tasted the well water: not much of it but it was cold and pure. The rocky headland stretching east would be a perfect picnic spot: she could call it Lookout Point. She took the island's measure, choosing a site for a house—a tall Bauhaus-modern slab of cedar and glass. "I've seen enough," she called.

Pruitt straightened, one hand on his back.

He wasn't a bad looking sort, Willi thought. A man like Pruitt could at least be relied on not to be impotent. Or queer. Not to be a man who sang in the shower "The Man I Love."

He could be relied on not to write a play that became successful, like Ben Hodierne, after which Willi was dropped, her private lines said all wrong? Not the type? Too old for the part of opening night?

She wondered what Pruitt would do if she walked up and pressed her stocking-clad knee between his thighs.

Don't be romantic, she thought.

Pruitt wiped his forehead nervously. There was his prospective buyer bending over in front of the shack's door. He watched her set their lunch, a thermos of coffee and two wax paper wrapped sandwiches down on a slab of granite by the clam shells.

"I hope you like peanut butter," she said to the door.

The wind harped through the grass, blew her hair. He was touched, thought her as tough as bullbeef and now this.

She saw him looking and stood up.

She was so close now he could smell her perfume. He felt sweat trickling down his neck. "Uh, what is it you do down in New York, Miss Beale?"

"I work at Beale and Thurston, an ad agency."

"What might you do there?"

"I'm attempting to inform you that I own the place."

"Own it? Oh, you mean, you and Mr. Thurston?"

"No, he's quite imaginary, is Mr. Thurston. You see, I just thought it gave the name a nice serious sound.

Her long-nailed fingers were on his arm, pointed and avaricious. He felt his skin jump.

"My but you're jumpy, Mr. Hoskins. May I call you Pruitt?"

No, he was just imagining this. He had always dreamed about it but women never were interested in him.

"I'm a sexual adventurer," Willi said. "Men go up the Amazon, I go down on men." She pulled off her sweater and began to run, shedding garments as she went. She glanced back and saw Pruitt with pants now at half-mast around his knees try to take a hobbled leap after her and fall.

Her laughter poured out, startling the gulls.

He was starting to gain on her now.

Eyes were watching them from the thin scrim of sumac, hackmatack. Willi thought she saw a dirt-dark face, tangled shrub of hair, a small animal? The eyes blinked and were gone.

And then Pruitt entirely nude now except for white socks caught up with her.

Under the overhang of rock the mosses grew thick and soft, sponging up water against her back. The spume of tide against the ledge rushed gurgling continuous as rain. She felt his thick white thighs, hairless as a woman's, press her thighs apart.

He thrust as if he were racing for an end-run.

But oh she felt: not like this, not for a long time.

He pounded her on the anvil of sex.

She was gold, heavy with experience and all the base metals pounded out. He wanted gold, did he, afraid to hope?

Afterward she walked back to the boat, picked up her soggy orange life preserver and strapped it on. Her knees were weak with feeling and with feeling, fear.

"So," Pruitt said. "I'm the seller. You buying?"

"I think Thrumcap's positively, absolutely, fantastically...just okay."

Emboldened, he said, "My advice's just to leave old Bartlett where he be. Don't bother him, he won't bother you. Haul him to the main and they'd just lock him up in the loony bin. A shame, wouldn't it be?" When she didn't reply, "Have we got us a deal?"

She was grownup now, Willi thought, and it was time she had a home, even if just for summer vacations. It was time the wanderer stopped wandering and put down roots. She might even be able to wangle old Pruitt out to visit her once in a while, so nice to have a man around the place.

A real man like her brother, her father. A man from Maine.

Hands on hips she laughed up at him:

" 'One half in goods received in part,
and cash to cheer the drooping heart?' "

His eyes sparkled brown and friendly across at her, not dull and embarrassed the way they had been just a moment before.

"Sure," he said.

"Deal. But you'll have to get rid of the crazy. I plan on sunbathing in the nude."

He turned around to stare at her as the boat pushed off. Behind them the gulls tore at the wax paper, devouring chunks of the bread within.

Serenus Bartlett lay as dead behind the hackmatack as Gooden in the mud. Their passion had made him feel again.

With Ma's rusty old kitchen knife he'd drawn an angry red mouth across his throat.

CHAPTER 31

1974 - Aguahega Island, Maine

She could stop dreaming about the wolffish in the ice.

Aguahega was only a summer island now.

Kezia stared at Alewife Pond. Summer people, their children and dogs splashed in the shallows of the 90-foot-deep murk of the water. Summer signs directed:

NO FIRES
NO CAMPING WITHOUT PERMIT
NO LITTERING
NO RADIOS

The Park Service decals were everywhere.

She was a summer person, here with a group, two couples and a woman, to camp and hike for the next three days. Then on to the Allagash Wilderness Waterway, 100 miles of lakes, ponds, rivers in Northern Maine's vast forest where they would spend ten days canoeing from Telos Lake to Allagash Village.

Far from Aguahega, safely inland.

It was at Ian's insistence they were here at all; he'd wanted to see where she grew up. "I grew up in New York." Still his fantasy persisted: girl island born, orphaned young, lost in storm. She loved Ian so she'd said Yes.

As long as they didn't have to see her family. Just come like any other campers, hikers, to see the sights.

"Let's go down, set up our camp, make some coffee," Brantley said.

"Coffee reduces virility, man," Gordy said.

Ian: "I don't know. I don't drink coffee."

They laughed, and all was back as it should be: a summer vacation, free and happy and clear.

They set up their tents, day-glo orange, olive drab and blue on the bottlecap-embedded dirt of Campsite #7, for which they had had to reserve six months in advance.

"What in hell is an alewife?" Gordy said. "And is she selling any? Her body, not the ale."

They were such outsiders they made Kezia the insider by default. "They're the Volkswagen of fish," Kezia said, "ugly but they get there. They come in early May, up Persistent Creek to spawn, gray-backed with fat yellow bellies—why they're called alewife. Full of bones. They home in on the scent of the pond, a few parts per million or something in the sea. They were born here."

"Do you *eat* them?" Libra Jean said. Next Wednesday was their second anniversary of going together, the entity known as Gordyand-LibraJean, which had met eyes across a crowded campfire.

"An *acquired* taste. But the smokers are fantastic: smolder over green pine covered in sawdust, pungent, that smell used to always be around in spring." Her voice was eager, on fire. She tried to drown it.

"No more?" Ian said.

"No more. Or, I shouldn't say that. I don't know. I don't live here anymore."

"Let's jump in for a swim." Libra Jean pulled her T-shirt off over her head with the confidence of perfect breasts. She wore nothing underneath.

"Wa-hoo!" Gordy too began stripping, dusty and grimed from two days driving north, like a hobbled horse stumbling, ankles bound with jeans. Brantley crawled out of her tent with a squeeze bottle of Dr. Bronners Biodegradable Peppermint Soap in one hand, stopped, gawked, looked over at Kezia and shrugged, peeled off her brown nylon tank suit with the runs in it and waded in.

The yellow float with the bunny head on the front stopped bobbing. The children stood up in the shallows and stared.

"Hey you guys." Kezia's voice startled herself. "Cut it out. Back with the suits, come on." Desperately she looked at Ian. He had to stop them: GordyandLibraJean were his friends, his age, they had started it all.

But the entity known as IanandKezia was in trouble. This trip would bring them back together, Ian had said. But neither heaven nor a double sleeping bag could zip together what the years had torn asunder.

Phhftt.

The strong protective mountain man of Kezia's imaginings had finally expired softly and sadly somewhere on the car trip north from New York.

They'd met after an all-nighter a friend threw. Ian had crashed next to her and when she woke up she said, "My name is Kezia and if you touch me I'll scream."

They had shared an apartment for two years with a dirty spot on the wall by their bed—fingersmudged from so many times Kezia had braced herself clambering out over his sleeping legs. His knees and the tops of his thighs had small places she loved to kiss on the way: bald of hair. One morning they had lain together and giggled; outside in the alley a mourning dove alternated with a police whistle that blew fifteen times (she had counted). They had laughed together because they could laugh in bed.

And yet they couldn't talk.

Covered with this blind cloak Kezia was speared by so many terrible hurts, bewilderments, pains, enormous angers. But she had no idea where they were coming from, or why, or who was out there threatening her, or whether she was only hurting herself. Until she said one perfect morning in complete blind naivete, "I'll never love anyone else."

"Don't say that," Ian said.

Until then she never knew that it wasn't totally perfect, that he felt (or must have felt) also the hurts, angers.

She was willing to talk about anything but not brave enough to take the initiative. They sat by Manhattan's East River for hours watching tugbouats and garbage scows go by—in perfect silence.

Now, at Alewife Pond, Ian was trying not to stare at Libra Jean. "Nothing to get uptight about, right?"

Libra Jean bent at the knees, pudgy in the shallows, splashing water up on her short thighs. Her mass of frizzy hair was matched by pubic hair so abundant it bushed between her thighs from behind. Gordy bellyflopped in, size thirteen feet and genitals to match, the longest balls Kezia had ever seen. Even Brantley looked a stranger, brown with a white "bathing suit" of untanned skin, breasts large and pendulous and between her breasts a patch of dark hair (her mother had it also) which she disdained to shave. Her long beautiful legs started out slim and grew slimmer on the way down. Her crossed arms were hugging her chest, one leg raised at the knee—August Morn.

"Brantley, please do it. Put your suit back on."

She dove in and reemerged spouting water. "See? Nothing shows now. Come on in, chicken. Take it off."

Ian looked at Kezia. "Come on, it'll be fun."

She saw the struggle in his face, the effort to be "laid back," to stifle his natural fastidiousness, to join in. He had looked the mountain man of her imaginings: he never wore suits or deodorant, spent all his free time in the woods. It meant a whole sexual thing in her mind, he would be totally natural about sex, could accept her birthmark, wouldn't get upset over "natural" functions. But the truth was he didn't feel any more natural doing things than anyone else. He was looking at Kezia now with a dark sorrowful look.

"Dive in, you Ivy League janitor," Gordy called.

She heard his zipper, then he pulled down his jeans. He was only 23. No matter how he felt he always went along, Gordy the leader, Ian the follower. Kezia was 31. "It's not my fault I'm eight years younger," he'd said.

She watched his hand reach for the waistband of his white briefs. They were ironed: he wasn't called "janitor" for nothing.

His hand rested on the sunny patch between her shoulderblades. They still loved each other, even though they knew it wasn't working out.

Blindly Kezia shook her head.

In the pond the children's parents, faces stiff and angry, were ordering them ashore.

"Not here. Not like this with strangers and your boyfriend's male friend around, Ian. Not at a child's magic place—Alewife Pond." Couldn't he hear the people they had driven off: slap of towels, angry words, slamming cooler lids? The families were fleeing to their cars.

Browned body, puff of pubic hair—Brantley clambered out onto a rock. She squeezed soap into her palm and began to lather up, totally without modesty. Kezia had always admired her for that before. She stood up: white bubbles in hairy armpits, crotch, down her legs, and then with a rinsing crash she dove off.

Oblivious, Gordy and Libra Jean were two heads close together, necking on a field of dappled blue.

"If you can't beat 'em, join 'em." The hand lifted, was gone.

Kezia tried to tell him with her eyes: she wanted above everything not to be too old, to be a part of things, to be free and wild and wonderful like Brantley and Libra Jean. But not here, not like this. She could hear giggling now from the water. Were they laughing at her?

At the sound Ian stripped off his briefs. He was all of a piece as only short men can be, compact and lithe. His nose and cheeks were feminine pink with sun, jaw gray with unshaved beard. His hair fell long and free. He looked androgynous—from the back almost a woman, from the front bony, craggy, hairy, male. His penis was beautiful: beige and thick skinned. But it had been a secret just they two had shared.

Fingers warm on her chin turned her face up. "I don't have fun with you," Ian said. "Even though I love you."

She watched him choose. For one moment his small hard bottom shone cleft white above the fork of tanned legs. Then it disappeared into the water, his dark brown hair trailing sleek and wet behind him like a seal.

Now the Ivy League Janitor was compulsively barreling in a crawl straight down the middle of the pond toward its northern shore: a distant mile and a quarter beyond.

Whose island was it? What right did these strangers have here?

Kezia crawled into the stifling low canvas tube of their tent, changed into her one-piece bathing suit. She peered out the tied-back flap of the door. The parents and children were long gone. A shrieking water fight created false white waves.

"Hey, great," Brantley said. "Here she comes."

Kezia sank into the water, the cold a sharp shock, and breaststroked deeper until her telltale bathing suit was hidden. Beneath the water their voices were gone, roaring silence like a shell's music in her ears. Her legs scissored and kicked through the icy cling of lilypad stems for as long as she could hold her breath. Fish grazed down the calf of her right leg. She kicked and the cold ached, rushed off the top of her head as she surfaced, gasping for air. She sank again and kicked, rose and breathed and sank in a rhythm of forgetfulness. Nothing mattered but this, swimming with the sun gliding above your wet hair.

When at last, reluctant, she surfaced again she heard a man's deep voice in mid-bellow.

"You hippies get the hell out of there!"

Kezia blinked away a veil of water.

"*Out*. Haul your brown-rice eating asses out now!"

Tall forest green uniform with glint of brass badge, gray Stetson, powerful legs planted far apart. Barrel chest heaving, arrogant authority above the brown bulge of a scuffed leather gun holster low at his hips.

Her fingers wiped dripping water from her brow, the choking vegetation of the pond hiding her body, moving green around her head. She rubbed her eyes, trying to focus on the park ranger's face.

The others were disembodied heads floating among the white lily pads. Brantley's voice croaked, a chastened frog. "We, uh, haven't got anything on."

"Yes. Twenty-five outraged citizens just drove up and told me."

"No sign said no stripping," Gordy said.

"OUT."

"What's he so excited for?" Libra Jean said. "It's nothing. Nudity. It's natural, isn't it?" But now she was clambering out, and then Gordy and Brantley. The ranger stood hands on hips scrutinizing the women as they raced for their tents.

Finally Ian started for the shore.

Solemn, fierce, the ranger's face peered out at Kezia from under the Stetson's brim.

Only her face was visible as she treaded water, heart loud in her ears. There was something almost familiar about him, but what? When? If only she could see under the brim of his hat.

"Come on, Kezia," Ian called from the shore.

Expectantly the ranger leaned forward, waiting to see one more nakedness rise.

Toe-dancing on the slimy weedgrown mud at the bottom Kezia pushed toward the shore, staring at him boldly as her body rose. Water poured off her shoulders, ribbons of droplets from her electric blue tank suit to the sharp hard pebbles of the shore. "Satisfied?"

His gaze took its time traveling over her, then looked her abruptly in the face. "Disappointed."

Her too-large hands met behind her back, tips of her fingers cold against her spine.

"You're only the *second* most gorgeous broad I've ever seen."

Still he was standing there when they all emerged from their tents dressed again, wet haired. "So? Which of you-all's coming back with me to pay the summons?"

"Summons for what?" Ian said. Beside him Libra Jean sat eyes downcast, fingers curled in front of her crossed legs. Brantley fidgeted in her sunburn on unaccustomed places while Gordy sat with knees insolently spread. They were all hurting for money.

"Public obscenity. Public don't even like to see hippies *clothed*."

Gordy's head tipped even farther back. "The naked body's beautiful, man. I'm not obscene. What's obscene is the war."

There was that look again, a steely compelling gaze from under the Stetson while beneath it his long body was deceptively relaxed, loose. "Look, kids, I'm not the Park Service. I'm ag'in 'em. Hell, I just work for 'em."

He cranked open the rusting door of the pick-up truck, yet another National Park Service deal fraying from its side. Weeds grew up between the truck bed's planks. "So which one's the sacrificial lamb?"

"I'll—"

Everyone looked at Kezia.

"Go."

"Wait a minute, honey," Ian said. "You're the one who *didn't*."

"Nobody's perfect, right?" She turned to the ranger. "Do you take MasterCard?"

CHAPTER 32

The road cut through the forest like a wound.

Kezia stared straight ahead, fingers white on the rolled-down window as the truck hurtled toward the ranger station.

The ranger drove one-handed, relaxed. "Sorry to put you through all this. But you people come down here from the city, and your ways don't go over so great around here, you savvy?"

"I savvy."

"People here are the conservative kind."

Where had she seen him before? She glanced again at his profile etched in hard lines against the soft flicker of the sun through leaf spaces of trees. His face was a drawn bow, immobile yet suffused with some barely suppressed tension. An edge of small molded ear lay tight to his skull above his thick powerful neck and broad shoulders. He didn't spare a glance back at her.

"Conservative, huh?" Kezia said. "Is that what the natives are?"

"Don't call them natives."

"Ignorant, benighted is more like it. I mean, can you believe it? This place isn't just the Dark Ages out here. What is it before the Dark Ages? Primordial ooze?"

"Where are you from?"

"New York. Hey—" The truck lurched from rut to pothole. "Do you have to go so fast?"

"I thought girls from New York were fast."

He threw her a wicked look. She could read the message in his eyes: danger—it drew her like Drown Boys Ledge. Its depth wasn't what you thought, nor its location—all disguised in the crystal refraction of water that boiled over kelp-covered fangs. She had floated in the skiff on a rare windless day, head over the side memorizing shape and size and still wasn't its master: when she started the outboard motor it ate her shearpin.

"I thought parks are for people—that's what it said on your literature. Yet you're hauling me in."

"Hippies ain't people. Let 'em buy fifty-pound sacks of nuts and berries and high-tail it to Vermont, not here."

"We're not hippies."

"Now, I can spot a hippie at a hundred yards. Hell, I had sensitivity training. I can spot dope, profanity, nudity, sex. Speaking of which..." He appeared to be staring at her left breast. "You go in for the killer weed?"

"What?" Kezia felt her still-wet hair drip on her neck.

"Your button."

It was still pinned to the T-shirt she'd pulled blindly on: "I've Gone To Pot."

"It means, not that it's any of your business, I've let myself go."

"Well, killer, we're here."

The spruce forest fell back on a naked clearing in which stood a wheelless trailer. Immobile home, it wore cement boots, sinking like some victim of the Mafia. It was painted avocado green like a refrigerator or a kitchen blender. Beyond stood the shingle-roofed redwood outhouse facing discreetly away. On its side boards someone had painted

SMASH THE COSMODYNAMIC COCKSUCKING
CORPORATIONS

and below that;

POST NO DREAMS.

The ranger was holding the trailer door open, and now he swept her a mock bow. "Some days you eat the bear, killer. Other days the bear eats you."

She hurried past him and inside where metal walls enclosed an orange shag carpet and mismatched filing cabinets, drawers askew. Kezia removed an old wasp's nest and sat down on the fuzz balls on the couch.

"Let's just make it fast, okay?" she said. "I just want to get back to my friends and the hell off this godforsaken place."

He pulled the manual typewriter closer across the battered desk. With an overgrown thumbnail he tapped his hat brim up and collected a sheaf of official-looking forms. "Paperwork and paperwork, the clerk-typist quit."

BUT WE ALWAYS DO IT THIS WAY IN YELLOWSTONE, a sign behind him on the wall read.

Where had she seen him before? Her gaze went to the letters on his brass namepin: "Reo Macrae."

But it couldn't be: 22 years ago, when she was nine. "What have we here?" he'd said. "The junior black sheep of the family?" "You let my Gran'sir go!" He was studying her now with the same pale green eyes beneath creaseless lids half-lowered, lazy. Dark flecks in the pale green, and she remembered how she had grabbed his arm, and before he realized it was just a little girl the flecks had flashed wider, darker until his gaze stabbed at her stony and dark.

She felt a stifling excitement, like fear.

"Just got to ask you a few questions, killer. Then you can go."

Name; address (Manhattan); age; driver's license. The money was paid. "Thanks"—he glanced at the paper—"Miss Beal."

"Thank *you*." Kezia stood up.

"So when can I expect it?"

"What?"

"The letter of commendation from the grateful tourist."

"Is this what you do for fun?"

"No."

"What is?"

"I trade insults with the public." He rocked back in his swivel chair, interlaced fingers behind his head, still wearing the hat. "Now we beat our money out of your hide, want a government-issue beer?"

He got up, came back with two beer bottles and a jar of pickled eggs. He opened both beers and they steamed their frost into the air.

She realized her throat was so dry it hurt. She watched his large thick hands with their blunt fingertips sprinkle salt on the white paper plate, fish boiled eggs out of the purple beet juice, roll one in the gritty bath of salt.

"Help yourself." Half the egg disappeared into his mouth.

She shook her head. Her fingers were laced together red and white, not golden like his skin. He wouldn't be attractive at all, she thought, if it weren't for his skin. She knew she should just walk away. Upside down on the memo pad on the desk in front of her was a list of twenty items under the heading "TO DO."

"Go on, take a beer, killer. They've got a saying around here, the natives as you call them. 'If you wet a board on only one side—' "

" 'it'll warp.' "

She saw the dark flecks widen in his eyes, unfiltered by eyelashes. What had happened to his eyelashes?

"I heard someone say it in the village," she said. "Not that you can really call it a village, nothing's there."

"I like it here."

"You've been here two months then, I'll bet."

"Nope. I was a seasonal here, back when I was eighteen, my first regular job. Paid a dollar ninety-five an hour."

"And you've been here for twenty-two years?"

He stared. "I'm forty, but how did you know?"

"Just a guess." He was looking at her the way she was looking at him: it kept going, too long, too intense. She picked up a beer and took a swallow, cold fire.

"I worked here for a while," he was saying, "then I was a smoke-jumper up in Alaska—"

"Smoke-jumper?"

"Parachute down. Put out fires. Real Smokey Bear, that job. Burned my eyelashes right off. Then I was at Yellowstone so many years they started calling me a homesteader and if you're a ranger, well, it's official policy: you got to *range*."

Kezia sat back down in the chair in front of his desk. "They made you come back here?"

"No. I asked to be sent here. Always liked it the best. Better even than Ellettsville—Indiana—where I grew up. Went to the Miss Ellettsville pageant they had one year, if you won you went on to the state. All these pretty girls, all smiling with these perfect little smiles. Then was the talent part of it and there was this one girl who forgot the words to her song. Everyone else marched on and performed like clockwork, right? But the one who just stood there, silent, she was the one who interested me."

"Why are you telling me this?"

"That girl who forgot her lines, her song. She's like you."

A cold tingle began at her fingertips. "What are you talking about?"

"You forgot to take off your swimsuit."

Kezia put her beer down on the edge of the desk. "I wish you'd take off your hat."

"Why?"

"I can't see your eyes."

"Only time I take it off's when I hit the sack."

He was looking at her again and she felt the mouse pulse hotter on her cheek.

"You with the little guy?" When she didn't say anything, "You know who I mean."

"He's my boyfriend, if that's what you mean."

Reo was idly cleaning his fingernails with the point of a Swiss army knife. "He's got long hair. You know what we do around here with men like that? Hogtie 'em and put the shears to 'em."

"His hair has a sense of humor." She stood up, turned toward the door. "I'm sure that's more than I could say about yours if I could see it."

"You think I'm an old burrhead?"

"I don't care what you've got. I'm leaving now."

Heat, warm animal heat from his body pressed near her, not touching. Tiny hairs on her body rose to meet the heat. A pair of uniformed arms came down around her, pinning her to the wall. She saw the reddened backs of his hands mined with veins and something else there on his right wrist. White as a cataract, a thick ropy band of scar tissue that circled his skin (from a burn?). Just for a second, still not touching, his body arched over hers where she struggled to remain still. Tiny shallow gasps for air: her lungs had forgotten how to breathe.

She smelled his sweat, individual as a fingerprint, a raunchy flower.

"Get out of my way." Her voice came starched as a schoolmarm, chalk streaked. For the first time she saw that above the heavy nose his eyes were black and stony again. Then the dark entity receded and his eyes were searching and somewhat pained. He blinked, and the expressionless mask was on his features again.

"Want another beer before you go?" Casually he turned away toward the little half-refrigerator.

"Waiter, check." She felt the anger heating out of her face, incinerating the vulnerable feeling deep inside. She hugged her arms across her chest, cupping each elbow in her palms like a fragile egg.

"Some shrink," Reo said, "claimed both boys and girls carry their books at their side—are you listening?"

"Yes."

"—until puberty, when girls suddenly switch to carrying them in front of their chest. He says it's because their hips grew too wide. But that's not it."

Her arms tightened across her chest. "What, then?"

"They do it to hide their breasts."

A drop of sweat slid near the corner of his lashes. As he handed her the opened beer bottle she whirled for the door, heard the bottle fly from his fingers and crash to the linoleum. Kezia felt the cold splash up to her knees.

Reo stared at the shards of glass and the spreading circle of wetness. "Sorry."

Kezia felt herself trembling: the beer had soaked her like a blow. Reo was mopping at her bell-bottom jeans with an already wet red neckerchief. She felt his fingers press her calf, then her knee. He's probably had every girl on here.

"Sorry. Can I ride you back to camp, out of town as the sheriff used to say?"

"I suppose you think all the female tourists are like that."

"What?"

"Some sort of harem waiting for your ministrations."

"No."

"No, of course not. I can't imagine why anyone would be interested in you."

"Ask yourself," he said. "You are."

Just as he was laughing, the door pushed open and a man walked through.

Thin, boyish body, old hands, old face: something familiar about this man in his ill-fitting plaid sport jacket that gaped at the back of his neck. His face was a red sea behind islet-freckles of brown. "Been a report of skinny dipping out at the pond, Macrae. Mind getting back to work and checking it out?"

"All taken care of." Reo grinned at Kezia.

"Can't have that kind of thing around here. Are you the one did it, Miss?"

"This is the one who *didn't,*" Kezia said.

"They paid the fine, it's all taken care of," Reo said.

The man picked up the sheaf of forms from the desk, then turned with a slow smile. "Kezia Beal? Don't you recognize me, hon? Well, I got pretty successful and all. Acting superintendent now that old Clyde up and quit."

"Ran off with the clerk-typist?" Kezia said.

"Just as much vinegar as ever. Don't you know me? Milo Gilley."

She knew him—the man from the Lobster War. He took her hand, and she felt his palm perspiring. "I'm the park superintendent now. Surprised? No one ever thought I could make good. Nose to the grindstone, that's all." Gilley looked over at Reo while still pumping Kezia's hand. "Knew little Miss Kezia here when I first come to Aguahega. Was a lobsterman living on the main then."

"She's from New York."

Gilley laughed. "Have you been feeding our boy here some nonsense? Well, go on, Macrae, clean up that mess there."

Kezia looked down at Reo who was on his knees with dustpan and brush, saw the color flushing up his neck. She waited until he looked up, gave him a Miss Ellettsville smile. "Mr. Gilley gave us some of his lobster catch back when my father was killed."

"Killed?"

"A lobster fracas—" Gilley began.

"A lobster war," Kezia said.

"Her sister's married to a Chancellor," Gilley said.

"You mean the Chancellors of Chancellor Parkway?"

"Both sides thought it was as bad as an interracial marriage," Kezia said. "We thought it just as bad as they did. And remember, back then seventeen states had miscegenation laws. Couples were arrested, told to leave the state and not return for twenty-five years."

"All that money," Gilley said.

"Yes," Kezia said. "Love makes passion, but money makes marriage."

"They probably used to do that before," Reo said, "I mean, up at the Point. But they didn't *marry* them."

"Well, I don't think about those things anymore. Past history. I live in New York."

"Going back soon?" Gilley said. White lines cracked his forehead, a high expanse topped with pale hair in greasy separating strands. Kezia saw some unexpressed urgency behind his gaze.

"This is just a vacation, two weeks' off. We're going to go on, canoeing, the Allagash Waterway."

Gilley seemed to relax. "Long's you're here, Kezia, come on in my office." His head turned back toward Reo, who stood as if to follow them in. "Can you manage some coffee for us, Macrae?"

In Gilley's neat office Kezia stared at the polished desk with its prim stacks of papers, corners lined up, so different from the chaos of the desk outside.

"So tell me," he said, "what are you working at down to New York?"

Reo stood there with a tray and coffee straight from the machine.

"I work in the smudged cubicles of Gimbels writing ad copy. Like for a shower head appliance, 'Two Screws And You're Ready For A Shower.' "

Gilley sat there nodding seriously as Reo poured the coffee. "Well, I just wanted to be sure you were all right."

"All right?"

"Well, after all that happened. Back then."

She felt a shaft of anger but she didn't know why. "Of course I'm all right. That was then. This is now. I have a career. We do good work, considering the budget."

"What's this?" Reo said. "Did I hear you use the corporate 'we'? You've sold out to Madison Avenue already?"

"Some thoughts on advertising as a career," Kezia said. "If you're going to sell out, make sure the price is right."

"Put me down with JFK. He said his dad told him all businessmen were sons-of-bitches."

"Ladies present, Macrae," Gilley said.

"In the next few years (if not already)," Kezia said, "required reading at the highest corporate levels will be the quotations of that son-of-a-bitch, Chairman Mao."

"Does that mean you like it, killer?"

"No. I hate it."

"Then why don't you quit?"

Gilley sat watching them, his coffee untouched.

"Can you type?" Reo said.

Kezia stared at him.

"We need a clerk-typist. If you want to quit."

"I don't think—" Gilley began.

"Sure. All she'd have to take is the general inventory test, not even a typing test, right? She'd be a GS-Three, or is it Four?"

Kezia saw it: fear on Milo Gilley's face, but why?

"I have a job already."

"Macrae, get back to work or you won't have one. So. You'll be here how much longer, Kezia?"

"Two days."

He nodded. "Well, have a good time." He was handing her a folded map, pressing it into her hands whether she wanted it or not, she could feel the sweat from his palms.

Outside the trailer she opened it, her right hand chilling on the creek-wet stone that weighted one of the four corners of Aguahega. It fought her, stretched taut, billowing starchy and new. The real colors of Aguahega weren't here: primary blue slashed with green, the pastels of Alewife Pond. Here was pea-green with yellow shading for the higher areas, mimicking folds and contoured hills. Solid red lines were roads, dotted red were trails. Familiar landmarks were renamed: Crotch Harbor sanitized to "Dunlap Harbor," the nameless cliffs now laboring under "Artists Point."

There was no white inholding left on the map. All was Norumbega Park green even down to Toothaker Harbor, even down to where Perley's House should have been.

"You don't need a map, do you?" Reo said. He had come up behind her, was looking down at the map.

Behind her the creek rushed its water-tumbling sound around a dented Sierra Club cup, an aluminum rock abandoned in the mud. Beyond the fringe of spruces came a louder sound, the intermittent drone of engines of the Fairfield C. Chancellor Parkway. If you concentrated hard enough, you could pretend it was bees.

Kezia looked up at Reo. If he hadn't been a ranger, perhaps...

But he was. He was the park. The park was him.

Whisgig Creek seemed to swell louder in her ears, bubbling merrily over the rocks the way it always had. Remember? Those bayberry bushes down at Whisgig, the bayberry wax bubbling musky and herby, green stained cheesecloth, voices laughing together: hers and Victorine's. The candles finally lit—Christmas Eve.

Now a sign at the creek read:

SURFACE WATER IS OF QUESTIONABLE PURITY

TREATMENT OF DRINKING WATER IS RECOMMENDED.

Kezia straightened, something dry and sharp in her throat. Norumbega National Park, the green map read.

Aguahega was gone.

But Victorine had bought back Perley's House from the DiBlasis, paying an outrageous price no one else could afford, cutting off the park's lower offer at the pass. With Chancellor money Perley's House was deeded back to Clara Beal. It was Victorine's first act of Chancellor largesse—collecting the bouquet of thanks like a brand-new diva taking bows.

Why was it easier to hate someone for doing good than bad?

Why was the inholding now green?

Kezia crushed the map back together again shapeless in her hands, thrust it at Reo. "You're right, ranger. I don't need a pictorial representation of reality. And Aguahega doesn't need you. All you redneck park people—you're all buzzards of a feather."

"I let it drop."

She looked at him: the mask was back on his face.

"The beer bottle. I thought it was better, don't you? Just to drop the whole thing."

"We're not here to see your damned park. We're leaving right after the Sheep Drive."

POST NO DREAMS.

CHAPTER 33

1974 - Sheep Island, Maine

"Faster, Ian," Brantley said, eager to see the Sheep Drive.

"Give him a break. Waves, sheep, and women can't be turned." Kezia heard the elation in her own voice. Clara Beal was waiting for her somewhere there on Sheep Island which bulked larger with every tug of Ian's oars. Kezia turned her gaze from the dark narrow shoreline of Aguahega, pinched between a wall of firs and the sea. Maybe that was why she'd had the thought in the ranger's office—to come to the Drive. Sheep Island was open, sunny, nearly free of trees—between its rocks an Emerald Irish green.

"We're leaving tomorrow, aren't we?" Libra Jean said.

"Sure, but you'll see. You wouldn't want to miss the Sheep Drive. Used to be a vacation from school. All the neighbors and a big picnic. First running the sheep, yarding them, then the shearing."

"Great," Gordy said. "It's the wild west."

"Nice," Libra Jean said. "But it isn't the Grand Canyon."

Gordy looked at her. "Just as long as we don't run into any more rules. More Smoky Rangers, more asshole cops."

The skiff was so heavy each pull raised Ian's bottom off the plank. He put the oars down, took hold of Kezia's hand. She felt her cold palm crimp, a lifeless part not attached to her. The dawning sun gave no warmth yet to the air.

"Lighten up, you guys." Kezia grabbed the oars, started rowing standing up the way she used to, the white paint of the oar handles flaking sharp and spiky into her palms. Ahead lay the thumbnail of an inlet and above it the sheep pen and the wooden shack to the right. Something moved on the hill, catching Kezia's eye—an old woman in a print dress so washed-out it looked white.

Kezia forgot to row. The swash of waves batted the skiff's nose.

The woman topped the hill, walking wide with each step, watching her feet and the ground. Her fingers were spread wide, aiding as if with invisible canes the reluctance of her high-laced black shoes.

Was this the person who had towered over her in might and anger so many years ago, forced her to drink the spring tonic called gargadee? It was milk from the Vannahs' cow that had just freshened, blue and clumped with threads stirring outward like kelp, *gag*adee.

The skiff clanged ashore on a wave of rusted cans. Clara Beal, 78, squinted at her granddaughter. The fire was gone or banked, covered now in white ash.

Didn't Grandm'am recognize her?

Kezia felt the immense weight that was her feet, and they slowed.

Grandm'am's mouth fell open, a round hole where her cheeks sucked in over loss of teeth. "Kezia." Reserved as always.

Kezia thrust herself desperately into the old woman's arms. They had got thin as the center of her body thickened, and Kezia felt the arms tremble and the pallid chill of the skin. When she pulled back to look at her, tears stood in the bleached, once-gray eyes.

"Remember what Gran'sir used to say, Grandm'am? 'The man in the wilderness asked me, how many strawberries grow in the sea?' "

Grandm'am's thin colorless lips smiled. " 'I answered him as I thought good. As many as—' " Her eyes clouded, paler still. A look of anxiety came into her face. She squinted at her granddaughter. "Pants too tight. Is that how you run about in New York?"

Kezia could hear the rocks resettle under her feet—*ping ping ping*. "I brought us some wine for lunch, Grandm'am. Red wine, the kind you like best." Kezia hoisted the leather wineskin.

"The doctor says no."

When had Grandm'am gotten so thin?

As she introduced everyone, Kezia tried not to stare at the woman in the loose dress, no more than a stick in a sack. Now Grandm'am bent over, tying the skiff's painter and then straightening, the dress empty around her, the painter's mark across its front—muddy and green and young with rockweed. The first light of dawn fell on Clara Beal's hands. The backs were dry and scaly with knotted veins, liver spots, venous lakes—flat vessels that had pooled blue and exhausted from the fight up from her legs. The light splashed pale on her neck dotted with skin tags—soft small protrusions the size of peas. Her face was shiny and flat, thin and liver spotted. Thank God for dappled things, some poet had said. Did he love old age then? It turned curdled, spotting the colors of youth just as it had Gooden Beal.

Kezia looked at the shears by the pen and the long burlap bags for the wool. "So tell us, Grandm'am. Let's get started. Tell us where you want the human corral."

The dawn breeze warmed and soon vanished. The drenching dew dried on Kezia's legs in air that had grown perfectly still. They all stood: a fence of bodies to funnel the sheep across the isthmus into the pen. The sheep trail was narrow and hard-packed, hoofprints cloven as satyrs in the mud. The path divided and redivided—to the left, right, up, down, sprinkled with droppings rabbit-small. All eyes looked north toward the hills and trees at the far end of Sheep Island where the men would soon start the flock running.

She hadn't seen Nate Vannah in ten years.

You don't look for happiness, you don't expect it, and yet suddenly it was there.

"Remind me before we leave, Brantley. There's a place I want to show you, where wild orchids grow. Just the color of your fingers."

"You were lucky to grow up here." Brantley had literally proved it true: you can't go home again. Returning for a visit last winter she had stood outside her parents' house, unable to go in. Her room had a view. Brantley did not. Hours passed. Finally her mother had seen her: it was snowing quite hard—a statue in an empty winter garden. Brantley had checked into an expensive psychiatric clinic for three weeks. The drugs had released her; she carried them everywhere in case the dosage failed.

"Yeah," Ian said. "Me in Brooklyn, you here."

Half a mile to the north all was unsuspecting quiet and peace among the flock: thirty-one sheep, thirty-nine surviving lambs. The ewes' heads were down, muzzles busy in the dense short grass. The lambs, born in April through May, alternated cropping grass and suckling, the sun warming their still dew-wet fleeces.

Now there were forty lambs. This newest one, black-faced, picked his way along the soft brown dirt of the sheep run to join its mother, late as always, slower than the rest. His gait was different, delicate, wide stanced. He stumbled now in the rocky meadow where pink granite threatened its warning, sparkly with galena, zinc, and copper. And there were the dangerous fluffs of eider nests too, gray down plucked from the female's breast and held together with tiny feathered barbs, shielding two to four large cream-greenish eggs. The nests hid in the grass and by the jagged shapes of driftwood—a trod egg was pain, shattered shell cut like stone.

But standing here in this dirt-soft patch the lamb felt safe. He lowered his nose toward the inviting green aroma of the grass, spindly legs tripodded apart. His pink and black muzzle lipped, small teeth tore through the blades of grass between forelegs that ended, fleece soiled, without hooves.

He had been born that way, a congenital anomaly. At birth Clara Beal had seen him from a distance, already standing and nursing, apparently as hardy as the rest. A year before she would have looked closer, during the count. But this year the sheep ran endlessly through her mind, nose to tail, she couldn't count because she couldn't tell the beginning from the end.

The sun dried the grazing flock's wool, burned into their withers with the promise of summer. And then the silence emptied out.

A manyheaded monster jumped up from behind the screen of raspberry bushes, drumming Indian war whoops against its many mouths with raspberry-stained fingers. Wild bleating now and the sound of hooves thudding, behind them hunters with blood-lust in their yells.

The lamb without hooves ran bloodied already, oblivious to all save the necessity of not being left behind.

Listening to the men's cries from where she waited to the south, Kezia felt the hairs on her body stand on end.

They could hear the sheep running now, topping the hill and pouring down, a white river that surged left, then right, then galloped straight at them.

Kezia's knees tightened with the urge to break and run.

Libra Jean went suddenly AWOL, darting behind Gordy. As if sensing this weak link the black-faced sheep in the lead veered toward her. Libra Jean ran toward the shore and the entire flock pelted after her, the sheep river overflowing the break and spilling out onto the seaweed-slippery rocks. Finally they stopped, looking back at the yelling humans and waving arms while the incoming tide plucked at the wool of their bellies, washing their tired legs.

"Damn it all!" Five hunters stood silhouetted on the hilltop. "Couldn't you guys hold them any better than that?"

Kezia squinted up at them. "What're you? A row of braves brave enough to squawk at squaws?"

Floppy rubber boots, dark pants, sweatshirt, an edge of brown hair, skull wide and plastered naked with damp. He was waving, dripping: the sweat clung glistening in beads and rivulets to his hair. Shock fell in her, separate blows down through her body.

Nate was fat. The work clothes hid his body but not the bulk. His face—once flat cheeked, hard chinned—was lost in padding, double chin. Only his eyes were the same above pools of darker flesh. On a street, in New York, she would not even have recognized him.

"Hello, Nate."

Was there anything still there when he looked at her, that power that was a will-o-the-wisp, the power that radiated, that gathered in that certain look in someone's eyes. Kezia had seen it blink out like a light switched off in Ian's eyes. It could be hard sometimes to know who had really switched it off. But once gone you could never recover it. Ian looked at her now like a sister, a sunset, a club sandwich—something liked, appreciated, even loved but something he could live without.

The hunters reformed, keeping abreast of each other in a line that stretched out to the edge of the rock-strewn water's edge, shouting and waving their arms over their heads. Two other island men—one tall, one small—and an even smaller island boy. One man from away, tall, barrel-chested, who was he?

The worn weave of the man's jeans gripped the muscled clench of his thighs. One jeans pocket was torn off, its outline darker than the rest. Against the pale sky the red and yellow plaid shirt armholed with sweat was bright as a flag. Now the blue mesh visored cap was snatched off, waved like a banner over his head. The ends of Kezia's fingers went cold.

Out of uniform she hadn't even recognized him.

Reo Macrae chased the sheep toward her from the shore.

The human fence had repaired itself and this time the sheep darted, veered wildly, finally followed their Judas leader into the pen. The gate was swung and latched shut. As the sheep pressed and circled nervous as herring in a weir, Kezia joined the others in a victory yell.

Reo looked at her with a sardonic smile, his fine ginger-brown hair soft on his hard bony face. His baggy low-slung jeans were drying out from the dew, laced workboots white with salt.

"Keezie, don't you recognize me?"

One of the island "men" stepped forward: it was Deenie Beal, 22. Years ago she had demonstrated her specialty whether you wanted her to or not—imitating a horse with a deafening whinny. The last Kezia had heard, Deenie was bucking men off like a rodeo. But now she was dragging one forward, center ring.

"This is Duane. Didn't tell anybody till last week but we've been married three months now."

Why was she always the last to know? "Congratulations. But—I mean, I still think of you as just so young."

Deenie's face closed, crimped. She was darker than Kezia and Victorine with crinkly brown hair, full cheeks and a prominent chin. When she smiled her eyes disappeared and lines formed like parentheses around her mouth, small and bright as if bitten red. She was not smiling now.

"Apparently not *too* young."

Duane Mackle shifted weight beside her, his broad flat face pricked with a sharp nose as if a potter thumbed out a pull of clay.

"We sneaked off, Duane and me, spur of the moment. Easier that way."

"It was some cold when we got hitched," Duane said. "So cold I saw a chicken with a capon. Huh huh huh."

"Did you ever see a ring this big?"

Deenie's hand reached out to touch Kezia's, skin as rough as Kezia's had been after the summers raking the blueberry barrens. Did Deenie rake berries too, a small bent figure one among scores of rakers moving across the barrens between the poles hung with dead gulls? On Deenie's left ring finger sat a huge spark of light, a half-carat if it was anything, beyond it her fingernail bitten to the quick. The end was raw and red as if she'd been sucking it. Just yesterday, but Deenie was all grown up now.

Kezia glanced at Deenie's abdomen, hidden under the men's work clothes. If she was pregnant it didn't show. "I just wished I'd known, Deenie. Would have baked a cake. I'll get you a present tomorrow, before I go."

"You're leaving so soon?"

"We're going on to the Allagash, then back to New York. Where are you two going to live?"

"Right smack here." Deenie slipped her ring-heavy hand through the crook of Duane's arm. "Did you ever see a ring this big? Bigger even than Victorine's, huh?"

"You're going to live on Aguahega?"

"Duane's going to haul, lobsters been good recently. We're going to get a boat first thing."

Duane's eyes hooded, his toe scraping the dirt. "I dunno. Plenty better life back on the main."

"You'll get to love it here, just like I do," Deenie said. "When I was a kid, just so great. The kind of place you want to bring your kids up in. No pollution. Everybody's friendly. Don't have to worry about some crazy hurting you."

"But, Deenie." Kezia tried to get her to meet her eyes. "The last time I talked to you, really talked, you said you couldn't wait until you were old enough to leave Aguahega. You said it was the most boring place in the world."

"I fell in love." Her fingers pumped Duane's arm as if milking a cow. Her eyes moved darker with warning.

"I'm happy for you. You know I want the best for you."

"Well, I've got it now." Deenie's face was bold with challenge. "Haven't I?"

It had got her.

How many months pregnant? Forget the wedding present, just buy a baby's layette.

"Children are what we need now," Clara Beal said. "Lots of beautiful children to keep the school open. There are only two of dozens of people left, you know."

"Twenty-three, including five children," Deenie said.

Clara Beal smiled, toothless gums in unashamed view. "People who year around live here, that is what we need. Deenie's children we need, the children soon in her body."

"But that doesn't mean Deenie has to be the sacrificial lamb, does it?" Kezia heard herself say. "She should give up her life to vegetate away out here? For what? For the good of the island? For the good of the state? That's communism, isn't it?"

"Of course," Clara said, "you do not believe in the family. You and Wilhelmina, always this career you must have. Selfish, selfish. Now you are this advertising manager—"

"Writer."

"Writer of managing. Makes no good for anything but yourself."

Kezia turned to look at Deenie. "Just stay out of the blueberry barrens then. They spray Guthion on the berries, and God knows what that'll do. Somebody had a miscarriage after a highway crew sprayed Two-Four-Five-T last year."

The silence raked around her head.

Brantley's hand was on her arm, pulling her away. "Come on over to the pen. They're taking bets on the 'horse race.' "

A clean length of canvas had been stretched out on the ground, and two ewes and two hand clippers waited. Nate and Reo started stripping off the wool with exaggerated speed, throwing quick glances at each other's progress, faces screwed tight with effort. The shearing began at the head, the amazingly thick slippery wool peeling off in one piece.

"Come on, Nate!" Kezia saw Reo glance up at her.

Nate threw his arms over his head in a victory wave as his sheep slipped free of its fleece, shook itself dispirited and thin as a Persian cat caught in the rain.

After the shearing came the lambs' turn, the docking and castrating.

"Kezia," Libra Jean said. "You didn't say there was going to be anything of *this* nature."

Ian squatted, arms comfortably across his thighs as he helped to hold a lamb.

The lamb with no hooves wedged unprotestingly against the far end of the round pen. He might be overlooked if he just stood still. His eyes were white-edged in the black mask as one by one his mates of the spring were hauled forth, held, legs stretched stiff, and then the dull axe bit their tails off and there were blaring bleats of fright and pain. They stumbled up with a bit of loose wool pressed on the stump to stanch the blood.

But if you were unlucky enough to be a male lamb there was worse: to be held by the back legs, back pressed against the human's sweating chest while the other human wielded the sharp knife, in one practiced movement cutting off the lower third of the scrotum, and then the balls within.

The knife's blade ran red with blood now—wiped on the men's pants legs, smeared onto the green grass. The lambs humped up, silent and dizzy with shock and pain.

Brantley and Libra Jean had retreated to the blue flag patch on the hill.

But Torby Vannah stood tall and stout, already helping, not afraid of blood. Kezia stared at Nate's child, a boy of seven. He had run to his father when the men pelted down the hill and Nate swept him up and Torby burrowed under the loose tail of sweatshirt, his face laughing from the V of the open collar. Nate was dripping with sweat: the beads clung glistening now on Torby's round laughing face.

"We have a child, let's name it Torby. Okay?" Now Nate had stolen Torby's name.

"Hello, sailor, come here often?"

She turned around, found herself looking into Reo Macrae's eyes. "Since when did rangers go slumming with the natives?"

"The natives seem to like the park: jobs, you know. It's the summer people who don't. I think they call that irony in New York.

But maybe you didn't know. Haven't been back here for a while, right?"

"I don't see much of my family these days."

"Oh?"

"I have my own life. In Manhattan. A family of friends. I don't depend on anyone here."

"I guess that's why people start their own families."

"The nuclear family is on the way out, or didn't you hear that way out here? It's the greatest boon to women's freedom since we got the vote."

"So that little squirt didn't ask you to marry him yet?"

"You are the most insufferable—I see no reason to talk to you any longer." She tried to rush bodily through the closed sheep pen gate.

He crossed the dirt and held it open for her with a mocking grin.

She knew he was staring at her still. Her feet churned through the rutted mud.

Woe from the sheep pen, lambs desperate to find their mothers among these new bald thin strangers, fleece left behind. Mothers answering, sorting them out. And then a woman's cry, louder than the blare of the sheep, Clara Beal's cry brought everyone hurrying back.

They stood looking down at the lamb with no hooves.

Nate dropped his head, pinching his forehead between finger and thumb. They kneaded the skin for a moment as if it were bread. He looked up, red crease still there. "Well, guess there's no use delaying the inevitable. Torby, what say you and me go back across and fetch my gun?"

Libra Jean began to cry noisily.

Kezia turned her face away, stared out to sea. Gran'sir always said the breeze heeds the tides, comes in with the flood and dwindles with the ebb. Now the wind lifted her long red-gold hair.

She was not going to get involved.

She didn't live here.

Tomorrow she'd be gone.

Nate and Torby started walking slowly toward their outboard boat. Torby's hand came up, found the large warm one that gripped his own.

"Nate!"

His shambling head swung its slow way around.

She ran to catch up with them. "Nate, let the lamb live for the summer. Maybe he can't make it through the winter but that's so many months away. Just let him have the summer."

Everyone now was crowding around.

"Please, Nate." She looked up at him. His eyes were the same bright blue, inexpressibly sad. But looking she saw that the light was still there, the Look not yet switched off into dark.

"Might get into all manner fixes, way he is, Keezie. Hard, I know but it's the most humane thing."

"Well, do the most sheep thing, then."

She didn't care if anyone was watching. She put her hand on his arm. "Please, Nate. I don't know why, but I want it so much. I've never asked you for anything ever, have I? Now I'm just asking for this. Let him have the summer."

"We don't sentimentalize animals on here, you know that now. Can't raise sheep and look on them that way. Way it is."

Torby was looking at her with eyes round and bright, as removed from her world as the eyes of a deer.

Reo was squatting on the ground, fingers playing with a clod of dirt. His flannel shirt had pulled up, his jeans tugged so low she could see the cleft of his buttocks golden like the rest of him, moist with a few downy hairs. The color of a pelt, not skin.

"If a woman wants something that bad," he said, "give it to her I say. Can't argue with 'em."

The silence stretched like a long silver line.

Reo's hand contracted, then released: the clod rained in loose dirt between his grimed fingers. "Can't argue with 'em because they always win."

"I don't know." But Nate's eyes were lowered, watching the toe of his rubber boot scrape a semicircle in the dirt. He looked up at Kezia, suddenly grinned.

She rushed to him, kissing him on the cheek, old fish smells, sharp sweet masculine Nate, the brush of unshaven bristles, he smelled like her father and it stirred her now.

Nate looked at Torby and winked. *"Women."*

"You won't regret it, Nate. We'll take care of him, you'll see, Grandm'am and me. All summer—"

She saw the shock on Ian's face, on Brantley's face, on Nate's face. "All summer?" Nate said.

Reo was standing with legs apart and boot toes turned out, thumbs hooked low in the pockets of his already perilously low slung jeans. His left eye looked larger than the right: the left was calm but the right was mocking.

"You mean I finally got me my clerk-typist?" he said.

CHAPTER 34

1974 - Thrumcap Island, Maine

"So you're going to stay?" Reo said.

"No, No. Of course not. Just a few more days and I have to get back. I've got a job, you know."

"This jaunt's just your fare-thee-well? Mama, don't let your girls grow up to be heartbreakers."

Did he care for her at all?

"Your heart's rusted and there's dust on your trigger," Kezia said.

"Don't bet on it."

Kezia glanced from the darkening swells ahead at his face dark against the cockpit lights. Framed in oilskin yellow was the man-in-the-moon profile, curving back at forehead and chin. He didn't spare a glance back at her.

She felt a tiny niggle of fear. They were going out to Thrumcap Island and would not be coming back before tomorrow at the earliest. They were stuck with each other for the first time overnight.

But this was what she'd wanted, wasn't it? Three times they had met after Ian, Brantley, Gordy, and Libra Jean had left, three times their hands had been all over each other, desperate kisses deep and wild. "Where can we go?" he said.

He lived in the back of the trailer with Milo Gilley. She was staying with Grandm'am in Perley's House.

"Thrumcap Island," she said. "My aunt's got a house out there and she gave me the keys."

In the next moment she was swept with doubt.

Yet here they were on their way out, course southwest, Thrumcap a squiggle of yellow outlined in blue on her chart, surrounded by waves of numbers that were depths, barred by ledges looming like a mine field. Here she was piloting Nate's treasured boat, and she'd assured him she remembered what she was doing.

"What're you *doing*?" Ian had asked, tearful night, angry dawn.

"I don't know."

As they passed Aguahega's southern cliffs in the warm summer afternoon air, fast-gathering clouds were massing gray beyond its rim.

" 'Short warning, soon past, long foretelling, long last.' " Kezia's voice was happy and secure. "This'll be over in no time. That's Grumpy Shoals over there. At high tide you can get close enough to haul your string of pots there."

Now the rain was beginning to fall, each drop striking with a separate hammer of cold. Kezia's fingers edged the throttle harder.

"Never sat before while a damn woman drove."

"You'll get to love it, Reo."

"I think the tom turkey ought to do the gobbling, don't you? Hen shouldn't crow."

"Go to hell, turkey."

"What a pair of ovaries! A girl who talks smart, cusses, drives great big boats in hip boots."

"I never said I was a southern belle."

"Did I ask you to be, killer?"

"No." She wished they were already safely there.

"Only one place you have to be a woman with me."

"Where?"

"In bed."

She could feel the heat of him even through her oilskin against her back. And then his arms came down around her where she stood at the wheel. Not touching, his body arched over hers while she struggled to keep the boat on course.

Like a mink, like a dog, suddenly she felt his strong white teeth seize the nape of her neck.

Her knuckles strained white on the wheel. His teeth pinched, hurting her there.

The hairs on her neck stood on end. Excitement struck her like a blow.

His teeth released her, and she felt his warm finger gently rubbing the moisture there.

Her heart jerked, and she felt the excitement draining out her fingertips, leaving her almost nauseated, trembling in its wake. The wet place on her neck stirred, cold now in the air.

What she felt was just a rebound to Ian's going, wasn't that right? This strange man meant nothing to her. But something had torn free in her after Ian left, like a leaf tumbling on the wind. Brantley had understood, had hugged her there at the end. Her eyes ached from staring into Brantley's eyes.

Kezia heard the beer can open, the fizz and then he held it frosty against her lips. She tried to reach for it with one hand but he tipped it against her mouth. Her lips opened, obediently swallowing, struggling to get it all in.

He took the can away and with one hand wiped her chin.

"So you grew up in Indiana?" she said. "It's just a frozen pancake, my brother-in-law said."

"Now *there* were storms. The whole sky would go gray, then turn ghastly yellow; you'd look for twisters to the west. Wind enough to knock you down. But the storms weren't the big thing. Chiggers were."

"Chiggers?"

"Picture yourself in Singapore, temperature and humidity in the upper eighties and that's at *night*. You'd shower, then run dripping nude to lie on your sheets, try and fall asleep while the evaporation's still cooling you. But still you'd feel those chiggers itch. Little red mites that burrow under your skin. Nearly drive you wild. Women's legs all scarred up from scratching at them, and I liked to look at women's legs."

"I'll bet. But wasn't there anything good?"

"Osage oranges big as grapefruit lying in the fencerows, Monarch butterflies orange and black, and bright blue dragonflies."

"So why'd you run away?"

"What makes you say that?" Reo said.

Through the three windows of the wheelhouse Kezia focused on the gray water pockmarked by drops of rain coming straight down. Even as she watched, the wind began again, bending the rain into angles on the waves.

"I just think you and I are alike. I ran away."

"Maybe. Maybe not. But I did run away. I was sixteen that summer, was going to be *the* radio personality of southern Indiana, well, maybe all of the county at least. Stepped off the porch. You could hear the swing stir on the roof-hung chains, creak in the wind. No hint of dawn, black cloud cover, the air sharp with Mom's marigolds. I'd just about made it to the sidewalk when I hear her. 'Reo Macrae! Now just a minute, young man. Tuck in that shirttail! Son, how do you expect to amount to anything in this world with your shirttail flapping like a loose tongue?' "

It was warm now in the space of the wheelhouse heated by the exhaust pipe, comforting warmth. Kezia wondered if the imprint of his teeth was still on her nape.

"So that's why you ran away?"

"Something happened. Just when I thought I had it all. In every class there's a freak—right?—who doesn't fit in. For as long as I could remember I was fat, I was the freak. Always last on the team picks. But that morning I was someone else entirely—Will Ray was the name I picked—Will Ray, the new early-morning deejay with that extra something, that special magic, the mysterious, bodyless, hypnotic Voice addictive as cream puffs that you *had* to hear. All summer, every morning from six to ten."

"What happened?"

"It started out great, the radio show. 'Bottom of the morning to you. This is Will Ray, the Early Worm. In the morning do you hate relentless cheer? Do your eyes look like poached eggs? Do you want to kill your alarm clock? Do you hate the joyful noise of happy deejay rise 'n shiners? Then here's a new breakfast club for you.'

"Then I did it. Just to introduce something new, you know? So I started saying 'If no one's told you yet this morning, let me tell you.'

"What?"

" 'I love you.' It was a live call-in show. People called in by the droves. Told me they loved me too. Told me they told people they loved them—people they hadn't told in fifty years. Written up in the papers, I was even interviewed on another radio show."

"And then?"

"Then a woman called in, had a brain-damaged daughter who never responded to anything anyone said. So I told the daughter I loved *her* too, and the woman said that the daughter smiled. *That* was written up; the thing snowballed, got totally out of hand. I got too involved with that woman and her kid."

"Involved? What about the woman's husband?"

"He'd run off years before. She was only twenty-one."

"Was she pretty?"

She heard his chuckle.

"Well, why'd you run away?"

"Aren't you glad I ran away, to here?" He was looking at her still from under his sleepy hooded lids. But when she glanced up she saw a reflected flicker that wasn't sleepy in his eyes.

"I feel sorry for anyone living here. Don't lump me in with the rubber boot set. Thank you, no. A good place to be from, maybe, not a place you can live."

"Why was it good to be from?"

"Summer was summer then and winter was winter. Real weather, real ice. Vivid light. But of course, I love New York. It's fun in the summer. The Philharmonic plays in Central Park on the Great Lawn. You tell your friends 'Meet me at the front section of the eastern side of the lawn near the baseball backstop. I'll be flying three green balloons.' "

"Well, I like it here, killer. It's very erotic—living on an island."

He's probably had every girl on here.

"Erotic?"

"It's the isolation, I guess," he said, "breeds romance like a shipboard romance. Lots of vibration down under the hold."

"Chance says it's like getting back to childhood—an island."

"Chance?"

The name burst within her, hearing it spoken, like a chrysanthemum of sound. "The Chancellor who married my sister. He says your whole world's a small place with known bounds. And you go barefoot and play."

"That's what I mean, play. Like when you're a kid, right? You're exploring with your hand. You know, first your bellybutton, then lower down..."

The sweat on her lip was there again. Her thighs felt glued together under her wool slacks and oilskin.

He seized her hand and his tongue licked the salt from her fingers. Like a mink, like a dog. She struggled to draw her hand away, slipped it through his grasp. He *has* had every girl on here.

"So why'd this turkey Chance marry your sister?"

"On her behalf, I thank you."

"I mean, he's so rich, right? And she's—"

"A peasant only."

"Something like that."

" 'They are happy perfectly,' Grandm'am says. 'Every couple should be as happy as Chance and Victorine, my only wish.' I got a letter from Victorine before we came up here. She wrote that her cup runneth over. Her *cry* runneth over, more like. The only reason Chance married her was to spite his grandfather. Fairfield always preached about 'All people are equally good in God's eyes.' So Chance hoisted him by his own petard, mocked their pious Christian Do-Good hypocrisy by carrying it to the *nth* degree."

"So what did he do," Reo said, "that was so Do Good?"

"Married Victorine. He got the velvet hand in the iron glove. But she got the Isles Beneath The Wind."

"What's that, killer?"

"Didn't you see the movie *Fanny*? The movie opens with the blast of an ocean liner and the boy looks up, eyes dreamy. He wants to see the Isles Beneath The Wind, where black trees grow, and when you cut them inside they are gold and smell of camphor and pepper. The point is, Victorine never wanted to go there, and did. I always wanted to go but didn't."

"You went to New York, didn't you? It's really about who leaves and who stays, isn't it? Like the pioneers. The leavers are smarter, maybe, more ambitious, more aggressive. Optimists, too. The ones who stay are pessimists: it's bad here but it sure won't get better anywhere else."

Kezia thought of Nate and her heart contracted. "You sure won't make the Aguahega Chamber of Commerce."

"When the guy got to the Isles Beneath The Wind, in the movie, what did he find?"

"Volcanic ash."

"And you've never married?"

"I thought about marriage; and then, I thought again."

"Too afraid?"

"Too courageous."

He shook his head. "A girl who doesn't believe in husbands."

"Or maybe husbands don't believe in me. I mean, marriage just isn't for me. I have a career, you know. You may get stabbed in the back in the working world sometimes. But marriage is people stabbing each other in the front."

"You don't mind running around with a madman, do you?" Reo said.

"No." Her eyes opened wider but only the rain looked back at her through the streaked glass, a roiling wall of dark and lighter grays where the boat's lights struck, bounced off, returned their glare. In the green-yellow flash of lightning she saw the anxiety on Reo's face. White foam blew now in streaks along the line of wind.

But there loomed the treeless hill of Thrumcap Island.

Kezia's hand reached for the security of the Morse lever. She felt a sudden overwhelming feeling of rightness and belonging. The fear was gone. She worked the boat around to the west of the rocks until she could see right up into Thrumcap's tiny harbor. She ran in on a course ESE, leaving another ledge to port.

Then they were running with the ice chests between them up the hill toward the hard-edged geometries, the modern slabs of vertical siding and glass windows that was Aunt Willi's house. Kezia stared up, raindrops flooding her eyes. Twin boxes sharply sloping were gathered into a topknot on the roof, a latter day widow's walk beneath a cedar ceiling veiled now with rain.

And the house dark and quiet ushered them in.

Kezia tried to unclench her stiffened shoulders, the points of her elbows digging in to her sides. Without moving she stood as far away from him as she could. What was this new strange place. The dense air breathed around her with the mystery of her aunt and her aunt's possessions. The sound of a machine started up, hummed now outside the door.

A light went on and Kezia stared at the new strange man. She hoped he would just leave her alone.

"I'm your classic Chief Ranger: commissioned lawman, champion shot. Able to start large fierce generators at a single bound."

She felt his cold wet hands now sliding down her arms. Her oilskin dropped in a puddle at her feet.

If only she were in Perley's House: it looked the way a house ought to, chimney-braced roof facing four square to the south to catch the brief winter's sun.

He was looking at her. "I think we need another brew."

The beer chilled her hand to the bone.

"You're not a moth, I'm not a flame," he said. "Panic is motivated by fear rather than danger. It's contagious. To control panic you just have to control unreasoning fear. A moment of 'stunned silence' follows immediately after someone is confronted with danger. At that moment the appropriate action or spoken word or gesture can control the situation."

She leaned over and kissed him on the mouth.

"Oh, yes, that's better," he said.

She stared at him, realizing that the reins of power she'd held so blithely on the boat were pulled through her fingers, gone.

He was staring at her. "I think an orgasm begins for a man when he first sees a woman, and builds up from there."

She heard her breathing—harsh.

"Here's the ground rules. We're going to stay here for three days—I brought enough food. And two two-fours.

"We're not going to wear any clothes.

"We're going to give everything to each other—even if it's only for three days.

"I'm going to make you come every which way."

His elbows thrust out at her as he pulled his soaked shirt off over his head. His hairless chest gleamed gold and ended in an inch of purple, orange, and green paisley boxer shorts hitched up over his lowslung pants. Below his navel a line of hairs, too dark for his pale head, pointed straight down toward his groin.

"Reo—"

"What's the matter? My brave little darling looks as skittish as a mouse."

She flinched as his hand reached for her, but his fingers were gentle against the side of her face. She felt his full lips tuck into the space above her eye. He kissed one eyelid, then the other. His tongue, like a cat, began to lick her face.

Kezia felt her stomach turn to molten ore—a core of heat that spread downward, dividing her legs, forcing them apart.

He was kissing down the side of her neck. He unbuttoned her shirt and drew it off.

"No," she said.

"Yes." He put his hands on her breasts, rotating them with the nipples in his palms.

She inhaled sharply.

His palm was on her belly, fingers splaying out as he rotated the now burning warmth within. She was on fire. Startled she heard the groan break from her throat.

"Good," he said, perfectly in control.

She fell backward as his thick fingers roughened her pants down. He tried to force her over on her back.

"No." The word extruded, thick and swollen. She didn't recognize her own voice. "Not here." She was on her knees and he jerked her face around against the jeaned bulge at his crotch. Her lips mouthed and moistened over, along the bulge. She could feel the head grow larger through the jeans. She struggled back up onto her feet.

She heard her voice as if from far away. "Let's go upstairs."

Desire was like a haze, she could hardly breathe. His face danced in front of her, red and rigid, shaking and yet immobile, paralyzed. He was kissing her, teeth hard against his lips.

She pulled away, started up the open risers of the stairs, conscious of Reo's gaze behind her at eye level with her thighs. She could hear her breath snagging out in little gasps—the tremendous excitement floated her as if through water—she was already far out beyond her depth.

The cold quilt on the bed grabbed her bare legs, fierce as pain. Then he was arching over her and there was heat and she stretched taut and out along him. When he entered her, she thought she would burst in two.

Suddenly he pulled out of her.

She heard her voice crying, greedy: "Don't stop."

One finger jammed inside her. He had hold now of her diaphragm and she felt it torn out, flung across the room.

"Kezia." His voice was harsh air on her cheek.

Her eyes flew open.

"Don't shut your eyes. Look at me."

But they weren't tender eyes looking at her; they glared harsh with excitement down into her face. A white welt had appeared across his cheek, horizontal, not following the contours of his face. His eyes watched her, drawing her up and out of herself and into his eyes until she came.

Afterward she lay still, the wild excitement just starting to subside. He put her limp arms up around his neck. She heard her own voice weeping out as her arms tightened around him: "I love you."

In his silence her words stretched long, longer, disappearing into the distance.

Fear moved in her, even as he began to move in her again.

But he loved her; she knew he did. If he couldn't say it yet well, soon he would.

Soon.

She looked up. Through Aunt Willi's skylight the air came cold and thin with a wisp of fragrance, beach roses and the sea. Above were galaxies of stars, large white diamonds to bright blue-white dust casting blue-white images down on their bed.

She looked down at their bodies—double star.

Soon.

CHAPTER 35

1974 - Aguahega Island, Maine

It wasn't a three-day blow, the time with Reo, clearing and then passing away.

"I'll call you," he'd said, and then "No, no phones, right? I'll drop by to see you tomorrow, killer, all right?"

Tomorrow was today.

Kezia ran under blue sky cupped close on Toothaker Harbor, the sun following her. Suddenly digging her bare toes deep into warm-wet tidal flat and arching her back, she shouted at joy and the passing day. Then hoarse and aimless she waded out into the waves.

The sound of a window thrown up made her turn around. Grandm'am was leaning out of Kezia's own bedroom on the second floor, white coronet of braid gleaming from the dark beyond.

"Kezia! I found the old deed that you wanted."

Kezia's fingers touched the cement marker where the oak Witness Tree, that had rocked her swing under its dappled light, once stood. She straightened, opening the deed, the sun striking on the blurred words.

> Aguahega May 25 1804. Whereas Mr. Amariah Beal did formerly give his great Farm to be divided between his two Sons Gideon and Isham it was fully agreed on ye day the yeer above written between the Parties concerned who have hereto subscribed that the Division-Line be forever stated and followeth that of Nore-West—End of ye Farm from ye middle of ye fifth line (allowing twenty Roods at ye Norewest End)...

Kezia began to walk the bounds. The skirts of the firs rustled and the hairs on her body stiffened, rose. They were here somewhere, the ghosts of almost two centuries of Beals. She turned and faced the house, imagining the farm as it was then: six cows, a yoke of oxen, fifty sheep, four hogs. She would have tended the poultry, churned butter, spun wool into crude sails for the boats of her father, brothers, her husband...

forever stated and followeth...

She was home.

"Victorine, I have something to ask you."

Kezia tried to think what to say next. The coastline turned in at Haley's Landing, where three ninety-foot piers reached out to sea. The phonebooth huddled at the land end of the south pier, and sharp messages of pain traveled upward: Kezia's knee bracing the door shut. Some internal spring had broken and the wood and glass pleats fought to burst open on the clattering rain.

Static snowed through the line.

In bed in New York, Victorine waited to hear what the "something" was. They had become strangers: no telephone and Kezia could rarely force herself to write. To write meant to summarize your life in a letter, an anxiety-producing thing you didn't want to do on sun-filled Saturday afternoons.

"Is anything wrong?"

"No, no. Everything's right! That's the point. I want to borrow some money, if you'll give it to me. To buy a lobsterboat."

"What?"

The word came at Kezia open-mouthed through the long silvery lines.

"I'm going to live on Aguahega again, haul again. I met this man, Victorine. This time it's the real thing."

"What?"

Love was a bell curve. Too often she'd acted too fast, sent the photo of him (whoever) and her, arms enraptured. Only to have to admit to long-distance questioning that it ended while the photo was in the mail. But if you waited too long to send the photo your breathless descriptions sounded already hollow over changed feelings, even as you tried to deny it to yourself, the end peering up to mock your words.

"We're getting married. Live in Perley's House. Do you think you could spare the money for the boat?"

"Kezia..."

The rain began to dance before Kezia's eyes.

"How can you want to haul again? After what happened to Daddy? You don't belong there anymore."

"You don't understand—"

"No, I don't."

"They catch poachers green-handed these days. Paint the lobsters with invisible green dye, shows up under ultraviolet light."

But her sister didn't laugh.

"If it were up to me..."

Victorine's words bent over Kezia, cliffs in her mind.

"It's Chance who says No, Keezie. He said give to institutions, not individuals anymore. Duane already asked us for money, it's got to stop somewhere, he said. We bought the house for Grandm'am, isn't that enough? He says if you give people money they hate you even more than when you don't."

"But what do *you* think?"

"Look, Keezie, I'm really busy, I've got to go. I'm sorry, it's just not up to me. It seems to take a whole day now to get dressed, go to lunch. Then exercise class. Shop. And dinner. I don't have a moment's rest."

"Shop? How *is* the price of cauliflower these days?"

"Kezia, did anyone ever tell you you're sounding like Aunt Willi? You better grab this guy now you've got the chance."

Clara Beal walked heavily up to her horsehair trunk in the attic. Lifting off the big domed lid, searching under a pile of outgrown baby toys, behind the loose paper in the tray she pulled out a soft knitted bag—the one she had worn around her throat across the terror of the storm-tossed Atlantic. She opened the drawstring and removed the thick fold of bills.

"Twenty thousand dollars!" Kezia drew back as Clara pressed the still crisp unused stack of hundred dollar bills into her hand. "But Grandm'am—where on earth did it come from? How did you come by so much money as this?"

"I earned it, yes, every cent of it. Oh, not that way, stop rolling your eyes like a spooked cow, Kezia. I earned it honestly and it is mine to give and I give it to you." She looked fiercely at her granddaughter, daring her to interrupt. "It is for starting new."

"But Grandm'am, honestly—I just can't take your money like this."

"Hush. Please, my Kezia, you are a woman alone. Take the money, go to the main, go to that dealer and buy the fine clean boat you want. It is clean money, from the laundry, that I saved."

For forty years she'd used the vacant Toothaker Harbor schoolhouse for her laundry business, running it alone from 1932 to 1972, miles of Seal Point sheets.

"Do not live by luck anymore, Kezia. Do not let your children live by bad luck. That is what I want, Kezia, to see you safe, settled somewhere."

"Grandm'am...I just can't accept it."

"It is too late for that, Kezia. I cannot take it back."

"Grandm'am..."

"Now what!"

"Grandm'am, what can I say?"

"Nothing! Keep your flapping trap shut for once in my life and I will be happy. Yes, then I will be happy."

Kezia looked full into her grandmother's eyes for the first time in years. The two women stood eye to eye now that Grandm'am had shrunk with old age. Under her grandmother's straggly brows, which drew quickly down and sought to conceal them, in the corners of the deepset gray eyes Kezia was surprised to see tears.

Kezia went out the back door, heading again for Haley's Landing, while Grandm'am went out the front.

For the first time, Clara saw the long white sheet of paper nailed under the overhang of the front door.

UNITED STATES OF AMERICA
V.
3.38 Of an Acre, More or Less,
Merion County, Maine
Tract No. 101-10, CLARA BEAL
YOU ARE HEREBY NOTIFIED

that a Complaint in Condemnation has heretofore been filed in the Office of the Clerk of the above named Court in an action to condemn an estate in full fee simple title in and to the said property, subject to existing easements for public roads and highways, public utilities, railroads and pipelines in anywise appertaining to the land described in the Exhibits attached hereto and made a part hereof for the use of the United States for the proper administration, preservation, and development of the Norumbega National Park....

Clara Beal expected to see Perley's House worn and old, and so the crumbling mortar brought her no pain. But she had forgotten that the Witness Tree had become just decaying debris. Its heart lay split open and charred before her, by lightning no doubt, and the unburnt remains were silvered-white with age. The few remaining branches bore strange knobs, like an old man's knuckles, which she didn't remember from years past.

Don't you remember? They came, they chopped it down.

She stood heavily, suddenly realizing that she was cold and damp, and that the things she had tried to do in life were things that had to be done over and over. Soon she would be gone, and then who would there be to do them?

She felt like crying. Strange. She hadn't cried in forty years now. She wanted to give up and cry but she couldn't. She had never given up. And somehow it seemed as though now all her tears had dried up within her.

The rain roared about her, streaming from the sides of her umbrella. She walked vacantly to the little valley behind the house. A drop of rain spattered from the edge of her broken-spoked umbrella, and startled, she blinked.

And then again there it was before her: the disorder brought back by the wild. The little water hole was throttled with weeds, lay still and lifeless beneath its rain-ridden surface. Thorn bushes jostled each other, inseparably linked by entwined barbs. Thistles raised their heads and a fallen log cut Persistent Creek, which had angrily driven two channels around it, spurting from either side. The valley stank of foul mud that the rain could not wash clean, only add to.

She thought it would be painful to remember, that the edges of her memories would be raw and throbbing. But perhaps because she hadn't used them for so long, they were healed. She was flooded with a deep warmth. Comforting warmth...

Picking weeds. Yes, that was it. She had been weeding out beyond Perley's House and discovered the miniature valley. She, whose life was so orderly, couldn't bear this insect-humming miasma. Indignantly she looked at the little cross-section of wilderness. The woods, littered with evergreen needles, she couldn't clean. But this was within possibility, just a little dip between two hills. She flexed her square blunt capable hands.

She liked her hands. They were strong, not like those limp white things Mary Stella Witney had. Her hands had done a great deal of cleaning for her. With them she would clean this valley as she cleaned her house and children: roughly, furiously.

Clara had stood looking around her, listing in her mind the tools she would need to tame the valley. And when she went back to the toolshed the valley had somehow changed. She had left the imprint of her vital personality on it. The insects buzzed less joyfully.

She rummaged about in the shed locating tools, prying open long-undisturbed but carefully labeled boxes. Then back to the valley she came with her brown paper bag of lunch balanced on top of her armload of tools. She believed in an ample, comfortable lunch.

Clara hefted the axe, accustoming herself to its heaviness. When the dead tree fell she paused to wipe her forehead on the back of her arm. A hot humidity rose from the stagnant water hole. Sweat pricked her underarms, made her thighs sticky, but she turned back to her work. She chopped the tree into pieces and dragged them over the hill. Then she dug in the fat thick mud and threw shovelsful into the stream to be washed away.

The sun was directly overhead when she put down her tools to sit under the shade of a birch tree. As she ate, tucking her wax paper in her pocket, she looked at her handiwork. She pictured neat little rows of petunias and marigolds with dwarf phlox as borders, the kinds of flowers they had up at Seal Point. She pictured the clean, pebble-surrounded water hole, and the ancient sagging water trough scrubbed and whitewashed.

"A grape arbor would be just right over the steps I will set in. It will get plenty of sun there. I can make grape pies that will win a blue at the fair." With the thought of wresting the ribbon from Mary Stella, Clara arose and went back to her digging.

What exultation when her shovel struck the clean slate! She could almost hear it breathing again in the open air. She let the water numb her feet as she watched the mud washing away. Then she bent and pulled at the harsh water plants with her bare hands, not heeding as their spiky edges cut her fingers.

"Next," she thought, straightening, "I will chop out all of that underbrush."

As the valley became civilized, a certain quietude came to her heart. This was *her* place, the place of the woman alone. She had taken it by the ear and wrung it, chopped it, scraped and scrubbed and beaten the wild back to the woods...

The house. Oh, yes, Perley's House. Her memories of the valley had been so warm she had almost managed to forget about the house.

Nothing would grow there: the soil was thin over granite bone. She remembered how empty it had been, how silent after the children had gone, first Willi, then her own sweet Johnny. And when Gooden died there was no one left to chide about dirty feet and unshaven beard anymore.

She remembered how painful the mercy of the DiBlasis had been. Dirty people, that was all they were. She had wanted to clean their house and children and lives more than she had ever wanted to clean anything.

She looked at the emptied bole of a tree, patchily covered by a desiccating skin of bark. Even in the rain she could see what had happened. And the valley had seemed completed to her, finished, final, because she had done it herself. It was gone, too.

She walked slowly back up the hill. She stood by the great curve of shingled gambrel roof that could no longer protect Perley's House. The rain came down now in gray currents around the perimeter of her umbrella.

"Let me die now. Please God, let me just fall down now and die."

She stood waiting for a merciful interception.

She waited a long time.

When nothing happened she finally threw the umbrella away from her, watched it skitter on its spokes like a live thing. Her face lifted to the coursing rain. She ripped her coat open and spread out her arms to the sky.

She stood there many minutes, letting the rain soak and cleanse her.

And then, once again, she saw the notice.

The rain had stopped and Kezia stood alone above Toothaker Harbor, looking down at Perley's House. She had said goodnight to Reo at the ranger station because she wanted to tell the news to Grandm'am alone. Tell her the park wasn't the thing she hated: the park could also be Reo Macrae. How the three of them would live together, have the old Christmases again, the way they used to be.

She shivered, pulling her jacket tighter about her. Soon a glass would be in her hand, a jelly jar washed, swishing with a brown liquid from which came the most tantalizing smell. It would rattle down her dry throat as if solid, as if pebbles, then flow warm and honey sweet: Grandm'am's apricot brandy, brewing in its big jar and upended twice a day for eight days, then opened, ready to drink.

And she would tell Grandm'am that soon she'd be pregnant: nothing Grandm'am loved more than babies, another for the island to keep it alive. Kezia hoped for a girl, one who would eat peanut butter in the morning and try on padded bras in the afternoon, who would spread out her beloved toy animals and weep with a sense of irretrievable loss at the boredom they now inspired, and experience mystical conversions whose religious nature she would dimly feel and so clutch an unread Bible in her hand until they passed. She would begin a thousand projects which disintegrated once the planning stages were exhausted, would giggle and shriek and cry her way through adolescence, wanting only, though perhaps extravagantly, to be good and beautiful and pure.

On the hill above Toothaker, Kezia began to run down toward the house. Grandm'am would be there through the kitchen door as she always was, strong prickly hedge to keep her rabbits safe. Grandm'am would make it right—the pain she'd felt when she discovered that she wouldn't be Reo's first wife. He had an ex-wife and daughter, Martha, back on the main.

Her fingers pressed the pearl ring Reo had given her until it cut into her skin. She wanted its mark blood red, deep and irrevocable as a birthmark but not setting her apart, a mark drawing her into the magic circle—the circle of gold.

What had Grandm'am said? But Kezia was no longer 'a woman alone.'

Grandm'am wasn't in Perley's House. Kezia went looking for her, spotted a flash of faded blue dress within the little burying ground a few yards from the path, behind a perimeter of wood-braced chicken wire. Kezia stepped onto fallen pine needles, the shallow roots of the pines making her stumble in her heels, the low entangling branches thrusting toward her eyes. At the gate Kezia tugged off the tight loop of wire. Inside, low-bush blueberries matted the spaces between the stones.

Grandm'am sat alone on the damp ground, a worried look on her face. She looked up now. "Kezia. I have been meaning to speak with you."

"What is it, Grandm'am?"

"Not here. Let us go farther away." The old woman rolled onto her side like a baby, levered her way up from there. She thrust away Kezia's helping reach.

"The man who owns the sheep. On Sheep Island, Kezia. We cannot steal his wool the way we did."

Afraid, Kezia looked into her grandmother's eyes. They were gray and translucent as quartz; they held no suggestion that anything was wrong in what she had said.

"Grandm'am, Nate owns the sheep. He was right there while we did the shearing, he was so glad for our help. He'll sell the wool and the money'll go right to him. He'll get his and you'll get your share like you always do."

The gray eyes blinked, looked out unclouded as before, but above them the black brows knit tighter. "That guy. That guy. That is not Nate Vannah."

"Grandm'am, I've got something I want to tell you. Something wonderful's happened. I—"

"I never saw that man before in my life!" The old fingers clutched Kezia's arm, she could feel the cold coil of each finger pressing tighter into her flesh. She could smell the old woman's smell that clung no matter how many times she washed: breath like cooked peas, a scent like old clothes left half-damp.

Kezia looked down, picked a few blueberries at her feet. They were hard and white, unready in her palm. She looked away from her grandmother, at the dull black wrought iron marker, a circle on a rectangle heavy with curlicues. At its base plastic lilies reversed growth, pushing down into the earth. On top of the iron circle a wrought-iron hand pointed heavenward. But Johnny Beal hadn't gotten there: the sea kept its own. *Full fathom five thy father lies...*

Kezia squatted suddenly in the mud, tearing the lilies out, white rubber with yellow rubber paint. *Nothing of him that doth fade...* "I hate fake flowers! They're so ugly and dead."

Clara was looking at her with a shocked expression.

"I didn't mean to offend you, Grandm'am. Did you put the lilies there?"

"It is Deenie who does that. She always does."

... but doth suffer a sea-change into something rich and strange.

"I am frightened, Kezia."

Kezia reached for her hand, but it wasn't red and hard any-more—white and soft in her strong brown one—it gripped for some-thing solid in her own.

She had gotten her child.

When they returned to Perley's House Kezia saw the notice on the front door.

CHAPTER 36

1977 - Scrag Rock, Maine

In a gutteral blast of sound, the Sikorsky H.H.3F. all-weather, radar equipped, amphibious helicopter lifted off the mainland and headed out to sea toward Scrag Rock.

Kezia and her mother, Loara Beal Vannah, 63, sat silent, rocked in the safety of their seatbelts while staring out the window at the loss of land, the spread of thirty-foot waves that broke white as snow-covered mountains far below.

It was too noisy to talk comfortably inside the spacious empty cabin. They were the only passengers. Loara sat tense and rigid, as she had for hours driving down in the car. The white, heavy bellied helicopter with the shield-and-anchors emblem and "Coast Guard" painted on its side was taking her home, pointing its long black "Goofy" nose toward Scrag Rock for what would be her very last time.

The cockpit curtain was pulled aside, framing Captain Laverty, a tall uniformed shape. They could see the pilot sitting just beyond. "Be there soon," Laverty said cheerily. He sat down across from them, his long legs jutting out into the aisle, shiny black shoes silently tapping—one two, one two—against the air.

"Your first time back in a while?" he asked.

"My parents had to move off when I was twenty," Loara said.

"Had to?"

"My father had a heart attack. They're both gone now." The Coast Guard had notified her a steel locker had been found in the old house. It had papers that belonged to the Pritchards. Did she perhaps want it, after all this time? Conversation had followed, and the Coast Guardsman, Captain Laverty, sensing her unspoken plea, had asked if she would like to see Scrag Rock one more time.

Unofficially, of course. Officially it was certainly against the rules. But then, "To think you grew up in such a place," Laverty said now over the noise of the copter. "Between hell and a hard rock, for sure. Of course it's all automated now. First a family light, then a stag light, now nobody out there at all. Airlifted the last Coast Guard crew off some two months ago. All machines now, better for humans, don't you think? Never was a place for humans anyhow."

The helicopter shuddered, blundering on through the wind. It took nearly an hour to get to Scrag Rock. From above it was a flat plate on steel of molten blue. Closer and there were the fifty-foot cliffs and a stone light tower that pushed up off the plate, and a white country farmhouse, incongruous with a red tile roof, a ladder stretched at the ready on the roof beside the single two-windowed gable. The house's lawn was rubble and rocks, its trees empty rusting barrels on their sides and standing on end.

Loara and Kezia stepped out onto a raised wooden platform beneath the slowing beat of the propeller blades, climbed down steep metal stairs protected with a single railing, and onto a road of four wooden planks that led to the lighthouse. The wind poured, beat, battled against them. Loara's gray hair whipped out at right angles to her scalp, her sight blurred in a sting of tears.

"Well, over here for the house," Captain Laverty said, stepping up onto a block of granite, offering his hand to Loara Beal Vannah.

"What do you think of it?" Kezia said.

Loara shook her head.

"Nothing leads to the house anymore," Laverty said. "Watch your step. Due to be razed next year."

"Shh." Loara had stopped, her arms bent at the waist, fingers open like antennae listening.

Kezia stared at her, while trying to sort through the cacophony of noise from the 137-foot conical tower above her. The diaphone fog signal blasted for 2.5 seconds, was silent for 12.5 seconds, not enough time for your ears to stop ringing, and then blasted again. Here, too, in broad daylight the light flashed in 15 second cycles, *but why was it going at all?* A white flash—5-1/2 seconds of eclipse—a red flash—2-1/2 seconds eclipse—red flash—5-1/2 seconds eclipse, and back to the white flash again.

The eyes blinked, the ears ached to shut it all out.

"A trifle noisy, I admit," Captain Laverty said.

"But why the fog horn and the light?" Kezia aid. "Can't you shut it off? It's clear as can be out here today."

"Well, you see, they run twenty-four hours a day, weather or not!" Laverty lifted his cap, smoothed back his hair, settled the cap farther down on his head. "There are instruments, state of the art, that can be tripped for dark and light cycles, or changing levels of humidity in the air. In light stations near populated areas why, sure, we certainly use that kind of device. Sun sensors and fog detectors. But out here? What's the point?" His hand sketched the thin ridge of rock surrounded by sea. "It's more cost efficient just to let the light and diaphone run straight on through."

Loara Beal Vannah turned to look at him. Her short hair tufted up in the wind above her head. "I was listening for birds. Thousands used to breed here. That's what you'd hear, the medricks at this time of year. White bodies, graceful, they would literally fill the air."

The fog signal screeched its 15 second cry, screeched again and again.

"I've seen an occasional bird here," Laverty said, "blown out from the mainland, though. But not a lot of birds, not in my time, certainly not thousands anyway."

Loara stood straight, her pants legs cracking in the wind. "Do you mean you've done something so the birds are gone?"

The diaphone screeched.

Captain Laverty dropped his shoulders as if he would as soon be done with both of them. "Let's take shelter from the wind in the house," he said.

The house was empty, board floors and windows interrupted by board walls. But in the steel locker, among the other papers, was a student pilot's license, dated 1931.

"Mother, I can't believe it! I never knew you were a pilot."

"A *student* pilot."

"Whatever. My mother the Red Baron. It's fantastic."

"Never got to solo, though."

"Why did you give it up?" Kezia asked.

"I married your father. The same old story."

They filed back out to the waiting helicopter whose blades were jogging through a circle in warm-up time. "I guess you feel bad, Mrs. Vannah, seeing the Rock shut down," Laverty said. "There's seventy-seven light structures along the coast here, you know, from Isles of Shoals all the way up there to West Quoddy Head. And heck, this is just one, they're all going automatic, it costs too much the other way."

Kezia gave him a quick appreciative smile, and looked at her mother in the seat beside her. Loara stared fixedly out the window as the blades above them quickened into a canter, shaking the air, the seats, the view out the window that wavered with vibration like an underwater scene. Her eyes were searching as if for something. Her shoulders huddled in the direction of her lap.

The helicopter's blades galloped now, packing the cabin tight with sound, and the ground fell away, the narrow unforgiving spine of rock that Loara knew she would never see again. Her hands held each other, rigid in her lap.

Crazed, heedless of the twenty-mile visibility and the bright sun, the light and the foghorn flashed and shrieked in warning behind them.

The helicopter shrank away to a dot.

Loara could still see the light: a white flash, a red flash, another red flash, and back to the white flash again. The lighthouse itself, and even Scrag Rock, were already gone.

It was several weeks later, over the radio, that Loara Beal Vannah heard the first word in many years about the little biplane White Bird who had crossed the Atlantic first. A lobsterman, the news report said, who was hauling his pots from the ledges off Casco Bay, near Portland, had raised a rusted instrument panel which experts were saying was identical to the one which had guided *Oiseau Blanc*.

Pilots old and bold. Are you still going to learn to fly? Tears were running down her face. She was remembering the pain of that evening with Johnny Beal so long ago, hardly over their honeymoon when he had confessed to her, " 'Seven crow secret never to be told.' "

"What do you mean, Johnny?"

"I made it up," Johnny had said. "All that. About seeing White Bird."

It's all right, Johnny, she thought now. White Bird really did make it across. For the first time she could admit what she had never admitted even to herself: she had loved Johnny Beal. She was remembering how his left eye used to twinkle at her, boldly wink. He had winked like that long ago when he drove the old open Franklin car into Clifton Pond. Of course it had dried up, been planted with grass, a pocket park in Medon on the main. Spurred on by her shrieks of protest, he drove straight down the grassy incline and raced along a placid brick walk lined with pansies.

Was the small universe she had had worse than the large one she had once glimpsed from the ends of an airplane's wings?

It was still the world. It was still life. You couldn't regret life.

CHAPTER 37

1978-1979 Aguahega Island, Maine

"Domesticity doesn't suit you, Mrs. Macrae?" Reo looked up at her from the kitchen table with his mocking right eye.

Kezia's hands stilled in the soapsuds of the slate sink, carefully towel-padded the way Grandm'am had taught her to protect the delicate blue willowware. Her hair—that she had spent an hour on, carefully brushing and twisting into its fat chignon—was straggling down now, fine red-gold wisps sticking to her flushed cheeks. Chance and Victorine were due any minute now with their two girls to spend the afternoon and Christmas Eve.

Everything had to be perfect.

Chance would see: *she* was the island maid now, not Victorine.

"Or does all this hurly-burly have to do with the imminent return of old moneybags?"

"Damn you, Reo." She glared at him. "Don't make trouble to-day."

"I'm nice to people who are beneath me."

"Where do you find them?"

"You shouldn't fancy a married man. Lest it's the one you're lawful wedded to."

"Please. Not today. It's Christmas Eve."

From the old black stove wonderful smells of venison and green-tomato mincemeat pies filled the air. In the dining room of Perley's House the table was under a clean patchwork quilt, a wood platter in the center filled with bright red apples hollowed out in the middle, each with a fat white candle within. The pine sideboard was laid with a rag rug whose faded pastels held wood candlesticks and Grandm'am's collection of wood potato mashers. They were having the traditional Christmas meal: roast pork and cabbage salad with sugar and vinegar, and hulled corn.

Everything had to be right: the way it used to be.

"What do you mean, not today, killer? I can't wait to hear it—Chance's next new career. He gets an award for perpetual student of the year."

The soapsuds ticked to nothing under her nose. She glanced across at Reo: flannel shirt, crumpled tail hanging, open on a t-shirt that read SUPPORT YOUR RIGHT TO ARM BEARS. His green eyes were bloodshot and his ginger-fine hair lay flattened with sweat on his brow. He was all Roman nose leading, the bony thrust of his face unsentimental, bared.

Couldn't he at least have put on a clean shirt? He was 45 but he looked older, with a dirty smear of beard where he still hadn't shaved. She watched his fingers snap open another beer.

Where had it started to go wrong?

It had begun in disappointment. She knew he was as disappointed as she. It seemed he spent every evening now on the main, drinking beer with his buddies in the Red Rooster Bar. "Just going over for a cold one." "Just going over for a brew." It was always early morning before he came home. Her anxiety and resentment grew. She had accused him of being selfish and unloving, and he responded by withholding love.

He had given her a set of mudflaps for her birthday.

She had stood for hours in front of the birthday card display, trying to pick out a card for him. But none of the loving messages seemed to apply. It was like a questionnaire of marriage there in the cardshop on the main. She checked box after box: Does Not Apply, Does Not Apply.

"Just because Chance is richer than you," she said, "better educated than you, more socially conscious than you, artistic, liberal minded, a better person than you—that's no reason for you to hate him."

"Maybe I hate him for having such a beauteous broad for a wife."

He always knew where to hurt her.

"I would look that way too if *I* went to Elizabeth Arden every week. If I had cultured, groomed, *dyed* hair that took hundreds of dollars to achieve."

"You're dyed in the wool jealous."

"She's a Fashion Victim: it was right there in *Women's Wear Daily*. A photo of Victorine under the caption 'Too Loose Lautrec?' "

Kezia stood rooted, hearing his workboots thud closer. He stopped, too close, staring down into her face and she forced herself to stay still, not step back, to stare up without flinching, her heart racing uncomfortably under her ribs. He smelled of oil and gas fumes from the mailboat he'd just come back on, acrid as smoke.

"You're not in love with your sister's husband, are you, killer?"

Kezia hurled the blue willow plate against the wall. Even as she reached for it she realized she had picked the one piece that was cracked. In marriage even your rage was banal.

Grandm'am stood in the kitchen doorway in her new shiny purple print dress. She picked up the two pieces of the plate.

Kezia knelt beside her, her red hair touching Clara Beal's white coronet of braid. "I'm sorry, Grandm'am. I don't know what happened. An accident. It slipped right out of my hand."

Reo fixed her with a mocking look.

"My willowware. That Gooden gave to me. It was the very first thing he ever gave to me."

Gently Kezia eased the two pieces from her hands and fitted them together. Only a few small pieces were missing. "I'll glue it back for you, Grandm'am. It'll be as good as new."

"It is spoiled! Spoiled! Christmas—it is ruined."

Clara Beal straightened up and ran from the room.

Kezia stared into the blue face of the plate, half in her right hand, half in her left. In her right was the wealthy mandarin's house set about with orange and lemon trees, the air heavy with jasmine and mimosa, the willow tree bending over the little bridge.

In her left the bridge crossed to the poor little house in the plate's corner, barren, with untended ground and only a fir tree for shade.

Tenhaven and Perley's House, the gulf that was between. It seemed she saw them everywhere.

"Well," Reo said, "now you've done it."

She turned away, saw her own eye, wet and weary, glittering back at her from the cabinet's reflection. The wash of color which held the tracings of her face warmed and dribbled about the eye, and she saw only the eye and wondered for whom it was crying. Her stomach ached and she pressed it against the cool curved sink and splashed cold water against her hot tears.

Then came the knock from the front door.

"I'm the Lord High Chancellor," Reo said. "But you can call me Spike."

Swirls of snow fine as mica blew from the frozen brittle ground. Colored lights framed the small windows of Perley's House, glowing now on the four Chancellors' faces, each in its long-tailed navy, red, and white ski cap.

Inside was dry and hot and light: the Chancellors' two Scottish deerhounds, gray and platinum and rust, filling all space, pounding at Kezia. Dogs barking, children's clamor.

"Sit! Sit!"

The voice was confident, domineering. Hands cracked together with the unfamiliar sound of authority. It was Victorine.

"Bear! Flearoy! Sit."

First one and then the other dog dragged haunches under, tongues lolling now between massive ice-encrusted front paws.

Chance had left the room. In the new bathroom? Kezia listened for flushing, the sound of feet.

She bumped down on the edge of the couch.

Nicole, 9, was still staring, fingers gripping the edge of the chair.

Why did children stare?

"Did you notice," Kezia said. "I still use the plain lightbulbs around the windows instead of all those blinking lights and things. We always used the plain ones."

"Did we?" Victorine said. "I don't remember." She and her daughters, 9 and 13, wore matching Fair Isle sweaters, pink and blue and white.

The clock above the mantel ticked loudly.

Grandm'am appeared with a tray and a pot of cocoa. A plastic dog toy crunched under her laced, thick-heeled black shoe.

In her lap Kezia's hands stilled. She could smell snow-melt on wool sweater and the scent of the soap Chance had always used: sandalwood. She saw argyle stocking feet, size thirteen, flat as ever. She looked up: darker than before, half his face hidden by beard, forehead unweathered, the same boy's eyes. Beard hairs curled crisp above yellow button-down shirt collar, Irish fisherman sweater. His long legs were molded in jeans washed pale blue and honestly worn, not like Reo's in stiff tunnels: new navy denim baggy as always in the seat.

Reo sat with yellow leather construction boot up on one knee, the cleated rubber sole pointing at her, a dangerous look in his eye.

Chance touched her arm. "Well, looks like you've grown up, Red. Matured."

"It's just my heart's got hard."

Beneath the cuff of his sweater she stared at dark hairs straight as silk.

His fingers left her arm. Her skin felt on fire, like the Bridal Laylock in fog hiding fireflies. "Well," she said, looking around, "we're going to have a real down-home island Christmas this year."

Vinca, 13, had her mother's large round eyes, blue as the flower vinca. She stood arms at sides, toes turned out, and like a Felix-The-Cat clock Kezia had once seen, her eyes darted first right then left as if connected to an invisible pendulum tail. She was plump and rosy with beginning buds of breasts braless under the sweater.

"I just read *Bonjour Tristesse*," Vinca said. "I like Françoise Sagan, don't you? The nihilism, the despondent drab fatalism. The sordid awakenings."

"Vinca! That's enough," her mother said.

"How old are you now, Nicole?" Kezia said. *Dunce.* Of course she knew. But what do you ask a silent staring child?

"Nine."

"What do you want to be when you grow up?"

"Ten." Nicole was dark like her father, Santa's cherub, vaguely threatening: you never knew what to expect from a child. She was dressed all in pink from top to toes.

"You look so pretty," Kezia said. "What a pretty purple top and green pants, and I love your orange shoes. Why doesn't your mother buy you pink shoes?"

Nicole: "These *are* pink shoes."

Kezia smiled at Chance. "Such a literal child."

"Keezie—" Victorine said.

The years opened.

"What's all this mess doing piled all over?" She was looking at the cardboard boxes and filing cabinets, the typewriter and mimeograph machine, the stacks of papers, leaflets, bumper stickers that covered half the living room.

"It's the Community For Aguahega Conservation Association."

"Known familiarly as CACA," Reo said.

"Do you want a free bumper sticker?" She handed her one in blue and white: KAPOOM—Keep All People Out Of Maine.

"Going to cost *me* my job." Reo dug under his nails with his knife.

Kezia picked up a stack of mimeographs, dealt them out for everyone to see.

BLANK CANVAS WANTED BY PARK SERVICE.
FAMILIES MUST GO.
STOP PARK SERVICE EVICTIONS.
SAVE THE AGUAHEGA 20.

"They haven't evicted us yet, have they?" Kezia said. "And now they don't dare."

Reo stood up decisively, looked around. "Sunset's at four, gang. We going skating or not?"

The sun was hidden now beneath a low cloud deck. It was blowing 20 knots and the first few snowflakes began to fall. Kezia's scarf end whipped, reddening her cheek as she looked out at Alewife Pond's surface glittering dark beneath the leaden sky. Black ice, that rarity, fine as a black pearl: water frozen with no seltzer mush of snow to make it bumpy, swept clear by storming winds.

"These were Gran'sir's family's ice skates," she said, handing the old pine and iron skates around.

"They look weird," Vinca said.

"They're handmade but we sharpened all the blades for you."

"I've got new ones, white ones back home."

"Well, these are special, Vinca. They were your Gran'sir's."

"Who's Gran'sir?"

"Your great-grandfather Beal."

"They didn't know him, you know," Victorine said, gliding without even a wobble of ankle onto the ice.

When the others, tired of skating, turned to Reo's bonfire and tending hot dogs, Kezia skated by herself up the center toward the northernmost shore. Under her feet flew herself, mirror image, skimming along. When she was out of their view she got down on her hands and knees and peered through the mirror down into the pond, Alice through the looking glass. Beneath her own reflection the ice led her eye down in columns as it had frozen, below to twisted forests of brown, two torpedo shapes that were fish hibernating at the very bottom. Kezia felt her hands trembling, already cold, damp through her mittens as they spread her weight on the surface. She searched for the wolffish in the ice.

She heard the sound of skates behind her but didn't turn around. Beach fleas darted in silver tracks beneath the ice, but no wolffish rose from below to take them.

"Time to get back, killer," the voice said. "The natives are getting restless."

Kezia sat back on the ice on her bottom, and the cold seized her like two reaching hands. She looked up at him.

"I'm not your knight in shining armor anymore, am I?"

"I never thought you were," she said, not realizing how it hurt him until she saw it on his face.

Had she really dreamed a wolffish who had her face? Was the truth only that the wolffish was her?

The ice groaned, shifting against the far bank as the daylight melted its mooring. As Kezia got up she heard its long breathy sigh. The wind was raw and tough, bucking her face. She felt suddenly lonely standing beside Reo in the middle of the pond.

They skated back, in time for blackened hot dogs crackling and running with amber juices.

From the "used car lot" behind Toothaker Harbor they picked out a car hood that lay beside a wheelless blue Studebaker. Vinca and Nicole tried it first, down the frozen slope and out skittering across the pond. Then Victorine and Chance together, then Reo—alone. Then Kezia—alone.

Kezia hauled it back to the top of the hill, careful of the rusted edges, steadying it while Chance got back in.

"Come on!" Chance pulled her in on top of him just as the ground began to rush by. Kezia held herself stiff, half-lying, bent, balancing on his left thigh as far away as possible from his lap. The car hood bumped harder and harder, faster and faster over the frozen slope. His arms tightened around her as both their bodies rose in the air. Back into the cupping hood, her bottom wet from sitting on the ice squarely in his lap this time. She felt something hard. It could be anything. The proverbial Swiss army knife.

They hit a bump, careening away from the pond and then in a blur of sky going the wrong way were thrown out, scraping through a gray-mauve haze of flattened blueberry bushes. Swirls of snow flew around Kezia's head resting so comfortably, clouds of snow clearing about her, parting to show the sky.

"Remember when we rolled down the hill?" she said to the sky. "Out behind Tenhaven and your grandfather got so mad, rolling, everything got dizzy in the ferns?"

Chance was looking down at her. He had grown up to be so tall. She watched him wave casually back to Victorine, then, hands semaphoring around his mouth: "She's okay."

Now his voice was beside her, close, urgent, "Come on, Red. Get back on your feet."

"I love you."

The wind poured over her lying at the end of the pond. *Lion, lo*—they chanted it in the African bush to ward off the hidden beast. *Lion, lo*: named you cannot harm me.

The three words that Reo had never said.

Had she said it loud enough? He was walking away. Did Chance hear? Was it lost in the wind? The pond glittered as Kezia stood up, hurting her eyes through air that spun multicolored as light through glass.

"I'm getting tired of just standing here," Vinca said, combing her thin waist-length blonde hair with her gloved fingers. She took it by the ends and laid it across her palm, offering her face on the platter of her hair.

"We'll go get the tree," Reo said. "That'll be fun."

Kezia looked at Victorine. "How about it? I'll even let you pick it out this year."

"*I* getta pick it," Nicole shrieked.

"Well, I don't know now," Chance said. "Is that right? Vinca, did you pick it last year?"

"I'm too old for that now," Vinca said.

"Well, looks like you're the one, Nicole," Victorine said.

Reo led the way to the stand of balsam firs.

"You always picked the ones that were weak-sided, Keezie," Victorine said.

"*I* getta pick." Nicole stood body stiff with will.

"Why don't we let Kezia pick it this year?" Reo said. "In our family it's her turn."

The small face crumpled in along its midline. "It's my turn. Mommy said." To seal her right, Nicole ran ahead through the damp skirts of the firs feeling each branch, letting the needles trail through her white mittens, whiskered with green.

Kezia walked up to a beautiful small tree, the scent sweet and familiar in her nose. Peering through the branches she saw on the cleft of limb and trunk a small woven-brown nest. "Nicole, look here. This one's got something extra special: a bird's nest."

Everyone crowded closer.

Even Vinca agreed. "That's really neat."

"We could put a little Jesus in there," Kezia said, hearing her voice rush too fast. She wanted this tree, she wanted it so badly. "What do you think, Nicole? Put the little baby Jesus in the nest, like in the manger when he was born."

"*No.*" Nicole's fingers clutched the hem of another tree. "This one. I want this one."

"Miss Nicole done knows what she wants," Chance said, checking the edge of the saw. "Okay, Miss Nicole. You got it."

As the balsam branches slid hissing and whispering behind them on the ground, a rope tourniqueting its ragged stump, Kezia felt six years old, in competition with Nicole the way she used to be with Victorine. She wanted her own way.

"Victorine, remember those bayberry bushes down at Whisgig? I've got a candle recipe to make them from scratch. I mean, if we went and picked some. If you wanted to..."

"Why make them?" Victorine's white fur apres-ski boots went *thunk thunk thunk* on the frozen ground. "For five dollars a box you can just buy them, you know." She hit her palm against her thigh. "Bear. Flearoy. *Heel.*"

All dog trainers, Kezia thought, were secret fascists: heel, sit, schnell!

"Aw, Mom," Vinca said. "I want to pick bayberries. Please."

"It's a nice idea," Chance said, "but it's too dark now. Maybe tomorrow."

Kezia ran out onto the frozen edge of Toothaker Harbor. The salt water ice was tough, sagging under her boots but not shattering. She heard only the sound of her ragged breath heaving out into the snowblind world of white. She turned around.

"That's my boat out there."

Everyone looked at the lobsterboat, *Bog Onion* painted across its flat stern.

"So you're really hauling, even in winter?" Chance was squinting out at her boat as if the sun were in his eyes.

"I'm back now to what I was, where I belong. Hell, Chancellor, lobstering's big business now. What you see floating out there, gear and all's worth fifty thousand give or take. The best fisherman's got the best boat, best gear and I *am* the best. Heads turn when we go by."

"It's dangerous," Victorine said, looking at Reo. "How can you let her do it?"

"No one *lets* me. All you need is a break in the weather, a 'chance.' " She grinned up at Victorine. "I only get out one, two days a week to haul in December, January. I've seen better 'chances,' but still, with this one I'd go."

"She's local color," Reo said. " 'Would you mind?' this tourist says, motioning her—'skins' and boots and all—to get inside the frame."

"But you can't actually *like* it," Victorine said, "slaving away at the crack of dawn?"

"I can't explain it. Hard work. Simple physical work."

Chance was staring at her now.

"The enormous satisfaction in that. I've made a place for myself here. Worked for it, earned it. I'm the highliner around here now, just like Daddy. I'm better than Nate."

"You see, even in winter," Chance said to his daughters, "life is still here. Those are eiders and old squaws out there, see—there among the whitecaps. And above the rockweed barnacles stand on their heads and feed themselves with their feet."

"Who's that funny looking man?" Vinca said.

A bent red-faced man dug with a clam hoe for clams buried no deeper than they were in summer.

Bent, mud-streaked, oilclothes with the Australia-shaped stain in the back, the rent by the hip where the lobster had seized and torn, her father's oilclothes?

Kezia called something: voice loud, high over the sound of the wind and the breakers.

The oilclothes turned: it was Nate.

Grizzled whiskers white among the dark. Oh Nate.

Wind blew the lowering darkness in their faces as they waved, he waved back.

"Brrrr," Victorine said.

"Yeah, the temperature's dropping something fierce." Reo's face, ravaged and pale above unshaved dark, looked skyward in the failing light.

Kezia looked away, home.

Perley's House had been banked against the cold, Reo shoveling two feet of dirt all around, and then wheelbarrow loads of evergreen brush piled to the bottom of the first-story windows. The window-panes were opaque with frost but there glowed the golden light of Grandm'am's kerosene lantern set by the base of the fan door. On the door hung Kezia's homemade wreath, bright with the fiery red berries of the white alder. Above it was the solid heart of pine cones—Gran'sir's wreath made when he was a boy.

Didn't Chance see? She was what he wanted now.

If she hadn't done it all for him, who then?

She heard the voices of her father and her grandfather, rising on the wind.

CHAPTER 38

There was a tension new to Town Meeting. Kezia looked with apprehension around the room. It was March 15, halfway up March hill. The sun that had moved south since September, until east-facing windows were dark of morning light, now had turned the corner, lighting the one-room schoolhouse once more with spring.

It was 10 AM, colder outside than in as the islanders assembled, seating themselves spread-kneed at the too small desks beneath the pipe that hung above, distributing heat from a central stove. The air warmed and thickened: damp corduroy, wet wool, spilled coffee. The door in the rear banged as children ran in and out: Deenie's three, Nate's one, Ernie Smallidge's two. Kezia remembered running in braids and layered sweaters with Nate in hot pursuit, in and out among the desks in the back as Torby Vannah was now doing. Running harder, air screaming in your lungs, the tops of the firs swaying dizzy with the thrill of pounding feet. And far from Town Meeting and grownups' supervision, out on the spit of land's end wild and unobserved. And when Nate caught up with her she resisted fiercely in the time-honored tradition. "What a wildcat!" And then he claimed his prize, the one she too was seeking, not knowing what it was for or how to do it, knowing only that it was forbidden gold, adult treasure now theirs to plunder: children under a vast sky meeting in a kiss.

"I thought you said old moneybags was going to be here," Reo said.

"Old Victorine doesn't like getting up early." Her heart moved faster: Victorine had remained behind, in their Fifth Avenue apartment in New York. She looked again toward the doorway; but only old Mrs. Smallidge stood there, refilling the coffee pot.

She looked around the room with a burst of love. These were her people, blessed with those greatest of island goods: stability and continuity. They hadn't learned skills to survive outside, but what did it matter? They were here. She belonged. She looked at Grandm'am, at Deenie and Duane with their children Grace Ann, Teddy, and Myra Bell; Beck and Loara; Nate and Caril with Torby, now 12; Ernie and the schoolteacher Mildred Smallidge and their two teenage sons; old Mrs. Smallidge but not her son Ross (who was "peculiar," stepping into the woods when he saw anyone, just to avoid saying hello). Miss May-ry was here, of course, crotchety old Mary Stella Witney who'd been postmistress now for over forty years. The new mailboat with its striped canopy and fake smokestacks had been christened with her name, spelled as she pronounced it: *Miss May-ry,* God help you if you said it any other way. Miss May-ry, a widow, sat stiffly, eyes as bright, as fixed as a hen. Under the hairnet her hair was still faintly blond though in fragile thin puffs like whipped cream from a nearly empty can.

Except for Ross they were all here: nineteen survivors from three to 94, all that were left.

Kezia looked up again, surprised to see Milo Gilley walking in. He couldn't vote but he took a cup of coffee anyway, sat down on a folding chair in his black shoes and gray suit with the white handkerchief points in its breast pocket, the only man here in a suit. Behind his freckles she saw him staring at her and Kezia looked away, all her old dislike for him surfacing in a rush. The Man In The Empty Suit, Reo had always called him. Now Reo had amended that to The Man On The Empty Cross. Gilley was a born-again Christian, so intrusive in his newfound zeal there'd been talk of the park removing him as Superintendent, perhaps substituting Reo in his place. Even now he was leaning across toward her: "Have you thought about Jesus today?"

The warrant of articles to be voted on crackled as thick-knuckled island hands flipped the pages. Article Two: elect officers, first the town clerk to record the minutes. Kezia scribbled her own name on the scrap of paper, walked to the front of the schoolhouse, dropped it in the cigar box.

"Just a fast minute there," Miss May-ry said. "How are we to know that that ballot box's not been stuffed?"

"Because I looked." Beck Vannah, moderator for the past twenty-odd years, brightened at this hint of controversy.

Miss May-ry was standing, her shoes pointing at Kezia like a bird dog trying to flush her from the brush. "Well, check it again."

Beck handed Kezia's ballot back to her, held the box upside down. "Now, then, Miss May-ry, how do your find the ballot box?"

"I find the ballot box fair."

"All those in favor of the ballot box manifest by hiking up your hand. *Right* hand, Mr. Smallidge. Contrariwise? Anyone else wish to vote, anyone else wish to vote, anyone else wish to vote?" He struck the gavel down.

Mildred Smallidge was just coming back in through the door: too late.

"By your vote you have so voted it, and I so declare."

The door kept banging as children ran in and out but now there was a disturbance and heads craned back. Chance stood there endless legs in old jeans, ivory shirt, and tweed jacket, his arm upraised doing battle with wooden ducks tilting at him from a mobile too low for him, high enough for everyone else. Above the ducks a red heart painted with a message hung. "Home is where you hang your heart," it read.

Kezia felt Reo looking at her and forced her gaze back to the front. Soon, filled with pride she was taking the oath. "I, Kezia Macrae, Town Clerk, do swear that I will uphold the Constitution of the United States of America." Now she sat with her leather record book at the front table and Chance was looking at her, that familiar half-mocking smile beginning on his face. And she thought she saw a certain jealousy, too. He wasn't legal, after all, not a voter. Just an observer from a far-off land overgrown with irony—Seal Point.

"This here's our One-Hundred Forty-Fifth Town Meeting," Beck Vannah was saying in his gravelly voice. "But things aren't so great this year. Price of food and gas from ashore keeps going up, but lobster prices don't keep up. State threatenin' to pull out our teacher for lack of pupils. A sense of desperation, we've all felt it. Under the gun. I'm proposing we skip ahead to Article Twenty-Eight, the budget, before the day's tore in half. And vote in the other officers last. A reason: we'll get to that."

"Second," Ernie Smallidge said as if he knew what the reason was.

Kezia sat up straighter. This had never happened before.

"What budget?" Duane called out. "We're near enough to piss-ass broke now."

"You're out of order," Beck gaveled.

"Of course he's out of order," Deenie said sharply. "Went outside for a pint of stuff."

Now the looks on the faces hardened, eyes darting suspiciously back and forth. It was time to vote on how to spend the island's meager funds.

Kezia picked up her pen and her fingers were cold. What was happening? What was the "reason" that Ernie Smallidge had known about?

"Article Twenty-Eight," Beck Vannah called.

Deenie Mackle was standing, pregnant again in her long brown plaid jumper over a turquoise turtleneck. "We have to work together now, like we've done with the Power Company. As your president, I've got bad news and good news."

"Look out," Nate called, "she's going to pass the plate."

Through the pounding of the gavel, the shifting and coughing, Kezia felt the dry taste of fear in her mouth.

"The Company goes to the heart of things here," Deenie was saying. "We can't have it fail now. Haven't had a rate increase since we started up five years ago. Time for one now."

"How much you planning to wet us in and out?" Miss May-ry said.

"Last year we lost five thousand, three hundred thirty-four dollars on operating revenues of eleven thousand, four hundred forty-three. We need, on an emergency basis, a thirty-nine percent increase."

Kezia heard this settle into the rush of outcries.

"Now for the good news. We can use the waste heat from our generators for a laundromat for the whole island, showers, and a greenhouse."

Everyone stared at her as if she were insane.

"Three-fourths of us here still don't have laundry facilities. Sixteen miles by boat, another few on the main to the laundromat there. We need one here. The greenhouse would be a community garden. Whoever wanted would work it, everyone could take from it what they needed, conscience being their guide."

Ernie's face had gone red. "Showers? Greenhouse? Nobody's going to tell me what to do."

"Ernie, that's not it at—"

"Sounds like communism to me," Miss May-ry said. "Nobody's going to see me work and some lazy gets my share."

"It's not communism, Miss May-ry," Deenie said. "We'd be helping each other this way, get something most of us need. So we're not just paying more money out, we're getting something back."

"You don't like it here," Miss May-ry said, "why don't you go someplace else? Like Russia?"

Kezia stared at the rows of eyes. "But we used to do communal things here. It worked then. Why couldn't it work now? The whole island helped put up Perley's House."

"Mrs. Macrae," Beck Vannah said.

"You don't have to call me Mrs. Macrae. You know my name."

"Mrs. Macrae. It's a plain fact no one can pay higher rates no matter what fool thing they get out of it. Should of stuck to our woodburners and kerosene lights."

Mildred Smallidge was standing, shoulders trembling. "Heating oil's selling for a dollar four a gallon. Gasoline skyrocketed just when the mailboat cut back from three times to once a week. Spruce don't give off heat. Can buy a cord of prime wood for sixty on the main, ninety delivered here. Split and dried's ninety-five there, hundred and fifty here. The store's shut: who can pay two dollars-thirty for a gallon milk, two-forty for a pound of hamburg. Steak?

Who remembers steak?"

The gavel's rapping was drowned in voices of assent.

"I move we vote on the rate increase," Reo was saying. "If Deenie says we need it—well, hell, she's conscientious. Why, then, we need it."

He sat slumped down in his desk seat, legs spread insolently wide, but Kezia looked at him with pride. This was the man she'd married, the one she'd been standing beside in the Visitor Center when the blind man came to "see" Aguahega. Reo had held the man's hands on the relief model of the park, guiding his fingers up and around and through. Then Reo led him to a tide pool where they searched its depth with fingers that could see.

"Maybe," Ernie Smallidge said, "it's time for it. We all of us. Go ashore."

Silence rolled in.

"Just for the coming winter," his wife said.

"Wait a minute!" Kezia felt them looking at her as she stood up at the table in the front. They were looking at her snug black jersey leggings, the purple socks above the black-and-white ankle high basketball sneakers. "We're having money troubles, all right. But we can handle them. We've always handled them before, haven't we? We're die-hard islanders."

"Yeah," Ernie said. "We're gonna. Die hard."

Kezia looked at Chance in the back of the room and tears filled her eyes. The room was awash in talk....

"Not you, Mildred. Never thought but you'd stay here till the day I passed on."

"Up to Ernie and he says we got to, is all. What can you do? You should come to."

"Nothing could move me off here," Caril said, "if the Good Lord willing and the creek don't rise. Here you can at least always eat...."

"Rose Smallidge—no way I'm letting you off island."

"Well, well, diabetes, Dr. Maynard says, and he's some bully, you know. Wants me right near where he can bully me around, I expect. Haley's Landing, it's near enough to spit."

"If you go, I don't know," Miss May-ry said. "Don't know who'll go next...."

"Ernie, dammit, been close to you as two babies in a basket. You leave and who's going to stay?"

"Different since the War. Turn around and everyone's greedy now, a-grabbing. Fish your grounds without a by-your-leave. Not enough of us here to keep 'em off anymore."

"They'd better steer clear of me," Nate said.

So this was the reason officers hadn't been elected earlier. No one knew who would still be here in the fall. "Mr. Moderator!" Kezia said.

Beck Vannah began pounding the gavel again.

Reo stood up. "I move the motion. There's a motion about the Power Company still on the floor."

"Dr. Maynard says he wants me on the main," old Mrs. Smallidge said.

Chance was standing, and as he looked around the room his authority, his very foreignness quieted the room. "May I make a suggestion? Maybe this will straighten things out. I know, from my sister-in-law Kezia there, that there's been a lot of talk about the need for a live-on doctor. What with all the young children here now and the hope for more."

"Why don't *you* have any children, Kezia?" Miss May-ry said.

The silence swung around Kezia's head. She looked at Reo, at the darkening flush up his face, the same way he'd looked when she came out of the gynecologist's office that day. "He says it's not me," Kezia had said. And then Reo admitted what he'd known all along, the reason that she never got pregnant. "All my bullets, I regret to inform you. They're blanks."

"But what about *Martha?*"

"Knew all along she wasn't mine, but hell. Linda didn't know I knew."

"Why didn't you *tell* me? Before we were married?"

"It never came up."

"But all along—you've been paying Martha's child support."

"She didn't ask to get born."

Now, on Aguahega, Miss May-ry was still looking at Kezia, and beyond her Kezia could see Reo and the fear on his face. "I can't have children," Kezia said.

Chance was standing up now. "That's no one's business. I came here, in fact I'm back on the island at all to propose something that may help you out here. I know it's been tough. I've found a doctor who's ready to move on. I've bought the old Farnswell place and the first floor is going to be the clinic."

"You mean," Beck said, "you're fixing to sell us that worthless house?"

"Give it to you. To the island."

The room erupted in cheers and the gaveling began anew.

"But it has to be for the doctor," Chance said, "or what's the whole thing for, right? That's the only stipulation I'd make."

"I move the vote," Nate said.

"I second it," Kezia said.

When the votes were counted Beck looked at Kezia, then at Chance. "The nays have it."

Kezia saw the shock, the disbelief of Chance's face and she got to her feet. "Have you all lost hold of your senses? Chance's giving us the doctor we've been waiting for."

"Look, friend Chancellor," Beck said. "Appreciate it, but—"

Miss May-ry held up her hand. "I don't want anyone telling us who we can and can't have homing here."

"Infringes on our rights," Duane said. "Might not like the doctor, want to use the house for something else."

"Is that all you can think of, how will this hurt your somewhat theoretical rights?" Kezia said, glaring at Duane.

"It's dictating," Beck said. "Appreciate the offer, Mr. Chancellor, but too many strings attached."

Chance opened the door and the cold draft of wind set the wood ducks to tinkling. The light swallowed him and only the dark door banging back against them remained.

"Do I hear a motion for lunch?" Beck said. In the back of the room the trestle table held beans and brown bread, macaroni and cheese, pie, and coffee. Already the children had come back, were eyeing the plates.

"May I have the floor for a minute?" Milo Gilley was standing, powerful hands on the shoulders of Ernie Smallidge's oldest son Seth, fourteen. "Someone broke in my house last year, as you all know, broke in twice. Kids, I guessed. First time, booze. Second time, booze and Mallomars. Now when I came and told you, you said it was park visitors, as I recall."

"Well, what did I tell you, you hoser," Duane Mackle said. "Get you a gun."

"Don't know how to shoot."

Reo was staring at Gilley. "What about that sweet little rifle I bought off you? It had seen some time."

Behind the freckles Gilley's face went white. In the silence Kezia found him staring at her.

"Like I told you," Gilley said. His voice scraped out. "Was my brother's gun. He was the gunner in the family. He liked to plink at cans, not me." His hands dropped from Seth, held his trousers as if his thighs were about to burst through.

Seth stepped forward and Kezia saw, sharply, the vacant fear in his eyes. He kept on walking toward the front of the room and she saw his face and its terror, held like a sacrifice but with the pride of the one chosen for immolation. The silence grew.

"I did it! I stole his booze!" Seth's face reddened above his shirt. "I did it! I did it!" he screamed and then began to cry in the midst of what he had done. His body bent inward and Kezia saw him withering back from the room.

Suddenly feeling the silent crowd and the shame and the jagged fragments of his burst childhood he ran from the schoolhouse.

Milo Gilley was nodding as if satisfied. " 'He who conceals his sins does not prosper, but whoever confesses and renounces them finds mercy.' "

Ernie Smallidge's voice came high and low and cracking into pain. "My son's no thief!"

"Your son has found mercy. 'If you confess with your mouth: Jesus is Lord, and believe in your heart that God raised him from the dead, you will be saved.' "

"Liar!"

"God loves you," Milo Gilley said, "whether you like it or not."

Clara Beal had been sitting quietly throughout the meeting but now her mouth opened, the few teeth yellowed inside. Into the silence came the sweet tumbling melody, its words the language that all her life on Aguahega she had refused to speak:

" '*Unter der Linden, Auf der Heide,*
Wo mein Liebster bei mir sass—' "

Her internal phonograph was off, the needle lifted. She looked around and her face was bright and eager. "German, it is easy, but the English! Mixed up, so many times I got! I said, 'There is a train in this room. Give me another ceiling.' The word for draft and train, it is the same: *zug*. Blanket and ceiling, it is *decke*."

Everyone was staring at her and for the first time she seemed to notice. "They hated me when I came first to Aguahega. I was not free to speak the German then. I was German so they hated me, everyone did. I ran away and the gravel went crunch crunch crunch. It was like the bones breaking under my feet the first time I went there, to the magic place on the hill. The place they call Tenhaven..." Her gnarled fingers now were grasping the top button on the front of her dress.

As everyone watched, frozen, her fingers slowly, deliberately opened the buttons one by one. She wore nothing underneath. Her right breast—white and formless pudding—oozed out.

"Grandm'am." Kezia's voice was thick with grief and fear. She felt her cold fingers against Grandm'am's warmth rebuttoning her dress, heard the sound of Grandm'am crying. Grandm'am smelled like lilacs purple-red and heavy bunched, thick sweetness falling in a haze of lilac rain. Kezia touched her shoulder. "Grandm'am, it's all right." She held her grandmother's trembling body and tried to still her own fear. She felt the shuddering shoulders gradually quiet, but the wet face as Clara Beal looked up at her held only a weary resignation.

Clara drew herself with a certain pride up out of Kezia's arms. She walked stiffly down the aisle between the desks and across to the door where Kezia knew she would somehow prepare herself for the shame that was tomorrow. Kezia wondered if she could explain to her grandmother before it was too late.

Outside snow was falling, the rising swells rupturing on the shore.

Snow out of season, after the birds had returned, the storm they called Robin Storm.

When they returned home Kezia saw the two bound booklets on Reo's desk: Draft General Management Plan—Norumbega National Park, Draft Environmental Statement—Norumbega National Park. There were a few loose sheets stapled together, an Addendum, folded back to a page headed "Appendix A Continuation, page 110(a): "In carrying out his acquisition authority under this section the Secretary shall give priority to the following:

> (1) completion of acquisition of lands for which condemnation proceedings have been started pursuant to the authorization of this project referred to in this subsection..."

CHAPTER 39

The shadows stretched black on the avenue between Tenhaven's tall oak trees. It was the day after Town Meeting. The March sky remained leaden as December and cold was approaching: the trees seemed to pinch in, flatten as Kezia looked. The lights of Tenhaven flickered on the hill like a campfire on a continent of dark.

Kezia pulled her mackinaw closer. One by one as last fall turned to winter the lights of the year-rounders winked out, their houses locked and left. We'll be back, they said. Only twenty had wintered over, and now next winter there'd be fewer still. Everybody was going ashore.

How few of them could keep things going, treating the symptom or the disease? Or was it just lancing a permanent wound?

Around the corner Tenhaven's lights tunneled, a clearing in the forest, and Kezia began to run.

She stepped through the round Moongate into Tenhaven's gardens.

Where was it now, the wrought iron table lost in summer—the milk jug of flowers and on the chairback a wheel of straw hat? Like a crime this was the evidence: melancholy, lonely, tarnished, heavy with debris. The stained face of a stone nymph stared into a dry pool. The tops of steps were bone white, the risers leprous with growths. The annuals were all torn out, the flower beds banked and sleeping under leaves and brush. Even the gravel of the paths had been shoveled up and stored, to be rattled through a screen in spring.

In her felt-lined overshoes and earflap cap, Kezia walked back around to the front of Tenhaven. She hung her out of season Maybasket pasted with pink crepe paper around its sides, its handle braided with pink and blue, on the latches of the Christian door.

Please God, let him be in. She wanted to run into Chance's arms, have him tell her everything would be all right. Just the way it used to be.

Her mittened fingers pushed the bell, and then she darted back behind the shrubbery. Only silence, the door unopened. Should she ring it again?

The voices raised in Perley's House still argued in her ears...

"So who's this for, this thing you're getting into such a lather about?"

"It's a Maybasket and I'm hanging it on Tenhaven's door."

"But who for?" Reo managed to drain the Pabst while reclining on the floor, dirty stocking feet up against the wall. Kezia watched with disgust as his adam's apple jerked to get the beer down. In the silence his toes twitched the fringes of the three wall hangings he'd bought: a unicorn in ropes, a tiger in red poppies, Elvis Presley in his double-chinned, jewel-encrusted white jumpsuit phase.

"It's for Victorine." Her suddenly cold fingers kept on crimping the pink crepe paper. "I'm sick of winter, sick of this house. It's a Maybasket because she won't be here in May."

Grandm'am looked up at them from her ironing, steam rising around her head.

Kezia thought: I don't love Reo anymore. It was more frightening than the fear that he had ceased loving her. Her fingers kept on shredding the silvery reindeer moss, patting it down in the bottom of the basket, ready to cradle her gift. She heard yet another beer can open.

"Well, give my felicitations to Mrs. Jetsetter."

The point of Clara's iron struck heated little blows on the starched shirtfront. "No, Reo. Victorine, she is at home in New York. Kezia said."

A parrot, a pansy, a shepherdess endlessly repeated: the original now faded maroon wallpaper stared back into Kezia's eyes. Grandm'am couldn't remember anything these days. Why did she have to remember this?

Reo's arm sent the neat stack of anti-eviction leaflets storming through the air. "Why don't you clean up this dung hill once in a while instead of primping up for rich bastards? Get this stuff out of my living room!"

"*Your* living room? What about the *park's* leaflets, all those campers playing tapes up loud to scare the sea ducks away. What about *their* leaflets: 'Duck The Drive, Leave Them Alive'?"

He was standing next to her and she could smell the beer on his breath, acrid sweat. He seized her wrist and she drew back, trying to twist her arm free. "Get your all domineering hand off my arm."

"So you can go up to see Chance? You do, killer, and I won't be here when you get back."

Now, at Tenhaven, Kezia rang the bell again, long and hard.

The door opened. A shaft of light from speeding clouds, swift parting, lit gold across the side of Chance's face. She saw the dense length of his eyelashes, blond tipped, the blond down softening the sharp edge of his cheekbone, the glint of red in the crisp brown curls of his beard. As fast as the light had come it faded, etching the four lines in his lower lip deep and sharp.

"Well. What in the devil have we here?"

"Hey." Her voice was unsteady. "You need an assistant?"

"I'm looking for one named Red."

"Oh, I know just the one. Devoted, professional, experienced even."

"But does she do windows?"

Were all her feelings naked for him to see? She didn't care; they were children again.

"What's this?" He picked up her Maybasket, heavy with the quart jug within.

"It's a Maybasket. For you. I decided to hurry up spring."

"A Maybasket?"

"So many boys I've 'hung to,' so many I've been 'hung by.' More than anyone on Aguahega. More even than Victorine."

"Counting scalps? Say what's in here?"

"Now that I've hung you, sir, you have to drink it."

He upended the jug, drank in deep swallows, then wiped the glitter of droplets from his beard. "Whew. First rate. Tastes like ginger ale with a wallop."

"It's the raisins and brown sugar does it, made it myself. Hey, slow down. If you get drunk on cider you're killed for four days. Only antidote known to woman is clam water and lemon juice."

"Doled out by you, I hope?" He paused, looking out at the woods. "Don't you love this time of year?"

"No, I hate it. All black and gray and no color."

Her heart moved dizzily as his arm gripped warm around her shoulders.

"There're plenty of colors, Red. Yellow leaves right at your feet. Sumac clusters fiery red—see, against the firs? Tree branches dusky violet, birches white. Do you see?"

"Yes."

Inside a fire blazed in his study, and he was drawing off her cold socks. From the voluminous pillows of the chintz covered couch she looked down at Chance cross-legged on the rug, the straight silk of his hair falling over his brow. His palms chafed first one foot, then the other while the cider danced in her head.

"Good God, can this be the foot I love? A bunion yet."

Heat crawled up and across her cheeks. She struggled to pull her foot free. But his hands gripped it tighter now, and she watched his lips kiss the offending bump.

"Unhand me, you fool." Her voice was sharp.

"Have you no romance?"

"I'm middle aged, sir."

"How did we get here?" he said suddenly. "So soon? Middle aged with dread."

"I don't feel old."

"I don't feel young."

"Nonsense, Chancellor. At fifty, Gauguin was still a bank clerk."

"At fifty, Mozart was pushing up daisies."

This wasn't what she wanted to hear. But his fingertips were scratching gently now around her heel, then drawing delicious long lines forward under her arch. Now they kneaded the ball of her foot and in at the root while her toes spread. The warmth from the fire began to grow up her ankle, past her knee, across her thigh.

"It's good to have some company," he said. He patted her foot as if it weren't connected any longer to her body, put it down. His back settled against the blossomy chintz, the glass of cider cupped against his knee. She watched him stare into the fireplace whose mantel was blanketed with more chintz. Its hem was hung with Victorian beads that stirred lazily in the updraft of heat. The rest of the furniture bulked white under sheets.

"Is anyone else here?"

"No. Surprised? I cook a mean can of beans."

"What about the workmen? The bronze workers?"

"They're gone. It sealed the pits and pores to some extent, got down to the bare metal. But it removed the sculptor's original patina, the fine shading of the statue. So I told them to just leave the others alone."

Think what you're going to say, Kezia thought—the way she had so long ago in 1958? Sinking down in the slithery bath bubbles, memorizing Conversational Topics because he was back in Manhattan, was due here at Aunt Willi's in an hour.

1. "Do you know how to cha-cha yet?"
2. "Were they right to let Nathan Leopold out after only thirty-four years?"
3. "Do you think Sherman Adams should have resigned over the vicuña coat?"
4. "Have you read *Doctor Zhivago* yet?"

Now she looked at him, and she had never loved him more. "Do you think Dr. Zhivago should have accepted the vicuña coat?"

He laughed, just as he had then.

"Listen, Chance, I'm sorry about what happened at Town Meeting. I wanted to come and tell you before you left, apologize."

"You have nothing to apologize for. It was them, not you. You're nothing like them now." His fingers played the pipes on his cider glass. She watched his fingers raise, lower in invisible sound.

"Don't say that. They're my family now."

"They're stupid, benighted."

"Chance. I've got my family back again. For the very first time. It's hard, I know, to get anyone to work together on anything. Everyone thinks first, how will this hurt me?"

"They said I was dictating. But everyone wanted the doctor, that's what's so hard."

"Mother and Deenie. They're poor. They're all poor. They have only one thing to give you, Chance."

"What?"

"Lack of gratitude."

Chance got up and opened the window. The night swallowed the fireplace's warmth. "I only wanted to help."

"You could still help."

He looked back at her. "I don't want to get involved with these things anymore."

"But that's what living here means. It's Perley's House. I have to get it on the National Register. Of Historic Places. There's an Advisory Council with citizens appointed by the President."

He was looking into the far corner of the room.

"Red, take my advice. Better put all this aside."

"There's a new citizen been appointed. But I can't get him interested in Perley's House. One building in four in this country's at least fifty years old, he says. One in four hundred's 'historic' under their criteria. But maybe that citizen..."

His shoulders pinched higher, then dropped.

"No, you're right," she said. "He wouldn't help. Good old grandaddy Chancellor. Scourge of Aguahega Island, Maine."

"What is it you want?"

"Just ask him, would you? He'd listen to you. I know you could convince him."

"What do you think I am—a Chancellor?"

"Please."

"Remember what he used to say about the year-rounders? 'Fixed like a plant on his peculiar spot; to draw nutrition, propagate, and rot.' "

"What are you saying?"

"Maybe he was right, Red."

She was on her feet, the floor drafts circling her ankles, staring down at him.

"Maybe it would be better for the islanders, for the whole island, if people moved away."

"Not better for me." Her voice was bitter. A queer stifling force gripped her chest. She saw something in his eyes, but what did it mean? She saw guilt endless in his eyes.

"Think about it," he said.

She saw the terrain of his face: winter marsh colors, buff of dried grass, shriveled red of rose hips and white skin like new snow.

He sat up, stiff and straight, and poured them both another glass of cider. His forearm was a golden-shadowed bar, the veins bulging at the wrist, vine twisted ore fiber, knotted gold now as his fist clenched.

Desire struck her like a blow.

"Chance..."

"What does our macho ranger think of his little woman hanging Maybaskets up here?"

"I don't want to talk about Reo."

"What does he think?"

"He thinks I'm a hell-bent renegade, like him. Better renegade than not free. 'I wanna be an airborne Ranger, live a life of sex and danger, blood, guts, sex and danger, Oo-Ah! Oo-Ah!' "

"Park Service anthem?"

"U.S. Army marching song." Bubbles of cider buzzed now, crowding behind her eyes.

"So. How are things going with him?"

She held the glass cold against her cheek. "I sometimes think the whole romantic thing keeps running through your mind and running through your mind and you never fulfill it. When I used to go up to his trailer to see him, I'd have feelings of ecstasy—feelings I've never felt since and yearn for. Every time I got on the trail to go see him, I thought how exciting it was—just this constant pulsating pleasure. He said I was the perfect woman he'd been waiting for all his life. He said 'I never knew what the lover I would meet would be like, but now I've seen you.' "

"What happened?"

She didn't answer. Then she said, "How about you?"

He paused. "You know," he said. "With the first baby you and your wife stand over the crib all the time looking down, holding hands. By the second baby you don't do that anymore."

"What do you mean?"

"What you were just talking about, those ecstatic feelings. I was thinking, I've never felt like that. I hear people go on like that, I see it in the movies, but I don't know what they all mean. It just seems silly—people acting like that—romantic stuff we've all been bamboozled into believing."

"You mean—you never felt that way about Victorine?"

"I was rich. She was flattered. What did she know then? Her heart never pounded and all that stuff. Mine didn't either, but we were married just the same."

"But the feelings are real." Why did you marry her, she thought. Couldn't you wait for me? I would have married you, I truly would have made you happy.

"Remember what you said once?" Chance looked away. " 'Is it good to go back,' you said. 'Or is it better never to go back, to find everything changed?' "

"What do you mean, Chance?"

"Does it hurt less when you find it all changed? Or does it hurt more?"

"What has changed?"

"Aguahega. It's ruined now."

His words shattered around her and in them she saw all her wild dreams vanish, only the stuff of dreams.

"Don't say that! Aguahega—you married it." She drew the pillow from his fingers, her arms reaching desperately around his neck. "I haven't changed. Don't you see? It can be the way it was. I'm the same."

She saw in his eyes that he did love her, saw pain and emotion warring there. The dark pupils widened as she looked, drawing her up and out. Get home before it's dark under the table, Gran'sir used to say. Kezia stared blindly down a corridor of time. What dark? Which table? She was always afraid she'd fall in, the opening to some deep bottomless cave.

A log shifted, settled back with a hissing sigh.

But his eyes weren't Reo's. It was dark under the table: soft as velvet, black as night. Her hands came up, drawing out one by one the pins that held up her hair. She felt slow, deliberate, as if under water. Metal slid cold beneath her shirt collar, the pin rollercoastering down her spine. Shivering, she pulled her heavy sweater off over her head and her t-shirt rode up, exposing bare midriff above her pants. She felt his gaze on her bare skin, on the t-shirt whose message read *WELCOME TO MAINE. Now Go Home.*

Her fingers stripped the rubber band off, felt her hair spill across her shoulders in the thin cotton.

His chest, broad in the yellow wool, rose and fell. His mouth tipped open, moisture gleaming along the line where his upper lip had rested. She saw the tip of his tongue. She could hear his breath now, halting in the middle of a race. His index finger was rubbing along the lip of his glass with a barely perceptible sound, as faraway, as not-there as a hawk's jess bells.

She saw it: he was waiting for her.

Her finger reached, and he was tasting the deep rich cider from her glass, her finger rubbing it there. His tongue licked the drop of cider and she watched as his eyes went darker, softer. A sheen of moisture gleamed on his forehead, down his nose, the thrust of his chin. She saw his full sharp-edged lips part. No words came out. The moisture grew slicker as she watched.

She heard her own voice. "No cider ever tasted like this." Her finger, wet with cider again, touched his lower lip. He took it in his mouth, on his tongue. His teeth bit the smooth pearly surface of nail, sucked now around its apple tasting warmth. "It's like the ice, Chance. We used to cut it from the pond. The way it tasted: perfect. Never been able to find ice like that again."

His eyes looked steadily into hers. "Is it the memories you want. Or me?"

She felt her breath coming hard. They stared at each other, two combatants, the way they had always been. She was back, she stared at him with all the furious intensity of a child. Was that what all relationships were—hate and love? The deadly intermingling—cruelty and romance?

"Memories? What memories? Before I set Bandit free?"

"Set free? You stole her. I never forgave you. I don't care what I said. Never forgave you for it."

"I never forgave you! For Victorine. You married her."

Her hands battled up at him and he gripped her wrists, forced her arms apart. "What are you so angry for?"

"Angry? I set my sights by anger long ago. It's not Victorine who has everything. It's you."

Even as she glared at him she saw his hands release her, his arms go wide. The suddenness of his embrace surrounded her. She felt her own burst of tears, shock. Her arms held onto him with all her strength. He was the only person she had ever met who really knew how to love: meet anger with love, understand that anger was only fear you weren't wanted, were being left behind.

Light burst behind her eyes.

And then he was gone.

Stunned, she heard her own sickening gasp for air like a beached fish. She tried to focus on his face but it shifted higher, away from her as he pushed to his feet.

She stared up at him, fingers at her throat, something pounding there. "I love you, Chance. You love me. Say it. Say it! I know you do."

"You don't know me anymore."

"No one knows you the way I do. I'm the one who loves you. Why can't we be together? We could stay here on Aguahega, we could be together again the way it used to be."

"I'm not a boy. I'm an ironist now." His eyes looked bleak and faraway.

She forced herself to smile. "Ironist? What does that mean—hard as steel?"

"I can't just see things clear. Feel them the way I used to do. The wages of sin. Or maturity, I guess."

"Growing up has nothing to do with it."

"Says you."

"You're saying you don't love me."

His thumbs held her forehead, gently circling. Remember? His fingertips sliding hot with neatsfoot oil from Bandit's leash, wet on her face as tears.

"Red, maybe all along it was better this way. Maybe I'm not the right person for you."

His wrinkled collar curled on the end. She stared at its stitching neat and small, rolling something stony from deep within. "I've lived long enough to know that when a person says 'I'm not right for you,' they mean 'you're not right for me.' "

She dared him to contradict her and in his silence she felt her heart break.

"It's a fantasy now," he said, "what we were then: before. I don't want to lose that, too. Do you understand? I don't want to learn that all along it was something else."

"It will be better."

"I looked in your eyes, on that hill that night we rolled down in the ferns. In your pupils I saw myself, a tiny harlequin only comical in his dance. But you looked up at me as if I were God."

"Am I my own competition? A kid with dirty bare feet standing right toes on top of the left? A child with a child's pure heart and I can't compare?"

"You see, do you? If I lose that, too, Aguahega's really gone."

Kezia felt the tears well, the sharp painful pressure unrelieved.

"Oh Red. Don't. I'm sorry I vented my logic on you. It wasn't fair." His fingers held her cheek as if a wounded bird. "Could it be somewhere back then I made a mistake?"

"Please." Her voice was frightened "Please kiss me."

She felt his fingers widen cupping her face. He was going to kiss her. The room shrank suddenly small. The warmth, the surprising hardness of his mouth, cider tasting, his lips suddenly open, furiously searching hers. She felt him pushing her back, the pillows flattening to cup her in softness, his hand on her thigh, somehow her wool pants had been opened and she felt his long hot fingers touch her thigh. A shivering broke deep within her.

She was a child in a garden. Chance stood there in the mystery of adulthood, a mystery not dispelled by his nakedness but only deepened...

She had wanted him for so long.

She pulled her shirt off over her head and he was looking now, and then the heat of his chest seared down on her naked breasts.

The "mouse" blazed in triumph. "You do love me. We'll be together. Here, or somewhere."

Where?

The cider deep and dark whirled in Kezia's head. She tried to stop the whirling, opened her eyes.

It seemed she could see Victorine looking back. "Kept having a dream about a cheetah, Keezie, isn't that a gas? The shrink says free associate to the cheetah so I go 'cheat, fast. Something fast that's cheating. Omigod, my husband was a track star in college.' "

"You mean—"

Victorine's round blue eyes stared Yes and it was as if the years were gone. As Kezia watched, they welled suddenly with pain.

"What?" Groggily. "Red, what's the matter?" Chance half sat up, fingers on the bulge of his crotch. He looked at her, on his face the bulge of desire, the yearning mouth, eyes passive asking as if helpless, helpless with desire.

"You're married to my sister." It was an agony to force it out.

She watched the light die back in his eyes.

"Red. It's been two years. Victorine and I haven't slept together for two years."

"What?"

"Things aren't always what they seem."

"You have children. I've got no children. I have to hold onto my family because they're the only ones I'll ever have."

"I don't understand."

"You're married to Victorine." Her voice seemed to come from a crevasse, deep with ice. "Even if you left her, if I went with you I'd lose my family. And I've got them now. For the very first time."

"We could be family. To each other. We could be everything we'd need."

She walked over to the window, looked out. It was raining, an anachronism to be laughed at, a silent movie reel dim colored and a trifle amateurish. The small warm squares of film had snagged, the heroes-to-be lay not yet born in reams upon the floor. One barren rainy scene this, and played silently again and again.

"I'm sorry," she said. "It's my fault. I came here, threw myself at you."

"Well, Maybasket night. Isn't it a fertility rite?"

"Not for me."

"I'll drive you home."

"No. I've got my boat." She looked, hoping to see the harlequin only comical in his dance.

"Do you see the harlequin?" he said.

"I see something beautiful."

It shattered, broken by the refraction of his tears.

Kezia took comfort from the warmth of *Bog Onion's* wheelhouse, the familiar voice of the engine that had always seen her through. But a great loneliness, the impossibility of ever really connecting with another human being welled up in her.

"I'm ready for coffee," Reo had once said.

"Not just yet. Wait a little while."

Through the gloom that was Toothaker Harbor she saw the welcome sun of Grandm'am's lantern. She headed inside and home. She would go to Reo, beg his forgiveness. Tell him there had to be a way to talk about all this, a way to find their way back again. No more dancing alone: she would pour coffee with the other wives and dance with her husband as long as he wanted to dance.

Under the oak-ribbed fan above the front door, the fan with the lucky horseshoe imprisoned wrong side down, she saw it: from a distance like a long careless swath of white paint. Now why would someone want to paint her front door?

When she took the sheets of paper in her hand she understood the guilt she had seen earlier on Chance's face. So he had known, even then.

Reo was gone.

The Eviction Notice was there in his place.

CHAPTER 40

In the attic Clara Beal looked at the big, sprawly chair and beside it the china-based electric lamp whose beam of light pierced through the heart of her stack of poems.

She had read the Eviction Notice, and Reo had explained what it meant. "The park wants to construct a visitor center with an administrative office and concession wings. I did everything I could to stop this. It was genuinely unstoppable. You believe me, don't you?"

What did it mean?

All the poems she had ever written sat silent and limp, waiting for her, and she knew that the whole action had been set in motion and now would creak slowly forward then quickly gain momentum, while her hand would slip off the controls, unneeded.

Washing on Monday, ironing on Tuesday.

She wasn't needed anywhere anymore.

She knew quite definitely now that she would tear up the poetry and so end the years that they had been. And it was almost a relief to know that she, personally, no longer had to account for her actions. She had sent it all down the chute, and the movements of her hands would tear at the poems when the time came with mechanical and irreversible efficiency.

She wondered how she would remember this, how the scene would construct itself in her later mind. She saw herself wearing a warm wrapper, looking out a window, raising the teacup to her lips, waiting for Gooden who never came home.

The gatherings of their years and thoughts and love and the people they had been lay in a pile beneath the china lamplight.

"Take me back," she said into the room, "I love you," and waited, and then began to tear up the poems one by one. She had at first wanted to destroy them fiercely, to disintegrate them by some violent act—perhaps burning—but she had suddenly felt a desire to wound each poem that had been between them, to touch and tear the fabric of her thoughts and love. She had always planned to sit comfortably in the future with her pile of poems and read them and muse over what she had been like and regret her white hair and read Gooden some little funny line.

And then the two of them would laugh in utter familiarity over a coffee cup, some late and placid evening.

She had not planned to cry again but there it was. Clara wanted Gooden's hand on her throat, which ached, and on the back of her neck where it was bowed and alone. She cried into the empty attic and the thick paper the poems were written on made her fingers red and sore. She took them at first one at a time, then three and four at a time and tore them up, and scraps drifted down into the wastebasket.

Suddenly she wondered what she had written on this one, with green ink. Her fingers kept on slicing and shredding until the poem in green ink was gone, but her eyes sought for the pieces as they scattered into the basket. She wondered if it would be possible to find all the bits and pieces and somehow fit them together and hold them with tape and have the poem in green ink again. Her fingers dove down into the scraps, but the delicate patterns it had once been melted to nothing on her hands—her thoughts spun apart into the alphabet, into 'r' and 'm,' into a lost adjective and consonant and verb, into phrases that juggled words without meaning.

Something tightened within her into a sudden apprehension. She saw Gooden's lips move, and not to kiss her, and even as she leaned forward to hear him his words dissolved away before she could catch his meaning. He had always tried to tell her but she had never heard.

"I love you," she said against his will, beating on her. But he had asked more. She picked up the next to the last poem and then the last and caught at the phrases that fell against her mind and went sliding off and sought a foothold and she reaching out but still they slipped away.

Into the attic the footsteps rang, and sought beneath her coverings for the raw emotions.

"Grandm'am," Kezia said. "What are you doing up here?"

Thickly out of her grieving and her hoping she heard her granddaughter. Within the paleness of Clara's face her eyes widened into a sudden blankness.

Kezia picked up a scrap of paper from the basket. " *'komisch,'* " Kezia said. "What does that mean?"

"Comical, peculiar, strange."

"Grandm'am, tell me. What're you doing here?"

Clara felt a brief terror at the empty attic before her and the little table shorn of its poems, which were forever gone. And then the terror subsided, and she knew her granddaughter only vaguely, she heard her voice and understood her words as from a great distance.

"I am looking for a way out," Clara Beal said.

It was gray and overcast, the end of May when Perley's House started to die.

Kezia heard the bulldozer, eating its way toward her through a forest of gravel, spitting out the stones.

No osprey rose up in the nest to give warning—the high rising metallic alarm notes when strangers appeared. There had been no ospreys at Toothaker Harbor for five years. The white Eviction Notice still on the front door was the new cornerpost: here rules the park.

Kezia ripped it off the door.

There was scattered applause from the islanders gathered in waiting: there was nothing else they could do. Two reporters, one with a minicam perched on her shoulder, aimed now toward the dozer's sound.

There had been a trial—that was the law.

Judge Fenster issued a memorandum decision, finding against Perley's House—that was the law.

Kezia's lawyers filed a series of T.R.O.'s—technical restraining orders to stall off the final eviction for a few months more. Denied. Denied. Denied—that was the law.

Two deputy sheriffs from the mainland arrived to oversee the final emptying of the house. Kezia and Nate had saved what they could: ripping out all the pumpkin pine floorboards, each one two feet wide. The planks were worn down now below the harder knots. Her fingers had felt them like hills on a plain.

Now the high yellow cab of the dozer swung the crane into position; the wrecking ball slammed into the second story, biting out a great chunk. The Park Service lawyer and two policemen stood arms crossed, not proud but, well, the job had to get done.

The roar of the motor, the grind of the gears, and the house boomed its way down. In a wet climate Perley's House was tinder dry: years of drying, an insect casing, occupant flown. It crumpled like a mummy preserved through thousands of years and then exposed to light and air and in seconds powdering away. Roof fallen, first floor rooms revealed now, small and low. The supports were oak and white pine, the spaces between bridged with roughly shaped timbers and small boards. Inside stood a bracing of bricks to protect against Indians and cold.

Now the ancient bricks crushed into brick dust and blew away.

It only took a day to raise the house. The neighbors smashed rum on the roof for luck.

"Here's to Millard's industry
and Emmadene's delight,
Framed in a day and raised
before night."

Razed in an hour.

The smell of soapsuds in the washtub by the stove: the Saturday night bath in a kitchen rich with molasses baking beans. Sunday breakfast was hurried beans and brown bread and rushing out to church. And then you came home.

Kezia breathed: a sticky denseness filled the air. Hydrocarbons, a newspaper had said, from the metropolises growing amoebalike from the south and west.

When she let her breath out she saw it: a little wooden box, two by six inches, sitting miraculous amidst the rubble. Before the dozer's treads moved to crush it she rushed out and snatched it up. Had it been secreted in the replastered ceiling, forgotten behind a loose board in the wall? It was scraped and dusty with a tiny lock on the front.

It wasn't locked: she lifted the lid.

She felt a queer, hurting disappointment. Nothing: just a pencil box. The wood was rough and hand-carved with a little partition down the middle, the rear covered with a lid and an open black-stained square where once the inkbottle fit. Kezia lifted the lid by its tiny round knob: more ink stains, nothing else. In the front only two pencils, still sharp.

She shut the lid and held it against her side.

The dozer ground over the house's remains. Timbers split like bones, more dust billowing down.

"What do you think of the park service now?" the reporter said, thrusting a microphone at Kezia.

"I think it's simply smashing."

"What are your feelings now your home is gone?"

"I want to tell everyone, it had a name just like you or me. Perley's House."

The dozer, still hungry, scented the old fish shack down by the water's edge. It turned, treads rolling, roaring faster.

"*No.* Not the fish shack. It wasn't served for eviction! It stays." She put the box down and ran toward the shack, her feet finding the slats nailed on its side leading the way up where the shingled roof always needed fixing. The shingles were leprous now, patches falling away. The top above the doorway sagged broken-mouthed.

"Mrs. Macrae," the lawyer said. "Please get down off that roof."

"I'll sue for everything you've got. The shack wasn't served!"

The man in the dozer sat with gloved hands on the levers, his eyes in the high cab level with hers. Now the fingers of his right hand were pinching the bridge of his nose. The minicam moved excitedly, taking it all in. The Park Service lawyer unrolled a map and he and another man bent heads together over it.

The shingles crumbled under Kezia's fingers as if the roof itself wanted to thrust her off. She remembered running through the open door, all crowded order within, rafters hung with the maroon and yellow buoys she had painted at 3¢ per. She breathed in the sawdust and sour hawser and paint smells, fresh-cut spruce branches heaped for trap laths. A narrow path among yellow wood of new traps and gray of old led to the potbellied stove. There stood the long workbench under the little window, her favorite place to sneak away and read another *Nancy Drew*. When the mystery got too scary, she slipped the moist fragrant curls of wood shavings on all her fingers like rings, and dreamed of princes and love.

The Park Service lawyer motioned to the dozer operator to proceed.

Kezia stood up on the roof and the wind swept her hair. The old globe of shark oil in its net of twisted twine still hung over the door: the watcher of the wind. Some winds brought dirty weather. Others, fair.

Her gaze clawed at the sky. She wasn't high enough.

"No."

She went limp.

One policeman's hands seized under her armpits, the other's grasping her ankles, swinging her down like a sack of potatoes. The dozer ground forward and shark oil flung free, staining the shingles that collapsed backward without resistance like a movie set.

"What's that box, Kezia?" Loara Vannah said.

Kezia picked it up again. "Just a pencil box."

Across the bottom was a child's printing: faded almost to nothing like the letters in the Beal graveyard melting from the stones. She squinted to read in the darkening light.

"This is my pencil box. Johnny Beal.
December 30, 1923.

He was nine years old.

"His writing, Mother. It looks just like mine at nine." The permanency and transiency of life: she would pass that way too and die.

"Mrs. Macrae," the reporter said. "Where will you and your grandmother go now?"

"We're moving to Sheep Island. Beals still own Sheep Island. We'll play Tchaikovsky's Last Movement."

"Last Movement?"

"He was evicted too."

CHAPTER 41

1979 - Sheep Island, Maine

May was when you took off your winter underwear.

On the last day of May that was still chill, Kezia sat with her mother on the hillside of Sheep Island and looked across the water at Aguahega. On the dark blue sea it floated black under a gold noon sky.

Perspective, the painters said.

When I was nine I was scared to death of life.

When I was 21, I was sure I could conquer all.

Now I'm 36.

"I hope I'm not a burden on my children," Loara Beal Vannah said. "Like Clara. Rather be put away. Rather crawl out under a bush and die like the animals do. Simple, the way it should be. Then wrap me in a sheet and just bury me."

"Don't say that, Mother."

"Why? It's true."

"Grandm'am's doing a lot better than you or anyone thinks." She looked at her mother who kept on gnawing the "smoker"—an alewife lightly salted, the first batch of the season, green-pine cured. The alewives had come back to Aguahega just as they always had, silver-gray turmoil through the waters of Persistent Creek and into the dark sanctuary that was Alewife Pond.

Her mother put the smoker down.

"And on your right!" a loudspeaker blared. "You have Sheep Island. It's been utilized for raising sheep since the mid-eighteen hundreds." The white canopy-topped tourist barge listed to starboard as its cargo rushed to stare up at Kezia and her mother on the hill. "There are fifty some sheep," the announcer said, "at pasturage there now. A spry little lady well into her eighties is their devoted shepherdess."

Kezia dropped her own smoker and flattened herself down on her belly, behind the rocks embroidered with mustard and orange lichens. She watched the boat churn past with her head down like a snake.

"Now hard by that sheep pen you'll spy an authentic—ladies and gentlemen—scaregull."

Squinting, Kezia could just make out a splotch of color—pink print with a microphone in hand.

"It's merely a strawman in an old rowboat to warn the seagulls away. Yes, seagulls have been known to attack sheep...Yes, ma'am, works just like our old friend the scarecrow. Maybe this one, too, can go to Oz and get a brain."

When the boat passed out of sight to the south on its way to view the cliffs, Kezia sat back up. On the ground, ants black as raisins swarmed over her golden-bronze paper-crisp smoker. She could feel all its fishbones as if stuck in her throat.

Across the boat's wake, waves still fracturing on the shore, she could see the water of Fiddlehead Cove, brown. Sewage had been dredged from the sea bottom at Haley's Landing, dumped five miles south of Aguahega, and yet persistent as the alewives, had returned.

Kezia stood up and hurled the smoker away.

"Mother, I asked you out here today because I had something to tell you."

"You're giving up this foolishness about Sheep Island, staying on?"

"Mother, I filed for divorce."

"Oh no. Oh no. No one in our family—ever. We've never had that"—her voice struggled even to speak it—"a divorce."

"I know."

"Has he...got somebody else?"

"No."

"Then what is it, Kezia? What is your problem?"

Kezia looked out at the horizon. Problem? Which one to talk about? Her mother's voice was honed with its disciplinary edge that still filled Kezia with dread. She turned to look at the face that was reddish pale, a darker mauve under the eyes, the skin roughened and tight. A shapeless blue-plaid shirt hung over her thickening waist. Loara's eyes looked small and distant and her broad gold wedding ring flashed.

"We're not happy together, Mother. No one's fault."

"Happy! Happy! Do you think that's your God-given right? For better or for worse, you said."

"I have a right to love someone, and I don't love Reo anymore."

"Love! Do you think I always loved Beck? Or your father? No, that's not what it's all about."

"It is as far as I'm concerned."

"You do your duty. Responsibility. You endure."

"I don't endure, Mother. I don't want to live life and just endure."

"What problem? What is the problem?"

Something warned Kezia not even to begin, but the silence was stretching longer and she wanted to justify her decision, to explain. To see love in her mother's eyes.

"Reo's a man of dark moods, Mother. I thought right from the start there's a way I could please him. I'd make wisecracks, make my 'squirrel' face, and I could get him right out of it."

Loara focused on her dubiously.

"He loved me for it, Mother. And I loved feeling needed. Then all of a sudden it was my job. He expected it, every time he was in a bad mood. I resented the expectation. Plumping him up like a sickroom pillow. Then he said I made him feel like a child, always asking after his moods. He no longer felt loved; I no longer felt needed. The very thing that had made us happy was now driving us apart."

"Moods! Moods!" Sweat stood out on Loara's upper lip. "Is that what you think marriage is—a mood? It's because of New York, isn't it? Willi. You'll end up alone like Willi, putting on airs, swollen up as an old toad sculpin. Dried out as a prune."

Kezia saw fear on her mother's face.

But who was it for?

"You'll be alone. You understand me? A woman alone. You get back with Reo. You bend your head."

"Mother! I just want to be happy. Is that such a crime?"

"Then do as your sisters; they're happy. Deenie and Duane. Chance and Victorine."

"I want to be myself. Didn't you ever want to be yourself? Doesn't that come first?"

"You're wrong. If you were right, my whole life was a waste, Kezia. Sixty-four years of waste."

"What do you mean, a waste?" Kezia stopped. Her mother was standing bent forward, peering out to sea through her binoculars. Several boats, distant, were plowing like a little armada through the waves.

"Did you hear what I said?"

Loara's eyes, remote and unfocused as always, looked at her briefly above the black binocular rims. Back up the binoculars went. She slipped behind their protection like a deer through trees.

"Damn them. Oh God. Oh God damn them." Loara's face went red with the white strawberry splotches, the way it looked in the heat of effort when she worked bent over in the vegetable rows. The communal garden Kezia had plowed for everyone on the island, that no one but her mother would use.

"Mother, what? What's wrong?" Kezia grabbed the binoculars from her hand. The round lenses swam with blue sky, sea. Now she saw a white-splattered islet of rock with its gaunt leafless skeletons of trees suffocated by bird lime. Three men large as giants strode over the miniature world from one bulky nest of white-streaked sticks to another, smashing eggs and chasing hatchlings, clubbing them in silence. The men were Beck and Nate and Duane.

"Mother—*why?*"

"Did you forget? Shags are ugly and awful. They say they smell everything up with all that lime. They say they clean out a pocket of herring before you can run it to market. They say a lot of things. Kezia, now you run along. I'm taking the outboard out there."

"I'm coming with you."

"It won't be pretty. Now do as I say."

"I'm not a child anymore."

By the time their little boat nudged the rough rocky islet the men were gone. The rock and soil, even the sticks of the many nests a foot apart were encrusted with gray-white layers of lime. The white was splotched here and there with pink and purple, mussels and other creatures whose pigments, digested, were all that remained. The air smote Kezia, solid with the violence of rotting fish.

In every nest the cormorants' powder-blue eggs, mottled with a chalky deposit, lay shattered. The chicks, too, were crushed and bloodied: black, shiny skinned, naked as snakes.

"Mother, are they all dead?"

Loara didn't answer. Kezia followed her from nest to nest. What was she looking for? Kezia felt her foot come down on something that gave. But it was only one of the little balls of shell and gristle regurgitated everywhere.

Cormorants were called shags because they "shagged," chased the fish in weirs. But nothing could make them deserving of this. At the far edge of the colony a few nettles and mustard plants struggled to grow. Something else struggled there: a long throat that gaped toadlike, thrusting blindly for food.

Loara knelt, gathered up the hatchling in her hands as if she'd been doing it all her life.

It lay huddled, collapsed, motionless now, both its legs and one wing broken. Loara lowered the bird to her lap. She took off a sock with a hole in its toe, drew it gently over the bird so only its bill and head were through.

"What are you going to do with him?"

"Heal him up, if I can."

"Where did you learn that?"

"When I was a girl on Scrag Rock. Thousands of medricks—arctic terns, you'd call them—on the Rock. They came back to us regular as alewives in the spring."

"Did you like them?"

"They'd swirl all around you like a cloud and you'd be inside the cloud, inside the cry."

"What was it like?"

"It was like being inside God."

Kezia looked at her. Her mother had never talked like this about Scrag Rock.

"But Father hated them," Loara said. "The noise and the stench, he said. And they spattered white all over the red roofs, and we used the roofs for runoff drinking water. He would kill them all if he could—just like Nate, just like Beck. But one morning they came in before a storm boiling up to the southeast. Crashed into the lighthouse, into the lantern, confused by the light. Before dawn we had a hundred some birds dead or stunned. Father couldn't stop her. My mother laid the stunned ones in shifts in the barely warm oven to recover. That's how I remember her, tending them like bread loaves in the open oven door."

"Did they live?"

"Some. Some not. We'd better get ourselves back if we want this one to."

Kezia's hand touched her mother's where it was holding the bird.

Can you remember the last time you touched her, you who slept in her body close as a pea in a pod? You can hear more truly with your fingertips than your ears.

"Men see something, anything that moves," Kezia said, "and *wham*: they want to smash it."

"Shags are different, that's all. Men don't like that. Freaks. I'm a freak."

"What do you mean?"

"I couldn't raise you right to be what a woman has to be. I tried but I never fitted in."

"You got married, had children. Isn't that what you wanted?"

"I didn't want to be a freak."

It was there again on her mother's face, the shame of emotion, the embarrassment of feeling. But around it the tears were pouring down.

"Mother, what is it?"

"We all do. Marry, for the wrong reasons. Maybe people always do. I married your father for the wrong reasons."

"What reasons?"

"Every reason you could name."

For the first time they looked at each other with understanding, an understanding of the deepest kind.

CHAPTER 42

1979 - Bangor, Maine

"I am ready," Clara Beal said, standing with a towel wrapped around her head, a pair of stockings tied in a jaunty bow around her neck.

The doctor would have to tell them, Kezia thought. Let the doctor tell them it was time for her and Clara to leave Sheep Island, time to go.

Now the intense lights of the medical center in Bangor whitened everything like a sterilizing mist. "Five six one oh," the paging operator's voice sang, "five six one oh, five six one oh."

"How are we today, Mrs. Beal?" the young neurologist said.

Grandm'am made no response. She sat slumped in the chair in front of his desk, head bent in the hat Kezia had substituted for the towel, a black velvet hat with big white velvet bows.

"How are we, Mrs. Beal?" Still cheerfully.

"I'd like to ask you a few questions. Would you like to answer them for me?"

Nod.

"What year is this?"

Clara was at once all schoolmarm, arch, contemptuous as Miss May-ry: "It is nineteen seventy-nine, any fool would know that."

And the season of the year?"

"It is the fall, of course."

"Fine, fine. Now the date? What month is it, and what day of the month?"

"It is...it is..." Clara looked abashed, an 83-year-old child being scolded. Her gaze roved the room, finally settled on Kezia.

"I can never remember the date myself," Kezia said.

"Just let your grandmother answer, thanks." His fingers were marking something on a paper—failing grade?

"Now then, Mrs. Beal. I would like you to spell a word backward for me. Would you be kind enough to do that for me?"

Nod.

"The word is 'world.' "

"Spell?" Clara's liver-spotted hands twisted in her lap. " 'W'-'o'—"

"No no no." His words came like waves, in threes. "Would you please spell it *backwards* for me?"

Clara's face tightened, an anxious fear of failure narrowing her eyes.

It was like being reduced to a child again, Kezia thought, your narrow knees trembling at the blackboard, hand poised all ready to write, already dusty with chalk but not knowing the answer, how to get to the answer, hopelessly blank and dumb. The teacher waiting, parental disapproval looming ever larger, the lines of desks and children fidgeting and giggling, calling "*Stu*-pid" behind your back. Backwards.

" 'W'-'o'—" Clara began again.

Silently Kezia tried it herself. It wasn't easy, not diffused like this with the rush of panic, the word a red pigment mixing in with blank white paint like the birthmark coverup she'd put on that morning, the word not sharp anymore, spreading in whorls and thinning to a creamy nothingness across your blank white mind.

"Uh, that's fine, Mrs. Beal. Just fine." Still writing.

Clara darted her chin up and down, lips tight with satisfaction. Her body stiffened with the old spirit of the fight and she winked at Kezia. "I got through that by the skin of my mouth."

"Now, then." The doctor picked up a wristwatch from his desk, its strap worn and twisted. "Would you tell me what this object is?"

Kezia felt herself relax: this one was easy. She shook the tension out of her back first to the left, then the right, crossed her legs at the knee and swung her foot. She felt better. She was not prepared for Clara's harsh cold voice.

"Of course I know what that is. You cannot sneeze that away. Why do you ask?"

"Would you tell me, please?"

"Of course I know what that is." Her voice had left its steady track, was vaulting rubberily through a field of obstacles.

"Can you tell me, Mrs. Beal?"

"There is more here than meets the surface. Just give me a minute, my head hurts. I know what that is."

"Well, that's fine now. Let's go on." His voice, crisp, signaled her defeat.

Her features tried to regroup to face him, eyes shrinking within.

"Now I'm going to ask you to do something for me. I want you to take this paper in your right hand, fold it in half, and put it on the floor. Would you do that for me?"

Clara's hand picked up the white sheet of 8-1/2 by 11 paper as if it were of fragile Chinese porcelain. Slowly she folded it in half. Her forefinger and thumb creased and recreased along its fold. Finally she lifted it as if to pass it across to the doctor, eyes studying his face, saw that this might be wrong, put the paper back down in her lap. Her left hand beneath the paper trembled its surface that quivered now as if alive. Her head bent as she studied the folded paper in her lap.

Kezia didn't see it fall. She saw only a darker white consuming like a wet fire across the paper as the single teardrop spread.

Kezia left Clara in the CAT scan waiting room facing a four-foot poster of the Pink Panther. Then would come the EEG, the ECG, the chest x-ray, spinal tap, blood count, urological workup. She herself was about to be hacked and bloodied: let the wound do the weeping.

She sat in the Laser Clinic waiting room, wondering why the fear was so bad, Ugly Duckling not yet pecked out of her egg,

Cinderella still in rags, glass slipper soon bleeding. She had read in *Vogue* Magazine about the argon laser, a " 'stain' remover," it said, "for your skin." Like Comet cleanser for old New York sinks.

The backs of her hands were purple and white tundra under the ventilator's arctic air. But she made no move to change seats. Others—some birthmarked like her—were sitting carefully spaced in other seats. To move was to see them—pink/red birthmarks to red to red/purple to purple (and they to see you). If she got up she might run from the room. It would hurt, the pain fierce and the needle anesthetic sharp and endless through her cheek. It was risky, no one knew how *your* face would do, dragging it forward like a steer to the abattoir.

"Mrs. Macrae," the nurse said.

Kezia's knees bore her upward while across the room a man was staring. *His* spilled deepest flagrant purple down a whole harlequin half of his face, the lips on the stained side protruding grossly, cobblestoned and coarse. He gave her the thumbs-up sign.

An ice cube held against the mouse in the nurse's clear flesh-pink-through-plastic glove: "Cold makes it violacious."

"Violacious?"

"More purple. And the darker the stain the better the laser works."

And then it: the coherent model 1000 dermatological argon laser, an imitation wood-grained table on wheels, insignificant control panel, fiber lead, neat slim probe.

"We're just going to do the test spot today," the doctor said, his acne red under the fluorescent ceiling light. Physician, heal thyself. "Just relax now."

She looked at him through her tinted protective goggles. His eyes were safety-goggled also, fishlike now as he opened his mouth. "Please keep your eyes closed during the entire procedure."

The room went dark behind her shuttered lids. There were a host of technical reasons why the laser worked. Still, she would rather think of it as magic: the weapon of a paring Jedi knight. She would sit here docile while he burned her to the bone, zapping her fierce dark Force away. The round metal ring of the probe's attachment rested lightly against her cheek. Heat—a pinprick slowly spreading...

She imagined the blue-green Jedi light stabbing through her skin, speeding through the innocent white layers, selectively absorbed by red, the darker places where capillaries had gone awry, drinking the blue-green poison to the lees.

She wanted to laugh but the heat was a wave now, flaring and spreading hot with the smell: the smoke from her own singed downy facial hair. And then it was over and she felt dizzy, her brain washing loose of its mooring through her skull.

In the resting room the nurse handed her a mirror. "You can look at it before it's bandaged, if you wish."

There in the mouse was a spot the size of a nickel, beautiful pale frosty white like a bouquet she had once chosen wrapped in paper from the sidewalk water-filled pail: one white carnation among red. Something dark was gone, something from long ago, the wolffish rising dark through glimmering ice? She watched the spot puffing up before her eyes.

"Remember it's a second degree 'burn,' " the nurse said. "It'll swell and weep and then form a scab. Just keep ice on it and wash three times a day with soap and water. Put this antibiotic ointment and dressing on it, just like this. Three to five weeks and it'll be healed. We'll check how it's faded back here two months from now, and if all goes well, we'll start the treatments then."

"I can't believe it. It works. It does, doesn't it?"

The nurse smiled. "You're a very pretty woman, birthmark or no."

Kezia looked in the mirror again. Suddenly she didn't want the mouse to go.

She left, knowing she wouldn't come back again.

"Now, then," the neurologist said four days later, sitting back in his high-topped leather chair. It kept making a nervous creaking sound. "Who will be the patient's principal caregiver?" His tone was kind between the rush of words: appointments were behind schedule as always, the waiting room outside overfull.

Kezia waited until it was clear that Willi Beale, who'd arrived from New York, was waiting for her. Somehow she had inherited Grandm'am like a piece of furniture from Perley's House. "Well, I'm staying with her through the winter."

"And subsequent to that?" His eyes behind the square framed black glasses moved to Willi.

She gave off cold air that steamed into the room: arctic fox jacket flung over the back of her chair, cream wool pants still damp at the hems with snow, ivory jersey hood. She whipped her owl-round dark glasses off, peered challengingly back at him. Under a spill of bangs her eyes dominated her face: dark pouches below, dark lid looseness above. The brilliant-lit flash of her eyes glittered more jewel-like now than when she was young, now in their dark setting. At 67 her face was fragile, as if it might lapse into old age at any minute, even as you watched.

"Well," Willi said, "at this point in time we don't quite know. What's best, of course. What do the tests show?"

The doctor matched his fingertips together, bending them up down, up down, a spider's legs on glass. "Mrs. Beal has incurred a condition known as M.I.D.—multi-infarct dementia. She has suffered a series of small strokes over the years that in turn have damaged her brain. She has a loss of ability to form new memories. There's a slight elevation of blood pressure but she's in remarkably good health otherwise. For her age." His hands, white and scrubbed looking under the intense lights, were busy writing. His fingers tore the two sheets from his prescription pad, the soap scent citrus-brisk wafting to Kezia as she reached for them across the desk. "I've prescribed some medications for her."

Kezia looked at them. "Persantine," one read, and on the other his handwriting was illegible. "What's this one for?"

"Multli-vitamin tablet. Unfortunately we can't undo the neurological damage that has already occurred, but we hope to prevent any further cerebral infarcts with the medications."

With vitamins? Kezia felt her panic rise.

The doctor's eyes were warm. They seemed to say he didn't want to rush so, but what could he do? He felt the press of others waiting, problems more severe than this. He sat forward, gaze busy with papers he sorted on his desk. Kezia saw the manilla folder of her grandmother's file close. His eyes met hers; there were friendly crinkles as he smiled. "See that she takes the pills—the pharmacist downstairs will give you a patient-information sheet which should answer all your questions."

He stood up, hand extended to shake good-bye. "Don't hesitate to call."

But doctor, tell me, what should I do?

"Thank you," Willi said.

The doctor was leaving them with Clara just as she was. He didn't have to live with Clara the way that she was. And getting worse.

He smiled and nodded them toward the door.

Heads lifted, eyes studied them as they wove their way back out through the crowded waiting room. Haunches shifted, patients anxious to be called next. An old woman sat in a wheelchair, face shriveled under a cotton bolus of white hair. A puddle of urine lay under her chair, the surface tension molding it round as a bubble.

The old woman screamed.

Kezia started, but the people next to the old woman ignored her. Around the room faces were busy keeping away. Kezia took their cue: this, then, was dementia, its voice not communication any longer, just noise.

Kezia widened her path to go around the wheelchair. She could see the scalp gleaming pink as bubblegum beneath the cotton candy hair. The old woman stared up at Kezia, eyes fierce, haunted, the toothless gums cracking open and her hand coming up, signaling frantically. "Taxi!"

No one reacted.

Kezia kept on walking—it was like a betrayal—out of the room.

CHAPTER 43

1979 - Haley's Landing, Maine

Beside her grandmother Kezia was watching the sea for no better reason than that it moved and changed before her. She felt a sense of lightness, of peace coming in. The golden glaze of late-September noon overlaid the water and formed a shiny patina on her grandmother's arms and every other object that had been burnished and sea-dampened and dried. The Haley's Landing seawall on which the two women were leaning offered up the same sun-harsh color, its lines and cracks erased by the incoming tide, then etched in again more sharply at the ebb. Even Aguahega's crabapples grew more gold than red this fall, and already puckered wiltingly at both ends.

"Kezia!" Victorine's voice sailed from the open window of their mother's red-painted Victorian gingerbread house. Beck and Loara Vannah had followed the Smallidges in their decision not to winter over, had rented this house on the main. Even Deenie and Duane had moved to a small fishing village down the coast. The Beals of Aguahega were no more.

"We'll be ready in a few minutes," Victorine was calling.

Kezia raised her hand in assent. Ready for lunch. Ready to decide in this committee of family what to do about Clara Beal. Everyone was here: Deenie, Loara, Victorine, even Willi all the way from New York. "Just us," Kezia had suggested, "a family reunion. No husbands, stepfathers, no men at all, okay?"

"Duane *is* family," Deenie had said but finally agreed.

Now they were here, back together again, grandmother, mother, a clutch of daughters who year after year had arranged themselves along the continuum of womanhood. With each summer there was at least one who sat at Daddy's cherry secretary in the hall and read countless romances, and another who teetered guiltily on a pair of beautiful legs and wore baggy shorts and affected an undershirt, and some distant-woman child who played and skipped stones across Toothaker Harbor and was much too aimless and relaxed to wonder if it would last.

Beyond the wall startled gulls flung upward before a pair of dry-skinned legs flashing under a short, loose garment. Kezia watched Vinca Chancellor's zig-zag flight across the small sand beach, dress billowing, her sudden plummetings upon a new-found shell or stone. As Kezia had been, now she saw her niece Vinca caught for one last season between childhood and adulthood—one second close and narrow and guarded, another sand-slinging and child-foot running. She was Chance's child: beautiful child. I wish that you were mine.

The screen door broke into the world with a loud crack. *"Keezie,"* Victorine called. The dim, cool interior of Loara Vannah's house crept back into obscurity at the bold touch of light. Kezia saw Victorine's eyes—pale as Loara's—dazzled by the glare of sun and water, autumn clear.

"Victorine—" Kezia had left her mother and her sisters a whole person and now she wanted to begin again, just as she was 27 years before.

"The food is getting cold."

Kezia watched her mother's large hands ladling lobster stew into eight blue willow bowls. From her earliest childhood she remembered these same dishes and all the countless meals marking the passing of time and all her sisters and the sea along the shore that never changed. She wanted to regain that, the changeless fabric of family, the essential quality of a female world, somehow virginal throughout the whole of existence. Her marriage had touched her as little as Vinca's tan—a brief, clasped gilding that would soon peel away. Kezia felt happy, and more than that, complete. That she should be sitting here in her mother's house was as natural as that there should be eight bowls instead of one. There was no question involved in coming back to her grandmother and mother and sisters, but only one in going out from them, in leaving.

Kezia spooned up lobster stew thick with canned milk and rich with green tomalley, a scarlet piece of shell for extra color and flavor floating by the rim. She dunked in a saltine and felt the nectar run down her chin.

She looked around at Grandm'am, Aunt Willi, Mother, Deenie, Victorine, and Vinca and Nicole. "Isn't this great, all of us here together like this? Four generations of Beal girls."

"Women," Vinca said.

"Remember what we used to do at New Year's?" Victorine looked across at Nicole. "We'd get up on chairs, jump together down to the floor at the stroke of twelve, holding hands, jump into the New Year."

"Let's do it now." Kezia pushed back her chair, dragged it away from the table toward the middle of the floor. "Come on, you guys. We can do it now."

Willi frowned. "It's not New Year's."

"Come on, we won't all be together then."

Kezia's nieces were already rattling their chairs next to hers. They pulled up a low footstool for Grandm'am to stand on and then they all looked at each other, holding hands on the circle of chairs.

"Grandm'am has to say Now." Kezia looked at her. "Say Now, Grandm'am."

Clara's face was smiling, confident, part of things. "Now."

They jumped together into the new year.

It didn't matter that none of them lived on Aguahega anymore, Kezia thought. She and Clara could still see it from their cabin on Sheep Island, but perhaps Aguahega wasn't important anymore.

"I think we should talk about you know what." Willi looked at Kezia.

"Don't talk about her as if she's not here."

"Nicole," Victorine said. "You and Vinca go show Grandm'am your scrapbooks in your bedroom."

"Aw, Mom."

"Do as I say."

The spoonful of stew held only shell. Kezia looked around and the warm circle seemed to recede somehow away from her.

"You want to take your pie with you, Grandm'am?" Vinca said.

Clara Beal sat with mouth tight-hinged, hands in lap. On her untouched plate the store-bought pie extruded blue like a stepped-on tube of paint.

"Take it with you, Mama, for crying out loud," Willi said. "We paid for it regardless, you know."

A scab was forming under the weight of Kezia's gauze pad and she wanted to tear it off, to rake her nails across the crusted angry flesh of the mouse. The treatment was a disaster, redder now than before the laser surgery (but that's just from the burn, the nurse had said).

"Maybe when you get her home," Willi said, forking up a piece of her own pie, "you'll be able to do something with her."

"I said don't talk about her as if she's not here."

Mother, please help me, keep Grandm'am away from me I can't help her I'm a child I don't know how.

Everyone looked at Clara who was staring unperturbed out the dining room window.

"Come on, Grandm'am." Vinca tugged on her sleeve.

"I am not eating that food." They were startled to hear Clara's voice, as if a statue had talked. She continued looking out the window but they could hear her hands busy with her napkin in front of her, tearing, shredding. "That woman poisoned it."

The drip of the leaking faucet in the kitchen sounded loud.

Willi grimaced. "She doesn't even know we're here."

Clara looked at Kezia, her face twisted sideways, one pale eye staring at her cannily, a bird after a worm. "That woman"—her head nodded knowingly toward Willi—"you know who I mean." Now she whirled, her voice rising higher, to a shriek. "Let us get out of here. Murderer! Before she kills us all!"

My God, she's gone crazy, Kezia thought. She has. Just wait till dawn, pack up and get out. Let someone else deal with her now. You're not her daughter, she's got Willi for that. They've said it and they were right: put her in a home. You said No, but what did you know? You could live in New York, have no responsibility here. Remember, New York?

Willi's face was scarlet. "Mama, it's me. Willi. Mama, come on now."

"Murderer!" Clara's lips curled, lifted as if independent of the structure of her face. "That woman is not my daughter."

"Oh yes I am, you ugly old woman. I'm your daughter, all right, but not Gooden's, am I? Oh no, not Gooden Beal's." Willi whirled, confronting all their faces. "I've had a private investigator after this for years. I always knew something wasn't right. And now he's told me. I've waited for this for years. My father was a German farmer named Schleicher, now dead. Gooden worked on his farm, he and Clara ran away. They never even bothered to legalize it and get married."

Loara stared at her. "What in the world are you talking about?"

"She lied to us." Willi's voice was as thin and high as a scream. "We're all bastards! Even Johnny, he probably wasn't even a real Beal either. He was probably a Schleicher like me."

Victorine stood up. "I don't believe a word of this. You're always trying to stir up trouble, Willi. Grandm'am, tell her. Tell her it's not true."

Looking, they saw the truth washing away, forever obscured in Clara's faded eyes, another wave going out and no waves coming back in. "That woman is not my daughter."

Kezia's hands were on Clara's shoulders, urging her out of the house. "Grandm'am, please don't make any more trouble, okay? Tomorrow we're going home—remember? Everything'll be all right there."

"Murderer!"

Loara Vannah was standing in the doorway beside the lacquered red door surrounded like the rest of the house with immaculate white gingerbread. "Kezia, can't you control her?"

Not a real Beal after all.

It was embarrassingly obvious: neither Kezia nor Willi wanted to share Clara's bed. Two beds for three people, and Kezia fought to get her own clothes off first before her aunt did when she saw Clara laboriously getting into the bed by the wall. Kezia yanked down the undisturbed coverlet on the second bed. The choice, and obvious statement, were left now to Willi who stood looking from one bed to the other.

Being old was a disease. Perhaps it's catching (oh yes, it's catching, you'll get it sooner than you think). Liver spots a plague of locusts bearing scourge. Odors, night sweats, fluids, diseases rotting like leprosy from within. This was called prejudice against the elderly—easy to deny, not so easy to sleep beside.

"It's cold. Think I'll slide in here with you, Kezia, if you don't mind," Willi said. "Warmer than over there. By the window."

Right.

She was dreaming of ice again.

When Kezia woke, the sheet rasped harsh across the chilled bumps on her skin. Beside her Kezia felt the welcome warmth of Willi, an inert mass still asleep beside her in the bed. The darkness of the strange rectangular space that was the Vannahs' second story bedroom gradually cleared.

Clara Beal was sitting—back bent below the flat-topped velvet hat, fully dressed on the edge of the other bed. The side of the bed faced the wall and so did she.

She was his mother. You owe her something, just for that, even if you wonder if the Grandm'am you loved is still there.

Kezia got out of bed, reached her hand out to touch her grandmother's shoulder. Clara's dress was armored with a stiff tight jacket, a pin piercing its lapel, necklace choking her throat, her hat aggressive with plastic-pearl-tipped hatpins that wove and winked now as her head moved, fireflies at dusk.

Crying: small dry coughs more like a clearing of the throat.

"Grandm'am. What's wrong?"

The noises stopped and the face looked up. "I am going home." Beside the bed her suitcase stood closed and ready.

The mattress sagged inward as Kezia sat down, too close: she felt the heat of her grandmother's body, smelled her peculiar mashed-pea smell. Kezia put her hand out to touch her grandmother's arm.

The arm was snatched inward and away, hoarded as the last piece of February-night firewood. Clara sat up straighter, arms pinned in at her sides. "I am going home."

"Okay, sure. We are. Going home tomorrow. But we have to wait till it's light out, you know. Have to wait for the mailboat."

"You—and that woman. You are going to leave me in the *hospital.*"

"No. Now that's just not true. That's Willi. She loves you. So do I. We wouldn't leave you there."

"I am going home." Her face pinched, crafty, darting glances here and there. Now she was on her feet, calves flashing pale above the black shoes with the treetrunk heels. "You stole my purse. You! You evil girl. You took it. You stole it."

In the flickering light of car headlights from the highway outside, her grandmother stood revealed, snuffed out, revealed again: red-faced, her thin hair released from its braid, spiking crazily down past her shoulders. Kezia stared at the waving arms, the fist pounding at her through the air. The voice came louder, sliding up to a higher frenzy. *"You stole my purse."*

"Of course I didn't. Stop that yelling!"

"Stole it!" The voice, unfamiliar, flung its violence at her and Kezia was suddenly afraid.

"Give it back to me!"

Willi was sitting upright in her bed, eyes swollen under the nylon nightcap, trying to focus, peering out.

"Why?" Clara's voice soared higher, thin as a thread. "Why are you so cruel to me?"

Remember New York? Rabid rabbit transit, New York? Kezia felt the thin Maine carpet cold under her bare feet. Her spine seemed to lengthen as she let out a sigh. On a shelf above the window sat a square black patent purse. Kezia walked over, lifted it down. "Grandm'am, is this your purse?"

It was worn and sharp-cornered, an old-ladies' many compartmented handbag with a tarnished imitation gold clasp that was two tiny hands praying.

Clara stood rooted, eyes wide, her pupils so dilated they turned her gray eyes black.

"Is this it, Grandm'am?" Kezia heard the anger in her own voice. Where had all the patience gone? She was no better than the others. "You come here. You come over here to me."

Clara remained still.

Kezia put the purse down at her own feet. "All right, if you want to be stubborn. Miss Stubborn, if you want it, it's here. You get me up in the middle of the night for nothing, you accuse me of God knows what."

Willi threw back the covers as Kezia got into the bed beside her. "Well, and it's back to everloving normal, Kezia. Wouldn't you say?"

The blankets smelled comfortingly of their origin: lanolin and sheep, and Kezia pulled them up to her chin.

Clara had sat down on the chair facing them. They heard the first trickle, not believing, then the slow gathering gush released to freedom like ice-out in spring.

The bedroom door opened, the overhead light flicked on and Loara and Victorine stood there peering in.

Urine ran from the seat to the edge of the chair, dripping down now to the floor.

"Five six one oh. Five six one oh. Five six one oh."

"Why does Grandm'am keep saying that?" Victorine said from across the breakfast table, sunlight pouring in.

"Paging at the hospital," Kezia said. "They kept paging doctors overhead. You know: 'Dr. Merton, twelve, Dr. Smith, six, Dr. Merton, twelve, Dr. Smith, six.' "

Willi buttered her toast. "And I wanted Dr. *Smith* to win."

Somehow everything was lighter in the daylight.

"I just found out my diamond's not real," Deenie said.

"What?" Victorine said.

"I took it to the jeweler. He said it's fake. I don't care if it's fake but I care that Duane lied to me. What do you think I should do?"

"I think you should *tell* him. He should be punished."

"I kind of thought, 'if it's not broke, don't fix it.' "

"Then," Victorine said, "how do you know anything about him is real?"

Deenie rubbed the top of her "diamond" with her thumb. "I married him. That's real."

"Real bad," Willi said.

"Shhh," Loara said. "The children."

Vinca sat with the window's brilliance outlining her profile, quiet and smooth-browed as always. Beside her Nicole, never still, flirted ceaseless motions with hands that flopped on the ends of wrists, with long, loose feet and big wedge of nose, twitching now with dismay.

"Marriage can be described by the feelings of two animals, right, Kezia?" Willi said.

All eyes were looking at her. "Right. The feelings of two animals, one engaged in eating the other."

"Kezia!" Loara stood up. "Come along. I want to show you what I've been up to these past few months."

On a shelf sat a dollhouse, a model of an old-fashioned soda parlor with a peppermint striped awning and tiny hanging sign. The shelves were a miniature village, dollhouse after dollhouse terraced up a hill. Kezia drew closer, peered into the paned window of the soda parlor: tiny stools, tiny people, tiny banana splits and a wooden ceiling fan.

"It's wonderful. Where did you buy it?"

Her mother let the silence travel until Kezia looked up at her. "I made it."

"All of it?"

"First one I got was just a kit. Then Beck made me a miniature lathe and a little jigsaw. Most of the things inside are bread dough—you shape it, bake it hard and paint it. See these cherries? They're tiny red beads. And the curtains—I sewed them myself."

"It's a lot of work."

"I'm going to build a whole town."

"And you'll be the mayor?"

"Maybe I'll be an atom bomb and tear it all down." Loara wouldn't look at her or meet her eyes. She kept her face averted toward the window, the way she had when the telegram arrived, when Josephine Drouot Pritchard, her mother, had died. No mourning, no outward grief, no tears. Kezia had stood paralyzed in the crush of emotion, the suppression of emotion that warred all around. Loara's voice had come flat, dry, calm—a rage of suppression: "Mother died."

Kezia had said nothing then; but she would say it this time, anything she had to to get to know her mother finally, for the first time. This should have been the time to do it.

"Mother, are you sorry you had to move here, leave Aguahega?"

"Sorry! Sorry!" Loara Vannah looked around as if for the first time. "All the times I wanted to leave, walls pressing in, island pressing in, sea flattening you against Aguahega, pounding you thin over meals cooked, floors scrubbed, vegetables canned. Squeezing you between the boredom of Ladies Card Party on Thursday nights and Men's Card Party on Wednesdays and the baked-on crust from all those potluck suppers, everybody so familiar it was like eating at home. My ears went numb with the tales of who left, who put on airs, who's sick, who died."

"But if you wanted to leave Aguahega, why did you marry Beck?"

"He promised we were going to leave. He'd had it, the Lobster War, fed up. I promised I would marry him and then, just like Johnny, he couldn't do it after all."

"You could have gone alone."

"We aren't what we plan for ourselves. We're what God plans."

"Mother, I don't believe that."

"Shhh." Her arms were bent at the waist, fingers open like antennae listening. Now she turned to look at Kezia, her short hair tufting up on her head. "Thought I heard the medricks, flying back, flying south. Orvilles, we'd call the little hatchlings. Watch them try to learn to fly."

Loara felt the stern, still innocent eyes of Kezia watching her. Kezia—who still idealized her father, who hadn't known him at all. Who still blamed her mother, in some obscure way, for what? Surviving, when Johnny Beal had died? Girl children always idolized their fathers; it was the curse their mothers had to bear. She had idolized Ridley Pritchard, too, in his stiff blue uniform; her mother, after all, only in constantly floured hands.

Was there ever a time I was very young above the earth, and very happy? Her spirit had left the earth with that first plane ride. It had never really come back.

Loara's voice, not distant now, focused painful as a point of light. In it Kezia heard her mother's love for the first time. "Don't give everything up for Clara, Kezia. She's a grand old lady but she's had her life. You're still young. Whatever it is you want to do in life—do it now."

When they walked back into the living room, Kezia saw through the window Vinca and Nicole on either side of Clara, leading her down the hill for a stroll. Kezia knew the moment she'd been dreading had arrived.

"I think I have the answer here." Victorine's voice was coiled with expectancy, tight as her braided blonde hair wrapped against her nape in a little bun.

It was a brochure of a Tudor mansion heavy in ivy, rolling green grounds. Inside were smiling pictures of elderly people, and there were nurses and pictures of bedrooms, neat and clean. Everyone else had already read it, it seemed.

Kezia put it down. "Why do they always have everybody smiling in these things?"

"This is an excellent place. The best. I did a lot of investigating about all this and you can believe me when I tell you, it's got everything she could want or need. Of course Chance and I'll foot the bill."

"Why can't she live with Mother?" Deenie said.

"Beck doesn't want her living with us. I tried talking to him. But Clara says *she* won't live with him. Ever since Johnny died, you know, and I remarried, she's had it in for him."

"What about you, Deenie?" Willi said.

Deenie sat back so her maternity blouse swelled rounder over her abdomen. "I'd like to, but I'm obligated with family right now. Where could we put another person, and what with this next one coming in December and all."

"Everyone's working," Kezia said, "or else obligated with family or—"

"Willi, she's your mother," Deenie interrupted. "It's your responsibility."

"Well, New York and all. It's an awfully long way. My apartment's small."

"A good excuse, anyway," Kezia said.

Willi looked at her. "What's your excuse?"

The living room was dense, tapestried with brocaded furniture and bric-a-brac like the ones in the photographic exhibit at New York's Museum of Modern Art. "A horror show of hinterland taste," the Times' reviewer had said. "Take a Rolaid and follow with the Monets."

Remember? At New Year's Grandm'am melted lead in a spoon, dropped it in the pan of cold water where it chilled, moving, then stilled forever into the shape forecasting the new year.

"Well, I'm wintering over on Sheep Island; those are my plans. I wouldn't mind having her company."

"Now see here, Kezia," Loara said. "This is foolishness. Clara is eighty-three. You'll both freeze yourselves to death."

"Nonsense, we're set up snug as can be. I winterized the cabin, you know that. Put up plastic sheets outside, nailed to the walls, then weatherstripping inside, laid down insulated foil, new blue carpeting on top of that. It looks quite cozy if I do say so."

"Wintering over?" Victorine said. "But why?"

"Lobster landings have dropped by fifty percent. You have to work longer, fish more pots to call it even these days. Sometimes I haul forty, fifty pots to get half a dozen lobsters in April."

"You can't live out there by yourself all winter."

Kezia wished she were there: the pot hauler gargling and within a few seconds twenty fathoms of slimy spray-flinging rope would fly upward, whip around the sheave and fall snaking in coils at her boots. The bottom of the sea would suddenly surface and she would own it, seaweed billowing: two traps, each three feet long...

"It's a business. I don't close my doors half the year through."

"You and Chance—you're both crazy. What is this thing about boats?" Victorine said. "I've been after him for years to sell *Pyed Cow.* He's always either working on it, sailing it, or planning to sail it. Neither I nor the kids like to sail. What is it—just an ugly old lobster sloop he keeps promising to sell."

"You don't mean that."

"Don't mean what?"

"Don't you even know?" Kezia saw the flush rising on her sister's neck as everyone turned to look at Victorine. "He's never going to sell that old boat. That old boat means more to him than you or I ever will. It's all that's left—from before."

The silence seemed to rise like a hedge.

"What right have you to say that! You don't know him better than me."

Loara Vannah thrust both hands deep in her cardigan sweater pockets. "You can hold on over the winter, Kezia. You can hold on to Clara, too. But maybe you should let her go."

"What do you people want?"

"We want," Willi said, "what's best for everyone."

"Grandm'am could die out there, Kezia," Deenie said. "Did you ever think of that? While you're out gallivanting—"

"Hauling."

"She could die."

"Even if she did, what's so terrible about it? We're all going to die. In ancient Greece they said it's how you die that matters. If you didn't die happily, you couldn't be said to have lived happily."

"No one dies happy," Victorine said.

"Even if she died, that's how people used to die. Is that worse than dying strapped down to a bed in a nursing home, full of tubes?"

Willi stood up. "Why should she have a death that's right for you?"

"I'm taking Grandm'am home." Her voice was too loud, she could hear it hunting around the room.

"No, you're not." Victorine's voice was hard, her hands tightening on Kezia's arms, face already sorrowing, already gone. "It's been decided, Kezia. That's all there is to say."

She was breathless. Victorine was suffocating her. She could see Clara walking wide-legged now, stiffly up the walk. She couldn't cry, she wouldn't let it start. She was struggling now to free herself but Victorine's arms resisted. Kezia's hand came up, she heard the hard crisp sound of her palm against her sister's cheek. Victorine's face stared at her, pinched in, swelled with shock, drew away.

"Oh God, I'm sorry. Victorine, it was an accident—"

Still staring.

"I didn't mean to—"

Victorine was walking away.

Kezia hadn't said it but still she hoped it would last, the feeling of family that had started. She was afraid but still she hoped. She was waiting for someone to tell her it would.

Silent, they were all storming out of the room.

Kezia could see Aguahega from the Haley's Landing dock, just another cloud under pink and purple clouds massing across the apple-green sky foretelling cold. Only Willi had come to see them off.

"Grandm'am, say something to Willi, now. She has to leave and we won't be seeing her for awhile."

"Murderer!"

People were turning, looking at them now.

Kezia forced Clara's stiff arms back down to her sides. She could see the sudden luminous welling in Willi's eyes.

"I'm her own daughter," Willi said, "but she never cared for me. Why should she remember you, and not me?"

"I don't know."

"Why don't you answer her back when she's nasty?"

Why, indeed?

"If you think no one's speaking to you now, Kezia, wait until winter. You're just keeping her to spite us, that's what Victorine said."

The wind blew cold.

The boat ride home was cold and wet and silent. After landing at Aguahega there was still the journey across to Sheep Island, the sea seizing the end of her oars, traveling with its relentless pull into her shoulder joints. But then the cabin door was shut and the stove warming, and Kezia looked around, glad to be home: a bunkbed, kerosene lamps bright in brass, an oilcloth-covered table with two chairs, the bright new carpet, fleecy and deep. She sat down on the lower bunk, beneath her the mattress pressing soft and thin down to the boards. But the sheet hem and pillowcase were white and clean, just the way Clara liked them.

Kezia dared a glance at her grandmother. Age is a stranger; after a while, even you'll get there. You'll look in the mirror and you won't even recognize your own face. You're looking at what's waiting for you.

"How old *are* you?" Clara Beal said.

"What?"

"How old?"

"Well, I'm thirty-six now."

"That is pretty old. Did you never get married?"

"I got married. Now I'm getting divorced."

Clara sniffed. "That is pretty old. No one else will want you now."

"Shut up!" All of the trip's frustrations came pouring out. "You cantankerous old woman, you just shut up!"

Her hand was raised, she saw Clara staring up at it, saw the fear in her washed-out eyes.

So, Kezia thought. You stand revealed—an old lady beater. Her hand fell back to her side.

Clara pulled out her dentures and set them smiling, Cheshire-cat bodiless, in her lap.

"See what you've turned me into, Grandm'am? Goddam it, I'm a mean old hag." Kezia heard herself laugh. Clara stared and then, toothless gums working, let out a wild rising giggle.

"Both of us! Reo didn't want us. No one will want us. We're over the hill!"

The voice that answered came transparent as water, the words slurred with loss of teeth but the voice as measured, as rational as any Kezia had ever heard.

"Yes. I am happy that Gooden is not here to see. I do not like this. This."

Kezia sat up, startled, and peered over the edge of the top bunk. Clara was bending over the lantern's flame, turning the screw at its base. The light snuffed out.

"This losing my mind."

CHAPTER 44

1979 - Thrumcap Island, Maine

On Thrumcap Island, Pruitt Hoskins stopped shoveling for a minute, leaned on the red-painted metal handle. "They sent me notice you're maybe not what they call the 'true owner' of Thrumcap."

"What?" Willi saw him look down, his silence an assent that chilled her spine. His head was nearly bald, his face flat and not much troubled with features, like an elderly Japanese gentleman taking tea.

"They say they can't find a title for Thrumcap earlier than Nineteen Thirteen."

The wind reddened her cheeks. She watched him reburying the bones that had surfaced so many times now it was getting to be a joke. The knolls kept surrendering to alder swamps, the beach rising to a sunlit knoll.

"Remember that fool register business in Seventy-Three?" Pruitt said, eyes focusing far out on the horizon.

"Coastal Island Registry Act? How could I forget it? My lawyer made a nice nest egg for himself out of that one." His fees were large but what she had ended up paying to the state of Maine was small: $10 to register Thrumcap. Now each of the state's islands with fewer than four dwellings had a number. Thrumcap was now officially six digits and hyphen in between.

Pruitt pounded the flat of the shovel on the new mound that covered Gooden Beal's bones. "They say they can't find a title for Thrumcap," he said again.

They went back inside where the logs shifted in the fireplace with a pungent hiss, nestling closer now, hotter. Willi sat deeper in the huge white pillows of the sofa—all the furniture was modern: white and black and red. "You can bet your ass, Pru, that this island is mine."

"July Thirteen, Nineteen Thirteen. After that, so they say, the state legislature put the kibosh on selling any islands owned by the state."

"You *sold* me Thrumcap. Gave me title to it."

"Well, now, Willi, the town did. Now it turns out the town was wrong. There's no written evidence of ownership before Thirteen, see, so the state says that makes Thrumcap theirs."

Willi laughed. It was not a pleasant laugh.

"'Course, title search, now," he said, "that's a long process. You and those lawyers can keep 'em going for another ten years. Or you could 'quitclaim' Thrumcap, and the state'll give you a twenty-five year lease. Rent'd be not much more than four hundred sixty give or take."

"You don't seem to understand. Thrumcap is mine."

"They've got some kind of damnfool coastal management plan. Talk about 'lost resource.' Want to turn all these pesky little islands over to the bird watchers, all that stuff. Two eiders were all they found at the turn of the century, and now they've got some twenty-five thousand pairs of the damn things."

"Ducks?"

She strode over to the great expanse of the window, one of the reasons it was never warm enough inside. Yet who could have thought then, when the architect had been drawing, that she'd want to come to Thrumcap any time except the summer? How it had grown on her. How she sat in her office in New York and it seemed she smelled iodine and sea salt, and heard the high curling cries of the gulls.

"There's no written evidence," Pruitt said, "of true ownership. What it boils down to."

During the 1800's the state had practically given islands away: three or four dollars would have bought her Thrumcap then. Now she had seen one advertised in the back pages of *The New York Times Sunday Magazine,* not larger than hers with a house not nearly so grand: $335,000.

"Coastal management?" she said. "Oh that's a good one. Well, I guess it's management of a sort. Now these islands are worth something, greed's reaching out to grab."

The crackling fire filled the silence when he didn't speak. She wanted him to speak, to comfort her, to say it would be all right. Outside the snow had stopped, and the great cedar frame that held the hammock above the hot tub loomed like an unnatural tree. No warmth of sweating, singing hands melted the frosted rime on the jungle gym. No young and humming muscles could wrench the wagon handle from its casement in the ice. No shrieking heart could brave the frosted metal slide.

She blinked: there was no playground there. If. If she had adopted a child.

Mutton dressing as lamb.

She whirled on Pruitt Hoskins who sat with a palm pressed flat for protection on each knee. "Why the hell haven't you left your wife?"

"Seems like he likes the light of day, don't it? Those old bones...."

CHAPTER 45

1979 - Sheep Island, Maine

The rich molasses smell of beans baking, of brown bread steaming on the stove filled the air of the cabin on Sheep Island, keeping the outside and the December cold away.

"Converted rice," Clara Beal said. Shrunken, naked, with her fist she hit the water in the big galvanized washtub by the stove, sending soapsuds flying.

"Cut it out, Grandm'am." Drenched, Kezia leaned over again, firmly scrubbing the washcloth down the frail white back. Clara shrieked, a cry innocent of message as a bird's. Her body, surprising steel still when her will got behind it, flailed about and a wave of soapsuds broke onto Kezia's shirt.

"Dammit." Kezia straightened, then stripped off her own soaked clothes. She clambered into the oval tub, hunkering down cross-legged, Clara's knees, elbows jutting like ledges in the sea.

Clara blinked at her, eyes humorous as a tortoise, mouth round.

"It saves water," Kezia said. "Shower with a friend."

"Five six one oh. Five six one oh. Five six one oh."

Soap bubbles ticked to nothingness in the air. Kezia felt a deep loneliness as the water began to cool. She picked up her grandmother's arm, the skin beneath the upper arm hanging loose as a breast, tried to drape it around her own neck. The hand slipped off as if lifeless, slick with water, and Kezia tried it again.

The hand fell away.

"Grandm'am—"

Clara's eyes blinked around the room without training on Kezia's face.

"Do you know what day it is? It's Sunday. Can you tell me your name?"

Clara looked at her hand in the water, surprised as if at sight of a strange fish.

"It's Clara, your first name is Clara. What's your last name—Clara who?"

Clara's face began to move and her hand reached up, patted escaping wisps of hair. "Who." Now her voice was angry, insistent, it was her name now and she repeated it. "Clara *Who.*"

"You're a Beal and don't forget it. A Beal of Aguahega."

"Clara *Who.*"

Kezia sat still, listening to sounds outside near the shed where they stored perishables in mouseproof containers. There were footsteps now, knocking at the door. She cringed in the tub in sudden fright as the door was pushed wide.

"Reo!"

He stood there silhouetted in the afternoon light, dark in the light in his park service work pants and zippered work jacket bright with the brass badge on its tab and the namepin. Above the knotted tie, crisp shirt collar his eyes were comical with surprise beneath their heavy lids. "This the ladies' bath house? I'm looking for the gents'."

The same half-grin, same easy-going slouch, toes turned out.

Water lapped against galvanized tin in a succession of waves as Kezia grabbed her grandmother, hiding her old woman's nakedness with her own. Water surged, gurgled now like a bow wave. Suddenly she wanted to get up, run into his arms. Had he come here for her?

"Hi, Clara. Good to see you again. I'll just wait outside."

The water settled back limp around her arms. Why was it now she was remembering all the good things about him? What about the bad? The doorway stood blank now, white with light, then dark again as he shut the door behind him.

"Need a bean sandwich, do you?" Kezia said when he was back inside. His body seemed to fill the room. She watched him take a huge bite of baked beans on the crusted end-wedge of brown bread as he looked around.

"Not a bad place here. What happened to your cheek?"

"Got into a fight in a bar."

He took his Stetson off, his blunt fingers with the dirty fingernails roughing back his hair. Now he rotated the hat in his hands. "I came to tell you I'm going away."

Her eyes squinted as if to shut out the light. "So. That's news. Where're you going?"

"Another island—Ellis Island, New York. Put my request in for a transfer a way back. Somebody kicked the bucket out there so they needed a fill-in. Get another step increase, and I should. Reports, paperwork, bureaucracy, crazies." His face gave her the old mocking grin. "Hippies swimming naked in ponds and washtubs."

"You're going to arrest me again?"

"So how're things going out here?"

"Fine. Fine."

"I ran into your mother on the main. She tells me not so fine. She says you've turned against the family, keeping everyone away."

"You would, too, if they wanted to put you away."

"Of course it isn't you."

"Reo, what did you come here for?"

His face, not giving anything away as always, looked at her as he thrust a long parcel wrapped in burlap into her hands.

"What is it?"

"Open it, killer."

Carved squirrels marching down part of a stair railing—Kezia felt a sensation that was like physical pain.

"Sawed it off before the dozer came. Gilley helped me but we only got half of it. Took a devil of a long time."

Kezia remembered sprinting through the bedroom door to the center hall stairs, her hand suddenly wet on the railing's carved squirrels. In 1871, Perley Beal, apprenticed figurehead carver, had found the clipper ship era past. So he carved up the old Beal house for his new bride, and love (like a lot of things, Gran'sir said), ran away with him. Every dresser front, mantel, picture frame, and corner whatnot was carved with lambs, eagles, sunflowers, and cloverleaves. But Perley's real weakness was for squirrels, which tended to sprout up like long-buried nuts wherever the eye turned.

Her fingers moved up and down Perley Beal's dark old wood, up and down. "Thank you."

"Five six one oh. Five six one oh. Five six one oh."

They both turned to look at Clara who was sitting on the bottom bunk bed, her wet hair so thin and plastered flat she looked bald.

"What's she saying?"

"Calling for the doctor to phone five six one oh."

"She needs a doctor?"

"Reo, we're doing fine." She hugged the railing tighter against her.

"Maybe we should go outside."

In the west the sun was setting in turquoise and streaks of fiery amber, through air that was cold. No sheep were in sight.

"Nice sunset," Reo said.

"Oscar Wilde said people don't value sunsets because they can't pay for them."

"Oh, so you're a cynic now."

"I'm not innocent anymore."

"No. Nor I."

"So I've heard. You going to marry that bimbo you've been shacking up with?"

"Kezia, it's okay to deflower a girl in the gazebo these days."

"Is that what you call shacking up?"

"She's gone."

"She's gone?"

"She's gone."

She felt his hand on her wrist, the power of his huge fingers encircling the bone. Suddenly he was kissing her, his mouth hard and sure and she gave herself up to it.

He pulled away. "Just for old times' sake." But his expressionless mask was gone and his face raw and red.

But he didn't love her; he had never told her he did. Kezia felt the sweat break out on her body, like the "rise" slick and warm: the yellow sweat-grease in the wool that helped the clipping shears peel off long clean cuts. Soon it would be shearing time again, the annual sheep drive.

"I guess I was no good as a ranger wife."

She could hear the snowmobiles from across the water on Aguahega.

"I had no complaints."

"I heard a few in my time, ranger-danger."

"It's just like those snowmobilers," he said, gesturing toward Aguahega. "They're willing to coexist with the cross-country skiers, but the skiers want to *annihilate* the snowmobilers."

"I think it's the rangers who're annihilating things these days. Rangers are the homewreckers now."

"I was sorry about Perley's House."

"Were you?" The wind whipped blood into her face. "Parks aren't forever wild. Forever politics. Aguahega was better off when the rich ruled things here. But fools that they are they gave it to the Park Service and what's that? Giving it to politics. And politics tries to please everyone: build, build, build, so everyone can come here and drive, eat, buy."

"Now you sound just like Chance."

A shiver still went through her just at the sound of his name, and she turned away. "When are you leaving, Reo?"

"Tomorrow."

A queer weightless feeling filled her head.

"You haven't signed the divorce papers yet," he said.

"I know. I've been busy." She thought of them in the table's drawer, like a deed in reverse:

> "WHEREFORE, I respectfully request that judgment be entered for the relief sought in the complaint and that the written Separation Agreement be incorporated but not merged in any judgment to be entered herein..."

"Reo, I'm sorry everything went wrong."

He pulled her into his arms, the hard beat of his heart dampening now under her tears. His hands turned her face upward to him, the warmth of his hands cupping her cold ears.

"It's Earmuff Day today, that's what I came over to tell you, killer. The great State o' Maine honors the great unsung hero of American invention, Chester Greenwood, creator of the earmuff."

Her hands came up, warmed his where they shielded her ears. If it weren't for Chance, she thought, I would have. Could he see it in her eyes? I would have loved you with all my heart.

She heard his boat going away, an endless mechanical sound blurring into the snowmobiles, but she didn't watch him leaving. Never watch a person leave until he disappears, she thought, like Gran'sir. Never, never kill a toad. Don't burn apple branches for firewood. Never, never count the stars.

When she saw the spilled cocoa, the damp trail from stove to table to chair inside the cabin, Kezia knew that something had changed. Clara's gaze, restless, beamed around the room. It came to rest on Kezia and the light in her eyes went out.

"Who are you?"

"It's me, Grandm'am. Kezia."

"I do not know you. Where is this place?" The early night settled darker around them. "I am afraid."

In the dark upper bunk Kezia watched the last faint red glows through the seams of the stove, listened to the gentle nudgings and settlings of the coals. The deepest oppression thickened around her and she felt completely alone.

She wished Reo in her hands, felt him close, and relived, dreamed, *wished* that he was here. And the clock struck twelve and she loved him intensely, even though a few miles meant not at all. Finally she dozed off, kissed him and touched him in her sleep knowing he was there, kissing his chest and sleeping troubled knowing he was not.

When she woke, surprised to have slept at all, the fire was completely out and the cabin black and still.

Too still: no sound of movement, no familiar harsh sound of breathing from Clara's bunk below.

Oh my God.

Kezia's feet swung out over the bunk's edge, dropped down to the floor. The lower bunk lay empty, covers thrown open, pillow cold. Kezia pulled on her jacket and boots, and in her long flannel nightgown ran out into the fresh cold night. The sky was black, cut through with stars, and a huge full moon hung white, misty-edged. The round hills lay silvered under frosty dew, the bare trampled places by the trough and the sheep pen a shine of frozen mud.

"Grandm'am! Grandm'am!" The enormous dome of sky swallowed her cry and she felt weak and small.

No sheep were in sight, nothing moving at all. Kezia began to run down the narrow rutted sheep track, stumbling over rocks and against the banked hoof-packed sides, her boots too wide to strike side by side.

She had crossed the isthmus when she saw the first sheep.

Protective, the ram had come part way down the hill to assess the threat of Kezia's presence. His head, huge on his bodybuilder shoulders, turned to stare at Kezia, ivory glint of horns backward curved as scythes, his upper lip and nose sneering as he tested the wind.

Kezia stopped, breath frozen fire-smoke from her open mouth.

He was a full-blooded Rambouillet ram, a hardy breed who could thrive on sparse forage, and heavy wooled he was over 300 pounds. His weight jerked forward now onto one two-fingered hoof, and with the other he began to claw up snow.

Kezia stared at his white-edged criminal eye. There was no reason to hate and fear him. He was a good sheep, sound mouthed, straight-legged, long in the hind saddle. He could breed thirty ewes in one night. He was shit-headed from sniffing into the muggy warmth of the ewes' hind ends, dirty brown-browed as the little two-week orphaned cossets who butted under an already nursing ewe's tail and grabbed hind teat when they could, loveless, pounding the milk in.

The ram's long dong, bull balls swung.

He had come to Sheep Island three weeks before, a slave trussed and struggling on the deck of Nate Vannah's Jonesporter. Once freed, however, he would be only too happy to do his work. The fifty ewes and six-month old lambs had stood on the hill, waiting.

Nate trimmed wool from in front of the penis, over the scrotum. "Big stick of TNT ready to bang."

"The ewes are kind of helpless, don't you think?" Kezia had said. "I mean, with that ugly critter loping around."

He laughed. "Oh, they've been primping for days for this—he's the sheik of Araby to them. They're looking forward to it, and so should you. Get yourself married again. Put some damn babies to your breast."

"Get serious." Kezia tried to catch the expression on his face. "And I suppose you're available as prime breeding stock. No fee, either."

"Well, I am a 'proved breeder,' as they say."

"Oink! Pig."

"Chicken. You're just chicken about everything, Beal."

"Bull. And it's Macrae." Kezia had avoided the flock for the next few days.

Now, in the middle of the night, the ram, having cuffed the snow-covered grass into submission, swung his head from Kezia and began to climb the hill. Was the band there, ewes and lambs mothered-up beyond the crest? Was Grandm'am there, too, counting the sheep to put herself to sleep? Kezia followed the ram's scrambling haunches, pink gristled between.

The sound came haunted on the cold wind, the tinny child's horn of a lone ewe blaring for her lamb. Down the other side of the hill Kezia saw the flock, sleeping legs tucked under, ghost-white in the moonlight. Clara was nowhere in sight.

The ram jerked heavily past where the lone ewe stood, went on to join the flock below. As he passed, a raven started up from mid-hill, slunk low-winged away from something white there in the grass. Kezia felt her heart race and she wanted only to be back, safe again in the cabin stoking up the fire because Grandm'am would soon come home.

Nervous, the flock below began to get up at sight of Kezia. The ram barrelled into their midst. Stiff with cold and dread, Kezia walked down the hill to where the lone ewe bellowed. The flock stared at Kezia now, round-eyed.

It is the stillness of death that surprises.

The ewe's lamb lay on its side like a grown sheep lambing, but instead of its head laboring straight up to the sky, its muzzle lay flat on the earth, head stretching away. Ribs shone silver and long ropes of dark color staked out the burial ground, which tried to blot up the color from below. The lamb's eye sockets were emptied and whatever had been within.

The ewe was silent now.

When had it begun to die? When she left on her trip to the main for groceries? The gulls and ravens had started to gather but the ewe drove the first sentinels off. The ravens waited until the lamb was unconscious to peck out the eyes. Still the ewe, baffled now, remained.

Down near the tidal flat the ram was leading the flock away from Kezia's predations, up and over the other hill.

Beside Kezia the lone ewe remained, calling for her lamb.

The ram paused on the smooth bowl of skyline, looking back, nervously tearing at the snow with his hoof. Kezia watched the decision made, his ungainly return end run to scoop up the ewe. He approached, struck his front leg against hers. He nuzzled her wooled cheek. He called, and now she called, deep voiced, not high and plaintive like before. Coy, her face turned away from him and her tail end swung invitingly nearer for him to sniff and then, still coy, she charged away.

He thudded after her, clots of mud tearing up between cloven toes, passed her and kept on going toward the flock. The ewe followed.

He returned, sniffed her again, reared on two legs and hopping clasped her. The lamb without eyes watched them white and cold under the moonlight.

Kezia turned away, back toward the cabin, and she saw movement, a darker shadow down among the shadows on the hill's near side. Running far ahead on the sheep trail, completely naked, was her grandmother, her loosened hair a thin white streak down the center of her back. It swung, a horse's tail, and her buttocks shone long and powerful, younger than the rest of her as they worked to carry her away.

"Grandm'am."

The ram withdrew, stared at Kezia. The ewe, the other ewes stared.

Clara left the shadows to cross the moonlight, an ink blot on the white plain of snow. She ran the long way across the meadow and paused at the edge of the little stand of woods, as if seeking safety among the black and white trees, then darted within.

When at last Kezia reached the trees she saw her grandmother lying beside a large hackmatack, arms folded across her breasts, body empurpled with cold. Her voice sang, cracked and thin:

"Unter der Linden
Auf der Heide..."

Her skin was so thin and shiny it looked varnished, hair hanging in dull strings around her face that caught the edge of moonlight as it turned, peering up at Kezia. *"Mutter, ich will nach Hause gehen. Und ich Werde nach Hause gehen."*

Mother, I want to go home. I will go home.

So much torment in her voice. All right, Kezia thought. Maybe you're right. Maybe it's time.

Kezia got her into the lower bunk, piled the covers high. "Grandm'am, in the morning I'll take you over to the hospital on the main."

Clara's eyes took on a look of terror and fiercely she shook her head.

She lapsed into a deep sleep and when she woke she was straining, neck tendons rigid, back arching, face tight as she pushed, pushed.

"Grandm'am, do you need a bedpan?" Kezia held up the pan, motioning to slide it under her but Clara shook her head. Her body continued to strain, to push.

"Grandm'am, Deenie's having the baby, not you. Are you in pain, hurt anywhere?" Again the shake of the head, No. "Can you just take it easy till morning? We'll go for help then." Wondering if she should leave Grandm'am now, or take her back out into the cold night in her boat.

But the thin body was relaxing, the eyes opening and clearing, wonderful translucent pale gray eyes.

"*Oma!* Why do you sit there with me like this?"

"You've been sick and got cold outside. Don't you remember, Grandm'am? *Oma*—what does that mean?"

A soft rain was falling through the worn places in her brown woolen cloak and she shivered as she stood looking out to the North Sea. She stood up on her toes: if she could just see far enough, she could look right across and see it—America.

"It means 'grandmother,' " Clara Beal said.

"It's me, Grandm'am. It's Kezia."

"What sickness did I have?"

Did? As if it were all over, as if it had never been.

"Stroke. Something that went wrong inside your head." Kezia chafed the feet that were as soft as a just-born lamb's hooves, still new, unused. The grass would grow darker, thicker, coarse-bladed where the lamb had died on the hill, where none of the sheep now would graze.

"I'll tell you a story, Grandm'am. It'll help you sleep. Once upon a time, there were two people called Hero and Leander. Hero was a girl, a beautiful priestess of Aphrodite who lived across the water from Leander. They took to loving each other like men and women do, and Leander swam across to her, guided by her torch on the top of a tower. That was the very first lighthouse, Grandm'am. One night there was a storm and the light snuffed out and Leander drowned. His body washed up on the shore where Hero found it and killed herself. And a god, the most powerful of all, took pity on the lovers and decided they would live forever. He placed them together—up in the sky as stars."

Clara was sleeping. For the rest of the night she didn't move, Kezia sitting beside her watching dawn grow when suddenly Clara became very animated, arms moving and she let out a moan.

She was pushing again.

Remember the ewe's bulging side shrinking within the prison of bone, then testing the bars, heaving out. "How long is this going to take?" Kezia had asked her grandmother. "No more than an hour and a half." Little toe dancer, the lamb's two hooves reached out first and Kezia pulled gently on the hooves that were soft as cat's paws. And then it slipped out, head swollen to twice the normal size and it lay still while the ewe fronted away, raw ended, eyes circling wide with fright. "Hold it up for me, by the back legs," Clara had ordered, cleaning mucus out of its throat, pounding on it, pumping its leg, puffing bursts of air into the lungs. Finally, exhausted, she paused, forearm raking sweat from across her face. Kezia was staring at her while the gulls had gone silent under the vast silent dome of the sky. And then so light Kezia thought she hadn't heard it: *sssssshhhhh,* breathed the lamb, its first breath.

In the cabin Clara was pushing again. Maybe you had to push to die. Like being born, pushing into light. Only this time you push into darkness and you die.

When the pushing stopped, Clara Beal was dead.

CHAPTER 46

1980 - Camden, Maine

It was May and all the lambs had been born. In damp hiding in the woods, fiddleheads stood six inches high; ready to be picked and steamed, salted and peppered and buttered, the pungent taste of coastal spring.

Whatever it is you want. The winter bending already into summer. *Do it now.*

Kezia pulled her black leather jacket tighter over her jeans as the still wintry 15-knot wind swept down from the Camden hills—Mount Battie and the notched mass that was the second highest peak along the Atlantic seaboard: Mount Megunticook. The name meant "Big Mountain Harbor" in Abnaki, "the high mountains of Penobscot," Captain John Smith had agreed, "against whose feet doth beat the sea."

Because Chance was here, out of place, she hated everything she saw.

Mainland tourist trap, the place where *Peyton Place* was filmed, but she would find Chance here, his houseman had told her, the *fool,* his voice seemed to say. Kezia searched for Chance among the harbor's forest of masts: the windjammer fleet at moorage before the seventeen-week season of cruising, tourists gaping at lighthouses and islands from slanting decks, photographing "local color": the woman in hip boots that was her.

Chance was totally out of place here renovating his new windjammer, as wrong as she had been renovating herself in New York City. He had made her see that—could she make him see it, too?

Behind her Camden's streets wound up the hill, black-shuttered white frame captains' houses with widows walks: still closed for the season. Beautiful houses but soulless as Nantucket's: no fires burned in the hearths and stoves. They were dark and cold here at the beginning of May, a museum before hours. The summer harp colony hadn't arrived. The guest houses, motels, specialty shops were closed. Through the plate glass window dust still softened "The Jolly Lobster" 's display: a lobster trap magazine rack, a lobster trap coffee table with "cord net trap opening." What were you supposed to find inside? Earrings still flowered on a brass tree, real lobster claws cleaned and lacquered blue and green and topped with feathers.

The summer fog that would wrap wild roses late into October was a season away. Kezia hurried out on the pier, and under the low cloud deck that might have been November she saw the ship. A "three-sticker" Gran'sir would have called her, one of only two surviving three masted coasting schooners along the entire Atlantic coast. Kezia wanted to hate her but she was all beauty and grace, 170 feet from the end of her jibboom to the end of her spanker boom, masts 80 feet high. Great sheets of plastic swathed her from top of masts to deck, a ghost ship sailing sailless through mist. From waterline to waist she gleamed bottle-green with black bulwarks and yellow cove-bead, underbody glinting copper red through the harbor's water. Gold leaf highlighted her name: *Carrie E. Fears.*

Beneath the shroud of plastic Kezia saw a man high in the rigging and she walked up the plank and slipped beneath the welcome protection of the clear walls. The world outside fell away. Her moccasins moved soundless on the tarpaulin-covered deck. She could see Chance now, army surplus overalls and a bucket secured around his waist. He leaned far forward, hands in heavy gloves tarring the rigging, oblivious to her standing there.

"Hey up there. This your dude coaster, cap'n? This here your damn rag merchant for sure?"

The tar brush came tumbling down. He vaulted down the rigging and he might have been a boy, she thought, this man almost 41. Gone was the beard. His skin was startlingly pale, the brown silk of his hair falling unkempt and long, damply over his forehead, wayward tendrils across his collar as he stood there smiling at her. She tried not to look famished into his eyes: so deepset they appeared as always off-center, looking back at her now with a squint.

"Red! What are you doing up in this neck of the woods."

"Brought you your Christmas present. A bit late."

He took the package. "Can I open it now?"

"Well, maybe not right now."

"So. What do you think of my little beauty here?"

"*Little?* Think you can shanghai enough dudes to fill up this thing?"

"Sold out already through the season."

"But why do you want to haul a load of dudes? You can afford to sail without them, anywhere you want."

"But they can't. That's why I want to do it, I guess. The beauty up here—just makes you want to share. Speaking of which, let me show off the below-decks and I'll even give you a drink."

"Chance."

"Yes."

"She's the most beautiful boat I've ever seen."

She was surprised at the rush of response across his face. "You're the only one I know who understands."

The acrid smell of tar from the bucket filled her head.

"Just look at this deck, Red." He lifted the tarpaulin on gleaming planks. "Did her all myself. One hundred thirty-two feet of her and God, she was a mess. Had to clean, then bleach, sand, then stain, then—"

"I know."

"Sealer, eight coats of varnish, sand again after every coat—"

"I know." She was grinning up at him now. "I'm such a perfectionist I'll only varnish after a fresh snowfall."

"I do it before dawn. If only we could transport the whole thing to the middle of the North Pacific—now that's clean air." As if in rebuttal, sand tapped like pebbles against the plastic wall, rattled harder now as the wind sprayed the sand hill of Camden's new sewage treatment plant. Hurriedly Chance let the tarp fall.

"Yep, you sound like just another new boat owner," Kezia said. "Of course, *Bog Onion*'s a *working* boat."

"But *Carrie is.* Was just the pick-up truck of those times, Red. Don't you know your history? She was no pleasure craft. A graveler, picking up her cargo on a gravel beach, then she was a rumrunner painted white and fitted with a short bowsprit, new name. One of the most daring, most notorious, they say. Captured by the feds and sold at auction, and now she's come down to me."

She watched his fingers caressing the brass binnacle, bright and newly cleaned, between the two brass lamps. He had a new plaything, a new fantasy because he had the money to make his fantasies come true. "What's Victorine going to be? Chief cook and bottle washer? Isn't that what the cap'n's wife does on a windjammer? Hash slinger *non pareil*?"

"She doesn't want any part of *Carrie,* so she said."

"Where is she?"

"They'll be going out to Southampton at the end of May."

"Don't you care?" Her fingers were clutching the brass-trimmed wheel and unconsciously they moved up, caressing the spokes that were capped with brass.

She saw the smile start at the edges of his mouth. "Victorine gets seasick in a bathtub and you can't keep your hands off that wheel. Two sisters, and how can you be so different?"

"We weren't so different once. Or if we were, it was the difference made you want *her*."

"So it's my fault?"

Skimming the edge, afraid to fall in, "I didn't come to see you to talk about Victorine."

He was enjoying himself now. "We could talk about your marital folly, er, Macrae. I mean, what was his deathless attraction?"

"He's all right."

"Got no eyelashes. Rabbit eyes."

"He *had* eyelashes. They got burned off." Her pulse jumped as his long fingers seized her arm.

"You don't want a man with fried eyelashes."

"Let go or I'll gnaw it off and escape." She felt his grip release and she stepped backward. "You want to know why Victorine and I are different? I struggled for everything, never got it. She never even tried and she got everything."

"What, everything?"

You. "She was always Grandm'am's pet. I was the one who really loved Grandm'am and Grandm'am always preferred her."

"She told me once it made her just as upset as you got, the fact she was favored. She said she knew it wasn't really *her*, just an adult whim."

"That's what I hate about her—she's nicer than me."

"You can't help it if you love her."

But I don't, she thought. I don't have any family anymore. "Do you?"

His eyes squinted off toward the horizon. "Let's just say I'm making the best of a diminished thing."

You love me, say that you love *me*. Instead she said, "Don't forget to launch *Carrie* on the eleven o'clock tide."

"You get the highest rise then, you monkey-wrench sailor?"

"For luck. I could use that drink now."

Chance lit the brass kerosene lanterns that hung on gimbals, smoke bells above to catch the carbon and heat.

Kezia stared around her. "It's like a railway car. The most luxurious old-time private railway car that ever was."

Butternut paneling, bulkheads, cabinets, brass fixtures glinting back in tall mirrors, built-in sofas fat with pillows. Chance squatted, relighting the logs in the stove that was soapstone-faced with a brass frame, still warm. A large green parrot squawked, then lapsed back into silence in an ornate cage.

"Does that beast have a name?"

"*Res ipsa loquitur.* 'The thing speaks for itself.' So. Want something to eat? Mouton forty-seven n' burgers?"

"Great."

He was gone behind more butternut that had magically opened into a door. Out on the sea a chop was running and here below decks every sound was magnified, waves slapping rhythmically against the hull. She imagined herself chief cook and bottle washer for the dudes while "Cap'n" Chance stood upstairs at the wheel. She listened for sounds of him behind the butternut, a queer stifling fear gripping her chest.

She smelled sandalwood soap and looked up. He had changed into a raveling, too short-sleeved tweed jacket over a sweater striped horizontally blue and green, and held a wine bottle carefully horizontal in both hands.

"Take off your coat?" he said.

Flushing she pulled it off and her sweatshirt tugged up, showing her navel above lowslung jeans. His gaze moved from her belly to her eyes.

She stood still, not moving until he turned to pick up the corkscrew. She watched him holding the shoulder of the bottle over the candle's light and in one clean motion pouring the dark red wine, dark as a bloodstone, into the decanter. Unwanted gold dust, the first trace of sediment washed into the shoulder and he set the bottle upright, poured them each a glass.

"Now let's get down to it, Red. What made you come all the way out here?"

"Open your present first."

He took out the card: spray-painted all around in red was the white imprint of a fern.

"Grandm'am helped me make them. Before."

"She touched a lot of lives. Remember how she always said 'Out of the frying pan, into the gravy'?"

"It's called the Christmas fern. You have to look close to see where it got its name."

Chance squinted, turning the card. "The fronds sticking out are like Christmas tree branches?"

"Nope. Turn the card on its side, see? It's the leaves."

"What?"

"The leaves. They're Christmas stockings."

Chance looked up at her, skin ruddy in the reflected light, and she saw what she'd always wanted to see in his eyes.

"I guess that's true for finding much meaning in Christmas in general," Chance said. "You really have to look for it." He was unwrapping the paper, revealing a nineteenth century oil on velvet painting of wild orchids that had hung above the couch in Perley's House.

"Perley Beal carved the frame. Do you like it?"

"It's quite a fruit compote of a frame. Yes, Kezia, I love it."

"It's the moccasin flower. It still grows on Aguahega."

"I'm going to hang it right over there."

She could smell the prosaic smell of hamburgers browning in the pan. "When we were little, we always wrote a letter to Santa. We put it in the stove and it went up to Santa in the smoke."

The wine was like ruby fire in her head.

"Did you write one this year?"

"Too sad to even celebrate Christmas, I guess."

"Let's each write one now."

She sat up, putting down her glass. "It's just for little kids, like Nicole."

"Every time you say you don't believe in Santa Clauses, a Santa Claus dies." He handed her a piece of paper and a pen. She wrote hastily, opened the stove door and tossed it onto the blazing fire. She watched the edges curl up in smoke. "Dear Daddy, please come home," and then the flames crinkled it like an impatient hand. Now Chance's letter, folded and secret, burned on top of her own.

He could only come back like Nate's uncle, wrapped in kelp. She watched it gray ash now falling between the grates.

The panel door of the cuddy yanked across. Fresh air and light poured in, hitting her like a blow. "I'm Chance. Where's your father? What happened here?"

Her fingers held the wineglass as if it were a lifeline. "Chance, I found out a way back that Mother always wanted to fly. She had a student pilot's license when she was just fifteen. But she never got to solo."

His eyes looked at her over the top of his glass.

"I offered to give her the money for flight lessons. But you know what she said?"

"No."

"She said, 'I don't want to dig all that up again,' as if it were worms. It was too late. She doesn't even want to fly anymore."

"Red, what's all this about?"

"I still want you."

Waves battered against the wooden hull, waves higher than her head down here in the hold.

He was looking steadily at her. "Something happens to a man in middle age. Remember Parsifal in triumph at Arthur's court? Then the hideous damsel rides up on a mule, sends him off to search for the castle again. Something like that's happened to me."

Was that what he was saying: she was too late?

"You asked what I care about. Sailing. Do you know what it's like to sail at night?"

She shook her head. He was saying he didn't love her.

"The water, the sky vanish. They're one. Silence except for the clink of the halyards, the suck of the bow wave. You cut through the one. Your lights are the stars, moon, buoys, maybe a lighthouse or few. You realize you never need any other light. It's all so simple."

"Simple?" She looked around at the opulence of the cabin. "I'd say simple was where I am, living on Sheep Island."

A phone was ringing: she looked around in confusion. A telephone on a boat.

"I'll just get it in there."

He disappeared through another door—she could see the bed beyond. And then the door shut.

Her gaze returned to the extension on the table at the end of the couch. Her fingers carefully eased the receiver up. It was Victorine's voice.

"*Three* children are more than I can handle. You were acting like a child taking Vinca's behalf against me. I read an article on problems caused when the father's weak, the mother's strong."

Chance (faintly from the bedroom, loudly in her ear): "You're acting like a child yourself."

"I think we need help. But I can't stand your parents interfering with my bringing up of the children. Vinca has very little sense of humor. She just can't tell when I'm teasing her."

"Well, since you know that to be the case, why do you insist on doing it?"

"In my family no one was considered specially. Maybe I'm not fit to have children. I thought I wanted them but that was before I realized I was going to have to be in a constant state of tension worrying about how I disciplined my children because others were not going to want them brought up the way I was brought up. And it's your fault because you were one way when we met and now you're another!"

Kezia eased the receiver back down. Victorine: shoulder bones starved into prominence, all the softness had left her face.

She was turning the hamburgers over when Chance came back out. "Who was that?"

"Your sister."

"Victorine? She *was* my sister. Not now, not anymore. None of them are. They blame me for Grandm'am dying. I left them long ago."

"I left, too."

His fingers touched her hand, fleetingly, for an instant. She held her breath until he touched her again. They looked at each other and at the same moment began to smile.

It was not going to be like her first love.

You could never feel that way again: light refracting through the water, the fish gleaming higher, askew to where it really swam. Like the osprey now she plunged not where she saw the fish but where it really was.

She drove her mouth burning hard and open against his. A massive force as if stone or earth crushed her body. His scent surrounded her, a wild pungent aura like a valley earth-wet with rain. Hands warm and dry, cool and cold and wet. Eager hands warmed by firelight reached out to pick more and still more of him. Her arms ached as if torn at the sockets holding him.

Her eyes opened to see his face draw back, hesitant. He was green, unready.

Couldn't he see? It was past time, past summer, but still there was something green in her that had never been touched.

He had nothing to fear.

Now that I have memorized your body, now that I have you...

She lay looking down at his naked body that gleamed white beneath the straight black hairs as if lit from within. A black and white photograph hand-colored at the center: the canting curve of his long white cock that was also blue and rose. They had been a week on his coasting schooner, coasting nowhere. She hated to think of ever going home.

Now that I have taken you into the whorls of my fingerprints and made you part of my body, now that I have you...

"I'd just as soon die now and here."

He laughed, reaching up from the bed into the night, arms above his head.

"No, I mean it, Chance. We have—what it is people want."

"And after we're gone other lovers will feel like this. That's immortal, that lasts."

"And I won't mind dying knowing I've had this. I've known what it's about when people talk about it. About love."

Now that I have you by heart.

"No one can take the memory away," he said. It was like an epitaph.

"We'll never stop loving each other like this."

"Other lovers will feel the same. We'll be gone but they'll go on."

She turned her face away and felt the tears, sharp, felt them grooving over her face and down her throat, and something ached beneath at their passing. She stood up suddenly and held her face with her hands as if it would break and walked into the bathroom.

When she came out, she climbed on his body, felt his arms reach up to hold her, felt herself rooted on him as he began to grow. As she moved she saw the tears fill his eyes and she leaned down and with one long kiss drew his soul like light through water.

The telephone rang again the following week.

"Who was it this time?" Kezia said when Chance came back, standing unmoving in the bedroom doorway.

"Uh, nothing. Nothing. Mother calling to say hello." He tried to hide it but she saw fear, banked like kindling against a draft.

"Come back to bed."

"No. No."

"No?"

"Think I'll make us something special to eat. Something in honor of your grandmother—German. Would you like that?"

"I've never been happier in my life."

She watched him brown a *pfannkuchen*—a foot-wide pancake in a round pan, flipping it out onto a tray, sprinkling it with powdered sugar and cinnamon and squeezed lemon juice. Then he ladled steaming tart lingonberries from a can over the top and rolled the pancake up with his fork and spoon like a jelly roll. More dusting of sugar and cinnamon, a sprinkling with *kirschwasser* and with a match and enormous flourish he set it ablaze. When she kissed him he tasted of powdered sugar but she saw his eyes watching her, afraid.

The fear that was in her now, beginning to grow.

He hadn't eaten anything. "You know that game," he said, "Truth or Consequences? I ask you something, and you have to tell me the absolute, God's honest truth. And you'll ask me and I'll have to tell you. And so on."

"You mean, like 'what IS the meaning of life, anyway?' "

"Something like that. And you have to promise to answer, okay?"

She put down her fork. "You mean, like cross my heart and hope to kiss a pig?" He nodded.

"Sneaky, Chancellor. So you get to go first?" She watched his eyes and his face for some sign of what he might ask. She hoped it would be something light, or something like "What do you think of me, Red? Do you think you could ever marry me?" She wanted to get to her question for him. She would ask—

"I've wanted to know—and always thought I should keep my stupid mouth shut, right? But I've been concerned for a long time and I wondered—"

It was not to be something light, then.

"—whether you still think about it...your father and how he died. When I found you like that on the boat...I mean, can a person come to terms with a thing like that? And if a person does, how does he do it?"

Her breath pushed audibly from her lungs as if she'd been punched. "Christ, Chancellor, isn't that below the belt?"

"I only ask it because I care."

Kezia examined the speckly bluish reddish mottles on the backs of her suddenly cold hands.

"I don't know, I really don't. That last summer I had with Daddy, being sternman finally and all of that. It was going to be the most wonderful summer of my life. I had no idea something like that could just end. You know what I said to my father? We were anchored in Crotch Harbor drinking tea."

"What, Red?"

She remembered how she had laughed. The sound carried high and clear over the harbor water, back into the listening trees. Someone had been there, watching and waiting, listening to her joy.

"I said, 'Daddy, what is it about the world that's so wonderful?' And he said, 'Hah! Every day with you it's a different word. Today it's wonderful. Yesterday it was fabulous. Day before, terrific, right? Make up your mind!' And I said, 'Is it silly to feel that way?' "

"How did your father answer you?"

"He said it wasn't silly."

"I wish I could have known him, Red. To have him die so young..."

"He didn't die." Kezia forced herself to look at Chance. "He was killed. It wasn't his time to go. I believe that God received him but he didn't take him. He didn't take Daddy's life. A man did."

"Red..."

"Someday I'll see that man dead. There's your Truth, there's Consequences. I'll pull the switch myself. I'll aim the rifle, whatever they want me to do. I'll kill him barehanded if I have to. I'll hurt him the way he hurt me. He'll pay for what he did."

He was looking at her with a remote watchful look. "Is that what your father would have wanted?"

"Yes! I knew him, yes! He was a real scrapper, the leader in the Lobster War. They met in our kitchen so many times. They were all there looking up to him, waiting for him to tell them what to do. He was President, head of the revolution. I was just a kid—it was incredibly exciting: that's my father up there. I was scared but I was innocent then. Couldn't imagine 'consequences' then."

"That doesn't mean your father would fasten on revenge for twenty-eight years."

"Chance. What's this all about?"

His eyes were empty as the lamb's under the moon.

"Milo Gilley."

Her fingers examined the arm of her sweater, picked off a tiny pull. She could see it was hopeless, a field of oatmeal pulled threads, dead chrysanthemums nodding to their knees.

"Milo what?"

"He confessed. He's over on the mainland with the sheriff right this minute. Turned himself in. He's the one, Red. Killed your father."

After a time he heard her voice which he had always loved, full and throaty. But now it had withered.

"I've been waiting for this day since I was nine years old."

CHAPTER 47

1980 - Medon, Maine

It was Milo Gilley's plea-taking day.

Crime wasn't supposed to happen here, in rural New England, in Medon: county seat. But "things go from bad to worse and from worse to Medon," Johnny Beal used to say.

Reporters and television crews thronged the sidewalks in front of the courthouse along with crowds who couldn't get in. It was a crime aged in aspic, a fly in amber, and that was news.

PARK SUPERINTENDENT ADMITS MURDER.

Lobster War Boiled Over 28 Years Ago.

Kezia walked alone between the maples, past the lawn sprouting groups of old men like crabgrass, too old to be routed out. She felt nothing except fear—fear of what she was going to feel.

"The word is the judge'll just let him off with probation," the female reporter said. "Could you tell us your feelings about that?"

"They used to release the guilty party into the custody of the island," Kezia said. "Not a bad idea. We'd know what to do with him there."

"If it's probation, would you leave Aguahega rather than go on living near him? He says he loves Aguahega and doesn't want to move."

"I'd do what they did in the eighteenth century, sentence him to public scorn. Put up a four by five sign in his front yard. 'Milo Gilley Is A Murderer.' "

"He said he's a born-again Christian, and that's why he confessed after all these years. Could you forgive him?"

"I don't forgive."

She walked through the door of the squat two-story brick courthouse with its white wooden portico, four white Corinthian columns entirely too grand. Up the stairs to the courtroom on the second floor: high, pale, hot. Bare ten foot windows were sealed closed, and a glass eagle in the ceiling skylight mantled over them as if they were prey. The rows of wooden benches were already full, buzzing now at sight of her. But there was space reserved in the front for the family, facing the witness stand, empty jury box, still empty judge's brown leather highbacked chair. At one of the long wooden tables was the back of Milo Gilley's graying head. He had been his own jury. "Guilty," he'd said. So say you all.

Loara Vannah was looking at her from the front pew, beside her Beck and Nate, Deenie and Duane. But Kezia remained standing in the back, her head filling with the smell of stale floorwax, cigar smoke. Milo Gilley had torn her family apart: he couldn't bring them back together again.

A ranger was looking across at her from the other wall: dark green dress uniform, Smokey Bear hat in one hand. The park service had organized a campaign, laboriously raised all the bail money which Gilley, refusing to be unruined, refused. It was the new ranger—young, nervous, the one who'd replaced Reo Macrae. "It's a tragedy," he'd said to Kezia, "but locking up Gilley won't bring your father back. He's a broken man. Have some compassion."

"I do! For my father."

" 'Revenge,' " the ranger said, " 'digs two graves.' "

The bailiff struck the gavel three times as the judge entered. "All rise."

The judge's voice, heavy as his robes, began to drone. The hearing was a "Rule Eleven Proceeding," the judge calling the defendant to plead. The prosecution outlined the state's evidence: there was evidence independent of the missing body, the bullet found on *Loara B.*'s deck and the gun that shot it retrieved from the old hermit Rowdy Richardson's well.

It was stifling hot in the room: banks of fluorescent lights above, flaking white-painted metal registers along the walls still turned on, you could see the hot currents rise. A huge portrait dominated the west wall: a reproduction of the one in Washington's Capitol rotunda, Pocahontas saving Captain John Smith, behind her the Indian famous for his six painted toes.

But Kezia neither saw nor heard nor felt anything.

The judge advised the defendant of his constitutional rights. Milo Gilley steepled his fingers, once massive shoulders thin now, hunched in the gray suit, the blue shirt, red tie. He pled guilty—so entered. The only question now was what the sentencing would be.

"Twenty-eight years ago," the judge said, "the applicable law did not distinguish between degrees of murder. Sentencing was not delayed because the court had no discretion in the length of the sentence. The current statute, Title Seventeen-A, came into effect in Nineteen Seventy-Six, and applies only to crimes committed after its effective date. If your lawyer wishes to move that the Nineteen Seventy-Six statute be applied here, I will consider such a motion. However, I wish to be frank that there appears to be little basis for the granting of such a motion."

"Your Honor, my client wishes to proceed under the old statute."

"Then sentencing must follow the Title Seventeen statute from Nineteen Fifty-Two. Mr. Gilley, please rise."

A hush deepened through the courtroom.

"I have no discretion, Mr. Gilley, but to sentence you to life in prison."

Intake of breaths all over the courtroom. Milo Gilley brought the points of his steepled fingers up to his forehead.

"Before you are remanded into custody," the judge said, "is there anything that you wish to say?"

Gilley's freckles were gone, frightened pale. "Your Honor, the Lord has moved me to repent my lies. Jesus rules my life now. I'm not concerned what other people think. I'm concerned what Jesus thinks. But I want to state that what I did, while it was wrong, it was a mistake. I only meant to frighten Johnny Beal, give him a good scare. I drew a bead on his colors, his lobster buoy nailed to the roof. Did the barrel move? Did he move? I only meant it to frighten—a mistake."

Kezia stared at him. *Here's to them that shoot and miss:* it was the falconer's toast. They all sat there, all the middleaged and old for a crime committed when they were all young. Now they were handcuffing Gilley's hands in front of him, starting to lead him off.

"You got to stop this!" came an old man's voice. "Your Honor! Stop this now!"

Over the commotion Kezia strained to see what was happening in the middle of the pews.

Like a wooden jointed doll she'd once owned, an old man was struggling to get to his feet, each joint bending separately, one after the other in slow deliberate time. He was half bent forward at the hips, levering himself up now with his braced arm and his knees. He straightened, stepping wide with one leg for balance, his dark cap salt-whitened across the bill, a day's growth of beard grizzled white around a mouth gone rubbery, loose lipped with age. Work clothes and a flannel shirt inside: just another none too prosperous fisherman.

"Order!" the bailiff called, gaveling.

"Nobody's killed me, you bleeding fools. I'm Johnny Beal."

The full moon silvered the patchy rock-strewn hillocks of the "Commons," the open heathland on Aguahega where once its thousand sheep had roamed. They were rough-wooled, too long in the leg, too thin in the chest, wild eyed. But shearing was a frolic, a school holiday then. Kezia imagined her father, small, too knobby in the knees as he ran after an escaping sheep.

She seized a rotting fence rail, smashed it into the leaning post until the rail shattered to wood dust in her hands. She uprooted the fencepost and attacked the great spruce that still towered three fathoms about in the pasture's center, having escaped becoming a mast for a ship, the sail yards. Noises raged from her throat, ached up from somewhere deep in her chest. She fell to her knees and tore up dirt with both hands.

In the courtroom, louder than the sound of the man's voice she'd heard the hiss of the radiator as it spat on her bare leg. "What a strange old man," she'd thought, watching his slow progression toward the judge down the aisle of silent pews. "Isn't there anyone around to help him?"

"I'm remarried," he said, "got me four kids. It's wrong. It's wrong but it's done. Planned it, many times but never did it. Then the noise of that gun must've put the startle in me. Fell in the sea. Would have drowned but for the currents got right hold of me, brought me back into the cove. Maybe I was in shock but I thought: to them I'm dead. I just kept going."

He turned around toward Loara, fingers gnarled as the pitch pine on top of the ridge. "My mother—is she still alive?"

"You came back for *him*," Kezia shouted from the back of the courtroom. "Not for me. Ashes. I've got Clara Beal's ashes. You'll never see her again."

Under the cap the old eyes peered out at her. He was like Grandm'am—he couldn't recognize her anymore.

"Kezia?" He took a step, fingers spread. "I waited. Waited till that boy in his sloop so fancy came back by. Waited till I saw you were all right, pudden stick. Wouldn't've gone if I thought you weren't all right."

The old man got farther and farther away, smaller and smaller. Now she felt the anger, the hurt, hate, betrayal, the passionate, furious aching inside. Was it for her father or herself?

"You died on me when I was nine years old. You're *dead.* You're still dead."

His name was "Harold Clintock," and he wanted to keep his new identity, the television news report said. He was a Pea-Eye (lived on Prince Edward Island), a Canadian now. Kezia had stared at the television image of his house, cramped dark ranch house with a small Japanese car in the drive. By the picture window a wrought iron tree grew, each "limb" blossoming with a white pot of plastic geraniums, pink and red. An overturned toy wagon in the grass: it belonged to a grandson, also a "Clintock" because he'd finally had the son Kezia was supposed to be. There was no image of his wife (fifteen years Loara's junior), a waitress named Margaret who would have no comment, the reporter said.

"One point eight million people are reported missing each year. Most come home. But three hundred thousand are never seen again." There was a policeman with the reporter's microphone under his face: "People leave home every day."

The image of Loara Vannah flickering: "We were happy."

The policeman again: "People leave home every day."

On the Commons under the moonlight Kezia heard that strange hesitation of wave: an absence of sound that marked the moment of the turning of the tide. Bruised, her hands bleeding, she walked down to the cove and sat for the rest of the night by the water's edge, until dawn came.

The wind strengthened from the west, a clearing wind. The fresh piny smells went deep into her lungs. She looked out to sea. It was the first high tide after the first full moon in May. She heard them in four inches of water, the mating horseshoe crabs. She could see them now, the hard shells clicking as four and five males surrounded each female, clicking louder now as they competed to push closer. Now there was the scream of gulls gathering to dive for the eggs that the waves would wash away.

The dark discs of the ancient round shells shone like pennies in the white swash of backwater.

She could never forgive her father. It was a hard knot in her like knots on the pumpkin pine floorboards of Perley's House, worn to prominence as the softer wood planed down.

She thought: I don't forgive.

CHAPTER 48

1980 - Aguahega Island, Maine

Johnny Beal, Loara Beal Vannah was thinking, was one of those people who had never fit even in his own world. And she, too, was one of these. Clothes betrayed her with lost buttons, sprung seams. When she walked she jerked like a rabbit fleeing hounds.

Certainly she had never belonged here at Seal Point.

She was sitting alone on the blue velvet settee, waiting for the housekeeper, Mrs. Simpson, to return with the money for her ironing. Loara was impatient to get back to her house in Haley's Landing. But instead of returning footsteps, all she could hear was the sound of her own breathing, too loud, too ragged. She wished, as she often had at Seal Point, that she held Alice in Wonderland's magic mushroom: the kind that eaten made you disappear. She looked around for a rabbit hole of escape.

But she was surrounded by Tenhaven. English oak paneling rose two stories, a rainbow through the stained glass window on the landing splashing the staircase with reds, yellows, blues. The Main Hall's fireplace gaped black: big enough to steer a lobsterboat through. The mantel was carved with hunting scenes; hunched gargoyles supported the shelf.

Loara started half off the settee. A clock, London made in 1732, chimed the first bars of "Un Bel Di." As if in response, a vast mouth yawned in the wall. Inside, the elevator glowed red and bright with lights that beckoned her.

Silence except for china tinkling somewhere out of sight, the sound of her breathing thunking like the blades of Clara's washer as Loara fed in more Seal Point sheets. The mouth smiled its invitation, the lights danced, and Loara rose. Her shoes disappeared into the clutching depth of the foreign "turkey" carpet. She hesitated for just a second and then stepped inside the wall.

In the close space she felt the warmth of four lamps above, and bent her head to peer up. Bright red enameled walls molded in gilt met a painted ceiling of clouds. In its center, braced by arms of gilded red, a hidden fan started up behind the lighting fixture's sun. Damp once-brown, now gray tendrils on Loara's forehead stirred.

She cast an appraising eye at the leather bench and an enormous shiny lever, cocked at the ready. Her left hand clenched firmly behind her back where it belonged. But her right of its own accord reached out, felt the cold delight of the metal lever, then yanked it over as far as it would go. The wall shut, she was inside, and a stone in her belly tugged toward the floor. The soles of her shoes vibrated as a soft purr of greased bearings rushed her up. Her peal of joy sucked through the ventilator and poured into space. It was like a magic red-and-gold candy box, she thought, as it bore her skyward, then earthward again and again and again. A considerable time passed. Loara could hear a muffled pounding on some faraway closed outer door, an island of sound that vanished as the elevator sprinted out of reach again. Then, in a screeching protest of emergency safety brake, metal snagged the guide rail notches. The magic ceased, the earth slowed, flight stalled.

The doors of the elevator irised open again.

"Oh, *Gaaahd!*" the matriarch of Tenhaven said. There towered Eleanore Chancellor, who often swept unseeing past Loara in Tenhaven's halls, the one Loara (under her breath) called "ritch-bitch." Now she was swole up as an old toad sculpin. The thunderclap of silence echoed on and on. The face gazed in at her, puffy and red and detached as a balloon, wobbling. "And at your age!" the matriarch cried.

Suddenly Loara was laughing. From the open window she could smell the honeysuckle-wrapped benches surrounded by lovage and sweet cecily, hyssop and anise. She felt as free as Johnny Beal when he'd driven the car into Clifton Pond.

And then Mrs. Chancellor was laughing, too.

CHAPTER 49

Kezia stood on the Aguahega village wharf watching *Miss Mayry*, the third generation "mailboat," now a huge ungainly car ferry churning in.

They were all out there on the deck looking back at her: Loara, Willi, Deenie, Victorine. Loara had written each member of the family and suggested they all meet, repair what had been torn and decide what to do: to see Johnny Beal again or never to contact him? Kezia raised her arm in welcome, hesitated a moment and then waved.

You're like the person in the Dylan Thomas poem, she thought, who sees the ship come in, sees the sailor with something in his hands. But you can't decide if he's holding poison or grapes.

But the answer was poison *and* grapes: it was the truth and the ambivalence of life. Like the island that she both hated and loved.

There were crowds around her—it was the height of the season, and now the first car came rolling off the mailboat. Instead of numbers, its license plate read: Maine 80
LOBSTR
vacationland

She could see Victorine spritzing her face with an atomizer of distilled water. Now they were all standing, staring, unsure what to do.

"We'll never argue again," Kezia said.

Willi looked at her. "Let's not go that far."

"We'll never get mad again," Victorine said.

"Let's not go that far." Willi looked around the circle of them through her owl-round dark glasses, and suddenly they all burst into laughter. Kezia put out her hands and the circle held.

She could hear Loara talking but beyond Victorine's head she'd glimpsed Chance on the far edge of the crowd of people waiting to pick up people, to ride back on the ferry. His hand rested on the weathered wooden frame that held the fog bell. The granite plaque in front of it was inscribed "FOG BELL of Hobbomocca Head for 60 years tolled the men home from the sea. Gift of the U.S.C.G. installed on this spot by H.P. Henry, J.W. Turpin, Sid Staples, 1973."

Still the circle held.

In that moment she saw Chance moving farther back in the crowd, slipping away, in his eyes the far look of the osprey after her hands had loosened the leather jesses. Immediately she'd regretted it, tried to call it back.

It would no longer answer to her call.

CHAPTER 50

1980 - Aguahega Island, Maine

"Distance lends truth," Aunt Willi said.

A haze was on the water and in the air—the late afternoon's light a golden confusing glare. Below, the sea was gray, flat and solid as a piece of sculpture crafted with welding iron and rivet gun. Aguahega was only a darker gray on this plate of gray, flattened too from this height, steel on steel.

They were the only two passengers save for the pilot on the Cessna 182 RG airplane that now wing-tipped and turned, descending, and trees and tiny houses sprang up on Aguahega, artificial as pasteboard backdrops.

Kezia adjusted the heavy earphones: they were set too wide, for the copilot if one had been along. Conversation between the pilot and the control tower still flowed back and forth—snap, crackle, words, pop. Kezia glanced back at Willi who was rattling her newsmagazine, a commotion of disinterest in the sight below. During a pause in the radio noise Kezia said, "Could you make a pass over that whale-shaped harbor down there? We grew up there."

"You got it!" The plane swooped lower and Kezia clutched the foot-high can of Clara Beal's ashes tighter against her chest. *A coelo usque ad centrum,* Chance had once told her, the ancient property law that meant from the heavens all the way to the center of the earth. Not any more: property owners now were subject to the rights of airplanes.

She looked out the window. Perley's House was gone. Well, what did she think she was going to see, the backhoe still there munching up the last few clods? Toothaker Harbor stood tenantless, and already the climax growth of spruce seedlings was jostling dark browed toward the water's edge. Was that what the park service wanted: impenetrable forest, no open spaces playing with the sun?

She couldn't read the official park sign but she knew it by heart:

> Here lived Perley Beal and his wife Sarah who raised
> a family of eight, six miles by tote trail to the village,
> and another sixteen, sometimes icebound, to the main.

Still no ospreys had returned. But Kezia could see the pole sticking up near the harbor, a huge wooden shipping pallet braced and screwed on top. Soon there would be a cage there with a pair of osprey chicks transplanted from Maryland, and a two-way mirror so observing graduate students could keep up their behavior charts. The chicks would be fed there, their food gradually reduced; and if all went well, hacked back to the wild. They would fly with tiny transmitters sewn to the base of their tailfeather shafts: you could pick up the signal 200 miles away. They would be imprinted with Aguahega—would they?—and like the alewives, return.

Dashes of memory pierced her mind, and she knew that for the rest of her life, in cities, wherever, the thoughts would come.

The plane shuddered in an updraft, then blundered through the wind again. "Well," Willi said as it came around once more. "You going to toss out the old dame's remains here or not?"

Kezia shook her head, fingers tightening on the can.

"Take all the time you need, ladies," the pilot said genially. Brown bristles along his chin, young hard-blue eyes looking back now out the side window as the plane dipped and turned. "Will you look down there!"

Kezia looked, expecting to see Chance's beautiful bottle-green three-sticker with sails in her branches like clouds. Would she be flying the night hawk, the long black pennant that told other ships she was homeward bound? The plane was sweeping out over open water but Kezia saw only waves dancing distant below. It was Sunday, the dude cruisers' day of rest.

"A hundred sure as we're settin' here!" the pilot said.

"A hundred?" Kezia peered again out the plane's window.

"Hundred thousand. I'm a spotter for pogies—menhaden—direct the purse boats to make the set from up here."

"We *know* pogies are menhaden," Willi said. "And where did you come from? Climb out of the wall?"

"Portland."

"Portland." As if it were a scandal just to mention its name.

The front seat was cold and riven with drafts. *"Oma,"* Clara Beal had called, her eyes pleading. "It's me, Grandm'am. It's Kezia." The old eyes had seemed to clear. "I know you are not my grandmother, Kezia. But it does not really matter, does it?"

Kezia looked at the pilot. "Could we make a pass over the northwest end of the island? Seal Point?"

"So you two good old gals are island-born, huh? Hardly anybody left there now, year-rounders I mean. Don't know how they stand it in the winter."

"It's difficult now for anyone," Willi said, "but especially younger people to imagine that one could be happy without cars, radios, TVs, washing machines, dryers, dishwashers, etc. Life was simpler, and I think better. People adapted their way of life to what was available. We cut our wood, carried water from the well whose ice we broke with a crowbar in winter. We had a freezer (the woodshed). It wasn't a bad life at all. A person can quickly adapt to different and simpler ways of doing things if he/she desires."

Kezia stared at her.

"Children didn't have many bought toys. We played outdoor games that didn't require props. We were more imaginative, creative than most children now. We were also more physically active. We ran and walked, climbed trees, fished, skated...."

Kezia could see them now, the great sprawling estates of the Point, gardens wide, pushing back the firs.

"Remember all those jack-o'-lantern seeds drying on the sill?" Kezia said. "Always going to plant those seeds. Have our own pumpkins. Somehow they always got lost or burned or thrown out."

Her right palm came to rest on her stomach and the sensation startled her, *komisch*: funny, peculiar, strange. It passed in a wave through her, like the game she and Vangie played in third grade. You held your index finger next to hers, a column of paired flesh, then ran your finger and thumb up and down, up and down, shivering, feeling the you and the not-you—someone else.

Her period was two months late but still she hadn't seen a doctor. She was island born, without a doctor, just a midwife.

There they were now; the towers of Tenhaven, square mouths of chimneys, tall witches hats. Kezia pressed her face against the vibrating window. Why was it that now she was leaving the island forever, she felt she had it for the very first time?

Her hands picked up her father's pencil box. Over the sound of the airplane it seemed that she heard the one-lunger laboring of Johnny Beal's ice-cutting rig. Another block of ice groaned as steel teeth hoisted it up from Alewife Pond, out into the fading red light of Aguahega's brief winter afternoon. Kezia had knelt by the 400-pound ice cake, staring into its radiance, breathing in its cold. Soon it would grow dark, smothered in sawdust in their icehouse. Yet now a sun rose within and beamed toward her, moved as she moved, the same bright yellow as her father's coat.

It was perfect ice, but that was then. She could finally stop looking for it.

No such ice can be found.

Memory is its own thing.

Far below her Kezia could see a table in Tenhaven's Scented Garden, people sitting around it so far below.

"Now!" She tore open the top of the can.

"What in the *world*?" The matriarch of Tenhaven, Eleanore Chancellor, sat upright as if goosed, white wine sloshing over her hand. A fine ash was drifting gray over the pink linen tablecloth, dusting over her arrangement of prize roses in the tall glass vase.

Fairfield Chancellor, 94, squinted up at the sound of the airplane as the shadow of its wings crossed the sun. He looked at Chance. "Is that, uh, what I think it is?"

Chance nodded.

"I hate to inform you, dear," Fairfield said, "but I believe it to be your former laundress."

Across the table Victorine smiled. "Bless you, Grandm'am. You always did like to have the last word."

From the screen of spruces Torby Vannah, thirteen, was peering out at them. Mohican-ing, he called it, seeing without being seen, his face hidden in the trees Indian dark with sunburn. He was staring at Vinca Chancellor in her white cotton sweater, white pants. She was the most beautiful girl he had ever seen.

If only she could see that he was different from the others, the natives. But he talked like one, walked like one in flopping, folded-over rubber boots, smelled like one. If it was the last thing he ever did, he would leave Aguahega, make a better life for himself by going ashore.

Maybe then Vinca would want him. Could she want him, a lobsterman deep in his bones, would she? Maybe then....

EPILOGUE

INDIAN LAND CLAIMS SETTLEMENT

Using a quill pen fashioned from an eagle feather, President Carter signed the $81.5 million Maine Indian Land Claims Settlement Act in October, ending almost a decade of conflict and confrontation caused by tribal claims to more than half the state....

The tribes argued that their ancestors lost the territory in agreements with settlers that violated the federal Non-Intercourse Act of 1790 which prohibited individual states from entering into treaties with Indians.

—*Down East* Magazine
December 1980